Fires of Life

By

Maria N. McMillan

Maria N. McMillan

Fires of Life

© 2016 by Maria N. McMillan
All rights reserved.
No part of this document or publication may be reproduced, stored in a retrieval system or transmitted in any for or by any means without the prior written permission of the publisher.

ISBN: **978-0-692-73645-6**

This is a work of fiction. All the characters, places, or events in this story are fictional and solely the product of the author's imagination. Any resemblance to any person living or dead, place or event is purely a coincidence.

Dedicated to my daughter

To the incredible woman you have become.
Thank you for all your patience, time, and suggestions during the creation of this story.

ACKNOWLEDGMENTS

I would like to acknowledge all those who took part in the creation of this book. Thank you for all your help and support.

Maria N. McMillan

Close your eyes.
Heed the Earth.
Hear her voice.
Feel her dance.
Smell her scent
Breathe her life.
Drink her spirit.
Taste her joy.
Find her heart.
Discover yourself.

Chapter 1

Moonlight streamed in through a small barred window above him. The cold dampness of the stone walls chilled him to the bone. He pulled at the chains that bound his hands and arms but to no avail. It was useless. They had chained him up like an animal, hanging him by his arms with chains around his neck and feet as well. The frigid metal cut into him but not nearly as much as the betrayal that had landed him here in the first place. He had trusted Almaik. They had fought in many battles together and become close friends, or so he thought. Almaik was the son of the king he had been fighting to restore to power, King Sevzozak, who was now no more than a mere puppet.

It was Vaulnik who ruled everything, controlling his outer lands by allowing the previous rulers to remain in power so long as they paid tribute to him and obeyed his laws. He had been fighting to liberate his people and his king from the tyranny that was Vaulnik's. Why had Almaik betrayed him? Was the aristocracy that afraid of his popularity amongst the people that they would deliver him to their enemy?

The obvious answer was, yes, as the cold hardness of the chains now told him. He pulled at them once more in frustration. Tomorrow he was to be executed. Vaulnik had little mercy for his enemies and instigators of unrest. His death would not be pretty. Vaulnik's propensity for imaginative, but exceedingly painful, gruesome executions was known far and wide.

Clavorn looked up at the moon as it shown in through the bars of the small window in his cell. Its fullness filled the gloomy space with beautiful soft silver light which contrasted sharply with the harshness of his surroundings. A breeze from the outside sent a cold chill across his bare skin. Pain racked his body, and his heart. Freedom had nearly been theirs. Oh, why had Almaik betrayed him, and more importantly, their cause?

Once more he pulled at the chains which cruelly held him in place. A tangible reminder of the bondage he and his people faced. Clavorn's long dark hair flowed about his bare muscular shoulders, providing him with the only warmth his stony prison could offer in this tower dungeon. His strong jaw and chiseled cheeks had taken more than their share of a beating before they had chained him up, as the ache in his head now told him. There had to be more to his life than this, but then if this was to be his end he would make it one for the legends. They would get no pleasure out him. No. He would not beg for mercy as so many others did.

What's that?

Muffled voices came in from the hallway just outside his cell door, braking his train of thought. The flicker of torchlight told him the guard had risen from his post. Shadows danced in the glimmering light, but he could still not identify what was going on.

Perhaps they are simply changing the guard. No.

A heavy slumping sound just outside his cell seemed to indicate that other matters were afoot.

Clavorn watched intrigued as the figure of an old woman came to his prison door. She had keys in her one hand and a basket in another. Her face and body were shrouded by the cape and heavy garments she wore.

Puzzled, he continued to watch as he heard the familiar grate of a key as it turned within the lock. Then the door to his cell opened and in entered the old woman. Promptly, she turned and shut the door behind her so as to make it appear as if it were still locked. Quickly, she came rushing towards him. It was clear by her movements and agility that she was no old woman.

"Who are you?"

"No time for explanations," she whispered, as she hurriedly began unlocking the shackles about his feet and hands, unlatching the one about his neck last. "Now bring the guard in and exchange your clothes with him." She ordered as the last of his chains fell to the floor.

It did not take him long to figure out what she had in mind as he swiftly made his way to his cell door. Cautiously, he opened it and peered out into the cold stony hall. Fortunately, all was quite. His cell was apparently in a remote section of the castle. He had been out of it when they had brought him in and chained him up, so this was his first good look outside his cell. Now, as he stared out into the hallway, all he saw was the guard slumped over next to the wall.

Quickly and quietly, he strode over to him. Immediately, he hoisted the unconscious guard up and carried him into his cell, swiftly deducing that she must have somehow drugged the man. Then he set the guard down in the center of the room, and began to exchange clothes with him, while his apparent liberator stood watch.

Before long he was dressed in the guard's uniform, with the exception of the breast plate which she was now helping him to secure.

"Alright, now let's shackle him up," she continued in a hushed tone, pointing to the guard on the floor.

He bent down and began to heave the guard into place, not expecting that the slightly built woman before him would actually assist in chaining the brawny guard up. However, he was amazed by her strength as she helped lift the man from the floor.

Soon they had the guard placed in the shackles which, till recently, had been Clavorn's nearly sole attire. He looked over their handiwork, and then glanced in her direction. Quietly, she motioned him towards the cell door.

Placing their bodies flat against the stone wall, they listened for any sound of guards coming down the hall. When all appeared quiet, she handed him the keys to the cell and readjusted her garments. Then nonchalantly, she opened the door and walked out just as an old woman might do when leaving her home; her back was slightly bent, her hands shook, and her movements slower as if from age. He marveled at her transformation.

Following her lead, he took up his stance as a soldier in Vaulnik's army and exited his cell; being sure to close and lock the door behind him. Glancing up, he took one last look at his prison hold with the guard now splayed in his place. But for his benefactor that would be him. Turning, he followed her down the short corridor to the winding stairs.

Torchlight flickered against the stone walls of the tower staircase. The rank smell of dampness mixed with other unsavory scents of sweat, decay, blood, and more as they paused before ascending. Moans and other sounds too echoed up the narrow flight of stairs.

"What about them?" he whispered, gesturing with his head in the direction of the suffering prisoners held captive by Vaulnik.

"No time," she told him.

"Make time," he insisted, grabbing her by the arm as she turned to leave.

"We'll never make it out of here," she replied turning her head back towards him, "There are too many. You are more important."

"No. They are equally important."

A brief silence filled the void between them.

"Alright," she acquiesced, "but be quick."

Immediately, he turned to the cell nearest him.

"Here," he said as he handed the keys to one of the men nearest him, "Wait a sufficient amount of time for our escape, and then get as many of them out of here as you can."

The man nodded and Clavorn returned his attention to the woman who immediately took off to continue their escape.

Soon they came to a wooden door. Quietly, the woman glanced down to see if anyone was coming up, then she quickly opened the door and motioned him through. Now they were out on the ramparts far from the castle entrance. She put down her basket and took out a long rope.

"We'll have to climb down from here," she told him in a hushed tone. Clavorn glanced over the side.

"What about the perimeter guard?"

"They only come around once every hour. If we hurry, we should have time," she informed him as she attached a metal claw hook to one end of the rope and lowered the other.

Surveying their area of the rampart, he wondered what had become of the guard posted there, when he suddenly spied a body hidden off to the side. However, he could not ascertain whether or not the man was still breathing, being as there was no obvious mortal wound.

"Come on," she whispered urgently, "We don't have much time. The guard on other side of the rampart is on his way in our direction."

He motioned for her to go first, but she shook her head and motioned him on. Then the two of them quickly and quietly descended the rope along the side of the castle wall. Once on the ground, she immediately gestured for him to follow her along the castle wall. Round the castle they surreptitiously traveled on their way towards its entrance. Soon they were in sight of a group of perimeter guards making their way in their direction.

Clavorn walked alongside her trying to act casual. Suddenly, she grabbed him and shoved him into a dark crevasse, pulling him to her and kissing him passionately as she grabbed his hand and placed it on her thigh.

What the…?

A group of guards glanced in their direction. Clavorn had no trouble following her lead and continued to kiss her back, making it appear to as if he was just a guard having an interlude with a castle servant. But his manliness could not help responding to her passionate display, and he could feel his heartbeat quicken.

"Will you look at that," laughed one of the oncoming guards.

"Glad some of us are able to enjoy this night," commented another.

"Be quick guard. The king will have your head if that Clavorn Remmaik escapes," ordered a gruff voice which he guessed must be the highest ranking guard of the group.

He nodded and motioned that he had heard the man while continuing to remain in a passionate embrace. The guard acknowledged his response and motioned his group forward. Clavorn listened to their voices and footsteps as they faded into the night. Finally, when he felt the coast was clear he released her.

"Come on. They'll find that rope soon and we'll be sunk," she whispered to him while pushing her way past.

He had wanted a momentary glance at his emancipator, but she had not given him any time for such a pleasure. A sigh left his lips, as his body betrayed his mild frustration at being denied a glimpse of his apparent benefactor. Clavorn turned and followed her quickly receding figure.

Soon they rounded a corner, and he could see that they were nearing the castle entrance. Horses and various street animals such as dogs, cats, and most assuredly rats, along with carts filled with stacks of hay and assorted items were scattered here and there. Peasants, servants, and guards milled about the grounds in the flickering torchlight.

Suddenly, his liberator slipped behind a cart filled with hay, temporarily disappearing from his sight. Clavorn stood near it trying to blend in with the dynamics of the crowd when, all of a sudden, she reappeared dressed in a soldier's garb. He guessed that was what must have been hidden under the haystack. Now, she strode at his side looking the epitome of a fellow guard, only a bit shorter and slighter.

Finally, they came to where two horses were standing tethered not far from the front gate. By her motions it was easy to see that these were meant for them. Clavorn nodded to a guard that passed them as he mounted the dark bay horse at his side. His benefactor was already mounted and backing her black horse by the time he had a hold of the reins.

The moonlight shown down on them as he turned his horse to face hers, momentarily affording him a glance into her face which he hoped would provide a glimpse of it. The dark shadows of the

Fires of Life

crevasse had succeeded in concealing her identity. Now he wanted to see her, if only for a second. But the helmet she wore cheated him of such a chance, the cheek pieces being far too large to allow a clear view, especially in the torchlight. Clavorn turned his horse again so that it faced in the same direction as hers, and together they trotted off for the gate.

Soon they slowed their horses back down to a walk as a guard stopped them on their way out.

"Just checking the perimeter as ordered," he told the guard.

The guard paused, looking the shorter of the two of them up and down as if unsure of his companion.

"He's new," he told him, "Time to break him in," he elaborated. The guard eyed her for a moment, and then broke down apparently satisfied with his explanation.

"Well, see to it he gets the royal tour," the guard told him.

"Oh, I intend too," Clavorn fired back with all the ease and confidence of one accustomed to leadership. He spurred his horse forward, and the two made their way over the draw bridge. Their horses' hooves echoed out into the night as they rode across.

Suddenly, just as their horses stepped off the bridge, they could hear the frantic sound of soldiers' feet, and then brusque voices.

"It's the prisoners!" They heard one guard yell in the distance.

He smiled to himself at the thought of the chaos now ensuing within the castle walls.

"Quick, follow me," she ordered.

Then with one swift kick to her horse she spurred it into action. Clavorn did the same and followed her into the forest. Quickly, they rode into the dark and foreboding woods. Soon the sounds of horns blowing and horses' hooves could be heard as the castle alarm was sounded and its soldiers roused into action.

Spurring their horses once more, they drove themselves harder into the woods weaving and dodging through the dense vegetation. Frantically, they wove their way through the dark trees and old undergrowth, branches splitting and tearing at their clothes as they flew past, scraping against their armor. Over a small stream they galloped, spraying water everywhere.

On they went. The horns of the castle alarm sounding in the distance. Clavorn wondered if she had a plan from here when suddenly her horse veered right and took off up a hill. Clavorn jolted his horse to turn in her direction. The beast reared slightly before following her.

Up and round the side of the hill their horses flew as deeper into the woods they went. Soon the land leveled. On they galloped down into a ravine till they came upon a fast flowing river where they pulled up their horses and came to an abrupt stop.

"Now what?" he asked.

"We enter it," she replied simply.

Clavorn raised one eyebrow in disbelief. The river was fast and it appeared to be deep. Without hesitation she slowly rode her horse in. Clavorn paused.

Is she mad! One false step and we will be at the mercy of this river and its frothy, turbulent waters. Or worse. A river in these woods, who knows what lies beneath its surface.

Stories of unnatural creatures which lived in the waters of the forest surrounding Vaulnik's castle abounded. The tales of those who had died by them were not pretty.

"Come on!" she ordered, "But stay right behind me."

He looked on for a moment in awe as she successfully navigated the raging water before him. At this point it was becoming quite apparent to him that his liberator had a much better understanding of the terrain around here than he did, and he wondered what circumstances had made that possible.

Dismissing his misgivings and questions about his benefactor, he reluctantly decided to follow her as best he could into the tumultuous river. Tentatively, he edged his horse to the water's edge, but the beast shied and backed off. In the distance he could hear the sounds of soldiers, and a castle in chaos. Soon they would discover him missing, if they had not already.

"Easy boy," he reassured his horse, "I think I know what she is doing."

Once again he tried to urge the beast forward. It shook its head, refusing his intentions.

He must think I am crazy, but then I can't say I blame him. I think this is crazy.

He tried again, more strongly, for his benefactor would soon be too far ahead to follow safely. This time his horse complied. In the distance he could hear the soldiers searching the woods. Clearly, they had discovered his escape.

Icy cold waters hit his skin, and Clavorn took a sudden breath as they reached up near his chest. He could feel his whole body tighten, bracing against the frigid water. Clavorn shivered and glanced up, then breathed a sigh of relief as his body adjusted to the freezing cold waters.

He turned his horse to follow her on downstream. Soon he and his horse found the area of the river she had apparently used. It was amazing to him, but she was right. The path she was following or creating, he could not decide which, was calmer. The waters outside it were turbulent, harsh, and unforgiving, but just behind her, while they appeared turbulent on the surface, were calm beneath.

He followed on, ducking craggy gnarly old branches that grew out over the waters as they went. Here and there a raven flew up from one of the trees by the water's edge. Their slower pace through the river meant that he had a chance to take in some of their surroundings, and they were anything but beautiful.

Spring, it seemed, was reluctant to visit this forest. The thick dark twist branches sported little in the way of leafy vegetation. Yet despite their lack of leaves very little light seemed to reach the forest floor, so tightly intertwined were the branches of the canopy above. The wood was old here, very old. He could tell from the size of the trunks of the trees. However, it was clearly not a healthy forest. No new saplings or other signs of renewal could be seen. Dark ooze emanated from some of its more twisted inhabitants, and a foul order permeated the air around them.

Spiders were plentiful here too and could easily be observed spinning their webs across the open spaces. Open spaces that, as far as he could tell, were the only reason they had been able to navigate it on horseback. What little undergrowth there was, was also old and much of it brambly. But what did he expect. This was the Forest of Thestaera which had once grown proud and tall, but that was before the dark times, before Vaulnik.

An eerie silence lay in the stillness around them. The sinister nature of the wood brought his attention even more into focus, as he followed the strange woman who seemed to know her way so well around this dark and foreboding forest. Suddenly, a bat flew down and he was forced to duck out of its way.

Moonlight danced off the raging water, and Clavorn continued to marvel at how they were able to navigate the tumultuous river. Most horses and people would never attempt such a feat on this river or any of the waters here for that matter. Stories of great demon fish that swallowed men whole abounded. Tales of unnatural creatures with multi-heads and numerous limbs that strangled or dismembered their victims were not uncommon. Whether the accounts were true or not was debatable, but he could definitely see how they were started.

"Who is she boy?" he mumbled to the horse after navigating the waters a bit further, "you know?" The horse nickered. "Figures, well I sure wish she'd tell me." The horse made no comment as on they trudged through the raging waters.

Clavorn ducked as a low lying branch nearly took his head off. In the distance he could hear the sounds of the soldiers as they continued to search the woods. Thankfully, they appeared to be far in the distance; for the moment anyway. He wondered if they would follow the river downstream on land, or if they would risk fording the rapid waters.

Follow downstream along the river bank. That's my guess. I doubt they have the stomach for these waters.

Suddenly, the river opened up onto a lake. It was amazing to him how glass like the surface of it was considering the nature of the waters they had just been in. Twisted overhanging branches reached out over the lake and an eerie mist graced its surface. At the far end of it there was a huge raging waterfall which cascaded down from a cliff opposite them. It stood approximately two dragon lengths high and nearly that in breadth as well.

To the right of the lake there was another falls only this time it emptied from the lake, spilling down over three times the distance as the first, to a much larger raging river below. The roar of these falls was nearly deafening. The woman kept her horse to the left of the lake where the water became shallower.

After a few moments, she stopped her horse and quickly dismounted without leaving the lake, though the water was still knee deep. Clavorn followed her and did the same. He was expecting a heavy undertow given the large falls at the end of the lake and was surprised to find none where they had dismounted, though clearly there was one at its surface as he watched a remnant of a log float quickly past.

"Take your armor off and tie it to your saddle with this," she ordered, tossing him some rope.

Catching it deftly with one hand, Clavorn did as she requested. When they were done she struck her horse on the hind end, and it went trotting off into the woods with his horse following suit.

"Now what?" he asked.

It seemed to him that they had just let loose their only hope of out running Vaulnik's soldiers.

"Now follow me," she told him as she turned, flinging her scarf around her face.

Is she deliberately hiding her identity from me?

Icy cold water swirled around his legs as he waded through the lake after her.

"I don't suppose you are going to tell me your name, or where we are going?" he asked as she appeared to be heading straight for the raging falls that was pouring violently into the lake.

"You'll see," was all she answered as she began swimming across the glassy water, the moon reflecting perfectly on its shiny surface.

I'll see. I wonder what that means.

He bent over and eased himself into the frigid lake as he acquiesced to her request.

Once again the icy water bit into his skin. He took a deep breath and began to swim, being sure to stay within her wake. Immediately, he could feel the undertow of the cold waters beneath him as they tugged and pulled, yet they were still navigable. Testing the lake, he took a stroke or two outside her path. Instantly, the waters there became deadly, threatening to pull him under into the depths of the icy chaos below. So, like the waters they had traversed before, the apparent safest place to be was right behind her.

As they neared the falls, he could feel the spray of the cascades as they hit his face. The thunderous sound from the powerful waters filled his ears, and he could sense their force thrusting deep into the lake beneath him. Shaking his head to clear the water from his face and eyes, he could see her swim to the right of the falls very near where the second waterfall spilled over into the raging river below.

What? How is it she is not swept down into that second falls?

The question would not leave his mind and only added to the mystery surrounding his liberator. However, as he continued to swim behind her, he could sense the lake becoming shallower, calmer.

Odd for such a lake, but perhaps there is a natural explanation for this. Right? And she just happens to know where the safest waters are.

His mind was in conflict as it viewed the huge rocks which were coming into sight the closer he swam to the falls. Soon there were stones beneath his feet. He stood up, watching his benefactor do the same. To his amazement though, she continued to travel straight for the falls in front of them.

Suddenly, she ducked down and went through the waterfall, disappearing from sight. Clavorn paused a moment in disbelief. The falling waters were powerful, rushing down like a giant curtain.

She's crazy. I know she is.

He shook his head and continued on till he reached the spot where she had entered the falls. Glancing about, he searched the area for a more viable solution. Roaring water raged all about him. The rocks below promised certain death, and there appeared to be no easy way to get to shore to explore the area for another way in. Seeing no other alternative, he took a deep breath and followed her.

Ice cold water hit him with a thunderous force as the falls bore down on him, pushing him deep into the chasm below. Down, down, down he felt his body tumble. To his surprise much deeper than he expected, but soon he could sense rocks beneath his feet. Up, he pushed off, and out of the turbulent wake from the waters above. When he rose he was amazed to find himself inside a giant cave.

The huge cavern did not appear to have any other entrance besides the falls behind him, and he was glad he had not opted to brave the journey to shore for an alternate entrance. As he swam forward, he could sense the water becoming shallower. Finally, he found hard ground beneath his feet and stood up, shaking his head and spraying icy cold droplets of water about himself. Then, in one swift motion, he brushed his hair back with a swipe of his muscular hand.

"Here," she said, tossing him some dry clothes. "You'll want these."

He caught them adeptly and continued to gaze around him in bewilderment. The loud roar of the rushing waterfall behind him continued to pour down and echo about the cavern.

Glancing about, he marveled at the expanse of the space before him. Unfortunately, the true extent of its size was difficult to discern, being that the only light available was that of the full moon as it filtered in through the rushing waters behind him. Peering into the deep darkness of the vacant space before him, he had the sense that it stretched far beyond the opening where he now stood.

Clavorn took the clothes she had tossed him and continued to trudge his way through the water towards the cavern. It was becoming readily apparent to him that their escape had been well planned. The dry clothes she had tossed him being evidence enough, to say nothing of everything else.

"Who are you? Who planned all of this?" he questioned, raising his voice above the falls so she could hear him as he made his way to the edge of the pool where the water finally became shallow enough for ease of movement. He had a million questions for her.

"I suggest you keep your speech to a minimum for now," she informed him, "We're concealed in here as long we make like a rock."

"You think anything can hear us above that raging falls?" he commented, almost shouting as he turned towards her and gestured to the torrent behind him. He could barely hear himself think above the noise of it.

"Do you want to chance it?"

No.

She had a point he had to admit, though he could not quite get over the niggling feeling that it was more to avoid conversation than keep them safe.

Clavorn continued to exit the water, and drew back to a corner of the cavern to put on the dry clothes she had tossed him. He assumed his emancipator had done the same, though in the darkness it was hard to discern much of anything.

After he finished changing out of his wet cloths, he went to sit by her near the entrance of the cave. The dry cloths felt good against his skin. The early spring air was cool, and he would have frozen if he had had to remain in them much longer. He sat down beside her just outside the spray of the falls on the bank before them.

Quietly they sat, both now adorned in dry clothes. The sound of the falls roared on. Clavorn peered through the falling curtain of water in front of him, but all that seemed discernible was the darkness of the forest on the other side.

Time passed. Silence filled the air save for the noise of the rushing water before them. Normally, a fire would have been a welcome sight, but, ignoring the fact that dry wood would have been nearly impossible to navigate in there, their need for stealth demanded darkness.

On they both watched and waited for any sign that their pursuers had found their trail, but only the rushing waters and empty forest appeared to lay in front of them. Clavorn was just about to make a comment, when suddenly she raised her hand to stay his voice. At first he was a bit annoyed, but then he paused following her gaze.

Suddenly, his eyes caught sight of something, but then it was gone. He strained them to see through the rushing waters before him. There, he saw it again. Through the waterfall he could just glimpse the flickering of torchlight clearly coming in their direction.

Will her ruse work? Will they follow the trail left by the horses into the woods?

By now he had deduced that was the reason she had sent them off into the forest with their armor.

The torchlight flickered a short distance away. Clavorn watched as the light danced and moved across the river, its riders apparently scouring the area for tracks. All of a sudden, one broke off and rode towards the falls, following the side of the lake. Finally, he stopped just outside their hiding place on the side farthest from the other falls which continued to pour forth into the river below.

"What are you doing?" he heard a guard yell to the one who had separated himself from the group. His voice, though muffled by the waterfalls, was still amazingly discernible.

"Checking it out?"

"They won't be in there? Look at those falls."

"Uhha, that's just my point."

The guard dismounted and waded part way in, apparently finding the shallow spot they had used. Wading forward, the man raised his touch and peered in. Clavorn could just make out his figure on the opposite side through the flowing curtain of water.

Why didn't we enter over there?

The thought briefly flitted through his mind as he observed the guard on the other side of the falls. Then he quickly decided that she must have had her reasons, though they were not readily apparent.

"Over here! I found tracks leading into the woods again!" someone else shouted from farther back. By context Clavorn guessed it was one of the other guards.

But the one with the torch just outside the falls lingered, peering through the waterfall. Slowly, the man edged his way towards the spot they had used as an entrance.

"Come on Ghent! Jovbet found their tracks."

"I'll be right behind you," they heard the guard named Ghent call out.

The woman slowly pulled out a knife from her boot, and Clavorn quietly unsheathed the sword he had confiscated from the guard back at the castle. Slowly, he backed into the darkness and made his way quietly to the other side of the cave, opposite her, where he figure the guard would most likely make his entrance.

"Ghent, I know what you're thinking. Come on! There's nothing behind that old falls but rock."

"I'm not so sure."

"Ghent, if we lose them we could lose our heads."

"That's why you go on ahead," he called back, continuing to gaze through the falls.

"Ghent, it's going to take all of us to take Clavorn down and you know it. More so, now that he has who knows how many men with him. Even if he is in there, which I doubt, he'll most likely slit your throat before you've even seen him."

He's got that right.

"Personally, I'd rather take my chances with the trail. Besides, if you're wrong you'll have gotten wet for nothing."

Fires of Life

The guard, named Ghent, paused and continued to peer through the rushing water as if searching for a reason which would satisfy him one way or the other.

"Come on Ghent! The moon is setting and they're trail will be harder to follow," shouted the one guard.

The guard on the other side of falls continued to search, the light from his torch filtering in through the rushing water and flickering about the cavern floor. Clavorn wondered if he would give in to his hunch and step through the waterfall. The silence that followed as the man on the other side considered his options seemed to linger on indefinitely. Clavorn felt his muscles tense as he readied himself to strike should the guard give in to his instincts.

"Alright, you win. It's an awfully cold night for a swim anyway," the guard named Ghent shouted back, finally turning and acquiescing to his companions, apparently satisfied that there was nothing behind the falls but rock.

Clavorn could see him turn to leave, as his torchlight flickered and began to diminish in size as he retreated to join the others.

Not long after that the torchlights could be seen fading off into the distance. There was an almost visible sigh of relief throughout the cave at the sight of the retreating torches. Clavorn made his way back to the woman who was just finishing replacing her knife back into her boot.

"We'd better get moving," she told him as he came up to meet her.

"I agree," he replied, sheathing his sword.

Clavorn began to take a step towards the falls, but his benefactor caught his arm.

"Not that way," she told him, "Come. Follow me."

Puzzled, but knowing the futility of questions, he followed her. She took his hand and led them deeper into the cave. When they could no longer see the entrance she stopped and released her hold on his hand.

Darkness had completely enveloped them. All he could see was pitch black before him. He could not even make out the woman who was standing right beside him. After a few seconds though, Clavorn began to notice a dim glow coming from her direction, he looked down at its source. It was a small rock that she had apparently pulled out from her pocket. The rock was emitting a strange cold blue light.

"It's what my mother used to call a moonstone," she explained. "For some the stone glows."

"How convenient," he commented the mystery around her growing, though somewhere in the back of his mind he thought he had heard something about that before, but where? The thought entered and left his mind almost simultaneously as he viewed their surroundings. The blue light from the stone played off the damp cavern walls giving it an almost surreal feel.

There was not much time to take in his surroundings though, for she quickly urged him onward. They proceeded forward with the stone lighting their way. However, as they continued Clavorn could see the cavern where they were was immense. The ceiling must have risen for what seemed like five dragon's lengths and its breadth only slightly smaller. Bats occasionally flitted about high above them, apparently startled by their presence, as great stalactites pointed down towards them. Several corresponding stalagmites could be seen throughout the floor, some small but others quite large. A few giant columns seemed to help support the roof of the huge cavern.

Soon, though, the cave narrowed and the ceiling lowered. Clavorn noticed several other cavern cavities and hallways branching off here and there as they traveled. On and on they continued on their journey for what seemed like hours. Clavorn noted that his liberator past dozens of would be tunnels and alternate routes without even so much as a second glance. She was definitely familiar with their route. The mystery surrounding her seemed to grow more as their expedition continued.

Who is she? Why is she helping me? How does she know so much about this place?...Where are the others helping her? Are there others?

These and other questions plagued his mind as they trekked on through the long cavern.

Time continued to pass.

"Is it me, or is that stone of yours growing dimmer?" he asked after they had been travelling for what felt like an eternity.

By now they had taken several twists and turns in their path. The thought of navigating this maze without light was not a prospect he was looking forward too.

"No, it's not. You are right. The stone is growing dimmer. It will be dawn soon," she informed him, stepping around a rather large column in front of them.

"Mind if I ask you a personal question?" he continued as they picked their way over the rocky terrain of the cavern floor.

"Yes, we're at the other end now," she announced as she came to an abrupt stop.

Clavorn looked up from the floor, and sure enough there was the beginning of daylight in front of them.

"I still would like to at least know your name," he pressed as he stepped over a large rock.

Suddenly, she turned on him as quickly as a cat to its prey she had him pinned with a dagger to his throat.

"Who I am is irrelevant. A ghost if you like," she told him fire burning in her eyes.

"You are a little too real for that," he countered.

"Then a mystery. The point is who I am matters little," she continued, pressing him further into the cold damp rock of the cave wall behind him.

"Ah, I beg to differ with that. Who you are matters to me."

A moment of silence passed between them, where she maintained the blade at his throat, as she seemed to consider his words for a moment.

"You saved my life," he added as he looked down upon her, the fervor still clearly present in her eyes as she considered this. If he wanted to, he was fairly confident he could arrest the dagger from her, however, that was not what this situation called for.

"I understand," she replied, softening for a moment, and for a brief second he thought she would release him from the dagger's embrace and tell him, "but you are just going have to accept my answer."

"But how am I to repay you?" he protested. Surely, she would not deny him some form of display of gratitude for all her trouble.

"You can repay me by winning this war," she told him the fire returning to her eyes.

He could feel the pressure of blade against his throat as it increased with the intensity of her emotions. Clavorn gazed deep into her catlike eyes. He could not tell their color in the gray light of dawn, but he could see they were rimmed with the most spectacularly long lush eyelashes he had ever seen. They were beautiful. He wondered briefly at the rest of her. By now it was clear to him that she had indeed been deliberately hiding her identity, and that it was not going to be forth coming any time soon.

"I'll do my best," he told her, continuing to stare straight into her eyes.

After a brief moment, in which she appeared to consider not just his words but him as well, she released him and sheathed her dagger, apparently satisfied with his response. Then she turned and walked up to the cave's outlet.

Relieved, he stepped away from the stony wall and began to pick his way forward amongst the rocks and stones which littered the floor in this part of the cave. Upon reaching the entrance, he saw her withdraw a strange tiny horn trimmed with silver details that he could not make out. He watched as she appeared to blow on it, though it did not seem to make a sound at all. More mystery, Clavorn made his way beside her, still a bit taken back by the ferocity of her display.

"What are we looking for?" he inquired as he surveyed the landscape. The foothills before them were rocky and full of low lying brush and wildflowers. Spreading out below them was a wide expansive valley heavily laden with mist and fog.

"Them," she replied pointing down into the misty valley below.

Out of the fog, galloping towards them was a pair of the most spectacular looking white horses he had ever seen.

Chapter 2

"We'll need to cross the valley before the sun has fully risen," she informed him as one of the gorgeous white horses came to a stop in front of her.

She rubbed its forehead and seemed to whisper something to it in some strange language that Clavorn had never heard before. The horse lowered its head, and then, to his amazement, knelt down so that she could easily mount it.

Clavorn stood for a moment staring, but not for long for the other of the white horses came trotting up to him and stopped before him. He stood gazing at it in awe, and found himself uncontrollably stroking its magnificent neck. Its long mane and tail gently undulated in the soft morning breeze. The sun glistened off its coat so that it seemed to shine like new fallen snow.

"Are you going to stand there admiring your horse all day, or are you going to mount it before the sun reaches its zenith?" she remarked to him, suddenly snapping him to his senses.

"Oh, yes, of course," he replied a bit embarrassed.

He stepped to the side of his mount and in one catlike motion lifted himself atop the magnificent steed. Clavorn patted the horse gently on its neck and gave it one more stroke. The softness of its coat amazed him for it felt like fine silk.

"Do they have names?" he asked curious.

"Yes, but they are hard to pronounce," she replied, turning her steed to face him.

"Try me."

"Nahhanahrilla and Nahhaelamana" she told him, pointing first to her horse and then to his.

"That doesn't sound so bad," he remarked, being careful not to try and repeat what she had just said. "Does that translate into anything in our language?"

"Of course, Wind Dancer and Song's First Light," she told him, again pointing to them respectively.

Then, before he could say another word, she turned her horse named Wind Dancer into the sun and headed down to the valley below, disappearing into the low lying cloud of fog.

Turning his body, as his hands twisted into the horse's thick mane, Clavorn turned Song's First Light to follow her. Mist and haze shrouded the valley, enveloping him as they descended the mountainside. It was easy to see why she felt it was important to cross before the sun had its chance to burn off their cover.

The fog was dense as he rode astride the magnificent white steed. He could barely make out the back of the mysterious woman he was supposed to follow. Every now and then, they would hit a particularly dense patch in which she would disappear entirely for moments at a time. During those moments, he had to rely on the horse she had summoned to know where to go.

There was no way to tell exactly which direction they were traveling. All landmarks were hidden from his view by the dense fog. All he could do was follow her and marvel at how she was so expertly able to navigate their way through the mist.

Yes, there is a definite mystery about her, he considered as he rode on through the thick haze, one that begged discovery but hinted at danger, just the sort of mystery to intrigue a man like him.

Gradually, the fog seemed to lessen. Soon he began to see trunks of trees and small shrubs. Before long, he could tell that they had left the valley and were now traveling through a forest. The trees here were also very old, and felt as if magic and fairies dwelt within them, as if they were from a time long before the wars, before men, when dragons had ruled the land.

"By Alhera, where are we?" he asked, the words just tumbling out of his mouth as they shed the cover of the mist. "It looks as if the dragons never left here."

"We are in a safe place. That is all you need to know."

"You know, one would think that since you want me to win this war, you would trust me enough to at least tell me where we are."

Silence followed as she refused to answer him and they continued to ride into the wood.

It was beautiful. Moss and ferns grew near the bases of the large trees and up their thick trunks, spreading along their ornate branches. Assorted spring flowers littered the forest floor and were spotlighted by rays of sunlight that managed to find their way through the dense canopy above. Here spring had clearly come earlier. Birds sang and flitted about. One very nearly flew into him as they made their way in. A deer glanced up at their entry but made no motion of leaving. He continued to marvel at their surroundings as they rode.

Mushrooms and toad stools sprinkled their way up the sides and base of the great trees, intermixing with the mosses and ferns. Wondrous flowering vines wove their way up the trunks of a number of these ancient inhabitants. Occasionally, he could spot a tree frog in the trees. Their song, along with others of the amphibian family, mixed with those of birds to create quite a chorus. Wafting through the forest was a glorious perfume of wild rose, hyacinth, and other flowering plants and shrubs.

Young saplings abounded. Here, life was plentiful. He had been in every part of the forests of his country, or so he thought, but never had he seen such a wondrous wood. Only in the stories of old had he heard of such forests, but then there were many mysteries in the world and it would be presumptuous of him to believe that had seen them all.

"Follow me," she ordered once more bringing him back to the task at hand. It was then that he noticed the change in their direction.

"Do I have a choice?" he countered.

"Yes, you are free now. You always have a choice."

Now she is beginning to sound like Qualtaric. Do they know each other?

But he immediately dismissed the thought almost as quickly as it had entered his mind. Qualtaric was an old warrior who had mentored him in the ways of war, and, given what he knew about him, it seemed unlikely their paths had ever crossed.

"That may be the case. But, as I am at a loss as to my whereabouts, it hardly seems like much of a choice."

"You are in the Forest of Calhador," she told him.

"Oh, right, like that is elucidating." The Forest of Calhador was known only in legends. "You expect me to believe that we are traveling through a forest known only in tales passed on by old men. No one knows where that forest is, or even if it really exists."

She halted her horse. He came up beside her on his and stopped at her side.

"It exists," she told him looking him square in the eye, "and you are traveling through it. It has been protected for millennia. That is why only a select few know where it is. Fortunately for you, it happens to be our safest route back to Avivron."

"Okay. Assuming I believe you and this is the Forest of Calhador, which I am not sure that it is. How can you say I have a 'choice' if I have no idea where Calhador is?"

"You still always have a choice, Clavorn Remmaik, son of Favorn, whether you are aware of your surroundings or not."

"But I could ride into Vaulnik's men if I choose the *wrong* direction," he pointed out.

"True," she replied as she nudged her horse forward.

"Then how is that a choice?!" he called after her.

"It's a choice to trust," she shouted back to him over her shoulder.

Clavorn rolled his eyes and spurred his horse to follow.

Women.

"Besides," she continued, "I know a place here where we can rest and recover before we continue on our way."

"Good, I'm starving," he shout to her.

The sight of a deer along the way had inadvertently triggered his appetite. They had eaten nothing since their escape from the Castle Shalhadon, now known as Kazengor Castle, or even less lovingly as 'The Castle of Horrors.' With his sense of urgency dissipating, his hunger was now beginning to set in, or rather roar in.

They continued on through the woods in silence. However, the forest itself was alive with sounds, a far cry from the Forest of Thestaera. There it had been mostly silent. Now, he took in the sounds and voices of the wood as a choir of birds and others sang in the canopy above them. Sunlight continued to stream in through the dense vegetation above them. He could almost believe this was the Forest of Calhador.

How had it eluded discovery? Magic must be strong here. Does that mean the legends are true?

Stories told by his grandfather crowded his mind, and he began to wonder at the possibility of the truth of them as they traveled on. He had believed in them once when he was very young, before everything changed, before the Dragon Wars, before the horror.

Could there really be truth in the old legends? If this forest is the forest she claims it is, then clearly there must be.

Still a side of him was skeptical.

After a while they came to a rocky hollow. Cascades of water flowed down the moss covered rocks and spilled onto the ground, disappearing into the earth below. Bromeliads, ferns, and assorted flowers along with mounds of orchids decorated the entrance to the rocky hollow. His benefactor was heading straight for the cleft which seemed to form a sort of passage.

A cool breeze shot through the narrow confines of the space as they passed through it. The jagged rocky walls stretched upwards for several dragon lengths and seemed to almost converge at the top. There vegetation could be seen growing over and above the rocky walls, clearly preventing any notice of it from the surface above them.

When they came out the other end of the passage, they were in what was evidently another forest entirely different from the one they had just been in. The vegetation was more familiar and seemed to hint to Clavorn that he was now in his homeland of Avivron, though he could make out no familiar landmarks.

The sun was high in the sky when they left the passage. Clavorn hoped this 'rest and recuperation,' which he assumed at least included some sort of meal, would arrive soon. His stomach was making so much noise he was sure even the gods could hear it.

Suddenly, his benefactor picked up the pace, and they were trotting and galloping up and down the side of a mountain. Weaving their way through trees and forest vegetation, which while sparser than it had been in the Forest of Calhador, was still challenging enough. Then almost as quickly as she had picked up the pace she slowed.

Clavorn looked about as they came to another river, though much quieter, calmer, and shallower than the one they had crossed the night before. Here the forest seemed to change yet again. Great giant willow trees were unusually abundant along the banks of this river. The wispy, ever weeping branches of the giant trees blew softly in the gentle breeze. Their horses crossed the shallow river and stopped.

"I take it we have arrived," he remarked as he looked about the place.

Flowering bushes were everywhere as far as the eye could see. Hawthorn trees were scattered along the mountainside between stands of pine and were interspersed amongst the willows along with other ancient deciduous trees. Their flowers were in full bloom, adding to the picturesque nature of what could only be described as an old willow grove. Sunlight caught on the tiny white blossoms that covered the Hawthorns, highlighting the bees and other insects who were partaking in their bounty. As before, birds sang throughout the trees and flitted about them, while a carpet of wildflowers lay at his horse's hooves.

"Yes. Come, let's eat and rest," and with that she dismounted leaving her horse to its own devices.

Clavorn did the same and followed her as she entered the old grove of willows, but not without turning to stroke the long silky neck of the magnificent beast which had born him there. Song's First

Light nickered, and he thanked the creature before turning his attentions back to her. The wispy branches of the ancient willows seemed to reach out to them as they entered, inviting them in. Clavorn marveled at their magnificence.

"Where are we now? We cannot still be in the Forest of Calhador." he commented.

"You are quite right. We are not in the Forest of Calhador," she replied. "We left that as soon as we passed through the Passage of Allethor. No, we are in Shyloran Forest, an ancient willow grove in your homeland of Avivron. It thankfully has escaped the attentions of Vaulnik."

It appears to have escaped the attentions of most men as well. I wonder how that is possible.

"If you are wondering, Shyloran is a protected forest. Few know of its existence."

There was no doubt that someone had guarded Shyloran. All one needed to do was glance about. The beauty and majesty of this forest alone spoke to its keepers.

The wispy branches swayed and swirled all around them giving glimpses of what lay ahead, and then disappearing them in a sort of dance. Clavorn was about to brush aside another branch when the trees seemed to part and there, in the center of the willow wood, was the oldest and largest willow tree he had ever seen. Its grand old delicate branches reached far up into the sky and drooped back to earth with such thickness that Clavorn thought one could almost hide a whole army within its canopy. Therefore, it was no surprise to him when she parted its dense weeping branches that there, displayed before him, were all the creature comforts he so craved. For the ancient willow was more like a vast wispy fortress than a tree.

Glancing around to one side, he noticed a very large old root that had been turned into a bed with soft leaves and grasses to cushion its hardness. A bear skin lay over the bedding with another set off to the side, presumably as a blanket. The trunk of the giant old tree was quite substantial with a large hollow in its center. It was difficult for him to make out whether or not this was a resting place, or an actual residence of sorts. There was also what appeared to be a place for a fire in the middle of the empty space created by the overhanging branches. In fact, as he moved in closer he could tell a fire had been lit in that spot before.

"Please sit," she told him.

"But where?"

"Trees have many roots, so I shall enjoy this one over here," she told him matter-of-factly as she sat down upon a root that was just opposite the one set up as a bed.

Clavorn felt ridiculous for not noticing it earlier, but then he could have sworn it had not been there a minute ago. Still, he may have been so overwhelmed by the place that it simply escaped his notice.

"Why don't you rest now," she told him, motioning to the place set up as a bed, "You will be safe here while I find us something to eat."

"I am capable of hunting for myself," he told her, feeling a bit odd that she should be the one hunting for him. After all he was quite a fine hunter and warrior. He did not feel as if he needed all this pampering.

"I know, but you have just escaped from prison, and you will need your strength for later," she replied, standing up and darning a bow that he could have sworn had not been there a moment before.

"So will you," he told her.

At this there was a slight pause in her hands as she readied her knapsack.

"I will be fine. Rest," she ordered as she turned and left the tree.

All Clavorn saw of her as she departed was her retreating figure through the branches of the willow. He tried to follow, to protest, but she was gone, almost as if she had vanished into the grove itself.

Clavorn turned around, his eyes falling on the inviting bed created out of the giant tree root before him. Suddenly, a wave of fatigue washed over him as he glanced at it. He had not noticed how tired he was till now. A rest would be good he decided, and so he went over and lay down upon the inviting bed.

The grasses and leaves were soft due to their freshness. The bear skins enveloped him with their warmth and comfort, the fur feeling soft against his skin. It was a stark contrast to the cold stone and chains he had been forced to endure earlier. Whoever had set this bed up had known just how much bedding to put in place, for he could not feel the hardness of the root beneath him.

Clavorn looked up into the branches of the great tree. Sunlight filtered in causing the leaves to shimmer as it reflected off their surface. The sweet smell of the wild flowers outside waft in, and it was not long before sleep overcame him. A delicately soft warm breeze blew in through the gracefully flowing branches, gently caressing his skin. He stretched his muscular body beneath the furs, pulling the one over himself, as he turned over and drifted deeper into the realm of slumber.

Chapter 3

    He did not know how long he had been asleep, but it must have been sometime for the light now seemed to be fading, and there was a small fire in the open space before him. Upon it was roasting a decent sized rabbit, but his benefactor was nowhere to be found. Stretching his long lean sinuous body, he sat up. Soon he could hear the sound of rushing water as if there was a waterfall not far off. Curious he decided to head in that direction.

    Following the sound through the dense vegetation, he trudged, parting branches and ducking under large limps. The orange glow of the late afternoon light glinted off of the leaves and verdure around him. Finally, as he parted the branches of a large willow, he was greeted by the roaring sound and remarkable vision of a tall fast flowing falls. A beautiful rainbow shimmered within its spray as the light of the setting sun shined down upon it.

    His eyes followed the flow of the water to its base. That was when he saw her. Startled, he stopped dead, for there she was, naked, bathing within the waterfall. Her long dark hair falling well past her buttocks, her beautiful white skin appearing almost magical as it contrasted with the dark rock behind her. He could not help but watch as the water danced down her supple body caressing her breasts.

    Embarrassed by his intrusion, he stepped back into the willow just out of sight, hidden by the weepy branches. He could not, however, steal his glance away from her, hopeful that he might catch at least a glimpse of her face. As he looked on, she turned and faced the waterfall, sweeping her long hair alongside her sinuous body. He starred on enjoying the beauty of her, her soft gentle curves, her graceful muscles, the delicate way the water played over her as it danced down from the cliff above.

    Suddenly, she changed the angle of her body so that her back was full to him. That was when he saw them, horrifying terrible scars crossing her back. He knew of only one thing capable of making such a disfigurement, Vaulnik's Dragon Whips. They were said to be made from descaled dragon's skin so as not to tear the flesh off a person too quickly, but specifically designed to inflict tremendous pain upon their victim. Pain, that burned the flesh like the fires of the dragons from whence they came.

To his knowledge, rarely was there a person who recovered from the wounds of such a whip. For the pain was rumored to last long after the wound had healed, driving most of its victims to suicide. He had only seen such wounds once.

It had been during the Dragon Wars, on an evening raid of one of Vaulnik's fortresses. They had found a warrior who had apparently been captured a few days prior. He remembered how they had discovered him still writhing in pain in the dungeon. How the pain had eventually driven the man insane until he had, in a fit of madness, committed suicide, choosing to fall on his sword rather than continue to endure the pain of his wounds. As he looked on, he could not imagine how she had survived such torture, for her wounds were more numerous than the warrior's. Let alone maintain her sanity.

Shocked by his discovery, and feeling guilty about his infringement, he quickly backed away from the falls and returned to the huge old willow tree to await her return. Clearly, there was much more to her story than he could imagine. But at least now he had an idea of why she so obviously wanted him to win the war, and quite possibly a piece of the reason for her secrecy. Not really sure of what he should do while he waited for her; he decided to fain sleep until she returned.

He did not have long to wait before she arrived fully clothed and completely covered, her face included.

"I see you're awake," she commented, her back turned to him while she checked on the roasting rabbit.

"Well, it was kind of hard to sleep through the wonderful smell of that creature you're roasting," he replied, hoping she had not noticed his intrusions.

Fires of Life

"Well, then you'll be glad to learn that it is done," she announced.

With that Clavorn rose and came to sit near her. He could not tell from her demeanor if she had noticed his earlier infringements. But if she had, she was certainly not letting on, and there was no way that he was going to let on either. They sat in relative silence as they ate. Both clearly famished from their ordeal.

"So what's the plan from here? If you don't mind my asking," he inquired as he downed his last bite of the succulent rabbit.

"The plan is to return you back to your men," she told him as she took a drink of water from her oil skin bag.

"But what of Almaik?" he asked.

"He is your issue," she replied simply, placing the oil skin at her side and handing him another that was beside her.

"What do you know of him?" he pressed her, after taking a swig from the oil skin bag she had handed him. He had to know if she knew anything of him, or had any more information that could prove useful in his understanding as to why he had betrayed him.

"He is the king's son," she replied simply.

"Do you know why he would want to betray me?" he continued.

She chewed on a piece of rabbit, clearly considering his question. He wondered if she knew that it was he who had turned him over to Vaulnik.

"There is much intrigue in the castle these days, but it is rumored that King Sevzozak has been paying Vaulnik ransom to maintain his kingdom, or rather should I say his throne."

"Yes, I know this, but you would think that he would want us to win so that he could have his kingdom free and clear to rule."

He still could not understand the logic behind his betrayal. His theory about the aristocracy's fear of him still did not seem to justify their preference for Vaulnik's rule.

"True, why do you think that you were allowed to fight this war for as long as you did?" she asked him as she took a sip of her water again.

Clavorn blinked, the question blindsiding him. He had never even bothered to consider why. He had just assumed that it was because he was aiding the king and his people. That Sevzozak was pleased with his success. After all his men were doing a better job at defending his people than Sevzozak's had. He considered that the king was just continuing to pay off Vaulnik to buy his men time, and to appear cooperative in order to keep his head for when he defeated Vaulnik. There was little risk involved for the king that way. If he failed, it was merely the uprising of disgruntled peasants. If he succeeded, then the king would reward him as a hero and that would be the end of it.

So of course he had let him and his men fight, but now the question hit him broadside. Was there more to this than he had thought?

"What do you mean *allowed*?" he asked, "It served the king, but we would have fought whether he allowed it or not."

"Precisely!" she announced. He looked at her, "That is exactly the reason."

"What? I'm confused."

"You brought to light his failure to protect the people. In short, you did what he, for whatever reason, couldn't or wouldn't."

"But I was fighting for my country, for my people, his people; always in his name. I just assumed he would want that."

"You assumed much."

*What? How could a king **not** want us to win?*

He still was just not seeing what her point was.

"What? How could he not?" he replied.

"The question is not so much about the king as it is about how the people reacted to you."

"What do mean?" he asked, suspecting that she was about to confirm his suspicions, or was there more. Something he had not considered.

"Are you sure the people who fought for you felt as you did? That they wanted to liberate Avivron *and* her king."

He considered her question.

"Those men fought for *you*, not the nobles. Did they not?" she continued.

"Yes, but..."

"But nothing. Those nobles could not arouse those people into fighting for them no matter how hard they tried, and tried they had."

"And the people fought with them."

"Yes, because they were obliged too. However, their hearts were not in it or they would have won, and Vaulnik would never have entered Avivron."

"Maybe," after what he had witnessed at the Battle of Quantaris he very much doubted if they could have, "still we will never really know since the king ordered them off in order to prevent their slaughter."

"This is true, or perhaps not. He could have had other motives. You are making an assumption."

"So are you," he countered.

"Yes, but he still did not have to let them suffer. Wasn't that why you began the rebellion?"

True enough, but he still did not see where she was going with this.

"Yes, but your point is?"

"My point is...along comes you. A man they can relate too. Not a noble, but a man of the people. One who has lost just as they have lost. One who knows their pain, and who is strong, brave, and knowledgeable in the ways of war. You teach them to fight. You show them how. You show them they do not have to tolerate the abuses. Who do you think they are going to follow, the noblemen? Their king? Or you? And you they did. In droves they came to follow *you*."

"But it was always in the name of the king."

"No, Clavorn. It was always in the name of the people. Don't you remember?"

He stared at her, as the revelation of what he had done began to sink in. It had always been the people first.

"Yes Clavorn, you fought for them, for this land, for everything that you hold dear, and everything they hold dear."

"But isn't that what…shouldn't that be what our king should want?"

"Yes, but you already know the answer to that. If our king held those things in as high esteem as you, he would have never needed you. The people would have gladly fought with him."

She was right and he knew it. Why hadn't he seen it before? It was all so obvious. Blinded by pain, by frustration, fresh from the battles of the Dragon Wars, was that why he had not seen it then? Her words confirmed his growing suspicions.

"So basically what you are saying is that he felt threaten by my popularity."

"Yes, don't you see?"

Yes, he could see it. He could see it all. His suspicions confirmed.

"But I don't want to rule." He protested, "I never wanted to rule!" he blurted out, his outrage being difficult to contain, bringing him to his feet.

He ran a hand over his head, his fingers combing through his long thick dark hair. Power was something he had never sought for himself. He just wanted his people to be free. Free of that overbearing and cruel King Vaulnik.

"Sometimes it doesn't matter what we want. It only matters what the people want, and like it or not, if given a choice, the people are likely to choose you over their apparent cowardly aristocracy."

Again Clavorn looked at her. He had never considered this possibility. It had never even occurred to him that the people would want him to rule. He was just a commoner like them. Well, maybe that was a bit of an exaggeration. His father had been First Knight to King Dakconar, who belonged to the house of Akalor, one of the oldest dynasties in Avivron. But that was before the king had died under questionable circumstances; a hunt gone wrong, a stray arrow in the chaos of the chase.

He tried to remember back to when it had all started. The images were blurry. He had been just a young boy at the time, but he remembered his father coming home and his mother complaining about how he seemed so distant. That was how it had started from his perspective. His father would then apologize to her, flash a big smile and he would be amongst them again, leaving the troubles of the kingdom behind.

They had been a close family, his mother, father, his sister, and himself. He remembered the stories his father used to tell, all sorts of stories. They were good stories, for the most part, till one morning he found his father sitting on a log just outside their house. He remembered how sad and distant he had appeared. It was all as clear as it had been on that morning so many years ago.

"What's wrong father," he had asked.

"I could tell you 'nothing' son. I fear that is what your mother would want, but you will soon be a man, my son, and times are changing. "

"What do you mean father?"

"Sit here," his father had told him patting the log he was sitting on. He remembered doing as his father had told him and going to sit down beside him on the log. The log was set on the side of a grassy hill which over looked the kingdom. In the distance one could see The Krimian Ridge and beyond The Mountains of Shylaharon in the south.

"Look there son. Tell me what you see."

"I see The Krimian Ridge father."

"And beyond?" his father pressed.

"The Mountains of Shylaharon." He recalled how his father's inquiry had perplexed him as he continued to question him.

"What else do you see?"

"The sun rising?"

"Look harder."

He strained his eyes to see whatever it was his father was seeing. At first he saw nothing, and then, like the coming of a dark storm he had seen it. Through the morning mist he saw it, an unnatural darkening of the land far beyond the borders of Avivron.

"Is that it?" he had asked his father as he pointed to the area on the landscape which seemed out of place.

"Yes, that is it son. We have been noticing it for some time now. It grows even as we speak. Scouts say the land there is dying, changing. All we know are rumors. A time may come for you to leave this land. If anything should happen to me, promise me you will seek out my old mentor, Qualtaric."

"But what of mother and Shalvera?"

"I have made arrangements for them. They will be safe," his father turned to him and stared him straight in the eye as he placed a hand on his shoulder. "You must promise me you will find Qualtaric. You still have the book I gave you?"

"Yes father, but why must I find him? Shouldn't I stay with mother and Shalvera?"

"No!" his father's emphatic 'No' had taken him by surprise, but something in the urgency of his father's voice had made him feel that there was something even more going on than he was telling him, and that this was what was behind his father's insistence.

"Alright father. I promise I will seek out this Qualtaric if anything should happen to you."

"Good," was all his father had said before removing his hand and disappearing once more into the depths of his thoughts. He remembered sitting beside him in silence wondering what his father's cryptic conversation could mean.

It was not long after that that things began to change. Slowly, intangibly at first, but he began to notice it. It was something in the air. Then one day it all happened so fast. The King was dead. 'Questionable circumstances' he had overheard his father say to one of his knights and confidants. He had taken to eavesdropping on his father after that day when he had shown him the darkness in the land beyond, and he had watched as it had mysteriously grown. The King's son, Sevzozak, was crowned the next ruler of Avivron. All appeared fine except for the growing restless nature of his father. Increasingly, his mother worried for him, but nothing she said could coax the reason from his father's lips. Then one night everything changed.

He remembered it well. His mother and sister were away visiting his aunt. She was having another baby and they had gone to help. Everything had started off so normal that evening. His father and he had gone hunting earlier in the day, and they had just finished enjoying the day's spoils; pheasant. They had joked how his mother and his sister would be jealous if they knew. He could see it. The fire was crackling in the hearth, candlelight flickering off the walls, while the smell of their dinner still lingered in the air, though it had long since been cleared off. When suddenly his father fell silent and hushed him. Then, without explanation, quickly rose and went straight for the wall behind them, motioning him to follow.

"Quick. Hurry son. No time for questions. You must hide. No matter what you see or hear you must promise me to stay hidden. Do you understand?"

"Yes, but why?"

"I haven't got time for explanations," his father had said rather abruptly as he moved a small stone in the wall and a secret entrance opened up. He guessed his father had had it made for just such an occasion. Fortunately, it was not far from where they had been seated. "Now go!" His father had urged as he hesitated, "You are just going to have to trust me. Promise, no matter what you see or hear you will stay here."

"But I want to fight if that is it father."

"No son. There will be another time for that. Now, stay here and whatever happens, stay quiet."

"Yes father."

He remembered how he had wanted to ask more, but his father had sealed him in before he had gotten the chance. Quickly, he had glanced around the space his father had concealed him in and found a small crack in the wall from where he was able to see and hear most of what happened.

"Good evening Zarik," his father had said in a voice which clearly conveyed his displeasure as he stood behind the table they had previously been seated at. At that moment a male servant showed a tall man with well-groomed dark hair and his accompaniment in. Consternation was written clearly over the servant's face, who had evidently tried to prevent them from entering. His father's gesture to the concerned man in response was, while succinct, designed to convey at once both his understanding and his gratitude for his efforts.

"Good evening to you Remmaik. May we come in?" The man who his father had called Zarik replied as he entered further into the room.

It was at that point when he could see the man more clearly. He remembered what had stood out most to him in the man's appearance. Aside from the impeccable nature of the dark black clothes he wore, was an unusually heavy gold and silver chain upon which hung a large menacing dragon medallion. The sight of it had never left his memory, for it was a rather unusual depiction of a dragon; gaudy and hideous.

"That is *Sir* Remmaik to you Zarik and clearly you are already in," his father had replied to him as he quickly turned his attentions from the servant to the tall dark well-dressed man in front of him and his men, "As to whether or not you are welcome, that is another matter altogether."

"I see. Well, pity," the man called Zarik had countered as he strutted even further into the room, "but the King has found himself a new First Knight and sadly well, it is not you."

"Don't tell me. Let me guess. He has chosen you."

Fires of Life

"Oh, how right you are," the tall overbearing man continued. "You know, you are truly a clever knight," sarcasm dripped from his lips as he moved closer to his father, "They say that cleverness is often rewarded," Zarik went on.

He remembered how he could feel the hair rise on the back of his neck.

"Clearly, yours has," his father replied, "but does he know where your *real* loyalties lie?"

"Well, whether the king does or doesn't is open for debate," Zarik responded as he edged his way further forward.

"I see," his father replied, "Well, we'll see about that."

"No, I don't think we'll see about that," Zarik told him as he ran him through with a dagger he had surreptitiously concealed till that moment.

He remembered how he had wanted to cry out. How he had almost torn through the walls of the hiding place his father had placed him in. If it had not been for the promise his father had so vehemently sworn him to, he knew he would have rushed the tall dark man called Zarik.

As it was, however, he could only observe as his father doubled over from the strike, but he did not go down immediately. As he watched, his father gradually rose, pulling the dagger out and using it to try and attack his assailant.

"Look, the fool is still trying to defend his king," Zarik mocked. "Poor deluded man. You are as good as dead."

"I can still…" his father had begun as he faltered in his attempt to try and right himself so that he could strike the dagger into his opponent.

"You can still what?" the tall dark man named Zarik taunted once more. "You can still fight? Ha, ha, ha," he laughed, "I think not my friend. That dagger was laced with poison. Oh, oops. It appears you are at a loss for words. Pity."

Then he heard the clang as the dagger hit the stone floor. Moments later he witnessed his father collapse onto the table in front of him. It appeared to him that his father had been about to strike Zarik when the poison had finally taken hold of him.

In the end, he had watched as the man called Zarik tossed his father's body aside like yesterday's garbage.

"Search the house. Find the boy…and the rest of his family."

"What shall we do with them?" one of the men with Zarik had asked.

He could still here Zarik's icy reply, "Kill them."

What followed had felt like hours of terrible noises as Zarik's men tossed the house, and killed anyone they had found living on its premise. All he could do was shut his ears to dampen the hideous screams of those who were tortured and killed in Zarik's obsessive attempt to find him and the rest of his family.

At the time, it had felt as if the nightmare would never end. And as they continued to search the house after they had tortured and killed those within, it had seemed as if they had been looking for more than just his family, but what had been the mystery. He knew his father suspected treachery within the castle. The events of that day had clearly proved there was.

But what had Zarik's men been looking for?

He never forgot the name of man who had taken his father's life. However, after his father's murder he had gone in search of Qualtaric just as his father had requested. All he could remember about Qualtaric from his father's stories was that he was a great swordsman who lived somewhere up in the mountains, apparently as a kind of hermit in his old age. His father had given him a book for his seventh birthday and told him never to lose it. Then he had shown him a special page and said that the clues to finding Qualtaric lay there.

The reason for all the mystery behind Qualtaric he had never understood. Now he only partially had an idea of. At the time, though, the clues his father had left had been vague, he guessed, for a reason. The old knight turned out to have been the mentor and an old friend of King Dakconar. But for reasons Qualtaric was never willing to share, he and the king had had a bit of a falling out. However, he and his father had remained in touch. But the reasons for that Qualtaric had never been willing to divulge.

Qualtaric always seemed more of a mystery than a man to him. Half Dragon Wizard, if there ever was such a thing, half warrior. He had finally managed to find him, after some difficulty, way up in a very remote region of the mountains. The old hermit had scared him a bit at first, apparently testing his courage and strength of character. Once he had earned his respect, Qualtaric had dropped some of his more ominous characteristics.

He had been about twelve when he first arrived at Qualtaric's hut, for it took him nearly six months of searching, between deciphering the map and codes, braving the elements and the magic, to find him. His hut was a rather small place having only one room that severed all manner of purposes except, of course, those which required one to go out doors to perform.

The old warrior had taught him everything there was to learn about swordsmanship and warfare as well as much about honor, duty, justice, liberty, and above all, freedom. At least as much as any man can. He taught him many of the legends too, though his father and grandfather had already seen too much of that.

But it was his apparent knowledge of the dragons that had fascinated him the most. Qualtaric seemed to be able hear them. Even speak to them, though he never let him in on any of his apparent conversations. No, he just seemed to prefer to act as if they had never taken place.

Nevertheless, he clearly remembered a few times when he had seen the old man out sitting near a dragon or two. It had always appeared to him as if there was more going on than what met the eye. He remembered questioning Qualtaric about it a couple of times, but the old man had simply brushed him off saying something about 'just sitting out with an old friend.' That it was easy to make friends with dragons up in the mountains away from civilization. But he had never been totally satisfied with that answer. With Qualtaric it was like there was always more there than what met the eye.

He recalled how on certain evenings he would find him looking far off into the distance past The Krimian Ridge, past The Mountains of Shylaharon, to the area of growing darkness that seemed to plague the earth, to the land known previously as Ishalhan. The land he would one day learn had been taken over by Vaulnik, the land now known as Zvegnog. One night Qualtaric sat him down and told him everything he knew or had heard about the growing darkness.

"Rumors started to grow before the king's death," he began one night after a long day of training. He could still picture it. A fire in the hearth, its flames licking the logs while shadows danced around the walls of Qualtaric's one room home as he began to divulge what he knew of the growing darkness on the land. "Rumors of a King Vaulnik who had come from somewhere way to the south of Avivron and the surrounding lands as a nobleman. No one seems to know exactly how he came to power in Ishalhan. Only that it was not the usual way, by birth. A bit of a mystery he is. Reports suggest he seized power suddenly, an uprising which overthrew the previous king.

"Mesmerizing and charismatic to the people in the beginning, he cunningly bought himself time. Then one by one the dragons of his land started to disappear. First, it was one then another. No one noticed much until the land near his castle at Shalhadon began to falter and change. Reports began to filter back of a growing darkness around the castle at Shalhadon and throughout Ishalhan. We did not understand it at first until more scouts began to bring word of dragons found dead in the woods and hills where the great change was taking place.

"Then we heard that many of the dragons near his land were trying to renew it, but it never lasted long. Almost as soon as the dragons were done replenishing the land did it begin to slip back into decay and ruin.

"We couldn't believe it at first. Who would? Dragons were created by the goddess Alhera to protect the Earth, her land, and her people. That was why she created the great Maltak, Mother of all the Dragons of the Earth. Yet, no matter how hard the dragons seemed to try, the land always slipped back into decay. We still cannot explain how he is able undo the magic of the dragons, only that it is so. Some say it is dark magic. Others say it is his twisted heart."

Clavorn remembered having been all ears as his mentor continued to recount the tale.

"Soon it was announced that Ishalhan had been renamed Zvegnog. Its castle and her city of Shalhadon were now to be called Kazengor and Kazengor Castle. Not long after that we began to hear of dragons being openly slaughtered. Apparently, Vaulnik had trained special assassins in the art of slaying dragons; Darzors. It turns out they were the ones responsible for the deaths of the dragons in the Forest of Thestaera. In the beginning, we were unsure of their cause of death. Dark magic, poison, disease these were a few of the ideas bantered around as explanations. But then the reports started to filter back. Dragons were being openly hunted and killed; killed by Vaulnik's Darzors."

"How can that be?" he had asked his mentor, "Dragons are sacred animals. No man knows how to kill them."

"No man till now, Clavorn," Qualtaric had answered, "Evil men often find ways to commit evil deeds. By the time we heard of them, the Darzors no longer seemed to fear retribution from the people. Vaulnik had convinced many that the dragons were the cause of the darkness on the land and the trouble it brought. Others were just too afraid to challenge him, and so the darkness around the castle continued to spread.

"Before long, we heard rumors that many of the dragons not far from the Forest of Thestaera were rising up to challenge Vaulnik, but it was already too late. Vaulnik used their challenge to fuel the people's hatred for them; claiming the dragons were deliberately ruining the land. He twisted their actions, even using their attempt at renewing the land as a way to say that they were stalling the people's revolt by trying to create false hope and expectations. Soon even many of his subjects were aiding in the genocide of these sacred creatures."

"How is that possible?"

"Some men can be very persuasive, using fear to change men's hearts and motivate them to commit heinous acts."

"Fear then," he remembered saying to his mentor, "is dangerous in many ways and not just on the battlefield."

"Yes. Sometimes just the fear itself is enough to provoke people into doing monstrous deeds. Fear and ignorance, are unfortunately, one of worst combinations for bring about the most abdominal side of us."

"Not me. I won't let that happen."

"Good. But you must be ever vigilant. This kind of evil is not always easy to spot. It starts small and grows like a seemingly innocuous weed. Before you know it you are its slave."

"Then I will be vigilant."

"Good. Now back to Vaulnik. The more dragons that fell, the darker and more twisted his land became. Even the people there began to change. Their evil deeds corrupting their hearts and changing their nature. By the time of King Dakconar's death, Vaulnik had taken over a good portion of the lands far to the south of Avivron."

"Why didn't we help fight him off?"

"The last time I had spoken with your father, the king was planning on mounting an offensive, along with many others from the outlying regions. But he died before he could mount such an attack."

"Why doesn't King Sevzozak fight?"

"I am told that he does not want to involve Avivron in such a battle. It is said, our king believes it would endanger Avivron."

"Oh, and what do you believe."

"What I believe matters little to this kingdom. I am just an old hermit."

Fires of Life

"No you're not! And it matters to me."

He remembered Qualtaric pausing as if to consider answering his question or not.

"Well, since it matters to you. I will tell you. I think that a fight is destined to come when evil such as this threatens the heart of all that is good. The trick is when to fight, not whether one should or not."

"But how is one to know when it is the right time?"

"One never really knows for sure Clavorn, but a snake is always easier to kill when it is young then when it is old and wise."

"So you think our king should have continued with his father's plans."

"I said no such thing, Clavorn Remmaik, son of Favorn, now may I continue with my story."

Always a mystery he was, never a direct answer. He recalled how frustrated he had been, sometimes to the point of driving him to near distraction.

"Are you listening?"

"Yes, yes."

"Hmmm," his mentor had eyed him from under his bushy eye brows before he had gone on "Well then, as I was saying, it was around that time, the time of your father's death and that of the king, in which the Dragon Wars began far to the south and east of Avivron, in the land known as Salvahook. It was there that Dragons from all over the surrounding lands began to band together and to fight alongside humans to try and defeat Vaulnik. Unfortunately, they have not had the success they had hoped for. Thus far, they have only been able to slow down his forces, not defeat them. Their fight continues as we speak."

"So this is the source of the fires in the sky I see at night over the lands that border the darkness."

"Yes, Clavorn, it is."

"I want to fight. I want to fight this Vaulnik."

"I thought you would, but now is not the time. You are not yet finished with your training. Patience, the time will come."

"You mean, if the war isn't over before I am able to join."

"Come now, the war is the war, and if it is finished before you are able to join in so much the better."

"Why is that?" he remembered asking.

"Because it just is," his mentor had replied in frustration.

"You only mean that if we win right?"

"Yes, of course boy. I would never want that Vaulnik to win."

He had known that, but he had felt the need to confirm it.

"But what if we lose?"

"Well, that would be a different story, but not a part of this one. And not a notion this old man is willing to entertain."

That last statement had ended the evening's conversation on the subject. But as time passed he had watched as his mentor seemed to grow increasingly more disturbed.

"It is not natural," he would say. "Dragons bring life to the earth and defend her. They have always been able too." Then he would shake his head, and look distant and concerned. He would ask Qualtaric about it. All his old mentor would reply was that dark days were afoot.

You need not have been a seer to know that.

Anyone looking over in the direction of Zvegnog had to see the darkness growing, spreading out in all directions like some evil cancer.

Finally, however, the day did arrive when the old man said he had learned all he could from him, that he was ready. In his elation he had immediately gone to fight in the Dragon Wars, in a land far to the West of Avivron known as, Hindora.

Hindora had been a prosperous country known for its shipping and fishing. The land itself had been volcanic at one time which had also contributed to her wealth in the form of fine minerals, precious gems, and fertile soil. During that time it had been the frontline of battle for the Dragon Wars.

He had been just seventeen then. The soldiers had laughed at him when he had shown up for recruitment. That was until they had seen him fight in battle. Qualtaric had instructed him not to reveal his real name to anyone at the time. He had not thought to question him then, now he wished he had.

However, as it was, he had listened to him and gone by the name of Shaltak. He had quickly risen in rank, becoming leader of his own command in just a few short months. It was not long before he had been known as Shaltak, Slayer of Dragon Killers; Shaltak, the Dragon's Protector. Or simply Shaltak, Protector of Maltak.

The Dragon Wars had begun in the southeast, in the land known as Salvahook, and they had gradually spread north and west till they had reached Hindora. It was believed, at the time, that Vaulnik was obsessed with controlling the world. But there always seemed to be something more at work as he continued to slay the Dragons of the Earth wherever he went.

In fact, the last straw for the Dragons of the Earth had been at The Battle of Quantaris. For in that battle Vaulnik had unleashed a new evil. An abomination so hideous no one would have thought it possible. They came to be known as Zoths; evil, vile dragons the likes of which were thought only to exist in Zezpok.

Until then Vaulnik's success had been limited. He and his men had dealt him several hard blows. Why it had only been a few months prior to The Battle of Quantaris that he and his men had all but wiped out Vaulnik's special army of Darzors. They had even begun to win back some of the territory under Vaulnik's control.

But The Battle of Quantaris changed everything. Vaulnik set dragon on dragon and changed the entire equation. No one knew how many Dragons of the Earth had fallen in that single day and night of fighting. Only that it had been enough so that only one Dragon of the Earth was rumored to still be alive; Viszerak, the Dragon of the North.

He remembered that battle vividly and recalled, with great sadness, how they had been forced to watch as the vile gray creatures that were Vaulnik's army of hideous dragons tore at The Dragons of the Earth, ripping them open. There was not much he or his men could do. This had been their first encounter with these awful beasts. They could kill Vaulnik's men and that they had done. But the abominable vicious greedy horde of dragons Vaulnik had created was just too much. The Zoths were somehow stronger and fiercer. It was speculated later that these great beast had been summoned from the bowels of Zezpok itself and set loose to destroy the very fabric of life.

However, he was not much for such dramatic thinking, though he had to admit that the Battle of Quantaris had him wondering. To this day the memory of how hard he and his men had fought during that battle still burned in his mind. No one had ever been forced to kill a dragon before, and that was just the weakness Vaulnik had exploited. His evil beasts went against everything he, or anyone, had ever been taught about dragons. The only vile dragon he, or anyone else, had ever heard of was Demonrak. Who, according to legend, was supposed to be confined to Zezpok.

No, those dragons had been a new aberration, an abomination before Alhera, before Allethor and Thelenor themselves. He had never had such a failure in his entire life as he had in that single day and night of fighting. There had been nothing he could do but watch as dragons on both sides ripped and tore at one another. And while dragons on both sides fell, it was The Dragons of the Earth who had suffered most, leaving many to believe they were all but lost to legend now.

As a result of their loss, Vaulnik had overrun the land, conquering most of the kingdoms in his way, including theirs. The kingdom of Avivron had been mostly a quiet kingdom under the rule of Sevzozak's father, King Dakconar. The forests and her people had prospered and the dragons were good to them. When the last of the dragons fell, and Vaulnik took over, things quickly changed, especially for Avivron.

Avivron had always prided itself in its simple yet prosperous way of life despite being known for its vast stores of Kriac Stones. Clearer and harder than diamonds, yet greener and brighter than new grass in spring, legend had it that they had fallen to the earth millennia ago in a great shower from the Shardon Lands sent by Allethor to renew the land. Only one other being was ever alleged to create the stones. That of The Great Maltak herself, Mother of all The Dragons of the Earth, and Breather of Life. It was her, legend told, who had endowed Avivron with the greatest amount of these precious stones. As such, the stones were thought of as Maltak's blessings on the land and left alone, for the most part, wherever they were.

However, Vaulnik could not resist the allure of the infamous Kriac Stones, said to possess the power of life itself. It was for those stones that Vaulnik had apparently come to Avivron. To this end he had raped and scared the land, leaving signs of his decimation everywhere. Being fabled to possess the power of life, the power of creation, meant that anyone who could learn to wield them could, in theory, become as powerful as the gods. The key was in learning how to tap into it and wield it. It was perhaps for this reason that only Dragon Witches were said to be gifted with the ability to use the Effora, or Power of the Stones.

From time in memorial, the various stones of the earth were said to carry the power of the gods within them. Each type of stone had a different gift. Only Dragon Witches had the ability to sense and use these powers. Of them, only a very select few were said to ever be gifted with the power to use the Kriac Stones. If a Dragon Witch did possess the power, she usually could only handle one stone at a time, not several of them at once. The only one said to be capable of that was the Shaddorak.

The Shaddorak, according to the stories of old, was a woman whose strength of character would be such that the goddess Alhera would bless her with the power to use all the stones, in particular all the Kriac Stones. Only she would be her representative here on earth, and only she would be able to possess the power of life. So the stories went.

When Vaulnik gained control of Avivron he immediately began his quest for the Kriac Stones and the legendary Shaddorak. According to some reports, Vaulnik had corrupted a high priestess of Alhera and made her a member of his court. It was her, so the story went, who had prophesied that the Shaddorak would be born in his time and come from a land rich in Kriac stones.

However, few outside Zvegnog believed it. The ancient legend of the Shaddorak was sketchy at best. Most considered it more a fable than a real prophesy. Nevertheless, the idea of the Shaddorak became an obsession for Vaulnik who would stop at nothing to find and possess such a woman. The consequences of his obsession had been felt far across the breadth of Avivron by her women. Any woman thought to possess the ability to use the Effora had been rounded up. Of them, those whose age was considered to correspond to the legendary Shaddorak were then carted off to Kazengor Castle never to be heard from again.

Yet, ruthless as Vaulnik was he was also clever, offering to leave those kings in power that chose to stay out of his way. The others he would cut down rather than continue to fight their resistance. King Sevzozak had been one such king who had chosen to let Vaulnik have control of his lands rather than resist him. Many thought he had decided to do this for the sake of the kingdom, perhaps even to bide time to mount an offensive. The lands who had defied Vaulnik, such as Hindora, had been laid waist. Totally destroyed, their riches confiscated to fatten Vaulnik's coffers.

After the defeat at Quantaris the few surviving soldiers had all but scattered. Many back to their home countries to help defend their lands. He had been no different. Choosing to fall back to his old mentor, Qualtaric, so as to regroup and seek his advice and counsel. Maybe he knew of a way to defeat Vaulnik. Maybe he knew a way to defeat the Zoths, or at least offer an explanation for their existence.

Unfortunately, his mentor only became more cryptic, insisting he must wait till the appropriate time to strike Vaulnik. But he was not a

Fires of Life

young apprentice anymore, and while he was willing to wait for a time, he was not willing to wait forever. To that end he had used his connections to stay apprised of Vaulnik's doings.

Regrettably, there had been nothing he could do the day Vaulnik had chosen to invade Avivron; the event coming too close to his return from the Battle of Quantaris. He remembered it well. Vaulnik's men had moved in quickly, burning many of the outlaying cities and villages. As soon as he saw the fires, he had wanted to leave Qualtaric, but Qualtaric had insisted that he remain in hiding and not join Sevzozak's army. He, however, had vehemently disagreed with his mentor and immediately left to join Sevzozak's army and defend Avivron.

Only as he rode up to the front lines, all he saw were rows of Sevzozak's army retreating, capitulating. When he stopped and asked one of the soldiers what was happening, he informed him that the king had given orders not to resist; that they were to cooperate with Vaulnik. Shocked and confused he had let the soldier pass. When he had questioned another of higher ranking, he had told him that the king had capitulated to the mad tyrant in order to save his people from Vaulnik's wrath and further destructive rampages.

He and his horse had stepped back in shock while Sevzozak's army continued to pass. In total and complete disbelief he had watched from atop his horse on that mountainside, as Vaulnik's men were allowed to march across their borders and take over Avivron. Sickened and appalled he had stood, mounted on his horse, and watched as droves of Sevzozak's men flew past. He remembered how he had called out to them in vain to wait, to fight, but no one was listening that day. They had their orders, and he was no one to them.

With a heavy heart he had returned to Qualtaric. But thoughts of his mother and sister began to plague him. He worried for their safety. His mentor and friend tried to convince him that it was better for them if he did not seek them out.

"Those who wanted your father out of the way want your whole family out of the way. If you go to them, you risk putting them in harm's way," he would tell him.

When he questioned Qualtaric why they would want to kill his whole family, the old man would just shrug and say it was because of his father's close ties to King Dakconar.

However, as reports began to mount of Vaulnik's cruelty, he began to grow increasingly restless. Finding it harder and harder to control his urge to do whatever it took to end Vaulnik. Then one day a report reached him containing news that the entire village of Evangraw had been plundered and burned to the ground. Most of its inhabitants killed. To make matters worse the report claimed that King Sevzozak had done nothing to stop them.

According to the report, the people of that village had failed to pay the proper tribute to Vaulnik, and so, had been made an example of. He could not see how Sevzozak could just stand by and let Vaulnik slaughter innocent men, women, and children in his land.

Many of his contacts felt the king was simply waiting for a time in which to strike back at Vaulnik, but to him it just did not feel right. A king was supposed to protect his people or die in the attempt. Still Qualtaric kept advising him to wait.

"The time is not right," he kept saying. But on the night he had learned of the treachery that had taken place in the village of Evangraw he and Qualtaric had fought bitterly.

"How can I stay out of sight and do nothing while Vaulnik continues to slaughter our people?! I thought you were on our side. I didn't fight in the Dragon Wars for nothing. We may have lost that war, but I will NOT stand by and watch as Vaulnik marches in and takes what he wants."

"You have no choice. If you take up arms against, Vaulnik you will place the king in an awkward position; a position that may force him to denounce you. Clavorn you must be smart about these things and bide your time. The time will come for battle, but it is not now."

Fires of Life

"If not now then when? When he has taken all of Avivron for himself? Oh, scratch that. He has taken Avivron, just left her *king* in charge. So do I wait till he has laid waste to it in his insatiable desire for those Kriac Stones?!"

"No."

"Then when?!"

"Clavorn, you will know, but it is not now."

"How can you say that?! Our people are dying! I MUST fight. No. Don't try to stop me. I am going and if you get in my way…"

"There will be no need for that. I can see there is no discouraging you, but think on this. If you are captured, they will kill you. Sevzozak will do nothing to interfere with your execution and the people will have lost."

"Lost what, their only chance at a real champion and freedom? Come now, Qualtaric, you do not really believe that. No. I am sure there are others. My death would not end a rebellion. It would inflame it."

"Maybe, but it can end their one real hope of succeeding against him."

"Seriously, old man, you do not believe that I am the only one who can defeat this menace from the South," he remembered telling Qualtaric while waving his hands about in frustration only to have them come slamming down on the table before him.

Qualtaric had fallen silent. At that moment he knew what his mentor's silence meant. That he had arrived at the real reason why he did not want him trudging off to war, at least not at that moment. His silence had made him pause.

"Look Clavorn," his old mentor had implored, "At least wait till the morning. Let the heat of this news settle for the night. In the morning, if you still feel you must leave, I will not stop you. However, I do implore you not to use your father's name."

"And why ever not?! I am home. This is my country. Why should I not use my father's name?"

"Well, for one, the name of Shaltak will both instill confidence among those you choose to lead and fear in the hearts of your enemy."

"I see," he had replied, but somehow he thought there had to be more to it than that, "But so too should my father's name."

"True. But you have made a name for yourself. One that is both respected and feared. It would serve you most."

"I'll think about it, but I make no promises."

In the end, he had given in to his old mentor and stayed the night, but by morning his mind was still made up. He was leaving. Then just as he was fixing his sword to his horse's saddle more news came. His mother and sister had been killed. Inadvertently betrayed by a simpleton who lived in the village where they were hiding out and murdered by Vaulnik's men.

Sorrow and rage had filled his heart. If he had only acted sooner, if he had only sought them out and brought them out of harm's way. But Qualtaric was quick to point out that there was no way for him to have known they were in danger.

"You trusted your father's judgment," he had said, "And so did I."

Still he felt as if he was somehow responsible. Then he remembered turning on Qualtaric.

"Why did Vaulnik want them dead? Tell me!" he had shouted.

"I cannot," his mentor had replied.

"Why not?!! I am not a child anymore. I *need* to know."

"That is not my place."

"Why ever not?!" he had yelled. "It is my family. Now, I am the only left. Why are we so important? What is it? Common on tell me old man."

"No. In this you must trust me. Time will reveal all. I have sworn an oath to the Grand Mother of all Dragon Witches. I cannot tell you."

With that said he had paused. Mystery and magic always seemed to surround Qualtaric, and though he had never actually caught him in the act of performing any magic, at that moment he wondered if there might be some reality to his suspicions.

"I always thought there was bit of wizard in you."

"There are no Dragon Wizards, Clavorn Remmaik, son of Favorn."

"No. But if there were, I would know I was look at one right now."

Qualtaric had said nothing to that, only that he should keep his name from the Dragon Wars.

"No. I am sorry, but no Dragon Wizard or Witch, no matter how grand, is going keep me from announcing who seeks Vaulnik's destruction. I *want* him to know."

"Did it occur to you that may be what he wants," his mentor had countered.

"Fine. Then I will give him what he wants and something he did not bargain on as well. I am done waiting. This business at Evangraw, and now the deaths of my mother and sister, has only made me realize that I have been asleep here for far too long. No. It is time."

The memory of that day felt as fresh in his mind as the day it had occurred. Clavorn turned his attention to the fire before him. The woman said nothing as he stared deep into the flickering flames watching them consume the wood which was their fuel.

Fuel

The very word conjured up images of that morning, so not so very long ago, when his grief had only added fuel to his desire to free his people and avenge his family.

He recalled the day well. The sun just rising over the ridge as he rode up to the village gates of Yomontril on an old bull disguised as a peasant, his sword cleverly hidden within the folds of his clothes. The cold morning air had caused wisps of smoke like vapor to leave his mouth. Its presence foreboding, almost foretelling the wave of death he was about reek upon those of Vaulnik's army.

When the first of Vaulnik's guards came up to him in greeting, asking what his business was, he had expertly pulled out his sword and removed the man's head. Then turned and stabbed the second guard as he came up to assists the first.

Once he was inside the village he had immediately begun to make short work of Vaulnik's men. Cutting them down with his sword and setting off traps he had lain in secret the night before. He had battled the entire regiment responsible for his mother's and sister's death. He figured Qualtaric would have been proud of how he had fought that day.

By the end of the battle he had had the peasants taking up arms and fighting against Vaulnik's men as well. They had fought valiantly with their pitch forks, axes, and any other implements worthy of a weapon. The cheers went up to the Shardon Lands that day as they declared their victory and announced their proclamation of war on Vaulnik and his regime. There were to be no more Evangaws!

That day had marked the beginning of his rebellion against Vaulnik. It was also the day he had proudly proclaimed the name of his father; he was, Clavorn Remmaik, son of Favorn Remmaik, First Knight to King Dakconar. But he had never bragged, or promoted his background. He was fighting for his people. For their right to live free of tyranny and oppression, free of bondage and slavery, free of obligation to Vaulnik.

The deaths of his mother and sister had only punctuated the plight of his people and fueled his rage. He could not stand to see them suffer. If King Sevzozak felt powerless to defend his kingdom, then he would give him a reason to oppose Vaulnik.

But no raving endorsements came, though neither did any real opposition. As his victories mounted, he began to catch the eye of the nobles and the king's son, Almaik. Before long they were fighting together, he and Almaik. He saw him as a friend. Though Almaik never displayed his colors on the field of battle or used his name openly. He just assumed it was his way of supporting him while still maintaining the appearance that Sevzozak was cooperating with Vaulnik.

Sure the nobles who fought with them appeared uneasy at times, especially when they could not appear to rouse the same fervor in the hearts of the people who fought under them as him. But he did not worry, for he had the friendship of the king's son, and so he believe he had the king's unofficial endorsement. What did he care how many of the nobles fought with him? He fought with the king's son; therefore it was only natural that he felt he was fighting for the king.

"But I always told my men that they fought for the king, Sevzozak," he continued, not wanting to embrace the reality of her revelation.

"No Clavorn, think, you told them they were fighting for their freedom, for their country."

"And their king" he interjected, staring her in the eyes, he clearly remembered stating that to them.

Why did she keep ignoring that?

"Yes, but did you really believe they were fighting for their king?"

Clavorn considered her question. A silence fell between them for a moment.

"I always thought we were fighting for our freedom and that included our king as well. I told them that. Zezpok! I was fighting with his son. I still don't understand how this all adds up to turning me over to Vaulnik? I mean, why? We were winning? Many of the nobles fought with us, including the king's son."

Couldn't she see that?

"But none were as successful as you in convincing the people to fight for them. Why should they fight for a rich noble who would only continue to oppress them? In the years following your father's death, and the death of King Dakconar, many changes had occurred amongst the nobility. Those that were less than enthusiastic about Sevzozak's rule were…well, removed. Those nobles who fought with you fought for the king, but they had also been the same nobles who had taxed the people into poverty. Not exactly a conducive recipe for inspiring men to fight for you."

"Still, we were succeeding."

"Correction, you were succeeding."

"You mean the people and me."

"Yes, but that is just the point."

He looked at her.

"The king and his nobles understood, better than you apparently, that the real power lies with the people. That ultimately if the people do not want them as leaders, then there will be little they can do to prevent them from taking their power and placing it in the hands of the one they feel should rule," she informed him coolly. His benefactor then looked him straight in the eyes, "Clavorn, whether you wish it or not, the mantle of leadership may be thrust upon you. That was what they were afraid of; that your popularity outweighed theirs. That in the end the people would choose the man who had led them to freedom over those who had stood by and let them be enslaved. In the end, the truth is there may be little you can, nor should do to stop it, save only by losing the war, or your life. The question you need to consider is whether King Sevzozak, or his son Almaik, deserves to rule."

"But what you are suggesting is treason!" he protested.

"Is it? Is it treasonous if the people choose you over their king? Is it treasonous for the people to want a good and just king over an apparently cowardly, corrupt, and self-serving one?"

There was little Clavorn could say against this. He rose and paced around the fire like lion caught in a cage.

Leadership? Me as king? No. Definitely not! But if I lead them to victory, then what? Is she right? Are not the people entitled to a good king? But me? Am I such a man? No. There has to be other men for the task; another who is more worthy. But what of the people? What will they want? Should that not figure into who should rule?

He paused to consider.

If the people are to be free, then should it not follow that it be their choice for who should rule? And what is the point of my defeating Vaulnik if Sevzozak, or his son, is to be no better?

Will you listen to yourself, this is treason! Madness! Besides, who said you were fit to rule? Power is a seductive mistress. Can you resist her? Are you worthy?

His mind was of two voices arguing within him as he paced before the fire.

No. This is nuts!

Is it? Is rule a right passed on down through a man's line regardless of character, or is it something more? If character is the true measure of leadership, then will I, therefore, have let my people down by turning over the reins of power to men who are no better than the one I wish to over throw?

His mind raced as he ran his hand through his long dark hair.

But am I really worthy of being king?

"We need to get moving soon if we are to meet up with Sefforn and his men…"

"You know Sefforn?" he turned and looked at her, and for the first time he could clearly see the color of her eyes in the light of the setting sun. They were a mesmerizing shade of green. For a moment, Clavorn lost his train of thought before she brought him back to his senses with the reply to his question.

"Yes, I know of Sefforn and all your men, but that is not your concern. Your concern is to get to them and win this war," she told him as she rose to put out the fire that had cooked their dinner. "It will be dark soon. I will be back shortly with our mounts."

Clavorn wanted to ask more of her. It seemed he had a million questions. The more answers he got from her the more questions popped into his mind. Such as, how did she know about Sefforn and his men? Although, he did desire to see Sefforn, they had been friends since childhood and had battled Vaulnik together. It would be good to see him again. However, he still would not mind the answers to some of his questions. Who was she for starters?

Clavorn finished burring their fire, and as much of the evidence of their stay as possible, and stepped outside the tree. The gracefully swaying branches of the willows with the shallow river running through them, along with the last rays of golden light from the setting sun, made for a serene picture. To his eyes, she was nowhere to be seen as they searched the tranquil landscape.

Then suddenly his eyes caught movement as the form of a shrouded woman leading two spectacular black steeds parted the dancing willows before him. He wondered at her apparent power over animals, or did she just have extremely good luck. It took him only a matter of seconds to rule out luck. In his experience, luck was something one made.

"Ready?" she inquired.

"Ready as I'm going to be," he replied.

Soon they were mounted and set to leave the safety of the wood. Clavorn looked back at the stream and the willows. If he did not know better, he would have been inclined to believe that a dragon lived somewhere in those woods.

Chapter 4

It took several days of travel by night over barren and hostile land, through inhospitable forests, and even less hospitable weather, before they finally reached their destination, The Mountains of Kilmeia and the great Forest of Klestovak. Here the wood was thicker and older than in other parts of the country, primarily because its dragon had been one of the last to fall prey to Vaulnik before he took over the land. These giant trees had also been spared his vile plundering for they had the good fortune of not living on land said to contain Kraic Stones.

"It will be light soon," he remarked, as they reached the top of a hill that overlooked both the mountain range and the valley below.

"I know. We will camp during the day and meet up with Sefforn this evening if all goes well," she told him, spurring her horse to move on the down the hillside and deeper into the forest.

For his part Clavorn could only guess at the 'if all goes well' part of her statement. He spurred his horse forward as he took its mane in his hands. Before long they were in front of the mouth to another cave, though this time there was no waterfall to hide its entrance. Only a large number of trees and bushes obscured its view. They dismounted and set the horses loose. By now Clavorn was becoming accustomed to their uncanny return every evening. He figured that it had something to do with the small horn she carried around with her, but the rest remained a mystery.

"You stay here," she ordered, "I will go seek out Sefforn."

"No," he grabbed her by the arm, "I want to see him myself."

"If you come with me, you cannot reveal yourself till we are sure he has not been compromised or killed," she told him her green eyes looking straight into his. He felt his loins harden.

"Fine, but I want to see him for myself. I am tired of waiting here and there. I am not afraid to die," he told her.

"I know you are not afraid to die," she replied in the most compassionate and understanding voice he had heard her use yet, "but you are this war's best chance for success, and I am not willing to risk your life."

Clavorn released his hold on her arm. Something in her words compelled him to let go.

"This way," she ordered, as she turned and made her way into the woods. Clavorn followed, ducking his head to avoid hitting a large branch, but when he looked up she was gone. He tried to see if he could find her tracks, but to no avail. She had outmaneuvered him. Now, his only choice was to wait for her return.

Clavorn stood and watched the sunrise over the horizon still searching the landscape for any clue as to her whereabouts, but none was forthcoming. Finally, he resigned himself to his fate, turned, and made his way back to the cavern she had picked for his day's interment.

Dusk came, night fell, and still she had not returned. Sleep had been difficult for him to find that day. Now, with her not returned yet, a sinking feeling was beginning to creep into the pit of his stomach. The stars twinkled down from overhead as Clavorn pulled his tunic closer about him. Nights here were colder than where they had been previously due to their elevation. An owl hooted, startling him briefly.

Where is she? She is usually back by now.

He decided to leave the safety of the cave and pick a lookout point from which he could view its entrance as well as the surrounding landscape. Time seemed to slow down as he waited impatiently for her return.

Suddenly, a movement in the bushes beyond caught his attention. It was her. A wave of relief passed over him as he saw her make her way towards the entrance of the cave. He paused a moment to be sure she had not been followed then slowly he made his way down.

"So did you find him?" he asked once he had entered the cave. For the first time since their journey began he saw her startle. She immediately turned on him, her knife glinting in the moonlight as she placed it instinctually before his throat.

"Hey, I didn't mean to startle you," he told her, his hands raised in innocent submission.

"Don't ever do that again," she told him through her teeth. He still could not see her face for it was always shrouded over, but her eyes were clearly angry. "I could have killed you," she remarked as she relaxed out and backed off, removing the knife from his throat.

"Don't worry, I got that. So did you find him?" he asked again anxious for news of his friend and comrade.

"Yes, but they've moved off from their usual location so it took me a while to find them. It appears as if Vaulnik's men have been combing the forest looking for you and your men. I found their tracks on my search for your friends. My guess is that when you escaped they immediately sent word, expecting you to come here. We'll need to be extra careful. You and your men will need to find a safer place to hide in."

Suddenly, a horrible thought passed through his mind. He grabbed her arm and for the first time he saw her wince.

"If you're trying to kill my men by using me, I can assure you Zezpok will look like Shardon before I'm done with you," he told her icily.

"Look, if you don't believe me, why don't you use your sword and kill me now," she told him calmly. "Remember, as far as the world is concerned I am already dead, so it matters little to me. My life was over a long time ago. The only thing that matters to me now is the success of this war."

"Yeah, but which side," he insisted still holding her tight.

"That is something that you are going to have to decide. For no word of mine will ever be able to convince you. Only your heart can answer that question."

She was right. He would never trust her words. But could he trust his heart? Clavorn stood a moment looking into her eyes and considered.

Can I trust her? Does she really want me to win this war? Or is she merely trying to gain my trust, so that I can serve as some sort of assurance for Vaulnik's soldiers that the men they hunting are indeed my men, and end the rebellion once and for all?

Icy, horrible thoughts of betrayal flew through his mind. Like knives they cut and tore at his soul. He would not hesitate to kill her if that were true, yet as he looked into her eyes something there told him otherwise.

But should I trust my heart?

Again the question beckoned in his mind. Sometimes a man could confuse his loins for his heart. Many a man had been betrayed by what he thought was his heart. He looked at her as his mind raced.

To take a chance?

He paused. A few moments later he let her go.

"I take it that means you want me to take you to him," she remarked, rubbing her arm a moment in the place he had held her.

"Yes," he replied simply.

He wanted to apologize to her. Tell her he was sorry for doubting her, but something held him back. Perhaps he was not totally ready to trust again after being betrayed by Almaik. Perhaps it was something more. Only time would tell. But for now he would trust her to take him to Sefforn.

"Okay," she told him, "follow me."

Fires of Life

Chapter 5

The forest was dark as the moon had set early. Now only starlight lit their way. All of Clavorn's senses were on high alert as they made their way amongst the trees and undergrowth. Suddenly, a clearing appeared in front of them and there, below them, were his men. He could clearly make out Sefforn's voice from their vantage point on the edge of the rocky outcropping. Looking around he saw no sign of Vaulnik's men. All was peaceful, save for the occasional gust of wind.

"I'm sorry I doubted you," he told her as he looked back at her in the darkness. No reply came from her lips, and he wished he had never corned her on the subject.

"Look," she told him, "this is where we part ways. I have delivered you safely home. Now just be true to your end of the bargain."

"I will do my best, but…"

She raised her hand and placed it gently over his mouth to stay any further comments, her green eyes penetrating his.

"I must go now. Remember, I am a ghost. I may return, but for now I must go," she told him removing her hand as she slipped off into the woods.

He watched her go, and then, just as in the woods with the willows, she just seemed to vanish into the forest before him.

I wonder if she really is a ghost.

The thought momentarily lingered in his mind as he stood there alone in the darkness. But then he remembered the feel of her touch, the softness of her skin, and knew that she was no ghost. Finally, he turned his gaze and attention back to his men.

"The note said he would be here tonight," a tall, blond, well-muscled man with hair past his shoulders said to another man of nearly equal height, only more slender with dark hair which he wore tied partially back, as they made their way around the perimeter of their encampment.

The fires were out throughout the camp, so there was very little light to be had. Only the soft low light from the stars filtered in through the opening in the forest canopy. The waxing moon had set hours ago; taking is pale glow with it. Ahead of them, voices could be heard, as the men gathered together sharpening blades, honing bows, or generally just milling together for company as they awaited their leader's return. Tension was high in the air, as there was some concern amongst the men that the note was nothing more than a ruse to lure them out and cut them down.

"It did. If you can believe it," the younger pointed out.

"You can," came a voice form the wood behind them.

The two men nearly jumped out their skins, immediately unsheathing their swords, as they turned in the direction of the voice coming from behind them. Their eyes widened as the figure of a man waltzed boldly towards them. His face and defining features shrouded, obscured by the darkness.

"Who's there?" questioned the tall blond.

"I am surprised you cannot recognize my voice, my old friend," the figure continued as it made its way towards them.

Suddenly, their eyes became wide as they began to recognize the man who had come forth from the woods. Both men immediately sheathed their swords.

"Clavorn!" the tall blond exclaimed as he embraced his longtime friend and compatriot. "But the note…it wasn't written in your handwriting," he remarked slightly puzzled as he stood back. "We were a bit unsure of its validity.'

"Sefforn, you know me. I like to make an entrance," Clavorn replied to his childhood friend and most trusted soldier, hoping his reply would squelch any further examination into the matter.

"But where is your help? We must thank them for bring you safely to us," Sefforn replied.

So much for trying to avoid awkward questions.

"Only the gods know that, my friends," Clavorn replied to his closest friend who seemed to be combing the bushes with his eyes for more persons unknown. With the dim light from the stars, that just penetrated the canopy above them, he could just see his friend's distinctive well-trimmed beard and mustache which contrasted with his often tussled and rugged hair, "Come on let us celebrate my good fortune and plan our revenge. It is time to put an end to Vaulnik."

"But surely who ever helped you escape would like some appreciation for their efforts," the man with the dark hair exclaimed.

His blue eyes and handsomely chiseled face, which always had the ladies swooning, were barely discernable in the faint light. Clavorn liked his sharp quick wit in battle. Despite his age, he was quite the asset on the battlefield.

"Sayavic, for now our illustrious benefactor would like to remain anonymous," Clavorn told him.

"Anonymous? But why? Surely not," Sayavic questioned. Both men appeared surprise and confused.

"Yes, I am afraid we have no choice in this matter. Shall we say it is best not to look too closely at fortunes fair grace?"

"Yes, I guess," Sayavic replied, a bit taken back by his response and glanced over at Sefforn to see his reaction to Clavorn's reply. By the look on his face he could tell he was just as perplexed and surprised as he was.

"Well, if your benefactor wishes to remain anonymous, then who are we to question it? But it is rather unusual you will have to admit," Sefforn replied.

"I cannot argue with you there, my friend. But come. We have plans to make, and I want to see how the rest of you have fared in my absence," Clavorn told him, as he ushered the two men off further into camp.

All eyes turned in their direction, as Sefforn and Sayavic escorted Clavorn into camp. Suddenly, a great commotion broke out amongst the men as recognition and word spread amongst them as to who the third man was with them. Clavorn was both happy and concerned by the vociferous nature of their greeting, for he worried that Vaulnik's troops might hear their cries and come to investigate.

"Look, I appreciate your sentiment, but we are not totally safe here. Vaulnik's men are searching the forest for us," he told them, trying to stay their jubilation.

"Oh, let them come. We will show them a true Avivronian welcome. Won't we boys," shouted a man that could only be described as having a purely medium appearance.

He was medium in height, medium in weight, and of course, medium in stature. His hair was a medium brown which he wore to his shoulders with a beard and mustache. His eyes were naturally also a medium brown. The most distinctive feature about his appearance was the ever-present pipe he almost never seemed to be seen without, the only exception to that, of course, being on the field of battle. As it was, there were now rings of smoke gently floating up around his head.

More shouts and hoots went up from the crowd at the man's statement as they nodded in agreement.

"True, true, Melkiar, and we will. But I would like that to be on our terms not theirs."

Hoots and cat calls sounded good naturedly from the crowd at Clavorn's last statement.

"I think you are spoiling their fun," whispered Sefforn in his ear.

"I think you are right," he whispered back. "Alright you win," he shouted over the din of catcalls which quickly changed to cheers as the men realized they had won the argument.

"Melkiar, since this is your idea, you take first watch with your men while we celebrate."

"Oh, come on," Melkiar protested good-naturedly.

"The price for good ideas, my friend," Clavorn told him with a smile as he came towards him before entering the crowd, patting him congratulatory like on the back as he passed by.

"Thanks," Melkiar grumbled clearly wishing he had not been so keen to speak up.

"Don't mention it," Clavorn replied with a smile as he melted into the throng of men.

That night there was much celebrating amongst his men, though Clavorn was careful to avoid too much of the wine and beer that was flowing through the camp. It was close to dawn when the festivities finally died down. Clavorn could not settle himself into sleep. The tent he was in failed to offer any substantial comfort despite all its appearances to the contrary. The only thing that kept playing in his mind was the conversation he had had with her, his mysterious benefactor, several nights before and the warnings about Vaulnik's men. When he closed his eyes and tried to clear his mind all he could see was her beautiful green eyes. He got up from his bed and went outside. His eyes searched the woods for any sign of her, but he knew she was probably long gone.

"What is it?" Sefforn asked as he came up to stand by his friend.

"Oh, not much," he replied off handedly not wishing to reveal the true nature of what was on his mind.

"Come now. Who do you think you're kidding? It's me, Seff. What is it?" the tall broad blond friend of his youth cajoled.

"It's Almaik. I want him."

"I want him too, but somehow I don't think that was what you were thinking," his friend told him.

"You're right as usual." *But how do I tell you that I'm thinking about a mysterious woman who liberated me? No. That would sound not only frivolous but absurd.* "I was wondering where Vaulnik's men were and where would be the best place to set up our camp. We can't stay here, not after last night. You know how the forest has ears."

"Well, I can't argue with you there, but the men needed that last night. Morale has been really low since your capture. Some were even thinking you were dead and that the war was lost."

"I don't blame them. I thought I was dead."

Sefforn gave him a sideways glance.

"Don't worry, my friend, I am here now," Clavorn reassured him as he placed a hand briefly on his friend's shoulder, "Wake the men. It is time to leave."

"But they just got to sleep."

"I know, but my gut says it is time to go. We cannot linger, and I know just where we should make our camp. Tell them to get some rations together. It is a few days ride from here."

"You mind telling me where this place is," Sefforn remarked as Clavorn turned and walked off back to his tent.

"Yes," was all Clavorn replied over his shoulder, and his friend was forced to accept his answer.

The sun was just beginning to shine down on the little camp. Long early morning shadows crossed the ground while the wet dewy grass dampened Sefforn's boots as he turned and began to wake the men.

Chapter 6

The sun had just cleared the trees on the eastern horizon. Far to the south one could easily make out the outline of The Mountains of Shylaharon and The Krimian Ridge. Clavorn pulled his horse up to a stop. Hawk blew and shook his dark black head, a puff of mist emanating from his inky nostrils in the chill of the early morning air.

"Easy boy," he told him, as he patted and stroked his glistening ebony neck. His long standing equine friend stood restlessly under him as Clavorn paused to look back over the way they had come. A telltale dark cloud of rising smoke in the distance told him all he needed know. Vaulnik's men had found their encampment.

"Looks as if your gut was right," Sefforn commented as he pull his horse up next to Clavorn.

"Yeah, looks like Vaulnik's men found our camp. We need a way to through them off our trail, follow me."

Clavorn turned his horse and began to trot off in the direction of the river he had seen from his vantage point. Sefforn and his men followed suit. Clavorn pulled Hawk up near the bank. Behind him he could hear the sounds of his men as they too pulled their horses to a stop. Moments later Sefforn was at his side with Sayavic.

"Why are we stopping here?" inquired Sayavic.

"Because we need to through Vaulnik's soldiers off our trail," he replied. "Sayavic, why don't you lead the men into the river and have them follow it down stream. Sefforn and I will follow in a few."

"Sure. No problem," Sayavic replied, as he motioned the men behind him to follow. Then he rode off into the shallow river in front of Clavorn and headed on down it."

"Okay, now what?" Sefforn asked.

"Now, we wait for just the right group of persons to ride past," he told his friend. What he failed to tell him was that he needed just the right set of volunteers. Clavorn watched as his men quietly walked their horses past on their way downstream. Suddenly, he spied just the men he needed. They were the youngest amongst them. He waved them over.

What Clavorn was after was a small group of zealous young men to create a false trail that would drive Vaulnik's army mad. Something in this group, besides their age, led him to believe they would be just the group to do it. Their names were Tilon, Feiorn, and Natteon respectively. The three of them were well known throughout camp for their pranks and feisty natures.

"No problem," the three young men responded eagerly after he had relayed his orders, "We'll send them on a wild boar chase they'll never forget," continued the tallest amongst them named Tilon, before they turned their horses and embarked on their mission of deception.

He and Sefforn watched as they rode off happily creating a spurious, misleading trail on the other side of the river.

"Well, I think you just made their day," Sefforn commented as his horse shifted nervously under him.

"I think you are right," he replied, smiling to himself as he encouraged his horse forward into the shallow river. Moments later both he and Sefforn had turned their horses downstream with the others.

They rode for a good while down the river. At one point Clavorn pulled his horse up to see if his group of conspirators had made it back to rejoin the troops. Sefforn paused with him, and the two men waited. Soon their quarry came into view.

"All done, sir," replied Tilon with a big grin as he rode his horse to a stop in front of them.

"Yeah, I bet they'll be traveling in circles for hours," remarked Natteon, his red hair shining like a fiery mop on his head. Natteon was the youngest of the three.

"Good. Well done then. Now why don't you join us? Oh, and boys, remember we need to make like we're invisible," he told them.

"Right. No problem. We got that down don't we?" remarked Feiorn as the others nodded in agreement. Feiorn tended to be the most level headed of the three. Clavorn thought he had the makings of a fine soldier.

"Good. Let's go then," Clavorn told them as he turned Hawk down stream to rejoin the rest of his men. Sefforn hung back to bring up the rear.

That evening the scene in the encampment was quite different from the night before. All was quiet. Most of the fires were put out early. Heavy furs were in order for sleeping. Clavorn over looked his men as they slept. Except for the sounds of evening insects, all seemed quiet. Yet he still felt on edge. From his vantage point he could see his three conspirators sleeping soundly in the moonlight. How he wished he could join them in that great careless sleep of youth. Hawk blew over his shoulder.

"I know. I know, boy. All is well. I guess you'd let me know if it wasn't. Still..." he paused a moment. What was he looking for in the forest? Was it her? Was it Vaulnik's men? He did not know. All he knew was that sleep was not coming easily once more. He glanced back over his men. Most appeared to be sleeping peacefully, a few stirred with the slight breeze.

"You know you need sleep too," a voice remarked from behind him.

Clavorn turned. Once again it was Sefforn.

"So who are you; my mother?"

"No. Just the voice of a concerned friend," Sefforn told him, "You just escaped from prison and last night you hardly slept either. If you keep this up, you're liable to fall asleep in battle. Should we have one, that is."

"You have a point. But I'll be alright."

"Yeah, sure. Look they might think you're a demigod, but I know you're human. Hawk and I will keep this watch. You go get some rest. We need you coherent, remember."

"Point taken. I'll be just over here though," Clavorn informed him, pointing to small patch of soft earth not far off.

"Don't worry. If I see or sense anything out of the ordinary, you'll be the first to know," Sefforn told him as he took up his place next to Hawk. "Now don't pick my pockets, boy. I am not your master. You take that watch and I'll take this one. Deal," he told the horse as he settled in next to him.

Hawk nickered and sniffed the ground near him then lifted his head as if he were on lookout duty too. Sefforn shook his head and took up his watch.

The next morning brought with it a cold mist. Silence was the name of the game, so there was very little talking amongst the men. Clavorn and Sefforn over saw the breaking of camp. Melkiar came up and asked what his orders were. Clavorn instructed him to take up the rear and keep a lookout. The rest of day went quietly, however, a slow drizzle had taken the place of the cold mist and remained that way for the next several days.

The mountains grew even cooler with the nights near freezing and it seemed no amount of furs would keep them warm. Fires were difficult in the wet. Moreover, they were traveling in stealth mode which meant they were, for the most part, forbidden anyway. So it was with a glad heart that Clavorn and his men greeted the sun when it finally broke the spring rains as they came over the ridge to spy the willows of Shyloran Forest. Clavorn trotted his horse down and stopped on the edge of the grove with his men following not far behind.

"Wow, how did you ever find this place," Sefforn asked, marveling at its beauty just as he had done not so very long ago.

"It's a long story. Remind me to tell you someday when this is all over. For now, just suffice it to say that I stumbled upon it on my way home," he informed him as he dismounted Hawk. "There is one catch though."

"Oh," Sefforn said.

"This forest is protected. We are to do our best to keep existence a secret."

"Protected? Protected by whom?" Sefforn inquired.

"You know I'm not sure. I believe the dragons. At least until recently," that was his best guess but as they were currently nearly extinct it did make one pause to wonder who currently looked after it. She had never really mentioned who and he had not thought to ask. "We need to honor them by seeing to it that we are the only ones who know of it."

"Well, it looks like they never left here," Sefforn commented from atop his horse.

Clavorn just smiled. That had been his very thought when he had left.

"Does it have a name?" Sefforn asked.

"Yes, Shyloran Forest."

"And you know this because?"

"Because it is part of that story I would like to tell you sometime when this is all over," he replied.

"More mystery," Sefforn commented, "Well, I hope it's worth waiting for."

"It is, my friend. It is," was all Clavorn told him.

He urged Hawk forward and the two men rode on further into the ancient wood. After a few moments Clavorn stopped and Sefforn joined him.

"We'll use the trees to hide our men and supplies, including the horses. I want this to look as if there is no one here, understood," he told him, dismounting his horse.

"Yeah, but how...?"

"Look at those trees, Seff. They're thick and if you follow me I know just the tree to serve as our Counsel Tree."

"Counsel Tree?"

"Well, we cannot very well call it Counsel Chamber now can we?"

"No. You have a point," Sefforn replied.

Sefforn dismounted and followed as Clavorn led his horse deep into the woods. The wind blew; swaying the dense weeping boughs of the willows. The Hawthorn trees were still in bloom. Some of their small white petals flew about making warm snowy swirls in the wake of the gentle breeze. Sefforn was surprised and awed by their numbers. The Hawthorns were sacred, but in the years following the demise of the dragons, their number had dwindled throughout most of Avivron.

Flowers continued to carpet the forest floor while the stream ran clear and swift over the rocks that lined its bed as it meandered through the middle of the grove of willows. In the distance he could hear the sound of a waterfall. Just the sound dampening device they needed he noted as he crossed the shallow river with his horse.

"Melkiar," Sefforn called out as he led his horse over in his direction.

"Yeah, Seff," he replied.

"Will you look after him while I see what Clavorn has in mind?"

"Sure. Where do you want him?" Melkiar asked, taking his horse's reins.

"How about that tree over there," Sefforn replied, pointing to one of the great trees across from them.

"Sure. No problem," Melkiar told him as he began to make off in that direction.

"Oh, and Melkiar…"

"Yeah."

"Why don't you organize the first watch. When you're done come and join us."

"No problem," he replied, "Say how will I find you?"

Sefforn searched in front of him. The dancing branches of graceful trees played before him as he sought an answer to his question.

"I'm not sure. Check the trees. If my guess is right, you'll be looking for a very large one."

"That's helpful," Melkiar told him with a touch of sarcasm.

"Sorry I can't do better than that," he replied.

Melkiar starred in front of him, searching the direction Clavorn had set off in, "No. I got it. That way somewhere."

Sefforn nodded, and watched briefly as Melkiar strode off leading their horses to the tree he had indicated before turning his attention back to Clavorn, who was now disappearing into the grove of willows in front of him.

The giant trees swayed their long weepy branches disappearing and reappearing Clavorn in a kind of illusive dance. Sefforn parted the branches and caught up to his friend. He was just about to ask him where this tree was that he was planning to use as a command center, when the branches of the willows around them parted to reveal the real king of the grove.

Sefforn stood in awe as he stared up at the huge dancing boughs. Clavorn smiled at his friend's reaction before he turned and entered the giant ancient tree.

"Will you look at the size of this thing," Sefforn commented as he stepped inside the enormous willow in the middle of the grove, "This, by far, has to be the oldest and largest one of these I have ever seen. By the gods! One would think it's been here since time began."

"Well, I doubt that, but I do have to agree with you that it is quite the spectacular tree, and no doubt the oldest one in this forest and perhaps in all those beyond. Quite the tree for a 'meeting room' of sorts, don't you agree."

"I couldn't agree with you more. Look at these boughs. They're dense enough, and their circumference is great enough, you could almost hold a real castle ball in here and no one from the outside would be the wiser."

"I take it then that you approve of my choice of hideouts and war rooms," Clavorn remarked with a smile.

"Definitely approved," Sefforn replied still in awe of the great tree. "I see why you referred to it as 'Council Tree.'"

Soon the men began to filter in. One by one, Clavorn watched as they each had the same over awed expression as his friend had had as they enter the enormous ancient willow. It was not long before Clavorn was seated inside the grand old tree with most of his trusted friends and advisors.

They were all seated on the roots of the ancient willow while Clavorn himself had taken up a large root nearest its enormous trunk. As he sat observing, all of his men seated around in the great tree, the thought crossed his mind about the apparent increase in the number of exposed roots of the ancient tree. For the moment, however, he dismissed it as one of the mysteries surrounding this forest and perhaps his benefactor as well. Mysteries that were best solved at a later date.

His focus at the moment was on the impending war and battles at hand. When he was sure they were all assembled he rose and went to stand the in the middle of the large open space created by the tree's overhanging branches. With a long stick he began drawing in the dirt as he was accustomed to doing. Before long they were deep in debate about who to attack first and how.

"We need to eliminate those of Vaulnik's men that are after us first, we all agree that must be our first priority," Clavorn was saying.

"Let's surround them and catch them off guard while they are asleep," was one suggestion from the group. "How about a frontal attack in broad day light," was another and on and on it went. Sefforn watched as his friend listened carefully to all the ideas put forward and a vote was called for. Two of the ideas seemed equally favored.

"Thank you gentlemen, I will let you know just prior to our assault which I have chosen to go with," Clavorn told them as the debate died down and the war council came to a close.

"But don't you trust us," an elderly old soldier commented.

The silver hair that graced his head was thick and long. He wore it partially tied in the back, his skin had the weathered appearance of a man who had seen many battles, yet his body was still strong and virile.

"Yes, I do Kevic, but sometimes even the trees have ears," Clavorn told him as the men filed out of the ancient tree.

Clavorn respected the old warrior. He had fought alongside his father and grandfather in many battles and had been well regarded by them.

"You know, you could really lead this mob if you wanted to," Sefforn told his friend once they had all left. The admiration in his voice was unmistakable.

"I thought I was leading this mob?" Clavorn joked as he sat down with a drink on the broad old root he had slept on when she had first introduced him to the grove.

"You know what I mean," Sefforn replied, coming to sit down next to him.

"And you know how I feel about that," Clavorn answered taking a swig of red wine from his oil skin bag.

Is there something in the air? Sefforn is now the second person to suggest I rule in a matter of a few weeks. But then he has always felt I would make a good leader.

His thoughts on the subject were still a jumble. While he wanted to see his people free, ruling was something he had always seen as the purview of someone else, in this case, the king. Until recently he had not even really entertained the idea, having dismissed Sefforn's previous comments as mere jokes. But now, here he was reintroducing the idea.

Can we just win the war first?

"So you still haven't changed your mind even after all that has happened," Sefforn commented.

"No. I wouldn't go that far, but I am not fighting this war to become Avivron's next king. I am fighting this war to free her people."

"Yes. I know. But you know Sevzozak and his son are sell outs to Vaulnik. They have to be. If you win the war and give this country back to them, then you mine as well just leave things as they are. Those two are just as bad as our enemy, may be even worse because they are doing it to their own people. How can you care so much about these people and let those two rule?"

Clavorn thought on his friends words and remembered what she had told him under this very tree not so long ago.

Maybe it's in the air here.

"Perhaps you are right my friend, but we have not won the war yet and such decisions are a bit premature. I can only focus on winning the war at the moment, not on whether or not I am worthy of governing a people. If and when that time comes, it will be for the people to decide."

Sefforn shook his head. Once again his friend had come up with a diplomatic answer and he was out maneuvered yet again.

"I will never be able to pin you down on that one will I," he replied.

"Not at the moment, my friend. Not at the moment," was all Clavorn said as he swallowed another bit of red wine and passed the oil skin bag to Sefforn.

The thought of ruling was still too new an idea for him to bother with, besides had no real desire to be king himself. He hated what he had seen power do to supposedly good men and did not want to become thusly corrupted himself. For now he would just focus on liberating his country and let fate decide the rest.

Sefforn took a mouthful and passed it back to him. Clavorn took another swig.

"Seff, I need a favor of you," he began.

Two days later while Clavorn led the men into battle against Vaulnik's men, Sefforn and a small contingent of men slunk off. They're direction, due north.

Chapter 7

Clavorn pulled up his horse and all the men stopped. The night air was cool and still. Hawk shifted under him in anticipation of the evening's events. Silently, he was pleased by the stillness of night's air, for it would make his plan easier to execute. The moon was also gone from the night's sky, providing them with just the right amount of darkness for his plan to work.

Silence was the name of the game this night, as he motioned his first group of men to begin their attack. Quietly, they dismounted and disappeared into the forest, leaving their horses in the care of the younger, unseasoned men who were really closer to boyhood than manhood.

From his vantage point he observed one of his men slit the throat of a soldier on watch. Not long after that came the first signal telling him that all of the perimeter guards had been dispatched. He motioned his men to take their positions.

Quietly, they moved into formation. Clavorn was going to use one of his many successful battle tactics. He wanted to send a clear message to Vaulnik.

At his signal his men lit their torches and unsheathed their swords. Their horses stirred under them. Then with a nod of his head his archers commenced their attack.

Flaming arrows filled the air, setting ablaze to the area within the encampment. Immediately, chaos ensued as Vaulnik's men began to awaken. Some grabbed for their swords. Screams and cries could soon be heard throughout the forest as his archers found their marks.

Now he sent in his second wave mounted on horseback. With their swords glinting in the firelight and shouts of battle in the air they hurled themselves into the fray. Soon the sound of steal meeting steel mingled with the cries of pain as Clavorn watched and waited. His prize had yet to come into view. But he did not have to wait long as the commander of this army appeared in the center of the battle wielding his sword.

Adorned with the familiar black cape and red embossed dragon on his breast plate, it was not hard for Clavorn to identify him as his mark. With one swift kick to his steed he spurred Hawk into action, driving him forward. Immediately, his horse jumped over the wall of fire that now ringed the area and came down practically on top of the commander. In that same instance he severed the man's head from his shoulders leaving Vaulnik's men without a leader.

However, he did not stop to reflect, as he continued to gallop through the fray killing and wounding men left and right in his path. Behind him, he and his horse were spewing oil onto the scene in a maneuver he had fondly named, The Dragon's Breath, after the path of fire it left in its wake. The trick with this was to keep moving forward.

Finally, Clavorn turned and looked back behind as one of his men shouted to him. That was his signal. Quickly, he cut the rope that tied the bag of oil to Hawk's tail. It fell to the ground bursting into flames just as he and his horse managed to maneuver out of the way. He glanced up, driving himself and Hawk back into the chaos of the scene. On he drove Hawk as he now maneuvered him on instinct, abandoning his reins as he battled the enemy's soldiers before him.

Fire and smoke mingled with sounds of battle as one of Vaulnik's men managed to acquire a steed and charge him. Clavorn wheeled Hawk around just in time for him to catch the man's blade. Up stroke, down stoke, the man was strong and brutishly built he noticed as he parried with him. He turned Hawk into the mounted soldier rearing him up. Then, just as Hawk struck the man with one of his powerful hooves, Clavorn struck down with his sword, knocking his enemy clean from his horse while mortally wounding him at the same time. Glancing back, he could see the man was dead.

On the battled waged, as cries and screams echoed into the cold spring night. Firelight continued to glint off swords while smoke and the smell of burning flesh filled the air. Before long the whole battle was over. He and his men had killed every last one of Vaulnik's soldiers while only suffering a minimal number of casualties themselves. Victory was theirs.

From on top of a hillside Clavorn watched with his men as the last of the blaze finished off what was left their enemy's encampment. By daybreak all that would be left of Vaulnik's contingent would be a large number of smoldering corpses.

"Do you think they'll understand the message," Melkiar asked as he pulled his horse up beside Clavorn who was still overlooking the scene of their victory.

"Well, if Vaulnik doesn't. We'll just keep sending them till he does," Clavorn replied. There was more to this message than simply 'I'm back' but he was going to keep that part to himself for now.

"And what of Sevzozak?" Melkiar continued.

"I think we'll let that play out for now," Clavorn replied.

"Fortunately, that ring of fire strategy seems to suffocate itself after a certain point," Kevic noted as he pulled his horse up next to Clavorn and company.

Clavorn agreed and silently he thanked his old master for showing him how to use fire in battle. After a few more minutes he turned Hawk and headed back to their encampment with his whole regiment following suit.

Sure enough when dawn broke that morning nothing was left where Vaulnik's soldiers had camped in the woods. All that remained was smoldering ash. Later a scout reported to Clavorn that Sevzozak's men had arrived to inspect the scene of the battle.

"So did you happen to over hear anything they said?" Clavorn asked as he took a swig of ale from his flask while he sat on a large old root.

The willow branches swayed gently in the early morning breeze as the sunlight filtered in through the leaves. The large ancient willow was a great shelter and meeting hall.

"No sir, but I got the impression that they were impressed with your work," the young man told him.

Clavorn thanked him and swigged his ale, he was just beginning.

Chapter 8

A few days later another scout returned with news. It was late in the afternoon and Clavorn and his council were discussing another attack, this time on a garrison over the border. Golden light was streaming in through the branches of the willow tree casting shadows on the ground below. A gentle breeze belied the storm he was planning.

"Yes, what news do you have," Clavorn remarked as a young man entered through the branches.

He was tall and gangly, owing to his age, but still fit. He had short blond hair which was often found in locks about his head. All the men in his war council fell silent the moment he entered to hear what he had to say.

"They are saying that you are dead. That Vaulnik had you executed in a most horrible manner, and that the attack on his men near the Mountains of Kilvain was done by those who wished to wreak revenge for your death."

"I see," Clavorn replied.

I wonder how he explained the prison break.

"Did you hear any news about a prison break?"

"Sir?"

"An escape. Did anyone manage to escape that night?"

"You mean besides you?" Kevic asked.

"Yes."

"Ah...I heard nothing, sir. If they did, Vaulnik is playing it down."

Of course, he wouldn't want it known that anyone had managed to outwit him. That is provided they were able to make it out of the castle....I hope some of them did.

"So they are saying that you are dead," Melkiar repeated as billows of smoke exited his mouth.

"Why would they do that when they have been looking for you?" inquired Sayavic, "And how are they going to explain the soldiers searching the woods?"

"They'll probably say they are looking for my supporters. As to claiming I'm dead, I think they believe it will break the will of the people and ruin moral," Clavorn replied.

"True enough I suppose. I heard rumors of some who thought this rebellion might be over with you gone," commented Falor a tall dark haired warrior, who judging by the scars on his face, had seen his share of battles, "though present company excluded."

That's good.

"Well, I know in my village there are those who think like Falor said, that this war can't be won except with you as their leader," Another man with slightly greying brown hair by the name of Koron told him.

Koron had originally been a farmer. His story was very similar to so many others in Clavorn's army who had suffered a loss because of Vaulnik's men. In his case, his family had been killed as they defended the forest on the edge of their land which contained the ever precious Kriac Stones. They had known it was the stones Vaulnik's men were after, and they could not let them fall into the hands of such a man, nor did they wish the forest to be destroyed in their pursuit. The only reason Koron was alive was because Vaulnik's men had left him for dead. When he had come-to all his family was dead.

"I doubt our success over his soldiers will count for much unless it was done by you. To them, it would likely just be seen as a stroke of luck. Not something they can count on," he continued.

"I don't know," replied Thalon one of Clavorn's best warriors.

He was tall with long dark brown hair which he wore partially back and braided. In his village he had been highly thought of and had been considered a leader of sorts. His wife had been taken by Vaulnik back to his castle along with all the other women Vaulnik suspected of being the Shaddorak. She had been his village's medicine woman and was known throughout as a great Dragon Witch. Many thought him lucky to have such a wife. Now no one knew what had become of her.

"I know," continued Thalon, "I for one would fight even harder knowing you were dead, and I know many other who would do the same to avenge your death and carry on the fight. I believe I can speak at least for my village. It seems to me there would be others who would do the same."

"I would have to agree with Thalon that there would be those who would carry on," Falor reiterated, "With the right man in charge it could prove problematic for Vaulnik."

"Seriously," Koron put in, "I think there would still be those in many of the villages who would lose heart. So many of them looked up to you, and received their courage and hope from you. I just can't imagine how devastating this news will be to them."

"True, but I still believe that it could just as easily fail them and become a rallying cry," Thalon told them.

"What do they offer as proof of his demise?" Melkiar asked the scout named Alcon as he sat, pipe in hand, on a root not far from the fire pit.

"They say he is dead," he repeated a bit bewildered and seemingly unsure of what Melkiar had heard him say.

"I know that. I mean; how can they justify saying that he is dead without proof?" the crotchety, pipe smoking warrior asked once more, gesturing towards Clavorn who was seated on a large root near the base of great tree's trunk.

"Word is that Vaulnik gruesomely executed him in front of a mob of people," Alcon told him, "though I'm told he…or, err, whoever it was, sir,…was pretty messed up when they brought him out."

That figures.

"Humm," replied Melkiar.

Silence permeated the space with in the giant willow as all there took in what Alcon had told them.

"Oh, they are also saying that any man who claims to be you is an impostor just trying to keep the rebellion going," Alcon continued turning to face Clavorn.

Clavorn sat in thought. A deafening silence permeated the great tree as all those present waited for his response. Tension hung in the air even as the branches of the old tree swayed gently in and out in the soft breeze. Golden sunlight flickered to the dance of the weepy boughs while the light scent of spring flowers wafted about. Smoke from Melkiar's pipe continued to billow upwards and filter out of the ancient willow.

"Fine," Clavorn announced after several minutes had passed.

"Fine?!" Melkiar blurted out, "They claim you are dead and all you have to say is '*fine*?'"

"Yes," Clavorn told him flatly.

Melkiar raised an eyebrow in disbelief as mutterings and whispers filtered amongst them.

"Why fight them? Why disagree with them? They want to claim I am dead. Then fine. I am dead. We just need to provide the masses with a viable substitute."

Thalon nodded, "It could work if done properly."

"But you're *not* dead!" Melkiar blurted out.

"You're right, my friend. But they have just publically executed a man in my place. You know it was not me, but you know me. The masses hardly know me well enough to know that. Besides, they're already saying anyone who claims to be me is an imposter."

"True," Melkiar agreed, "But I still think it madness."

"Maybe not, if we find the right substitute like he said," Thalon replied, "And it's presented right."

There was a brief pause as everyone, especially Melkiar, considered Clavorn's proposal.

"Alright, say for argument sake I agree with you, which I am not sure that I do, who do you propose this illustrious substitute be?" Melkiar inquired with a bit of sarcasm, "Presuming, of course, that you have one in mind that is."

Fires of Life

"Shaltak," Clavorn answered.

"But sir, no one knows where he is, or even if he is alive," Alcon remarked.

"Yeah, I am told no one has seen him since the Battle of Quantaris," Koron put in.

"Well, that is not entirely true," Clavorn replied.

"Oh, this ought to be good," Melkiar exclaimed. "Have you seen him? No. Waite." He told him as he was about to reply. "I know. You want to impersonate this Shaltak."

"No." Clavorn replied flatly.

"You're not suggesting..." Melkiar continued before suddenly being interrupted.

"Wait! You mean you ARE Shaltak!" Sayavic exclaimed, "Shaltak, Slayer of Dragon Killers and Protector of Maltak and Dragons."

"No?" Melkiar questioned, and then hesitated as he apparently considered Sayavic's revelation.

Clavorn sat unmoving as he waited for them to draw the appropriate conclusion.

"Well, I guess he could be," Melkiar finally conceded, "or at least he could pass for him."

"No need to pass for. I *am* him," Clavorn finally announced.

"That was you!" once more a surprised exclamation came from Sayavic.

Since Avivron had not participated in the Dragon Wars none of those present, or within its boards or out, knew he was Shaltak.

"Yes, my friend," Clavorn responded.

"His heroics, I mean yours... I mean they were legendary amongst the people of my village. Now I know why you reminded me of all those stories I'd heard of as a boy." Sayavic was the youngest man on his council. "But why did you not use your given name during the Dragon Wars?" he inquired.

"Because Qualtaric, my mentor, insisted that I withhold my name and the name of my family," he told them.

"Why?" Sayavic persisted, "Your father was well known."

"Perhaps it was a test to see if you could make a name for yourself without your father's reputation behind you," Alcon put in.

"Perhaps," Clavorn replied, briefly considering this angle for the first time.

"So you hid your true identity," Melkiar persisted, restating the obvious, "But then why did you want go back to using your name and that of father's?"

"Out of anger; out of pride," Clavorn told them. "After the massacre at Evangraw, and my mother's and sister's death at the hands of Vaulnik's men, I could no longer contain myself. I wanted Vaulnik to know who sought to challenge him and…Well; you know the rest of that story."

"And of course Sevzozak let you wage his battles for him while he played the inept king who could not control his rebellious peasants," Kevic put in, "Until he believed your popularity threatened his crown."

Clavorn could see the light of understanding begin to grow throughout the group gathered in the great tree.

"Or his cowardice got the better of him," Melkiar put in. "Remember he is still paying Vaulnik to keep his throne."

"Then doesn't that call into question whether or not Sevzozak is truly loyal to his people or simply his regency," Falor pointed out.

"It does. It is for these questions and more that perhaps you will understand why I think, that for now, we should play along," Clavorn told them.

"No," Melkiar replied flatly.

"I don't follow," Kevic commented, the old warrior clearly having trouble seeing the sense in Clavorn's proposal.

"I do," Thalon replied, leaning on his battle axe as he sat next to Kevic on a root near the center fire.

"But I'm not sure I understand," Koron remarked, trying to get his head around everything.

"If we let them believe that they have successfully pulled off their little ruse," Clavorn explained, "Vaulnik is liable to pull back for now. We can then use this time to rally the people and bolster their confidence, which, if I am right, will perhaps force our good king to choose a side or recommit his previous crime. One we would be prepared for and, therefore, better able to expose he treason."

"Maybe, but why would he pull back?" Koron asked.

"Yes, and if he knows you are not really dead. Won't he suspect you are Shaltak?" Falor asked.

"Perhaps, but whether Vaulnik believes I am the real Shaltak, or just using the name to garner support, won't really matter. He may even just simply believe he has two opponents to fight instead of one," Clavorn explained, "The outcome is probably going to be the same. I believe he is likely to pull back his forces to reinforce the idea that I am dead and make it appear as if he does not see us as a threat. No matter what he believes about my identity it still works in our favor. At this moment only those gathered here, shy of Qualtaric, know the truth."

"Still, he could also redouble his efforts," put in Koron.

"Why? When he has Sevzozak," Thalon replied, "He is more likely to just put pressure on him to quiet his kingdom."

"Yes, but I hate to state the obvious," Melkiar put in, "but Shaltak, I mean you," he said, stumbling over himself, "was defeated at the Battle of Quantaris. A battle, I might add, that saw the decimation of all the Dragons of the Earth, save one; if you believe the rumors."

"True," Clavorn noted.

"Then how will it help us to have you claim that you are Shaltak?" Kevic inquired.

"Oh, I got it!" Alcon piped up, "Because of the defeat Vaulnik will not feel threatened."

"Yeah," Melkiar replied, "and because of that defeat, and Shaltak's disappearance, the masses will likely be tentative about following us. I still think this is a bad idea."

"Maybe, but I believe that if we have a big enough victory, and show the people Vaulnik is vulnerable, we can turn the tide of public opinion. If we can show that Shaltak is still strong. Perhaps even stronger than before, and that he is out to finish what Clavorn started, that he supports them and their cause, then we should be able to use their ruse against them."

"Pardon a proverbial sceptic, but I still don't see how this helps us over just simply proving he is a liar?" Melkiar commented; smoke billowing about him as he spoke.

"First, we would need to prove I am Clavorn. Since he has just displayed my dead body, they will likely believe Vaulnik over us. All Vaulnik would need to do in return is claim that we are so desperate to defeat him that we will stop at nothing to try and lure troops to our side. Forcing us to spend a lot of energy just trying to prove I am alive."

"Alright," Melkiar conceded after a moment of silence, "now I see the sense of it. Still, what of Sevzozak?"

"Well, if I am right he will most likely do some version of a repeat performance."

"You hope," Melkiar pointed out.

"A leopard rarely changes its spots. Besides, you have a better plan, my friend? Now's the time," Clavorn told him.

"Sadly, no," he grumbled, "but couldn't Sevzozak just claim our victories as his?"

"Only if he is willing to go to war with Vaulnik, which I am betting he is not. Not yet. His dilemma is the same as before."

"Only now he has angry peasants who want revenge for your death," Thalon said, "They could pose a threat to his crown."

"If he feels threatened by them," Clavorn told him, "Do you really believe he feels threatened enough to sacrifice his current position?"

Thalon considered his words, "Not yet perhaps. They would have to start rioting, and then direct that towards him which they are more likely to direct their anger towards Vaulnik. No. You are right. He will most likely wait to see how things play out."

"By that time it will be clear that Shaltak has taken up your cause of leading the rebellion," Sayavic added.

"And if he feels he needs to keep his face…" Falor put in.

"…Then he will side with us," Clavorn finished.

"But won't Vaulnik force him to put an end to us?" Melkiar remarked still questioning the viability of Clavorn's proposal.

"Then we'll be fighting two fronts. The people would have to choose to fight, not just Vaulnik, but their king as well," Koron declared.

"True, but Vaulnik was unable to get him to do that before," Clavorn replied.

"No. He just got him to hand you over instead," Melkiar fired back, "All-be-it surreptitiously of course."

"So isn't he more likely to do that again?" Falor asked.

"Oh, I see where you are going with this," Sayavic announced. "You are trying to force him to repeat his treachery."

"And when he does…," Thalon began.

"We'll expose him," Clavorn finished.

"Still, what is to stop him from handing us all over," Melkiar continued.

"Nothing, but the treachery will still be the same. The betrayal of his people," Clavorn told him.

"It is a big gamble," Melkiar observed.

"True," Clavorn replied, "but one I believe we should take."

Clavorn looked into the faces of all those present. Silence once more permeated the space within the giant willow as they all considered his proposal.

"I'm with you," Thalon announced after a few moments had passed.

"Me too," added Sayavic.

"You can count me in," declared Kevic as Falor and Koron followed suit.

Before long all those present under the ancient tree had answered in agreement except Melkiar.

"So, what about you, my skeptical friend, what do you say?" Clavorn asked of his ever pipe smoking friend and counsel member.

"Well, I still say it is risky. We're all most likely to end up dead from some double cross or other but…" he puffed on his pipe, "I am with you. Freedom was never won without risk."

"Then it is settled," Clavorn announced, "Alcon," he said, turning to the scout who had born the report to them, "spread the word that I am no longer to be called Clavorn, because he is dead. That I am Shaltak, Slayer of Dragon Killers and Protector of Maltak, and I have come here to lead them into battle against Vaulnik at Clavorn's request."

"I still don't know about this," Melkiar told him. "I think your most difficultly will be in convincing them that you are Shaltak come to fight in your name. I mean, by Alhera! We celebrated your return. How do you expect them to swallow that?"

"He has a point," Thalon admitted.

"I know there will be those amongst them who will not believe the story. If fact, I doubt very much if any of them will, especially at first."

"Then what's the point," Melkiar asked.

"The point is not so much for them as for our enemy. It is more important that Vaulnik and Sevzozak believe that I am Shaltak. So the story will stand as is. We will keep repeating it as long as it takes to become believable. There will be sceptics, but hopefully they will have the good sense to play along."

"Why not just tell them," Melkiar put in.

"Because the trees always have ears, my friend, and while we are safe here, the forests outside here has no shortage of spies. The story must stand as is in order to preserve the ruse for our enemy."

"I follow," Thalon said after a brief pause.

"I still don't like it, but I understand. If they all know, there could be one or more amongst them who may unwittingly speak of it openly in the wrong place or to the wrong person. We will be garnering more troops in the future, if all goes well, and it could be a source of our undoing. Still, I am not fond of the idea," Melkiar told him.

"Neither am I, my friend. Neither am I," Clavorn replied. He then turned to Alcon who understood his orders and left to carry them out.

It was late in the evening as Clavorn sat on a rock under the stars with Melkiar near the waterfall. The moonlight danced off the water and shimmered down the falls. Clavorn loved to watch the light play on the water. He thought back onto his first visit here. He remembered stumbling across her bathing in the waterfall. Her long wet dark hair falling down her back. The way the water played on her naked skin, and then the sight of those scars.

What happened to her? Will I ever see her again?

"Where are you tonight?" Melkiar asked, breaking in on his thoughts.

"Oh, nowhere in particular, just considering the events of the day."

"Uhm, I doubt that," Melkiar grumbled as he took another puff on his pipe.

"Now you are starting to sound like Sefforn," Clavorn commented.

"Well, someone has too," he replied. The smoke billowed up around his head before a gentle breeze sent it on its way. "Say, that brings me to the question I have been meaning to ask you ever since he left. Where is he? And where are Clovak, Sorenavik, and the rest?"

"He is on leave. His family needed him back home," Clavorn answered trying to be as matter of fact as possible.

He hoped Melkiar would not pick up on the subtle uncomfortable state he was feeling at having to have to answer his question. He did not want to give away the true reason for his friend's departure.

Fortunately, Sefforn had family near the northern territories, so his departure in that direction would seem perfectly natural. At least, that was the theory.

"So he took Clovak and Sorenavik with him, along with a small troop?" Melkiar remarked his voice riddled with apparent disbelief.

"The lands between here and his home have become infested with bandits."

"Bandits like us?" Melkiar replied, raising an eyebrow while puffing on his pipe.

"Melkiar, Clovak and Sorenavik are needed with him," he replied simply, hoping he would drop the subject.

"They are also some of our best men," Melkiar blurted out, "Shouldn't they have remained here? Clovak is quite possibly our finest archer and Sorenavik one of our top swordsmen. Shouldn't they be here with us?"

"Perhaps, but that is not possible at this moment," he told him, hoping his answer would suffice as he ran his hand through his hair in frustration.

He knew what Melkiar had to say was right, and he wondered how many other men had come to the same conclusion; that Sefforn was on some sort of mission.

"Look, they'll be back soon," he blurted out.

"Before the war is over I hope," Melkiar replied.

Clavorn could not help but share his sentiment.

A moment of silence passed between them. Melkiar puffed on his pipe while Clavorn remained lost in thought.

"You still object to my taking the name, Shaltak, don't you?" he finally blurted out after the brief pause in their conversation.

"Yes. I think it is a mistake. How will the people know who to rally around? Many will despair at the news of your death. Not to mention whether or not the men will even believe the fairytale you just had Alcon spin."

"The men might not buy it at first, but, as I said before, it is not so much for them as for our enemy."

Fires of Life

"You sure Vaulnik or Sevzozak will believe it?"

"Again, whether they believe it or not, they will be forced to act as if it is until such time as they can prove otherwise. And they would only do that if it served them in some fashion or other. Whether I am Clavorn or Shaltak matters little to this war. I am still a person the people can rally around, and that is all in regards to me that would matter from their point of view."

"Then doesn't that make you a target?"

"Only if they believe it would end the war. But if the people come together around another, such as Shaltak, it shows that this uprising has more legs than simply one man with good oratory can garner. And that, my friend, is more powerful and more threatening than whether or not I am Clavorn Remmaik, or Shaltak, Slayer of Dragon Killers."

"You still have to convince the people though."

"Well, as for them, that is why we will give them new victories and a new hero. Then when the time is right we will reveal all. You will see. They will be pleased."

"I hope you are right, my friend. I hope you are right," Melkiar replied nodding his head as he took another puff from his pipe.

Silently, Clavorn hoped the same.

"You know, that pipe has a better chance of giving us away more than anything else," he remarked jokingly.

"Oh, Dragon's Scales! A man needs some vice to pass his time," Melkiar protested.

"It's alright, my friend. I'm sure you're safe for tonight."

"You know, you sure know how to ruin a man's pleasure. Now how am I supposed to sleep tonight?"

"The same as always I suppose," Clavorn told him with a smile, "Tomorrow we strike the garrison at Latcon."

"But isn't that on our side of the border?"

"Yes, but after today's news, a victory here at home that the people can rally around would be good."

"I see your point."

Melkiar puffed some more on his pipe, as the two men sat in silence enjoying the relative quiet of the evening. Meanwhile, around the camp whispers and stirs could be heard as the men digested the news Alcon had spread around the encampment. Some men had been inclined to give Clavorn sideways glances as he moved amongst them earlier that evening. He could tell there were questions in their eyes. But none had been so bold as to actually come up to him to inquire about the truth of the new information, and he was glad for that. Tomorrow would bring enough challenges without having to address the matter now.

He breathed deep and drunk in the sweet smell of even flowers, damp rock, and awakening soil. If he closed his eyes, he could imagine spring as she brought to life the forest, with its apparent obliviousness to the pain, suffering, decimation, and chaos that existed elsewhere in the world.

He opened his eyes. Stars shined down on them from the Shardon Lands while the moon waxed its way across the evening sky.

"You know, we could use a few more archers for this assault on Latcon," Melkiar announced, breaking into his brief mental respite after a short pause in their conversation.

"I know, but the men will do fine," Clavorn replied, trying to sound confident.

He knew that ideally Melkiar was right. They needed more archers for the attack. But he also knew the forest had ears and that under these conditions rumors spread fast through a camp. He needed his men confident for the attack.

Melkiar took another puff on his pipe as a cool breeze blew through the trees. The two men sat in silence now, each absorbed in his own thoughts, trying to enjoy what there was of the evening before it was time to retire. Smoke rose up from Melkiar's pipe to meet the stars above them, but not before another gust of wind came up and blew it up over the cliff behind them.

Chapter 9

Dawn broke over the horizon. The day promised to be a good one. There was not a cloud in the new morning sky. Only a strong wind rippled through his long flowing dark hair. Clavorn and his men readied themselves for battle. There was much to be done, as last minute preparations were more than usual. He had wanted to keep the location of the attack secret for as long possible. The tradeoff now was that it caused at bit more commotion than there otherwise would have been. He figured over time the men would learn to be prepared for any sort of attack. It had been that way during the Dragon Wars, so it would be now. Before security had not been as great of an issue, after all he was fighting for a king and court he believed wanted the same thing. But now, now he was not so sure.

The biggest buzz about the camp, however, was the new revelation about his identity. A few more of those sideways glances he had experienced the night before made it more than clear that the speech he expect he would have to give was definitely essential.

"Melkiar!" he shouted over the din of activity. Melkiar lifted his head from lacing his boot, and Clavorn motioned him to come over.

Grumpily, he set his foot down from the log he was using and trudged his way over to Clavorn. The morning had been a trying one. What with all the number of men asking him to explain the recent revelation, and him having to put them off or give a repeat answer of what they already knew. He was not quite sure this was the best tactic, and so he hated having to answer their questions.

"Yes?"

"How are the men?"

"Confused, but that is to be expected," Melkiar commented, "It's not like it was easy news for them to swallow. I've been letting them know that you plan to speak before we go?"

"That's good. Hopefully I will be able to arrest their questions," Clavorn replied.

"That would be good," Melkiar told him not wanting to go into exactly all the many reasons why that was so. He had a feeling Clavorn already knew.

"Well, pray it is so, my friend."

Melkiar nodded.

"Now, I think we both best finish our preparations don't you," Clavorn told him as he placed a hand on Melkiar's shoulder before stepping away to do just that.

Once again Melkiar nodded, and then returned to his preparations which first included finishing lacing his boot. A problem he quickly solved by availing himself of a nearby rock which he used to set his foot on while he completed the task.

A short while later Clavorn was mounted on his horse staring down rows of bewildered and sometimes hostile faces. As he looked down at those rows of men, all mounted on their horses, he could only hope his speech would clarify their questions and assuage any fears or doubts that they might have about him. He hated lying to his men. It felt wrong. Yet, he had a sense that it was the right strategy for the moment; disinformation more for his enemy's benefit than his men's. Their purpose had not changed just who he 'was.' Ultimately, he hoped his speech would both unite and inspire them.

The wind whipped the eagle feathers in his helmet. Hawk snorted and shifted under him. He wondered if his equine friend could sense his uneasiness regarding his upcoming speech. Mounted beside him was Melkiar. His bay horse, like Hawk, shifted uneasily in the wind and tenseness of the moment. Silence moved through the crowd of men as they readied themselves to hear him speak.

"Avivronians, today we unite to fight our common enemy," he began.

Great cheers went up from his men. Clavorn raised his hand to stay their voices while his horse shifted its weight once more under him.

"I know you have heard the rumor that Clavorn is dead."

Loud jeering went up from his men, and once again he had to stay their voices.

"It is true. I am not Clavorn."

At this news, he could sense the disappointment and skepticism in the crowd as murmuring rippled through the ranks.

"But we celebrated your return!" a voice went up from the group gathered before him.

"Only Clavorn rides Hawk!" another shouted.

Melkiar gave Clavorn a sideways glance from atop his horse, but made no comment, as he and his horse stood beside him facing the throng of men gathered before them.

"I know. It was what Clavorn wanted," he told them. "He said I should ride Hawk so that you would know that it was his wish that you follow me."

At this a hushed silence fell over the men. Melkiar shifted uncomfortably in his saddle.

"It was his request that I finish what he had started," he continued. "I am Shaltak, Slayer of Dragon Killers, Protector of Maltak and Dragons."

Once again murmurs ripple through his ranks at his revelation.

"We share a common foe," he went on, "I too have lost loved ones and many of my people to this tormentor from the south. I know your pain. I knew his for I have it too."

Here he could see more whispers circulate amongst them. Would they believe his story? He could almost hear Melkiar's reservations echo in his ears.

"He was a good man, your Clavorn," he continued, a dead silence once again spread throughout the throng of men before him, "who wanted only freedom and dignity for his people, you. It was what he craved most for you; freedom from tyranny and oppression, freedom from injustice and persecution, and most importantly freedom from bondage and slavery." He paused, "Today, let us fight in his name."

The men nodded. Clearly he had their attention now.

"Let us send a clear message to Vaulnik that we will no longer tolerate his scourge upon our lands or his tyranny upon our people. I know many of you do not know me, but I can assure you that I know you. Your bravery is legendary. So today gentlemen, let us begin a war that our children will sing about for generations to come. Today, let us continue what Clavorn and you began. Let us take back our lands; for our children, for our families, and in the name of Clavorn Remmaik!"

As he raised his sword on his final words, hoots and cheers went up from the men gathered, and Clavorn knew he had made the right impression. Glancing to his side, he could see Melkiar was sufficiently impressed with his handling of the situation. He turned Hawk into the wind and set off towards Latcon with Melkiar following at his side, and his men all following in their turn.

Chapter 10

Latcon was no more than half a day's ride as the crow flies, however, Clavorn wanted to keep the location of Shyloran Forest a secret. Shyloran had been kept safe by the dragons for millennia, then, presumably, by others. Who, he did not know. If it was that important for them to look after and preserve, then he did not want to be the first to expose it. To that end he had taken his men the long way around, traversing a small mountain range just to the west of their intended target. Once they were there they would wait in the forest near the garrison till the cover of darkness.

No fires were lit at their make shift camp. In fact, not much activity took place at all while they waited for darkness to settle in, save for the quiet preparations of a few special items Clavorn had requested. In the time that passed, he went over his strategy with his ranking officers, and last minute changes were made according to the reports given to them by their scouts. All was ready. Swords doubly sharpened. Extra arrows loaded into quivers. All supplies checked and recheck.

Silence was once again the name of the game. The men had been extra careful during the day to move as stealthily through the forest as possible. Even now conversation was at a minimum.

At Clavorn's signal they all readied their horses and took their places. Darkness was their cloak this evening just as it had been several nights before. Tonight, however, silver rays from a waxing moon lit the evening sky. As Clavorn watched the night, a shooting star passed overhead. He hoped it was a good omen.

Latcon stood on a hill partially surrounded by forest. It was this forest he and his men were currently exploiting for the benefit of surprise. The walls of the small village were high and well-fortified despite its size, owing to the garrison contained within its borders. Guards paced along its walls at regular intervals.

Inside there was a central well, around which were various village shops and such, with the fort being placed on the western end of it.

The fortress itself had high stone walls which melded into the exterior fortifications of the settlement so that the entire western end of Latcon was dedicated solely to it. This made it the dominating feature of the town, with its menacing watchtowers and great metal door.

Atop the watch towers were large stone dragons heads from which fires spilled forth into the night from their large gaping mouths. Black flags with red dragons blew in the breeze at regular intervals along the stony battlements. Inside its menacing walls was housed a large contingent of Vaulnik's army known for their particular brand of brutish and unethical tactics. One of the many reasons Clavorn had selected it.

It was here, on the western end of Latcon, where Clavorn intended to concentrate his attack. His goal was to minimize civilian casualties. At his signal, Sayavic led the first wave of archers.

Moving stealthily through the forest to maintain their cover, they positioned themselves along the exterior walls of Latcon, concentrating on the garrison. In the meantime, a second wave of men was already positioning themselves to move in quickly once the full attack began.

From his position in the forest, along the northern wall, Clavorn could see Vaulnik's soldiers pacing atop the ramparts. The black tufts of feathers on top of their helmets silhouetted against the night's sky, while their dark mail blended into the inky firmament. Clavorn watched as two guards exchanged words on the parapet and then went on about their way. All was quiet. The night air was ominously still. A raven flew up but made no call. Only the flap of its feathers broke the thick silence that hung in the air.

Now!

He gave the signal to begin the attack.

Quietly, arrows flew upwards to meet their marks. Immediately, guards along the rampart walls began to fall. Quickly and silently, his men moved in with ladders to scale the walls of the fortress closest to them. They were half way up the wall before a guard from across the rampart noticed them and sounded the alarm.

Swiftly, Clavorn gave the signal for the full attack to commence. In a matter of minutes, mounted archers surrounded the village and began their onslaught. Arrows once again flew from the bows of his archers as his men on horseback, and on foot, went around to Latcon's main gate.

He could just barely make out the forms of Kevic and Koron as they reached the top of the rampart and began to engage their enemy. Before long there were sounds of steal meeting steal as sword met sword high up on the settlement walls. Soon this was mixed with the familiar cries of the injured and the dying which rung out into the night air.

Moments later more of Vaulnik's men joined the others on the ramparts. In droves they came as they tried to defend their garrison. Clavorn could see Vaulnik's archers as they rained arrows down upon his men. With another signal from him, a second wave of archers began pelting the fortress with fiery arrows. So far things were going well, but he worried that Melkiar might be right, that they needed more archers.

He looked down at his men trying to open the main gate. From his vantage point he could see Thalon shouting orders to those in charge of ramming the gate. However, the tree they had cut for the battering ram seemed to be having little effect. This concerned him, but it was still early in the battle. His men along the western wall, however, had managed to gain a foot hold along the rampart walls.

Now for his other version of Dragon's Breath; with a wave of his sword, huge catapults came forth out of the woods closest to the garrison. These were the surprise he had had a few of his men spend their time on after their arrival, readying and manufacturing, taking great pains to do so as surreptitiously as possible. Now, large leather balls were being fitted in them.

Clavorn raised his sword, pausing momentarily to be sure all his men were ready. Then with one swift motion he lowered it.

Suddenly, all the balls were lit and sent hurtling over or onto the rampart walls, exploding in a mixture of hot oil and fire. The giant balls of thick leather were designed to burn through or burst on contact, showering the occupants with flaming rain. One after another of these fiery balls were sent hurling over the ramparts, exploding inside the garrison. Soon Vaulnik's men were not just battling his men, but the raging fires within as well.

Clavorn glanced over at Latcon's main gate just in time to see his men successfully crash through. Hundreds of peasants poured forth in panic. Clavorn raised his sword again to stay the fiery balls and allow the villagers' time to escape. Soon, however, Vaulnik's army began to race out from the entrance of Latcon. Immediately, Clavorn's men closed in around them doing what they could to assist any of the townspeople through the gate safely while simultaneously engaging Vaulnik's men in battle.

At another signal from him soldiers began loading some of the catapults with large stones and hurling them at the garrison walls. On they pelted. He could hear them as they flew past him and crashed into the outer fortifications of Latcon. Suddenly, a breach appeared in the wall before him. Upon seeing this he spurred Hawk into the melee. Sword raised he rode straight for the opening followed by a contingent of his men. With one huge leap over the remaining rampart wall, Clavorn and Hawk were in the thick of battle. Left and right he flung his sword beheading some, killing or maiming others.

After a quick exchange of blows, in which he had successfully killed several of the enemy, Clavorn paused and took a quick glance about him. Smoke and fire blazed around him as the chaos of the battle raged before his eyes. He gazed across the battlefield to the where the entrance of the garrison lay. It was then that he saw him, the infamous Dark Knight, with his telltale black helmet shaped like the head of a dragon which obscured any identifying features. Raven feathers furled in the wind from atop his helmet and about his shoulders where his dark cape was attached. The only color on him was from the large red dragon that was emblazoned on his black metal breastplate.

The eagle feathers atop Clavorn's helmet whipped in the wind. For a moment he stood, mounted on Hawk, starring at the vision before him. Through the smoke and commotion of battle, the enemy's most infamous warrior stared back at him. His dark steed pawed the ground while his black cape continued to furl in the wind, giving him the appearance of an apparition from Zezpok, a demon befitting of Zagnor himself.

How oddly fitting.

Tales of the Dark Knight's vile exploits were known from Avivron to Shallungar. Many of which had him all but coming from Zezpok. Hawk snorted under him, and he could feel the anticipation mounting in his trusted equine friend.

"Okay boy, time to end him," he muttered to Hawk as he spurred him into action. Simultaneously, the Dark Knight rode towards him. The two men had no other vision in the battle except their respective opponents as their horses thundered towards one another.

CLANG! CLANG!

Their swords hit in a quick exchange as they passed one another. Clavorn turned Hawk to face his opponent again and charge as the Dark Knight did the same. Once more the two were charging full speed towards one another. This time a longer exchange of blows ensued, as the two warriors battled from their respective mounts. Down sweep, up sweep Clavorn fought with his sword always matching his opponent. Their horses danced to match their movements in perfect time. Fire and chaos raged around them. Smoke billowed in the air as the two warriors fought one another.

Then suddenly, from the corner of his eye, something glinted from around the neck of his adversary as his sword rose to meet his. At first, it failed to register in Clavorn's mind, as he finished the exchange and turned his horse once more to face the Dark Knight.

But then, as he eyed him from across the short distance which stood between them, Clavorn saw it again, a glint off the Dark Knight's breast plate.

He was about to dismiss it when suddenly he caught a full glimpse of the object that was catching the light of the fires of battle. Like a bolt of lightning the recognition of it unexpectedly split through the chaos and heat of the moment; transporting him back in time to another, not so glamorous, battle between the man before him and his father. The hideous dragon medallion told him all he needed to know.

He was Zarik, the man who had killed his father all those years ago.

But how?

Sevzozak's First Knight, Zarik, was supposed to have been killed; burned in a fire. The details were lost to him, broken pieces of overheard conversations spoken years ago before he was a man, before he was a warrior. Somehow he had survived. Again, the question was how? Or perhaps a better question was, did he ever really burn at all?

If he had not burned in that fire that was supposed to have ended his life, then the only other conclusion was that he had been part of a plan all along, a plan which had most likely been orchestrated by Vaulnik. But had Sevzozak been involved? Had he conspired in the death of King Dakconar and potentially his father's as well? Had the reality been that King Sevzozak had allowed Vaulnik to take over Avivron? If so, why? As the questions filed into his brain, faster than shooting stars, Clavorn's anger began to burn even more.

For now, however, the questions as to how much King Sevzozak knew, and how far did his treachery extend would have to wait. This moment demanded justice. The Dark Knight, Zarik, was not only responsible for his father's death, but for the deaths of countless others. The monster before him was guilty of an untold number of atrocities. He was a traitor to his country, to their world, to life.

Suddenly, all the pain and frustration of everything flooded into his heart.

Time to remove his head.

He spurred Hawk into action. Zarik followed suit. In a matter of seconds the two men were engaged once more in mortal combat. Memories of the poisoned tipped blade that had been the undoing of his father flitted briefly in his mind. He would have to watch Zarik's sword.

CLANG! CLANG!

Sounded once more in the air as Clavorn swung out with his sword, but Zarik met his blade with his. He wheeled Hawk around to meet his enemy. Again, the steal of their blades met. Fire glinted off their swords as they fought. There was no parting of the foes this time. No. This exchange was for the end. Only one man would remain standing when this was through.

They fought hard as their horses danced underneath them. Blow after blow it went. Each ending in a clash of steal until, in one exchange, Zarik sliced at Clavorn's head clipping him in the shoulder, penetrating his chainmail, and nicking his skin. Clavorn cried out briefly from the pain and swung his sword up and into Zarik's gut, temporarily throwing him off balance as he doubled over slightly from the impact. Clavorn swung his sword down to take off his head, but Zarik was too quick and reeled around blocking his stroke. Hawk reared and struck out forcing Zarik's horse to move. In the awkwardness of the exchange, the two men were both knocked from their horses.

Quickly, Clavorn rose to his feet, but a slight dizziness began to cloud his mind. He shook his head trying to clear it.

"I will gut you, you Avivronian scum," Zarik shouted as he rose to his feet.

Clavorn shook himself again trying to focus his mind. He starred across the chaotic scene around him to the Dark Knight before him, his vision alternating from blurry to clear. Anger welled up inside him, adrenaline flooded his body. He would not be taken down as his father had been.

He surged forward to strike out at his vile foe but, just as he was about to make contact, he faltered and missed, stepping past his opponent. As a result, Zarik easily moved out of his way and in one quick motion reached out, grabbed Clavorn's helmet, and removed it from his head as he stumbled past him.

Clavorn struggled to remain standing, his back to his opponent, the poison working, threatening to overtake him. Once again he shook his head trying to clear it, his vision continuing to alternate from blurry to clear.

I have to work past this.

"You know, I so enjoy seeing the faces of the men I kill as they expire by my hand," Zarik, the Dark Knight gloated, as he waltzed over and seized a hold of Clavorn's hair pulling his head back so that his face was to his, "Let us see who you are."

Clavorn's vision faded in and out of focus as he tried to gain a clear picture of the ugly black metallic face of a dragon that loomed before him. Malicious eyes starred down on him from inside the infamous dragon helmet.

"Ha, ha, ha," Zarik laughed, "Well, if it isn't the son of the great Favorn Remmaik now too weak and feeble to wreak the revenge he so desperately desires. Such a pity, but then the house of Remmaik has always been a pathetic one."

Surprise showed on Clavorn's face.

How?

"Yes, Clavorn," Zarik goaded as he spoke into his face, "Surprised? You shouldn't be. You are so like your father." Then he sniffed the air above him, "The stench of weakness runs in your family like a disease." Disgust dripped from his voice.

Clavorn narrowed his eyes. "At least we're not diseased!"

"Ha, ha, ha. You have your father's wit. I have to admit," he continued, the sarcasm and venom oozing from his lips as he placed his sword at Clavorn's throat, "it was a cleaver ruse you pulled off at the castle. I assume it was you who let all those prisoner go. I'm sure you'd love here they all got away, but I must report, no. Though they did give the castle guard quite a time..."

I'll bet they did.

"...before they were all killed."

NO!

"Ha, how glorious," he gloated waving his sword about in the air, "you should have seen it." He spat in his ear.

"Sorry I missed it." *You vile sack of dragon's dung.*

"Ha, but here is the best part," Clavorn could see him smile behind his dragon helmet, "Now I can end you here. No credit will you receive. Being dead as you are."

By Alhera I will NOT end here.

"Then why are you trying to kill a ghost?" Clavorn commented, as he vied for more time. He could feel his strength trying to return with each passing minute, though he was painfully aware of the poison's growing hold as his vision continue to fade in and out. For just a brief second, though, he could see his enemy's eyes slight with anger as the smoke billowed and blew around him.

"I'm not. I am just giving truth to the rumor and ending your little rebellion," Zarik spat, as he readied himself for the fatal blow; lifting his sword above his head.

Determination burned inside Clavorn, spilling forth in one quick outburst as he lashed out, elbowing Zarik, and causing him to release his hold. At that exact moment he then turned his sword in his hand so as to lash out at his opponent. He was not going down without a fight. However, Zarik easily countered his move.

Once again their swords clashed in the smoke filled night. A brief exchange of blows followed before Clavorn was forced to step back and break contact, drawing in heavily laden breaths as the poison worked its way through his body.

"You know, I rather enjoyed your mother and sister before I ran them through," Zarik announced as he slowly paced toward Clavorn.

Clavorn's eyes narrowed.

So it was you!

A great furry of rage welled up in him as he realized what Zarik had done. He had never known the identity of the one who had kill his mother and sister. Now, he laboriously lifted his head and glared at Zarik with a new burning hatred.

"Now, at last," Zarik jeered as he continued to pace closer, "it seems I have the pleasure of finally finishing what I started all those years ago."

He swung his sword to attack Clavorn, but Clavorn caught the blade with his.

"Not if I take your head off first," he replied, as he pushed back on his opponent's sword with all of his remaining strength.

Zarik was forced to step back, but not for long as another violent clashing of blows ensued. The stage around them was a chaotic storm as both armies continued to battle one another. Clavorn could feel himself struggle against the poison as he fought, but he was not going down, not yet.

Bodies littered the ground and fire raged about them. Suddenly, Zarik lunged for him, forcing him into a rapid exchange. Firelight danced off their swiftly moving swords as Clavorn was driven backwards, tripping over a body lying on the ground near the center well of the village.

Dizziness nearly overcame him as he felt his body hit the hard ground. Zarik took advantage of the opportunity and struck hard, causing him to lose his sword. Instinctually, he kicked up into Zarik, contacting him in the groin. At this Zarik doubled over and almost dropped his sword. Simultaneously, Clavorn fumble for and grabbed a large two handed sword off of a dead man on the ground near him and thrust it up into Zarik's belly, catching him just as he doubled over. The force of the two actions pierced Zarik's armor and went right through him. Zarik dropped his sword which Clavorn seized as he staggered to his feet. Then, in one swift motion, he

Fires of Life

raised Zarik's sword and swung it downward with all the grace of his experience, removing Zarik's head from his shoulders.

Clavorn stood a moment and watched, with drugged vision, as the head of his foe and killer of his father, mother, and sister rolled off onto the ground and came to rest near the body of a man not far from him. A strange sensation filled his soul as he looked upon it. His vision blurred momentarily. He shook his head to clear it and took one more last look at the end of his vile enemy, and source of much pain throughout many lands.

All of a sudden a man rushed at him from the side. Instinctively, Clavorn turned to fight him off, but the poison was still in his system, and he staggered again falling partially to the ground. He tried to adjust his vision, but it kept fading in and out. Clavorn lifted his head a moment, and was about to counter the man's potentially fatal blow, when just then he saw the head of the man who was attacking him come off and the face of Melkiar appear.

"Are you alright?" he asked as he helped him to his feet.

"Behind you!" Clavorn shouted as one of Vaulnik's men swung out at his friend and comrade. Melkiar turned just in time to run the man through with his blade. Clavorn could hear the sound of armor coming towards him and quickly wheeled around swinging up into the sword of an enemy soldier.

Sword met sword. Clavorn fought hard in a brief exchange of blows through the effects of whatever it was that Zarik had put on his blade. Finally, however, in one last exchange, his vision blurred and his strength failed just as he finished cutting down his opponent, and he felt himself fall to the ground at the man's side.

In the great distance of his mind he heard Melkiar cry out "Clavorn!" While the far sounds of battle raged around them. Then all went black.

Mist and fog swirled round him, clouding his vision. Suddenly, from somewhere in his mind, a dim light began to grow. About the light grew a strange mist. As he peered into the distant haze, a white horse appeared. No. It was not a white horse. It was a unicorn.

It galloped towards him, the light behind it silhouetting its magnificent form. Upon the unicorn rode a woman. Her long hair gracefully rippling, furling, billowing out in back of her while the light from a distant source intensified behind her. The unicorn stopped at his side and she dismounted.

He looked up into her face, but he could not see her features, for the intense light overpowered her form and shrouded them from his sight. A slight wind blew the soft silky cloth of her dress, revealing the outline of her svelte figure. Mist and fog surrounded them as she bent down and touched his wound.

"Rise," she commanded, taking his hand.

Clavorn felt himself lifted to his feet.

Instantly, he was back in the melee of battle, sword in his hand. He glanced about him, but the unicorn and the woman were nowhere to be seen. An enemy soldier came up from behind him but was fortunately shot dead before he could strike him. Clavorn turned to see Sayavic, bow in hand, and nodded to him in gratitude. He turned to find Melkiar, but the battle had drug him off into itself again, as he saw his friend battling in the distance.

Clavorn felt his shoulder where the wound from Zarik's blade had been, but to his amazement it was gone. His mail repaired.

How...?

Unfortunately, he did not have time to contemplate what had just taken place as another of the enemy's soldiers came rushing at him. Clavorn immediately responded as instinct took over, allowing him to easily dispatch his foe.

Smoke now filled the air where he was as the wind changed direction, blowing it up around him. Suddenly, out of the smoke and flames Hawk appeared. Within seconds the horse was at his side. Expertly and effortlessly, Clavorn remounted his steed and headed out of the smoky conflagration, wielding his sword at every enemy

Fires of Life

soldier in his path. Once he was clear of the worst of the smoke and fire he abruptly pulled Hawk up and surveyed the battle. From what he could see it was all but over as Zarik's men began to realize that he was dead and defeat was eminent.

As daybreak made its way over the horizon that morning a smoldering, fowl mess lay where Vaulnik's garrison had once stood at Latcon. The village itself lay in partial ruins, but it was free, liberated from the bondage of Vaulnik's soldiers, and Vaulnik himself.

Shouts of joy and praise went up from the grateful townspeople who had survived the attack as Clavorn and his men began to ride out of Latcon on their way back to their makeshift camp that morning; victorious. Flowers littered their path as joyous peasants lined their route out of the village.

Suddenly, a woman came up from the crowd and stopped Clavorn's horse. Clavorn pulled up short.

"Sir!" she cried out, "who may we thank for this glorious victory?"

"Shaltak, Slayer of Dragon Killers and Clavorn's Right Arm," he told the woman simply.

"Praise be to Shaltak," she replied as she stepped back from his horse in awe. After a brief moment she began shouting it so that the entire crowd took up the cry.

Chapter 11

A gentle breeze swayed the tops of the weeping willows as the stars shined down on them. It was just the previous evening in which they had been embroiled in a battle to liberate Latcon. Now Clavorn sat apart from his men who were busy celebrating their great victory. They had dealt Vaulnik a serious blow. The loss of the garrison at Latcon would not go unnoticed, not especially since it meant the loss of the Dark Knight, his prize commander.

Briefly Clavorn wondered how long it would take him to replace the infamous Zarik, but in Vaulnik's sphere of influence he doubted if it would be long. Evil men always seem to attract other evil men. Still, for now he hoped it would at least send a message that he and his men meant business.

"So what has you in such a brooding mood?"

Clavorn turned his head in the direction of the familiar voice.

"Oh, not much," he replied to the rugged, ever pipe smoking man who had fast become a welcomed friend.

"Well, it has to be something otherwise you would be over there with the others and I would not be here."

"Well, if you must know. I was thinking of the battle," he told Melkiar.

"Brooding over a victory, now that's a new one. I thought one was only supposed to brood over defeat."

"True, but this is just the beginning. We have hardly won the war."

"All the more reason to revel in our victory. So what is keeping the man of the hour from joining in the festivities?" Melkiar inquired as he sat down on a log nearest to him, a mug of ale in hand, while smoke escaped his lips from where his pipe was held firmly between his teeth.

"Oh, wait. Don't answer that. Let me guess," he continued as he set down his mug and removed the pipe from his mouth, "The death of The Dark Knight, Vaulnik's favorite commander."

"You're right. Only you left out the part about him also being the man responsible for my father's death, and the raping and killing of my mother and sister."

"Well, correct me if I'm wrong, but shouldn't that be all the more cause for celebration?"

Melkiar always had a way of coming to the point. However, all he could see of his departed enemy was his head as it rolled way and came to rest near the body of another man, his eyes staring emptily into the night. He should feel great victory over the defeat of such a man, and yet, for some reason he could not explain, he felt empty.

Perhaps it was because he had carried his hatred for him for so long, that cutting off his head was like removing one of his own limbs, with the ghost of its presence still being felt despite its clear lack of being there. Perhaps it was in the revelation that Zarik had also been responsible for the death of his mother and sister, and what that meant. Or perhaps it was just how one felt after defeating a long time enemy. Whatever the reason, he only he knew that while he was happy over their victory, there was a part of him that could not relish it the way the rest of his men did.

"Too true, my friend," he told Melkiar, "but I think that perhaps he has been part of the fuel for my rage for too long. I fear that, like the loss of a friend, he will haunt my mind even after he is gone."

"Nonsense! He has just been a part of your life for too long, and now your mind has no idea what to do with itself. Trust me. Once your brain has accepted he is dead, and by your hand, the emptiness inside will leave."

"I hope you are right," he replied, "I hope you are right."

"Of course I am," Melkiar commented, but Clavorn could only wonder if he was telling him that to placate him, or if he really meant it. "Besides, I thought I was supposed to be the pessimistic one around here. You know this camp won't survive two of us like me."

Clavorn could not argue with him there as a wiry smile made its appearance upon his face.

"Now don't you think it was time you joined in the merriment. There will be plenty of time to brood I assure you. Take it from me. I'm an expert. No, this is one of those brief moments life hands us, especially in a time of war, and I suggest you take it."

Clavorn looked over at Melkiar and for the first time he noticed the second mug of ale. This one he was holding out for him. Clavorn took the mug from his friend's hand and drunk deeply. A much needed drink. His only regret was that it was not much stiffer.

Sounds of music and laughter filtered into his consciousness as he glanced in the direction of the celebration. Perhaps Melkiar was right. This feeling was just a shadow of what had been. Still, as he considered Melkiar's words, he could sense an odd quality to the empty storm inside him. For while he felt a great void of emotions on one hand, there was simultaneously a huge mixture of emotions on the other which combined and clashed. The two extremes felt as if they were swirling together to form a complex soup which no single word could describe, nor group of words explain, for its reasons were far too numerous. Like a giant knot consisting of various threads, the only way he would gain understanding of it would be to pull each thread apart and examine them individually. Unfortunately, now was not the time. He took another swig of the ale Melkiar had brought him.

"Come on. It will do you good," Melkiar insisted as he stood up inviting him to follow him back to the festivities.

"You go on," he told him, still from his place on a rock not far from where Melkiar had been sitting, "I'll join you in a minute."

"Alright, but if you don't show up soon I'll gather up a group of us to come and drag you down there."

Clavorn smiled.

"Yeah, well I don't think that will be necessary," he told him, taking another deep drink, "I just need a moment to be alone then I'll follow you."

"You're sure?" Melkiar questioned, raising a bushy eyebrow and placing his pipe back in his mouth.

"Of course I'm sure. Look, will you stop hovering. You'd think you were my mother or something. I'm fine. I'll join you in a minute."

Melkiar paused a moment, once more removing his pipe from his mouth and pointing it in Clavorn's direction as he spoke, "Well, alright, but…"

"I know. I know. But you'll be back for me if I don't show up soon. Stop worrying. I'll be there. Now go. Before they all think we have both deserted them."

Melkiar replaced the pipe in his mouth, and making no more inquiries into his wellbeing, strode off to join the group in their merriment. Meanwhile, Clavorn once again found himself alone. A gentle breeze blew through the long wispy branches of the trees about him and riffled through his long dark hair. He looked up into the night sky and deep into the depths of the starry abyss.

"Father, if you can hear me. Zarik is dead. The Dark Knight is no more. You, mother, and Shalvera can rest in peace in now," he uttered into the darkness of the night hoping it would travel across the great chasms which were between him and his departed family to reach their hearing. "I will finish what I have started. I will free our people, or die in its pursuit."

He paused. No sound or reply came from the silent Shardon Lands above. Only the sounds of revelry in the distance filtered into his consciousness, yet somehow he felt more at peace than he had earlier. A loud roar of laughter went up from the merrymakers, and he took that as his cue to join them. But not without one last glance up into the night sky.

As he stepped off in the direction of the celebration, a shooting star crossed the darkness of the starry sky. In the silence of the shadows another graceful being moved off into the wood, satisfied all was well.

Chapter 12

It was now two months into his campaign, and while they were winning victory after victory against Vaulnik's men, no help was ever offered from King Sevzozak. In fact, the king still had not shown who he supported in any clear fashion. An uneasy feeling was beginning to grown in the pit of Clavorn's stomach.

He should be happy with their victories except he could not shake the uneasiness growing inside him. Had the Dark Knight been that integral to Vaulnik's army, or was their another explanation? Every time he went over it in his head, the idea of another explanation always won out. If he voiced it to Melkiar or Kevic, they would say he just was not giving himself enough credit. Only Thalon seemed to share in his disquiet.

King Sevzozak's silence did not aid matters any. Clavorn was beginning to wonder if he was simply letting his men wear themselves out. Almost as if he wanted them to fail, yet they kept winning.

His popularity as Shaltak was growing throughout the villages and cities of Avivron. Recruits had never been higher. He imagined if the king was in league with Vaulnik, that this irritated him. Perhaps that was why he had heard nothing from him yet. The rantings of Zarik during their exchange at the battle of Latcon only added to his suspicions about the king.

How had it come to pass that the Dark Knight was King Sevzozak's First Knight? Were they in league together? Or had their good king merely been the victim of well-played court intrigue? These and many other questions plagued his mind and were the reason for him letting things play out.

The one truly bright spot that had come to pass over the last two months was the news that, contrary to Zarik's claim, the prison break he had helped facilitate had been more successful than the great First Knight of Vaulnik claimed. A few of them had managed to sneak out in the confusion created and escape. Some of them had even made their way to his camp and were now a part of his army.

Some evenings, in the quiet of the night when the moonlight filtered in through the gently swaying branches of the giant willow, or when he sat under the stars near the waterfall, he thought of the woman on the unicorn.

Who was she? Was it her? Was the woman on the unicorn the same as the one who rescued me from Kazengor Castle? Or is it just wishful thinking on my part? Maybe it was all a dream. Something as a result of the poison as my body assimilated it.

Then he remembered her touch as she lifted him to his feet.

No, it had been real. But who was she?

However, that afternoon, as he sat starring at a map drawn on the back of a large piece of deer skin, such questions were far from his mind. He ran a hand through his now much shorter hair contemplating his next attack. Clavorn had cut his hair and let a nicely trimmed beard and mustache grow, in order to change his appearance, so as to go along with his new identity.

He lifted his head from the deer skin just as the branches from the tree parted, and a scout entered carrying a message. The scout was one of his. A young man from a village he had just recently liberated. Melkiar was pacing at the side of the willow opposite the boy's entry, while Thalon was seated on a great root near the trunk of the large tree sharpening his axe. Upon the boy's entry he ceased his actions and set the axe down.

The message the boy bore was apparently from King Sevzozak. He had obtained it second hand from a messenger to Sevzozak himself while on a wide patrol. Clavorn kept several layers of patrols; one he felt should be far enough away so as to disguise their location.

The young scout had apparently been on such a patrol with two others when he had run into the messenger seeking out Shaltak. The others with him told the messenger he would have to give the message to them and that they would forward it on. That was how he had apparently come to possess said communication.

"According to him, sir, he was to relay to you that King Sevzozak would be honored to have you dine with him at Escadora Castle," the scout told him.

Clavorn could hardly believe his ears. He had just been wondering when, or if, the king was going to respond to his actions just that morning.

"I was told that he wishes to make it a great event. With much feasting and dancing," the scout finished.

"How was it that he knew where to look for us?" Melkiar asked, always the skeptic and Clavorn was often glad of that.

"Sir," the scout appeared puzzled. It was clear that he was a bit confused by Melkiar's question.

"Well, boy, we are trying to keep our camp here hidden, even from the king," the boy again looked confused, "It... it protects us from Vaulnik's spies. He is most likely watching the king's every move as a way to find us."

By Melkiar's reply Clavorn could tell he felt awkward about their situation, for he could hardly tell him that they suspected the king of betraying his people.

"Also this forest's very existence and location has been kept hidden for millennia," Clavorn told him, jumping in to rescue the situation. "I do not want us to be responsible for its discovery and subsequent destruction by Vaulnik, or anyone else."

"Oh...uh, yes sir. I'll remember that," the boy replied.

"Good. Now, how are we to know this is a genuine offer and not some false message sent by Vaulnik?" Clavorn asked of the young scout.

"Oh, I almost forgot. The messenger said to give you this," the boy told him, handing him an elaborate scroll with the king's insignia and seal emblazoned upon it.

At this Melkiar raised an eyebrow.

"Well," exclaimed Melkiar, looking on expectantly at Clavorn.

"The boy speaks the truth," Clavorn replied simply as he handed the scroll to Melkiar who took it and read it himself then handed it to Thalon.

"Find this messenger again," Clavorn told the boy, "and tell him to convey to our good king that I would consider it an honor and would be glad to accept such an accolade. But…"

"Merrik, sir," the boy put in noticing Clavorn at a loss for his name.

"But Merrik, I want you to be extra careful on your way back. Take the long way home and be sure to take one or two of the more experienced scouts with you. Also take care that you are not followed. Do you understand?" Clavorn instructed.

"Yes sir," the boy told him. Then turning on his heels he left.

"Are you mad?" Melkiar commented after the boy had left, taking care to keep his voice down. "It's not like he doesn't know you. The minute he recognizes you he'll expose you for who you are and accuse you of impersonation and treason, or better yet simply accuse you of treason and skip the whole impersonation thing."

"I'm afraid I have to agree with Melkiar on this one," Thalon put in. "This gesture is surely nothing more than a ploy and quite likely a trap."

"You're forgetting one thing gentlemen."

"What?" they both asked simultaneously.

"This is first indication we have that Sevzozak has chosen a side. As such, I'm betting that he is in no position to eliminate me yet. Victory is not within his grasp. Not yet," Clavorn responded also taking care to keep his voice down, "Besides, if he is in league with Vaulnik, then he may believe there are two men he needs to worry about, Clavorn *and* Shaltak."

"It is still unclear what Sevzozak believes, and I still think it could be a trap," Thalon said. "But I do see merit in going. If he really is not ready to give you up, then he may simply be on a fishing trip much like us."

"Humm," a puff of smoke went up in the air as Melkiar considered his friends' response, "Let us hope you are right about that. Otherwise it will be a very short dinner."

"True, but I still believe he is not ready to try an assault on us, not yet," Clavorn told them. "Our popularity has grown beyond that of before."

"And if Vaulnik is pressuring him like last time? If he is feeling threatened?" Melkiar asked, pointing his pipe at Clavorn.

"Then I shall be prepared this time," Clavorn told him with finality. He needed to see the king. He had many questions, questions that needed answers. Ones he felt could only be answered by seeing Sevzozak face to face.

Chapter 13

    A gentle breeze blew in the air that evening causing the branches of the grand old willow to gently sway back and forth. Silvery blue moonlight streamed in through the leaves that decorated the ancient boughs, lighting the interior of the great tree. Clavorn slept on the large root much as he had the first time he had encountered the majestic old giant. All was quiet in the camp as the men slept save for the few lookouts on watch.
    It was a much more peaceful evening than the one they had a few nights before. That night a storm had raged through the forest, shaking trees and soaking those with no substantial shelter. Unfortunately, that meant a large number of them had suffered a rather unpleasant evening. In no short part due, not only to the nature of the camp, but the fact that many of them were recent recruits.
    Tonight, however, was different. Peace and calmness seemed to mark the evening. Occasionally, the sound of an owl hooting could be heard within the distant reaches of the surrounding wood.
    Silence filled the air. Once more a gentle breeze swayed the graceful wispy branches of the giant willows. Moonlight shimmered off the fast flowing shallow stream which meandered through the grove. Only the random sound of slumbering men, or the footfalls of a guard, could be heard breaking the apparent serenity of the night. However, on the edge of their encampment movement stirred.
    A dark shadow of a figure crept carefully into their midst. Using the vegetation as cover, it artfully avoided those on guard. Hooded and cloaked, the secretive being gradually made its way to the great tree. Stealthily, the silent presence glanced about before parting the branches of the ancient willow and entering.
    Smolder embers burned in the center space created by the weeping boughs. A soft breeze blew causing the supple branches to slowly billow in and out. The surreptitious intruder paused a moment to take in the surroundings. Outside the peaceful sounds of a forest at

rest could be heard wafting their way in while inside the occasional crack from a dying ember sounded.

Spying its quarry, the furtive being swiftly went over to the sleeping figure of a man. A glint of steel glistened in the moonlight as the silent infiltrator quickly placed a knife to the throat of the unsuspecting Clavorn.

Cold steal pressed against his skin as a hand came down over his mouth, startling him into consciousness.

"We must talk," whispered a familiar voice, "Follow me."

Clavorn guessed the woman did not want to be discovered, and that she must have felt in need of more privacy, so he followed her out. Something in his mind still wondered if she was the apparition on the field of battle, and he wanted to ask her but for the timing.

Quietly and covertly, they crossed the camp, through the shallow stream, and into the woods beyond. Moonlight lit their way. Occasionally, the sound of a small animal scurrying off could be heard, but for the most part the forest was quiet. Only the chirping of crickets and buzzing of other nocturnal insects broke the relative silence.

They traveled for some time. In the distance Clavorn could just make out the sound of rushing water. Louder and louder it became until finally they arrived at a glorious waterfall. Two dragon lengths high above them, the water billowed and rushed down from an overhanging cliff. He could see through the falls a dark empty space which he assumed was a cave, or cavernous like space.

Sprays of water droplets rained down on him as they neared the falls. The cool breeze created by the force of the falling water chilled his skin. He followed her, as she parted branches and pushed her way through the lush vegetation beside the waterfall.

Suddenly, they were through. Darkness enveloped the empty space before him. Only the silvery light which shown through the falls gave any shape or form to what was inside.

"Please sit," she told him, as she motioned him into the cavern and in the direction of a large boulder. The roar of the falls nearly drowned out all sound. Only the hollowness of the cavern within made the hearing of her voice possible. It was easy to understand why she had picked this spot. No one from the outside would be able to see or hear them through the fast flowing curtain of water which now shielded their presence.

Clavorn availed himself of the large rock she had indicated. Then she did the same, choosing one opposite him.

"You must not meet with the king," she told him.

"Why?" He already had his suspicions, suspicions which Melkiar had voiced earlier in the day; now her.

"Because he has plans for you, and they have nothing to do with honoring you."

"You mean he wishes to discredit me, or otherwise ruin my face for the people."

"In short, yes," she told him.

"I suspected as much," he replied though betrayal and not defamation had been more his preference. Easier to prove someone is disloyal if he betrays you than to regain your reputation.

"There is more," she went on.

"Oh?"

"Yes," she replied simply.

"What's the rest?"

"That Vaulnik is playing with you."

He raised an eyebrow. The thought was not a strange one to him. It had crossed his mind several times, but to hear it voiced.

"I have suspected this," he told her, "though I was not certain till now. The question is, why?"

"Because he loves to toy with his victims. When your numbers are at their highest, when you think you have victory within your grasp that is when he will strike you down hard."

Memories of the Dragon Wars and the Battle of Quantaris briefly flitted through his mind.

"Why didn't he the last time?" he asked.

"Because last time there was an easier way," she told him. "Because last time he figured if he could just kill the man, then he could kill the rebellion. This time you have shown him that if he kills the man the rebellion will likely live on. No. He wants to smash your followers as well, and send a clear message that any rebellion will be met with fury."

"And the greater our numbers the greater the impact."

"Precisely."

"Then why should I not attend the king's invitation?" he inquired, "Clearly, then he's not interested in my capture."

"No, but that doesn't mean that Sevzozak no longer feels threatened by your growing popularity. He cannot simply kill you. Not without a reason. He must find your weakness and exploit it."

He considered her words. They were not new ideas. Just ideas made more tangible.

"If his son identifies you as Clavorn and not Shaltak…"

She hardly needed to say any more. It was one of the reasons why he had since changed his appearance, grown a beard, and cut his hair.

No. I have questions that need answers.

"I must go," he insisted. "If the king and his son try to discredit me, then I will use it to show the king as being in league with Vaulnik."

"I know this is your desire, but how are you going to prove it?"

He looked at her and was about to say something when she continued.

"Now is not the time. Say you are busy and send someone else in your sted. Say you're sick. Whatever you like, but now is not the time for this."

There was a pause as he took in what she had said. The roar of falls sounded throughout the cavern as the two of them sat in silence, encased in the cool dark damp stony confines.

"You know his Zoths are still alive and well," she informed after a few moments.

Her words took him by surprise.

"So that is why he doesn't care about his loses," he remarked, "I thought he had not sent them against us because he did not consider us enough of a threat, or had had them destroyed."

"No, they are still very much alive. In the beginning he did not consider you much of threat, but now he is just waiting like a cat," she told him.

His dark eyes probed the inky blackness before him. He wished he could see her face to know the truth of her words.

How does she know all this? Who is she? Is she one of the legendary Dragon Witches who haunts the forest and uses magic to see into men's minds?

She certainly haunted his dreams. When he was not considering battle plans there she was, her green eyes staring at him through the emptiness of his mind. The image of her fair complexion set off by the darkness of the rocks while the water caressed her body entered his mind.

Has she cast a spell on me?

He shook himself and returned his mind to the present.

What of Sefforn?

He needed him to return successful.

"Sefforn will not return successful," she announced, "He will fail."

Immediately, he turned on her, rising from his seat on the great rock, and rushing forward.

"How can you know that? That mission was of the strictest secrecy! How can you know they won't accomplish it! Who are you?" the anger in his voice was unmistakable. Now she had gone too far. She had invaded his inner circle, intruded into his mind.

A sword to his throat stayed his advance as she countered his aggression.

"I am a ghost. Remember? As a ghost, I know things. I do not exist as you do," she replied calmly.

"But I *can* kill you," he told her through his teeth.

"Yes, and you would accomplish what? To finish what others have started," she remarked coolly.

His face softened at her words. He did not expect her to admit that she had been a victim, but of whom and why? The scars on her back suggested Vaulnik's doing, but was there more to this? He could feel that there was. However, he decided to drop it for now.

"Tell me, why is it that Sefforn will not accomplish his mission," he asked, backing down and once again sitting himself on the rock. She lowered her sword.

"He will not accomplish his mission because what he seeks is not where you sent him," she told him.

"Then where is it?" he asked, skipping the whole idea of asking her how she knew where he had sent him and for what. Clearly she knew. How? Well, that was another matter, one not likely to be answered.

"Only where a worthy man can find it," she replied simply.

Great! A riddle! As if I have time for such things. Besides, I thought I sent a worthy man.

He ran a hand through his thick dark hair in exasperation. "And where do I find such a man if Sefforn is not him?" he inquired, the frustration clearly evident in his voice.

"You already know him. You just need to realize it for yourself," she told him, "Once you do the place where it is hidden will be obvious, and he will find what you seek."

"But how am I to know this man?"

"I must be getting you back," she announced as she ignored his question and rose abruptly from the rock she had been sitting on, "Dawn will be upon us soon."

Just like a woman. Gives a man a riddle, gets him all worked up, and then...time to go.

"I can find my own way back," he protested, as he got up from the boulder he had been sitting on. He wanted to be alone with his thoughts, to think on what she had said.

"I am sure you can, but you are not armed and the forest is not safe."

"And whose fault is that?"

"Mine. I know. So you see. I cannot leave you to the mercies of the forest."

"I can take care of myself you know," he told her, but his benefactor had already started to pass him on her way to the exit of the cave.

Silver light from the other side of the falls gently penetrated into the cavern highlighting her form. At his comment she paused, turned, and looked at him. Her catlike eyes penetrating deep within him while the rest of her face remained a mystery, shrouded by her coverings.

"I know," she replied simply, in a soft tone, and turned to leave.

He wanted to stop her, to make her reveal herself, but something inside him stopped him. Perhaps it was because he knew it would be futile. Perhaps it was because a part him was enjoying the mystery. Whatever the reason he found himself simply following her out of the cave without further discussion.

It was just before dawn when they reached the edge of his encampment. Clavorn moved ahead of her. From his position he could just see a couple of his men as they paced the perimeter keeping watch. The sky was a deep shade of indigo and the stars twinkled overhead. The light from the sun was just beginning to brighten the horizon. Once again a gentle breeze blew in the air, but now the sounds of the first morning birds began to play within it.

"Will I see you again?" he asked as he turned around to say goodbye, but just like mist and smoke she was gone. The only thing that remained to remind him of her visit was the small object she had handed him just as they had arrived back at camp.

"Keep it safe," she had told him.

Now, as he felt it between the folds of his clothes, all he could think of was what a mystery she was.

Chapter 14

As he exited the forest and strode into camp, he came across a young man washing up by the shallow river. Immediately, Clavorn recognized him. His blond hair and scar that came across his right arm made him easy to identify in the early morning light.

"Good morning, Alcon," he said to him as he walked up to the stream on his way to his quarters.

The wispy branches of the ancient tree seemed to call out to him from across the grove of willows which grew up around the shallow river as he caught glimpses of it through the gently swaying limbs of its younger compatriots. The spectacular old giant seemed to beckon him to enter within the softly undulating folds of its weeping boughs, there to be lulled into a deep slumber. However, there would be no time for such indulgences this morning. There was too much to do, too much to consider.

"Oh,…ah, good morning, sir," the young man replied as he rose up from splashing his face in the cool shallow river.

For a moment Clavorn paused as if in thought, took two steps past the young man, and paused again. Alcon was about to resume his morning ritual when Clavorn spoke once more.

"Alcon would you mind doing me a favor this morning," he asked.

The young man ceased his doings and turned to him, "No sir."

"When you're finished there would you mind finding me Melkiar and telling him that I wish to speak with him as soon as he is able."

"No sir. I mean, certainly sir," Alcon replied, stumbling over his speech, "I'll find him and give him the message."

"Thank you, Alcon," he said, resuming his journey back to the majestic willow in the center of camp.

When Melkiar entered the venerable old tree Clavorn was seated on one of the large roots with his back against its trunk. Rays of pinkish orange light filtered in from the sun as the early morning

Fires of Life

sunlight peaked over the horizon. A soft breeze gently rustled through the long weepy branches of the great tree. Dampness filled the air about them along with all the sounds of the forest and stirrings of the camp coming to life.

"You know it occurs to me, Melkiar, that we must have the oddest encampment ever in the history of warfare," Clavorn remarked to his friend as he entered through the boughs of the ancient willow.

"Well, I can't argue with you there, but I highly doubt you called me here for such a revelation," Melkiar replied as he sat down on a root near Clavorn.

A small fire burned not far from them in the center where his benefactor had roasted the succulent rabbit just a few months before. Clavorn sat up and reached for his oil skin bag. He took a swig of the bitter contents before continuing.

"Too true, my friend, too true. No, I brought you here because I have been thinking that perhaps you are right. I should not go to the castle."

"Oh, praise to the gods! You finally came to your senses. May I enquire as to what act of providence brought you to this conclusion?"

"No. But I have decided that you will go in my sted," Clavorn announced.

"Wait, I take that back. Are you nuts?! Have you totally lost your mind? I have all the diplomatic skills of a young dragon on its first flight."

Young dragons were known to be notoriously awkward on their first flight. This seemed to be one of the main reasons why no had ever seen a dragon's clutch, or even knew where one would be, though speculations did abound.

"No. I haven't lost my mind."

"That's debatable," Melkiar mumbled.

"What?"

"Nothing," he replied, "Go on."

"I was thinking you would apologize for my absence and say that I was unfortunately too busy, or something which I have yet to solidify, to attend, but that I sent you in my place to graciously accept his hospitality."

"That's if he doesn't decide to kill me in your sted, or I you," Melkiar exclaimed in exasperation.

"I don't believe he will," Clavorn answered, rising from his place by the trunk of the ancient willow to avail himself of a bit of leftover bread from dinner the night before. It was situated on a nearby root which was large enough to double for a small table of sorts. "He would need a really good reason. My lack of attendance would hardly qualify," he continued as he turned to face Melkiar. "Why would he kill the representative of the one who they are all gathered to honor? No, my friend, you will be just fine. Besides, just think of all of the good food and wine you'll be getting to enjoy. Not to mention the women."

"Yeah, all while I keep my wits sharp as I pretend to be having a good time with a group of men I'd sooner rather slit the throat of than dine with. Are you sure this such a good idea? You know how I hate such political trivia," Melkiar replied. By now he had removed his pipe from its usual and customary place in his pocket and was packing it with tobacco.

"Yes, I'm not exactly fond of it myself, but the practice might do you some good," Clavorn told him, while taking another sip from his flagon.

"I'd rather practice in a den of Zoths then. At least those you can fight with a sword."

"Not exactly."

"Well, you know what I mean."

There was a short pause in their conversation. Melkiar reached over and grabbed a twig from the fire with which to light his pipe.

"You know, Solonavic is much better at this sort of thing than I am. Perhaps he should go," he continued, puffing on his pipe to lite it, causing billows of smoke to encircle his head.

"No. I need someone I can trust for this job, someone who is not going to lose himself in court."

Solonavic was very adept with court politics. Clavorn had watched him at once resolve the most difficult diplomatic situation while almost simultaneously weaseling his way out of the stickiest of circumstances. His good looks and charm always seemed to serve him well. Unfortunately, his fondness for all that glisters, and not necessarily jewels, tended to place him in rather compromising positions, and this was not a time to risk any such happenings.

"True, Solonavic enjoys his women just a bit too much, but isn't there someone else you can send? Like Thalon or Falor…" Melkiar pressed, but before he could make another suggestion, Clavorn interrupted him.

"Thalon. I considered him," he told him, "And at first-blush he would appear the logical choice, since he held a position of leadership in his village, but that is precisely the reason I feel he should stay."

"What? I don't follow."

"Well, he is exactly the kind of person the king will be expecting. Calm, knowledgeable in the ways of politics, and skilled in battle, in short too level headed to trip up. No. I need someone who is at once close to me; skilled in battle, but perhaps seems a bit inexperienced in the ways of court. I want him to feel comfortable being exactly who he is. I know he will not be able to pull one over on your eyes, yet he may believe he can and that, my friend, is what I am hoping for."

"Oh, I get it. I think." He replied slightly confused, "I assume you mean this to be a complement."

"It is, my friend," Clavorn told him, placing a hand on his shoulder, "It means that I believe you are shrewder and more observant than he is likely to give you credit for. And that, my friend, makes you the perfect candidate."

"Terrific," Melkiar replied with an edge of sarcasm.

"Believe me I have thought this through. If Sefforn were here, perhaps there would be an alternative, but he is not."

He released his hand from Melkiar's shoulder and stepped back over to where he had been sitting earlier, then reached down for the flask so as to have another drink before he sat back down.

"Speaking of which, when is he supposed to return?"

"Soon."

'He will fail.'

Her words came back to haunt him, and he could only trust that 'failure' did not mean the death of his longtime childhood friend. Sefforn was more like a brother to him than a friend. His death would be a great loss, and not just militarily.

"In short, you don't know," Melkiar replied, briefly removing his pipe from his mouth and intruding into his thoughts.

"Perceptive as always, and you doubt my choice for you as my representative," Clavorn told him, trying to deflect the conversation.

"It seems you have me there. Still, it would have been nice to have them here during these past few months,"

"I can't argue with you there, but it couldn't be helped," he told him.

"I know. So you said before."

There was another brief pause in their conversation. The smoke from Melkiar's pipe was now collecting above his head as a sort of great misty cloud. The top of which was slowly being wafted out of the ancient willow by a gentle breeze that blew through its branches. Melkiar broke the silence by returning to the subject of their original conversation.

"Why not send Kevic? He is more experienced at this sort of thing than I am and way more level headed."

"True, precisely the reason not to," Clavorn informed him grateful to have their conversation returned back to its original subject.

"Okay, I'm confused. Why not," Melkiar asked, a bit befuddled as he removed the pipe from his mouth.

"Again, because they'll be expecting that, not you," Clavorn explained as he sat back down, while taking a swig of ale from his flask.

"Alright, I think I get it. Though I am still not sure whether to take that as a complement, or not, but seeing is how you leave me no other option, I'll go."

"Good!"

"I'll keep my head up, my eyes sharp and my tongue in check. Which unfortunately means little drink," the last bit being mumbled under his breath. Melkiar clearly was not at all satisfied with the situation, though evidently at a loss for a better solution.

"That's the spirit, my friend," Clavorn praised as he raised his flask in solute.

"I don't know about that, or the friendship part," Melkiar remarked back good-naturedly, "but I'll do it anyway." With that he took a swig of ale from the flagon Clavorn offered him.

"Thanks," Clavorn told him more seriously, "Take Kevic and Sayavic with you if you want."

Melkiar near spat out his ale at Clavorn's last suggestion, "Hold on. Didn't you just say they'd be expecting Kevic?"

"Yeah. But not as a simple council member."

"True. In that case, I think I'll just take Kevic. Sayavic is too young, but Falor or Koron might be good alternatives."

"Yes. But remember, I do need a few of my council members here. They cannot all attend this 'honorary' dinner."

"No, apparently not," Melkiar grumbled, "just your most expendable."

Clavorn laid a hand on Melkiar's shoulder, "That is definitely not the case, my friend. I trust you more than you know with this mission."

"Really?" Melkiar replied with a mixture of skepticism and sarcasm.

"Yes, my friend," he told him, "It is that keen sense of yours for what is not right that I am counting on to sniff out the truth. There is no one else in this camp I would better trust for that; lack of diplomacy or no lack of diplomacy aside."

Chapter 15

As they rode up the hill towards Escadora, they could clearly see the castle. Its walls and spires lit by added torchlight for the evening. The golden wings of the gilded dragons that made up its roofline glistened in the moonlight. The huge twin dragon sculptures of the city gate stared down at them as they neared her entrance; their sculpted fires breathing out into the night to ward off any oncoming enemies. Hard to imagine that when closed the two of them fitted perfectly together as one seamless gate. Melkiar had always been impressed with their appearance, however, tonight they seemed to have an ominous quality about them as he and his two companions drew near the city's entrance. Kevic rode alongside him as did another man in a hooded cloak.

"Who goes there?" asked a tall rugged looking man. He was dressed in the traditional garb of the high guards of Avivron. The emerald green standard, with the king's crest clearly emblazoned in the middle of it, rustled in the wind high atop his spear. His matching green cloak, which was securely attached to his steal breastplate, whipped about in the wind.

"I am Melkiar, son of Afileszon," he told the guard, "and we are here on behalf of Shaltak, Slayer of Dragon Killers. The king is expecting us."

The guard eyed him suspiciously then moved on to his other companions.

"My orders were to allow Shaltak through along with any who accompanied him. Is anyone of you Shaltak?"

Melkiar had been dreading this question, now to see if Clavorn's excuse would hold up.

"No. Not a one of us, sir," Melkiar replied. The guard turned his attention back to him, narrowing his eyes, "You see Shaltak could not make it tonight. He sincerely regrets his inability to come and hopes that our presence will more than make up for his absence."

The guard raised one eyebrow, clearly not sure what to make of his answer.

"Wait here," he told them as he conferred with his companion about the situation. Soon Melkiar could see that he had dispatched a courier back to the castle to notify them of the situation.

Melkiar tried to act natural as they waited. The plumage on top of the guard's helmet fluttered in the wind. Melkiar's horse shifted under him. Kevic shot him a look while they waited. The man with the hooded cloak appeared undaunted as he sat upon his steed. The guard eyed him suspiciously but said nothing for the moment.

Time passed, as they awaited the courier's return and news of the king's decision. Kevic's horse shifted, momentarily catching the guard's attention. The air was thick with anticipation as an owl hooted in the night. Melkiar began to become increasing more uncomfortable with each passing moment. The man in the cloak and hood, however, continued to remain impervious.

Once more the captain of the guard came forward from his post and eyed the man with the hood and cloak. But just as it appeared as if he were about to inquire more of the man the courier returned with the king's reply. The guard turned to receive the message.

"It appears as if the king will grant you entry. You may pass," he told them, stepping aside to let them through.

Melkiar almost visibly sighed at the news before spurring his horse on, nodding to the guard on their way past as the three of them rode through the gates of Escadora.

The sound of their horses' hooves echoed off the cobblestone streets as they traveled on their way to the castle. Everything in Escadora appeared as one would expect it to be given the circumstances. Here and there they passed villagers, or town's people, as they peered out of windows or doorways on their route to the castle. Most of them simply appeared curious while others continued on with their evening routines. Still, there was an odd quality to it all. Something Melkiar could not quite pin down but tingled down his spine.

Was it the way the added torches played on the walls and shadows of the city, or was it the looks people gave them as they rode past? Or was it simply his imagination getting the better of him? For now, he would just remind himself to stay on task, but keep his guard up and eyes sharp.

Once again he glanced up towards their destination. The graceful wings of the dragon spouts that adorned the outer walls of the castle seemed to have a special air about them as they rode along on their way to the castle entrance. The torches danced and played in the windy night, giving life to the inert statues which peered down on them from the roofline above. On the main castle building fires were lit in the mouths of the large gilded dragon sculptures which adorned the corners of the roof, giving a life like quality to the normally passive beasts.

Melkiar returned his attention to the main road ahead of them as he pulled his horse up short to allow an elderly man to pass in front of them. Up ahead, he could see the main gate which led to the castle proper. Its large bronze doors stood open, ready to welcome the night's guests.

As they rode up to the main castle gate, he could see where other royal invitees were making their entrance ahead of them. Melkiar glanced over to his hooded companion, but no expression was forthcoming. Kevic remained silent.

Soon they stopped and dismounted. A couple of young boys quickly came up to greet them and take their horses. As they mounted the stairs, Melkiar could clearly see the brass doors of the castle proper which led inside. He admired their workmanship as another guard came to greet them with similar questions as the first. Once again Melkiar explained their situation. Fortunately, this time the guard was aware of their situation and simply let them pass, giving them directions to the great hall.

Up some stairs and down a long hall they went, past paintings of long dead ancestors. Elaborate tapestries with scenes from old legends, and handsomely carved gold framed mirrors with dragons sculpted on them, were scattered between the portraits. Melkiar could not help but notice how their footsteps echoed off the marble floor, while sounds of music and merriment floated through the air and resonated throughout the passageway.

Soon he saw another guard at the entrance to the Great Hall along with a line of other would be guests waiting to be introduced. It was not long before they added themselves to this group.

Now, as they glanced about the entrance of the Great Hall, it was clear that the king had planned a grand celebration. There were many courtiers dressed in all their finery. Ladies arrayed in beautiful flowing gowns of silk, in all manner of colors with gold trimmings, and jeweled necklaces of rich design. The men were also handsomely attired. Melkiar looked to the tall hooded man standing next to him, who had come in with him, and the two exchanged glances. Kevic stood solemnly behind them.

A well-dressed man clothed in a green velour tunic, the color of king's standard, with a large similarly colored hat, sporting a single white feather stood at the entrance. His stance and actions clearly denoted him as the one in charge of formal introductions to the court. He now turned his attention to them as those before them entered the Great Hall.

"Who do I have the pleasure of introducing this evening?" the man asked.

Melkiar informed him as to their respective identities and the man thanked him, but not before pausing and giving the man with the hood an askance glance. He then turned to make his formal announcement to the court.

"My lords and ladies may I present, Melkiar, son of Afileszon, Kevic, son of Riconovic, and, Mentak, son of Joseavic," his voice rang out clear above the din of conversation "They are here as representatives of our champion, Shaltak, Slayer of Dragon Killers and Defender of Maltak." At this announcement all within the Great Hall turned and starred at them as a hushed silence fell about the room. From across the hall a finely dressed man rose and came towards them.

"I think we are a little undressed for the occasion," Kevic commented, whispering to the men in front of him. For while it was true that they had put on their best attire in honor of the occasion, their tunics and clothes could not compare to the finery displayed before them. A faux pas for which, at present, Melkiar was all too keenly aware of.

"Fortunately, we are the honored guests, so our lapse of etiquette should go without too much embarrassment. After all we are fighting so they can enjoy their fine clothes," replied the man with the hooded cloak in hushed tones.

"Uhm, we shall see," Melkiar commented under his breath as the tall, very finely dressed man came up to greet them.

His dark hair was well groomed and trimmed about his shoulders so that it blended in with the dark black color of his vest which was finely embroidered with gold and silver thread. About his head he wore a fine hat also adorned with a huge white plum, though it was clearly much finer than the one worn by the man who had announced their arrival. Around his neck was a thick necklace of gold emblazoned with the king's crest which was set off quite nicely by the vest he wore over his dark green, nearly black tunic.

"Good evening gentlemen," he said as he came up to greet them, "Which one of you is here to represent our illustrious Shaltak?"

"I am," Melkiar replied as he cleared his throat, feeling a bit awkward in the situation.

"Well, the king and all of those present here would love to extend our warmest and sincerest welcome to you and your comrades here. Shaltak and you have been doing a remarkable job liberating us from the scourge of Vaulnik, and his men. Come please. The king requests the pleasure of your company at his table," the man told them as he extended his hand inviting them into the room and to a grand table that had been finely set up at the end of the Great Hall. "Oh, I am sorry. I forgot to introduce myself. I am Yodonovic, Grand Vizier to King Sevzozak and you are?"

"I am Melkiar, son of Afileszon, this is Kevic, son of Riconovic and Mentak, son of Joseavic," Melkiar replied, as he introduced himself and his companions; each of whom bowed their heads in turn as they were introduced. Behind them could be heard the announcement of more arrivals as the din of conversation once again flowed about the room.

"I see," replied Yodonovic, "and why does our good friend Mentak wish to hide his face. We are all friends here."

"Yes, my lord," answered Melkiar, "but he has suffered much terrible scaring on his face of late and does not wish to offend the ladies."

"I see. Well, I am sure they would be fine with it, but if it makes him feel more comfortable."

"It does, my lord," Melkiar replied quickly, running over Yodonovic's speech while the tall hooded man standing next to him nodded once in affirmation.

"I assume we shall here from you later, sir," Yodonovic remarked to the one named Mentak, clearly regarding him with suspicion.

"Yes, my lord," the man responded, bowing his head once more, "I did not wish to offend my lord by not answering for myself."

"No offense taken. Shall we," replied Yodonovic, once again gesturing to the richly adorned table at the far end of the room.

As the men came upon the table, they could see a most sumptuous display of food and finery. Several large gold dishes held a variety of succulent meats such as roasted pig, duck, venison, and peacock. Others were full of various exotic fruits, breads, vegetable dishes, and more. Carafes of wine were beside a magnificent pair of golden candelabra encrusted with rubies and diamonds. Gold goblets and dishes were also wonderfully set before the occupants of the table. The small company of men could not help but notice the extravagant display.

"Your Majesty, my lords, and ladies may I present, Melkiar, son of Afileszon, Kevic, son of Riconovic, and Mentak, son of Joseavic," announced Yodonovic gesturing to each man respectively.

Seated in the middle of the table was an elderly man dressed in the finest of clothes, and to his right a younger man sat similarly but slightly lesser arrayed. Upon the head of the first was a golden crown studded with rubies and diamonds. At its center was a very large ruby surrounded by diamonds.

He was dressed in black, which offset his thick white hair. The garments he wore were finely adorned with gold brocade which was richly studded with rubies and diamonds as well. On his hands he wore all manner of rings. The lesser was presumable his son. He too wore a golden crown, though; it was not quite as richly ornamented as his father's. Likewise were his clothes, which, while also black with gold brocade, were not studded with diamonds or rubies.

Both wore necklaces of gold, though from the king's hung a very large ruby on a much thicker golden chain than his son's. Below it was a much simpler silver chain in which a very large clear Kriac stone was set flanked by two silver dragons. Melkiar and his companions all bowed before the king and his son as Yodonovic introduced them.

"I trust you gentlemen are hungry," the king remarked as he remained seated upon his throne; a wonderfully carved chair made of deep rich brown wood embellished with the crest of Avivron at its crown.

As he stood before the king, Melkiar could just make out the two handsomely carved dragons which seemed to constitute the majority of the king's throne. Their bodies appeared to make up most of its supporting structure. Upon their heads rested the king's hands while part of their back and wings made up the armrests. The rest of their wings swept up to create the back of the royal seat. High up above the king's head rested the crest of Avivron supported by the meeting of the two inner wings of the dragons which comprised it. Their outer wings accented the king, giving him a rather imposing appearance.

The crest itself was quite elaborate, and Melkiar thought rather ostentatious. He knew from rumor that the king had had a new throne made after the death of his father, presumably because the previous one had been too simple. This one before him was anything but simple.

The shield on the crest appeared to be made of silver with ruby red enamel as background which contained a single silver dragon adorned with ruby eyes at its center. The dragon was holding a large green Kriac stone in its talons. The shield itself sat in front of a delicately carved Hawthorn tree which was elaborately embellished. Gold had been used for its trunk. Beautifully carved emeralds mixed with ones made of silver for the leaves. Dotting the stone carved leaves were small rubies for its berries. Flanking the tree were two slightly smaller blue dragons made of sapphire which held the shield before it.

His son's throne was similar but slightly lesser, he presumed, to denote his position. Missing was the queen's throne. She would normally have sat to right of the king; however, she had long since passed away, so there was no throne to accompany the king's. Glancing down the long table, he saw various other high ranking court officials and their wives seated on richly adorned chairs, but none naturally met the grandeur, or complexity of the king's.

Almaik sat silently watching; observing the company of men as they stood before his father, the king. His dark, well-trimmed hair and beard bore equal measure as to his place and status, adding to the air about him.

"Yes, your majesty we are most certainly hungry," replied Melkiar simply, trying to portray an image of confidence and ease he did not truly feel.

"Well, then come and sit with me. Here, Yodonovic, please see to it that these men have a place at my right side tonight."

"Yes, my lord," replied Yodonovic as he made motions for servants to clear the places to the right of the king.

When all was prepared he gestured for Melkiar and his men to follow him, and showed them to the empty seats to the right of the king and his son. Then taking his place he sat down just to the left of the king.

"I am afraid I must admit to being a bit disappointed that Shaltak could not be here tonight," the king commented around his son once they had all seated themselves.

"Yes, I am sorry, my lord," Melkiar replied raising his voice above the din of the room, "Shaltak asked us to convey his sincerest apologies, but he was gravely indisposed this evening. He had the best intentions, I assure you, of attending here tonight to accept this great honor that you have bestowed upon him, but it could not be helped."

"Well, I hope he will still be able to continue to fight the war and that this indisposition will not interfere with any of his objectives. I trust he is in good health."

"I can assure you he is in excellent health, and that save for his death, Shaltak will not in any way be indisposed for the completion of this war, my lord, sir," Melkiar finished as a servant came by and filled their goblets with wine.

"I am glad to hear that," the king replied, "May I enquire as to the nature of this grave indisposition, if it has nothing to do with his health?"

This was the part Melkiar was not looking forward too. The dreaded question, the one he was fairly certain could put a quick end to this festive occasion was now before him.

"Just be natural," Clavorn had told him.

Right?! Be natural now? Was he crazy! Wait don't answer that. Breath...Just be natural.

"Yes, my lord," he began, trying to sound as normal and confidant as possible, "He had to attend to one of his most trusted and valuable men, sire. He fears this man may not last the night and wishes to be at his side during this grave hour."

"I see. Is he so valuable that he out ranks his king?"

"No, sire. But this man is more than simply a soldier in his army. He is like family to him and hopes that his majesty will understand."

"I see. Well, send him my best regard and tell him that I do hope this man of his recovers, but that his presence here was greatly missed by this court. And I, as his king, would hope to measure a bit more importance in the future."

"Yes, your majesty, I will convey this to him, and I am sure he would want me to impress upon you his deepest gratitude for your majesty's understanding."

At this the king grunted and nodded before clapping his hands, indicating that the festivities were to begin. Melkiar nearly breathed a sigh of relief at having gotten past this awkward, sticky, and potentially dangerous hurdle.

Now to get through the rest of the evening.

Courtiers took their places at the tables set alongside the walls of the Great Hall while jugglers, court jesters, and musicians made their way onto the floor in front of them. Servants began to busily buzz about the Great Hall as they catered to their charges for the evening. Sumptuous food and an ever flowing presence of wine were served nearly nonstop to all the guests.

"So how are you enjoying yourselves gentlemen?" inquired the king part way through dinner as he leaned over around his son towards Melkiar so he could better hear him.

"Just fine, my lord," replied Melkiar, again with a raised voice as he took a sip of his wine.

"Good. Then perhaps you won't mind helping me with a bit of a problem of mine later on this evening," he continued, similarly taking a sip of his wine from his jewel encrusted goblet.

"No, my lord. We would be glad to help his majesty with any problem he has," Melkiar replied, though he felt a tingling sensation of uneasiness beginning to grow within him.

Fires of Life

"Good," Sevzozak replied simply as he turned to his son.

Melkiar took a bite of the roasted duck before him and gave Mentak a sideways glance.

The evening continued with much wine, music, dancing girls and festivities as could be imagined. The men were all quite satisfied by the time the king clapped his hands again for the attention of whole court. Yodonovic stood up.

"May I have your attention," he began, pausing a moment to be certain all was quiet before continuing, "Lords and Ladies your king, King Sevzozak, son of King Dakconar, Keeper of the Dragon and of the Earth, would like to have your attention please."

Silence filled the Great Hall as Yodonovic reclaimed his seat. Kevic and Melkiar exchanged glances briefly while Mentak remained focused on the king.

"My good subjects, lords and ladies," here King Sevzozak stood up as Yodonovic was seated, "it was my pleasure tonight to present to you our most esteemed warrior, Shaltak, but as luck would have it he could not be with us tonight."

Moans of disappointment filtered about the room at the king's revelation.

"Instead," he continued, "I present to you his most trusted advisors, Melkiar, son of Afileszon, Mentak, son of Joseavic, and Kevic, son of Riconovic who have dined with us in his stead, " the king paused as he gestured to the men seated at his right hand. "Will you all please join me in toasting to their success and to their continued success in this campaign for our liberty."

At this all the courtiers lifted their goblets in a toast and Clavorn's men did the same.

"Now, gentlemen, I am sure you will recall that at the beginning of this fine dinner I asked if you could help me with a problem that I had. Is that not true Melkiar, son of Afileszon?" King Sevzozak continued.

"Yes, my lord, that is very true," he answered, placing his goblet back down upon the table as once again a feeling of foreboding swept through him, though he did his best to conceal it.

"Well, now is your opportunity," he announced.

At this the king motioned to some guards in the back of the Great Hall. Immediately, they turned and opened the large, imposing brass doors to the room. Clavorn's men watched while the guards proceeded with what was apparently a well-planned event. Melkiar felt the hair on the back of his neck rise and glanced in Mentak's direction. But his hooded companion remained stoic.

Soon three men in chains were being dragged into the hall. It was clear from their condition that they had not had the benefit of a fine meal. Their clothes were torn, their faces and bodies bloody, and dirty. It was quite apparent that the king's men had had their way in mistreating them.

All three men were roughly lined up and placed before the head table. Gasps and whispers were heard coming from the courtiers around the room. A prickling sensation rippled down Melkiar's spine.

"You see, gentlemen," the king continued, "my men found these vagabonds traveling into my lands from the northern border." Melkiar raised his eyebrow and briefly glanced at Kevic. The two exchanged knowing looks before he returned his attention to the king.

"Now, as you can imagine, I do not like spies on my lands, so my men brought them here for me to deal with. But you see, gentlemen, these men pose a bit of a mystery to me, for their style of clothing is not that of men from the northern territories. It is that of men from our good land, Avivron," at this revelation the king paused while a hush of whispers filtered about the room.

"At first it was assumed that these garbs were only meant to better able these men to infiltrate our sovereign lands. However, as we began further examinations of them, it became clear to this throne that these men are not men from the north, for they bare none

Fires of Life

of the traditional ritual markings of these peoples. Therefore, it can be concluded that these men are indeed men from Avivron." The king paused for effect at this revelation.

Silence now permeated the hall.

"So you see, gentlemen, I began to wonder, if these men are from our fair land of Avivron, what would possess them to travel to the northern territory and back. Were they traitors who had gone to my enemy seeking his help in waging a war against me? Or were they men on a mission, of which I knew nothing about and had not been approved by me, thereby also making them and their leader traitors to this crown? I cannot decide what these men are. None of my subjects, as far as I am aware, have kin in the northern territories so why would men from my lands travel there?" At this the king paused, waiting for their reply.

"I do not know, my lord," answered Melkiar uncomfortably sensing a trap.

"Well, you see I thought you might know because they were carrying this," and with that the king produced a Kriac stone, but not any Kriac stone, for it was clear from its color and the silver decorations surrounding it that it was quite special. "It is the legendary, Stone of Maltak," the king announced.

Gasps were heard circulating about the room at the king's revelation.

The stone was known to everyone, for it was the only known Kraic stone of it color, a flawless emerald green with a hint of blue at its inner core. It was said to possess many powers, none the least of which was the ability to locate dragons.

"You see, gentlemen, the last known possessor of this stone was my father, King Dakconar, but it was not found with his belongings at the time of his death. How is it, do you suppose, that such a stone found its way into the hands of these men?" the king inquired, gesturing to the men before them as he continued to grill them.

"Again, my lord, I am at a loss," Melkiar replied, becoming more uncomfortable by the minuet. For now it was clear to him that the king wished to implicate them, not only as traitors to his crown but also as harbourangers of the murderer of his father, King Dakconar. "Did not your guards find any useful information from these men?"

"No. They did not," the king replied. "Whoever these men are, they are not forthcoming as to their reasons for traveling into Avivron from the north, at least none that this crown is willing to entertain as truth."

"Then how is it that my lord thinks we can help?" Melkiar replied, trying to counter the king. "Why not have them executed immediately?"

"Your Shaltak has shown himself to be a leader of men. I was hoping to ask him this question myself, because I do not wish to execute men needlessly," replied Sevzozak with apparent compassion. "You see, gentlemen, shall I tell you what I think," Sevzozak went on.

Melkiar nodded in reply.

"I think that someone sent them on a mission to find a dragon. The only dragon thought to exit after the Battle of Quantaris is said to live way up in the northern territories. You know the one, Viszerak."

A shocked gasp was heard about the room.

"This would either be the greatest act of treason known to this crown, or the bravest act of courage. I cannot decide which. I was hoping that Shaltak might be able to shed some light on this, or at least give this crown some advice as how these men should be dealt with. However, since he is not here I am now forced to ask this very question of you."

Melkiar paused as in thought, "If you will excuse me, my lord, while I consult with my esteemed colleagues here and consider your inquiry."

"By all means, take your time, but not so long as we grow old while we wait."

A laugh could be heard rippling through the crowd at the king's last comment.

Melkiar turned to Kevic and Mentak, and whispered, "What are we to do? You know who they are!"

"Yes, my friend, but more importantly the king appears to have us right where he wants us. If we admit they are our men, we are essentially admitting to treason, if we denounce their actions he will slaughter them right here before us," Mentak whispered back.

"We could just claim they are brave men to go in search of the dragon," Kevic put in.

"That is just the bait Sevzozak is hoping we take," Mentak replied calmly.

"And how is that?" Melkiar asked confused.

"If we simply say they are brave, he will ask how we know this. We will then be forced to come up with an explanation, an explanation that does not lead us into a trap."

"Oh, right," Kevic replied as the revelation sunk in.

"So what do you proposed we do?" Melkiar asked, feeling very much like a rat caught in a trap. Mentak and Kevic thought for a moment.

"We will propose a test," Mentak replied matter-of-factly.

"What kind of test?" Melkiar asked bewildered, "I know of no test that will prove these men innocent."

"But I do," Mentak announced, "Just turn it over to me."

Melkiar raised an eyebrow but said nothing.

"What are your thoughts Kevic?" he asked, turning to their more seasoned companion.

"I say a test sounds good," he answered, "But it could prove tricky."

"True, but it is our only shot," the man in the hooded cloak replied, "Melkiar?"

"I don't see how we have any other option," Melkiar replied wishing for a smoke. "Alright," he continued, "it is agreed then."

Kevic and Mentak both nodded in the affirmative, with that Melkiar rose and turned to the king.

"Do you have an answer for me?" King Sevzozak inquired apparently surprised by their quick response, but also not wanting to reveal it to the crowd before him.

"Indeed, we have an answer of sorts, my king," Melkiar replied.

"Go on, please, enlighten us," the king said as he gestured about the room with a slight note of sarcasm.

"We propose a test," Melkiar announced.

"A test?" questioned the king who clearly was not expecting that for an answer.

"Yes, sire. Mentak here knows of a test that may shed further light on this subject. If I may...?"

"Yes, yes, please let him speak. This court is all too interested to hear of this test," frustration and sarcasm mixed in the king's voice as Mentak rose to continue.

"It is said, my lord, that The Stone of Maltak will only glow for a man who is true to the dragon Maltak," he began. "Therefore, would you not agree that any man or group of men who are found to be true to the dragon Maltak are, by extension, true to the people of Avivron, and thereby to you as their leader, my lord?"

King Sevzozak paused a moment before answering in the affirmative.

"Then, my lord, we propose that if any of these men are capable of using the stone, then they must be deemed brave and true to your people and thereby to you as well."

"I see," Sevzozak responded considering Mentak's answer, "And how shall we know if these men can use the stone since they have returned without the dragon."

"We propose that you have someone place the stone in the hand of each of these men. Then have him ask the question, 'Am I true to the dragon Maltak?' If the stone glows, then you know his heart is true to the dragon. If the stone does not glow, then he is not and..."

"...I have my answer," the king finished.

"Yes, my lord," replied Mentak, bowing his head in acknowledgement.

"And how is it that you know this information when even my most trusted advisors do not?" asked Sevzozak.

"Because, my lord, my grandfather was, Savorn Remmaik, Keeper of The Dragon Legends and Tales of Allethor. It is well known that as Legend Keeper he knew more about the legends and fables than any man in the kingdom. I am afraid his untimely death may have put your advisors at a disadvantage." he replied.

The king paused in thought a moment.

"Wasn't he the grandfather of Clavorn, son of Favorn Remmaik?" he asked coolly, eyeing Mentak.

"Yes, my lord, but Clavorn is dead and Savorn had many children of whom my mother, Marona, was one," Mentak replied glibly, "and she married Joseavic, The Dragon Caller; my father."

"Do you have any proof of this?" Sevzozak inquired.

"I do indeed, my lord," Mentak replied, "I have her ring which bears her name and the family's crest which I keep with me always as a reminder of her," he continued as he drew from his pinky a small silver ring.

On it was the head of a dragon holding one side of a small ruby in the shape of a rosebud. Upon the stone was the engraved crest of Savorn's family. Supporting the other side of the stone was a silver leaf apparently imagined to belong to the rosebud. Along its stem and down the leaf was engraved 'Marona, my beloved rose, keeper of the dra....' the last few words faded out as they had been worn away by use and time. Yodonovic came by, took the ring and examined it.

"It does indeed bear the crest of Savorn and the name Marona, my lord," he announced after he had examined the piece and handed the ring back to Mentak. "But how are we to know that you are the son of Joseavic, The Dragon Caller?" Yodonovic continued.

"Because I have his horn," he answered as he took out an object that he had inside the folds of his clothes. At first it appeared to be a simple, ordinary horn. The leather strap and wrappings gave it a common appearance. However, when Mentak unwrapped the average looking instrument, a beautiful iridescent green horn was revealed. It was obvious to all those present that it came from one of the smaller horns of a she dragon.

The light from the candles which lit the room shimmered off the horn's iridescent surface in a rainbow of color. Around the mouth of the horn was a silver rim in the shape of a dragon with rubies inlayed where the eyes should be. The wings of the dragon were open and arranged along the body of the horn. Delicately placed silver Hawthorn leaves formed the mouthpiece. The total effect was quite magnificent.

"I believe we can safely establish that your horn is the horn of Joseavic, The Dragon Caller. I recognize it. Your father was a well-respected man in my father's court. His untimely death was keenly felt. However, it was rumored that his son died during the Battle of Yonis and the horn lost. Tell me, where have you been if not dead?"

Melkiar stiffened in his seat at the king's reply.

"There was much confusion during that battle," Mentak began. "I was injured early on and rendered unconscious. When I came-to all that was left was a smoldering field littered with bodies. Injured, disoriented, my memory lost I stumbled my way into what was left of the forest where I found a stream and some shelter. It was there that I recuperated and regained my strength. I understand that because of the nature of that battle few bodies were recovered so I am not surprised by the confusion. It took me sometime to regain my memory. By the time I did the Dragon Wars were over. The Battle of Quantaris lost and our dragons gone.

"Oh, I still had the horn. Its beauty spoke of its importance, though at the time I could not recall. I kept it with me always, much as I do now. It had come to me after my father's death. As your majesty knows, the power of the Dragon Caller does not pass down from father to son. It is a calling marked by Maltak and discerned by the current Dragon Caller, who, at the proper time, seeks out his replacement to mentor before his death. However, with my father's untimely passing such discernment was not possible, therefore it fell to me to keep the horn safe.

"After the Battle of Quantaris the horn seemed simply a vestige of a lost age. Yet I still kept it in case, by some stroke of luck, a dragon had managed to survive and the age of Callers might begin again. Though I had little hope of this, or that we would ever be free again, that is until Clavorn.

"When Clavorn's rebellion began I joined. However, with the dragons dead I dropped my father's title. I was no Dragon Caller. There seemed little point in raising hope where none seemed possible. Nevertheless, in honor of our lost dragons and my father, I have kept the horn safe all this time."

The king was silent as he considered Mentak's answer. Melkiar could feel the tension rise in his body. He glanced over to Kevic. From the look on his face it was obvious he shared his concern.

"I see. Well, since you have his horn, and no trace of his son's body was ever found, I will, for now, accept your explanation and acknowledge you as his son and heir," declared Sevzozak almost flatly. "You may keep the horn in honor of your father, our last Dragon Caller."

"But why not discern another Dragon Caller now and have him use the horn to call upon this last dragon. Surely, then we can use the dragon to help us win this war," called out a finely dressed man from the crowd before them.

"Because, Lord Ekton," Almaik expounded. It was the first time the king's son had spoken all evening, "You should know that simply discerning a Dragon Caller will not automatically mean that he can successfully call upon a dragon. It takes years of learning, hence the need for the previous Dragon Caller to not only discern his successor, but also train him. We do not have the time, knowledge, or even the confirmation that this dragon from the north exists, to even begin to consider this as a viable option."

"I see," replied Lord Ekton apparently satisfied with Almaik's answer.

"Will you do us the honors then, Mentak of removing your hood so that we can properly honor you as the son of Joseavic, the Dragon Caller and grandson of Savorn our Legend Keeper," King Sevzozak said, turning to Mentak.

"Sire, I am afraid that my appearance may offend some of the fairer sex amongst us, but if that is your wish..."

"It is my wish," King Sevzozak interrupted coolly.

Slowly, Mentak raised the hood of his cloak. A horrified gasp was heard throughout the room as many of the courtiers were shocked by the revolting sight. Horrid red puffy flesh covered the entire left side of his face and part of the other. Only his right eye was able to partially open. His beard appeared sketchy as the proud flesh extended down into it.

"I see what you mean," replied the king, "Thank you for complying with the wishes of this crown. I now formally acknowledge you as the son and heir of Joseavic, the Dragon Caller. You may replace your hood."

"Thank you, my lord," responded Mentak gracefully as he returned the hood of his cloak to its original position.

"Now, if you would do the honors of placing the stone in these men's hands and performing this test," requested the king.

"By all means, my liege," replied Mentak as he then made his way around the table, taking The Stone of Maltak from the king. Then placing himself in front of the first prisoner he began his inquiry.

"What is your name?" he asked of the man before him.

The man had long disheveled dark hair that had clearly been partially braided at one time for ease of sight. His face was badly bruised, as was his body, and his wrists were severely chaffed from the chains. He looked up at Mentak who was now standing on a step in front of him. Despite the beard and swollen nature of the bruises on his face, one could just barely make out the finely chiseled features that were his.

"I am Clovak, son Clomaik," he replied simply.

"Very well, Clovak, son of Clomaik, please take the stone in your hands and ask the question, 'Am I true to the dragon Maltak?'"

Chains rattled; echoing throughout the hall as the prisoner before him raised his arms to take the stone. Reverently, he took the beautiful clear green stone with its blue heart from Mentak. The stone glistened and sparkled in the candle light, reflecting all manner of colors. The beautiful silver dragon that encased it contrasted handsomely against its emerald green coloration, while the rubies that formed the dragon's eyes flashed red.

Clovak held the stone out before him. A hush fell over the entire crowd gathered in the Great Hall. The air was thick with anticipation. All eyes were on Clovak as he cleared his throat.

"Am I true to the dragon Maltak?"

His voice sounded broken as he spoke and echoed ever so slightly in the cavernous space of the hall. At first nothing appeared to happen. The dead silence of the room felt ominous as the stone sat apparently inert in Clovak's hands. All was quite. King Sevzozak stood haughtily and was about to open his mouth when suddenly, to the surprise and amazement of all the court, the stone began to glow.

It began at its heart. Clear beautiful rays began to shine out from its center. An audible gasp of awe was heard about the room as the stone became a blaze. Before long its light began to refract into thousands of golden rays each breaking apart into their own prisms of dancing rainbow colors that shimmered around the room. Everyone present appeared awestruck by the sight.

"Thank you, Clovak," Mentak told him as he took the glowing object from Clovak's hands.

The stone immediately went dim, and he continued on to the next prisoner. For each prisoner Mentak asked them to perform the same ritual, and each did as he had been instructed, and for each the result was the same. Every time the stone's radiance graced the hall the crowd gasped in awe. Mentak looked the last prisoner straight in the eye as he took the stone from him, then turned and faced the king.

The chains of the tall blond rattled as he resumed his place with the other prisoners.

"Your majesty, as we have all seen, each of these men has clearly passed the test which proves their loyalty to the dragon Maltak. This being so, I would have to proclaim these men as true and loyal ministers of the dragon Maltak, Mother of all Dragons and Breather of Life, and, by so extension, to yourself. If it would not be too presumptuous of me to say that I would judge them to be brave men indeed. I would like to suggest that they be allowed, if they so desire, to join Shaltak and his men in their fight to liberate your kingdom," Mentak both declared and proposed simultaneously.

"I see, well I cannot argue with The Stone of Maltak," replied Sevzozak clearly a bit taken back by the results, "however, I would like to know how these men came to have the stone of my father."

The prisoners all looked to one another for a moment as the king made his way around the table to stand before them.

"Tell ME!" The king shouted, clearly impatient for an answer.

There was a brief pause before the tall blond prisoner spoke. He too, like Clovak before him, cleared his throat before he began. Once again the sound of rattling chains echoed about the room.

"Sire, we know not the man who gave us the stone. He did not reveal his name, and remained hooded and cloaked while he spoke to us," the prisoner replied.

The tall blond looked to the floor when he finished. His tattered clothes and beaten appearance added to his air of defeat. It was clear from looking at them that they had taken their mission seriously and now felt as if they had completely failed.

The king was furious with his reply and immediately grabbed the stone from Mentak's hand. He was about to hit him with it when Mentak jumped in between them.

"Sire, it is quite possible these men are telling the truth," he said, causing the king to stay his hand.

"Oh, and how would you explain it?" Sevzozak inquired suspiciously.

"Well, it is quite possible that the man, whoever he was, desired to keep his identity secret. That is if he did indeed steal the stone from your majesty's father, or if he even acquired it through other means, he clearly would not have wanted anyone to know who he was. I am afraid your majesty may never know what truly happened to the stone before it came to be in the hands of these men before you, but as loyal subjects of the dragon Maltak we can be certain their intentions were true," he explained.

Sevzozak eyed Mentak suspiciously for a moment as he considered his words, pacing around him and finally coming to stand before him.

"Perhaps you are right," he acquiesced, "Perhaps these men are not traitors, but brave men who were led astray by some hooded stranger. Though why they would follow the orders of some stranger is beyond me. If they are loyal subjects, then they are perhaps the DAFTEST in history!" Once again the king raised his hand containing The Stone of Maltak and made as if he was about to hit the tall blond prisoner before him.

"Stupidity is not a crime, sire," Mentak put in, quickly stepping in front of the king once more to block his path, "If I may," he bowed slightly as a gesture of deference to the king.

"Sire, the man claimed he represented you. He said he had come in secret at your request," the tall blond added from behind Mentak.

The king eyed them both suspiciously, "Perhaps you are right," he went on after a brief moment of consideration, "Perhaps they thought they were doing a good deed by Avivron, and so perhaps believed they were, in fact, aiding us. For now I will accept this story, but should I find out otherwise the full wrath of this throne shall be levied upon them," the king announced, relaxing his arm so as to hold the stone comfortably before him.

A nearly visible sign of relief could be felt about the room as the prisoners relaxed. The king then turned his attention to Mentak.

"Though I would like to know, if you don't mind, how long you have had to be thusly arrayed. No offense meant of course, but this man's description of this… this conspirator, spy, surreptitious would be benefactor…" the king was clearly at a loss for the right word to describe the man who had sent the prisoners before him on their quest, "this whatever," he finished waving his hand about so as to include any other name one might give him, "does rather fit you. You understand."

"Certainly," Mentak replied graciously calm, "Unfortunately, I acquired my injuries in our last skirmish, that being approximately a week ago."

"I hope you do not mind if I send for my surgeon to verify your injuries and the recentness of their acquisition," the king remarked.

"No. Your majesty may do as you must," Mentak answered confidently.

The king nodded his head to a guard in the back of the hall who immediately left to retrieve the king's personal physician.

Melkiar adjusted his position in his chair as he gave Kevic a sideways glance, and the two exchanged looks of concern. All present waited in silence. Fortunately, it was not a long wait as the guard returned with a short bald man with a fat pudgy tummy. He appeared much the nervous sort. One would have normally thought him to be amongst the crowd; however, it was clear from his nervous nature that such events were not a part of his repertoire of comfort. So much so was his discomposure that he must have apparently been excused from attendance.

"You sent for me your majesty," he inquired, bowing awkwardly before the king.

"Yes. I would like you to tell me the age of this man's injuries please."

The king's physician glanced tentatively in Mentak's direction, "Certainly, your majesty," he replied.

Meekly, he made his way over to Mentak who graciously removed his cloak for him. The shy man wrinkled his nose at the sight of the angry red flesh before asking him to bend down so he could take a closer look. Mentak appeared to have no problem obliging his request.

After several minutes of inspection, which included a rather squeamish bit of poking and prodding, the little man announced that he could not say as to the exact date of their manifestation, but that he could only conclude that they were rather resent in nature. To this end the king thanked and dismissed him. The pudgy little physician bowed awkwardly and scurried out of the hall. Apparently, all too relieved to be done with his majesty's request.

"So it appears I must apologize for my suspicious nature. I hope you understand these are difficult times," the king conceded, gazing in Mentak's direction though clearly he still held some suspicions.

"Yes, so they are indeed, my lord," Mentak replied and bowed his head replacing his hood.

"For now then, let it be said that these prisoners are but brave men who did indeed seek out to find the dragon in the name of our people. As such, they may indeed, if they so desire, join the ranks of Shaltak, Slayer of Dragon Killers and Protector of Maltak," announced the king in a conciliatory voice, "What say you?" he then asked of the prisoners before him in a more authoritarian manner.

The prisoners looked from one to another before the tall blond lifted his head and shoulders, whipping a lock of his hair out of his eyes as he took a step forward to answer, his shackles resonating about the chamber.

"I, Sefforn, son of Vistovak, believe I speak for all of us when I say that it would be an honor to serve with Shaltak, Protector of Maltak, your majesty, sir, and that we are all indeed grateful for your majesty's understanding in this matter."

"Then so be it. Be sure to show your gratitude on the field of battle," announced the king, "Guards!" he shouted, "Release these men and give them back their weapons. Also see to it that they are given proper attire before they leave here tonight."

"Yes, sire," replied a guard whose cape and helmet signified his rank as captain.

"Now let us return to our feasting and merriment, carry on!" cried the king with a wave of his hand as he turned and returned to his throne carrying the Stone of Maltak.

Immediately, the musicians began to play their music again, and the air began to resume its previous aura of lightness, though there was much murmuring amongst the nobles present. Melkiar noted that the king did not seem entirely satisfied and guessed that it was because his plan had apparently failed.

"That was close," he whispered under his breath as Mentak returned to his seat next to him.

"I know," Mentak replied simply as both men resumed their casual appearance.

Chapter 16

The moon had long since set when the six of them returned to camp. Dawn would be breaking in a few hours. They had taken care on their return journey to be sure they were not followed, so it had taken longer than expected. Fortunately, the king had seen fit to give Sefforn and company their horses for the return journey. No discussions took place on the way back to camp least the forest have ears.

Happily, it was still dark when they arrived at Shyloran Forest. This meant they would have time to talk before the camp started to come alive with activity. Most of the men appeared to be sleeping with the exception of a few on watch. Quietly, they made their way to the ancient willow in the center of their encampment. Mentak nodded to one of the men on lookout as they passed on their way to the great tree.

Once there Mentak parted its branches and stepped in, taking off his cloak at the same time, and immediately going to stand in front of the slow burning fire that was in the center of the space created by the ancient willow. Melkiar and Kevic entered behind him making their way around the 'room' the tree created, and seated themselves on a couple of comfortable roots.

"Alright, what's going on? Where's Clavorn? And **don't** tell me he is dead." Sefforn asked, a bit annoyed and confused as he entered through the weepy branches. His men filed in behind him creating an apparent wall beside him.

"Yeah, why has this Shaltak decided to reappear now?" asked Clovak, removing his bow from his shoulder, "I thought he disappeared after the Dragon Wars."

Speaking of which, where is he?" piped in Sorenavik, "Shouldn't he be here to great us?"

Silence permeated the great tree following Sorenavik's last comment. Pent up suspicion and frustration leaked from Sefforn and company as they postured themselves on the interior rim of the space created by the huge magnificent willow.

Melkiar glanced at Mentak who was still facing the fire with his back to the questioning men. The guard on duty had lit it earlier that evening in anticipation of their return.

"Did you hear me?" asked Sefforn to Mentak more emphatically, his hand now on the hilt of his sword, indignation and frustration pouring forth in his voice, "Where is Clavorn?! And who are you and what have you done with him?"

Mentak, whose back was still facing Sefforn, stood silently as he placed his hands about his face and grabbed at the horrifying red flesh. The new arrivals watched from behind him in confusion and horror as Mentak pulled at his face. Bewildered, they searched the faces of Melkiar and Kevic for answers.

"Ahhh!" exclaimed Mentak.

Sefforn and his men immediately turned their attention back to him, hands on their swords, as he continued to pull at the red injured flesh about his face. They watched in horror as part of his face appeared to be separating from the whole.

After a few minutes a pile of red, horrid looking tissue lay in Mentak's hands. They then continued to watch as he dropped the gruesome flesh into the fire before him. Smoke welled up as the flesh sizzled on the flames. Soon an awful smell permeated the space and all those present were thankful the area was created by a tree and not solid walls.

Coughing and choking a bit from the smoke created by the burning flesh, Sefforn and his men looked on at the horrific scene before them, not exactly sure of what to say. Mentak took a cloth from his pocket and began to wipe his face. Confusion now replaced frustration as Sefforn and company stared at the back of the man before them. The tension within the great tree was palpable. Slowly, Mentak turned around and lifted his head so that he starred straight into Sefforn's eyes.

"Clavorn?" Sefforn exclaimed tentatively with a mixture of surprise and confusion, for the man before him was a bit changed from the man whom he had left all those months back. The mixture of pine tar and blood did not help his identification any.

"Yes, it's me, the one and only," Clavorn announced to his childhood friend, and those with him as he wiped his face once more. He was more than glad to be ride of the awful flesh that had served as his disguise.

"But..." Sefforn began clearly at a loss for words.

"Yes, I am also dead as you have heard. I am Shaltak now, Slayer of Dragon Killers..."

"...and Protector of Maltak, I know. I mean....I heard. Surely you're not really this Shaltak?"

"Yes, he is," Melkiar confirmed from his place by the tree.

"But how? We've known each other since childhood."

"Except for those years that I went away after my father's death, you remember."

"Yes, but I thought you had gone into hiding."

"I guess in a way I had, though I never thought of it that way. You remember. I told you about Qualtaric, my father's old mentor?"

"Yeah."

"And that after I found him how he schooled me in the art of warfare and trained me to be a warrior," Clavorn continued, wiping his face once more. The sticky tar he had used to attach the flesh was proving much easier to apply than to remove.

"Yes, I remember. You told me all this when you came looking for me to join you."

"Yeah...well, what I didn't tell you was that when he thought my training was complete he sent me off, and I went to fight in the Dragon Wars," Clavorn explained, "However, he instructed me not reveal my name, or the name of my father, to anyone."

"Why? Why was it so important that you not use your name or that of your father?"

"He doesn't know," Melkiar interjected, "Though he suspects it might have something to do with the death of his father and that of King Dakconar."

"Oh," exclaimed Sefforn as he turned back to Clavorn, "So you took up the name, Shaltak. Now it's starting to make sense," Sefforn said revelation clearly evident in his speech. "But why didn't you tell me this earlier?"

"I was more concerned with the battles at hand and defeating Vaulnik, than recanting my past."

"I see," replied Sefforn, "But then why did you suddenly decide to start using your name again?"

"Pride," Clavorn explained simply, "After the massacre at Evangraw I knew I could no longer remain with Qualtaric. When news arrived, at nearly the same time, about my mother's and sister's death I could no longer stand not using my father's name any more. I wanted their slayers to know who was coming for them."

"I'm lost," declared Clovak a bit confused.

"I'm with you there," Sorenavik told Clovak before turning to Clavorn, "All I know is, as long as you're not dead, I will be happy to call you whatever you want," he remarked, making his way to a large root near the trunk of the massive willow to sit.

Sorenavik was a burly man, tall with dark brown hair he wore to his shoulders and pulled back in a ponytail for ease during battle. Now his great physic seemed to mirror the ancient tree. Upon reaching his destination he sat and placed his sword down beside him.

"Wait a minute what about Marona, she wasn't your mother," inquire Sefforn.

"No, she wasn't. She was my grandfather's fist love and wife, and eventually, my grandmother. The ring was hers given to me by my grandfather," Clavorn explained as he tried once again to remove more of the tar and blood from his face.

"Okay, that's great, but won't he figure out that she was his wife and not his daughter," Melkiar commented, removing his pipe from its customary place in his tunic. He had dearly missed using it during their 'honorary' dinner. Now, he was all too glad to be able to avail himself of its rich tobacco.

"Wait, didn't Savorn have a daughter named Marona," put in Kevic from his seat by the tree.

"Yes," Clavorn replied.

"So she must have been named after her, his wife," Kevic continued with his back resting against its ample trunk, "I didn't know he had a wife named Marona too. He never spoke of her."

"Most people don't. They were married quietly, up in the mountains, as Marona's parents did not approve of the match. They lived up there for a short time till she died giving birth to twins, Marona and Alsandra, my mother."

"So who we know of as his wife, Harona, was his…I'm guessing his second wife," deduced Kevic.

"Yes, that's right." Clavorn turned to face him, "he married her shortly after the twins were born."

"So Marona, his daughter, married Joseavic?" Sefforn continued, trying to follow all the loose ends.

"Yes, she was my aunt," Clavorn replied, rubbing his face where a particularly difficult clump of tar would not come off. There was a moment of silence as the fire crackled behind him.

"Well, however you explain it. I'm just glad we're all here safe as young dragons clutched," Clovak commented as he sat down on a root not far from Sorenavik and leaned his bow up against it next to him.

"I'll second that," remarked Sorenavik, taking out his flask for a drink.

"Now, as far as we are all concerned here, I am Shaltak," Clavorn declared, wiping his face again to finish removing the sticky pine tar he had used to attach the animal flesh.

"Tell me. Why are you going by Shaltak now? What's the point?" Sorenavik asked still a bit confused.

"It's a long story," Melkiar put in, tamping out the old tobacco from his pipe, "but suffice it to say that we're trying to out fox the fox."

"Oh, I think," replied Sorenavik still having a bit of trouble following it all. The exhaustion of everything he and his companions had been through interfering with his ability to put it all together, for the moment.

There was a short pause in the conversation as all those present tried to catch their minds up to what Clavorn had just told them.

"I will give you credit for that disguise. You sure did fool me," remarked Sefforn, breaking the silence that had briefly filled the area of the great tree.

"Well, that was the idea. It had to be convincing and yet disgusting enough that no one would want to look too closely," Clavorn explained, "Though I have to admit I was not expecting to pass the king's physician's inspection. I guess I did a better job with it than I thought."

"I told you you'd fool your own mother before we left," Melkiar interjected from his seat near the trunk of the tree as he stuffed his ever-present pipe with tobacco.

"True, I am glad I took the extra time with it," Clavorn remarked as he finished wiping his face for the last time, tossing the cloth he had used into the fire. Sparks flew, and flames welled up temporarily from the tar that was present in it.

"But what about all that stuff with the Kraic Stone?" asked Melkiar as he reached for a small twig from the fire with which to light his pipe, "How did you know they would pass the test?"

"My grandfather, Savorn, told me about the stone. It was he who gave me the stone for safe keeping," he explained, "Apparently, King Dakconar gave my father the stone when he suspected that things were going badly for him in the castle and had him hide it. My father had then given it to my grandfather believing it would be safest with him."

"But how did you keep it hidden all this time?" Sefforn asked.

"Ah, that is a well-guarded secret my friend," Clavorn told him with a smile.

"But how could you be sure they would pass the test," Melkiar pressed now drawing in deep puffs on his pipe, the smoke making rings as it floated upward.

"Because, I'm guessing, it was him in the hood and cloak that put us all through the test before we left," Clovak replied.

"Correct," Clavorn acknowledged as he went over to the trunk of the tree to find his oil skin bag for a drink.

"But why did you use a disguise? Why not just use the stone as you were?"

"Because I did not want it known that I had it, least the king find out and accuse my father of murdering his."

"That makes sense," Melkiar remarked simply, taking another puff from his pipe.

"So where do we go from here?" Clovak inquired, "Sevzozak will be looking for us to make a mistake since his plan didn't work. I think he was hoping to expose you and label us all traitors, thereby providing his guests with a spectacular end of party entertainment."

"I'll agree with that idea," Melkiar put in. He had spent most of the evening on pins and needles, "I have to admit I thought he had us there for a while."

"Yeah, well now aren't you glad I insisted in coming along at the last minute," Clavorn remarked.

"Alright, you win this one, but next time my friend…" Melkiar told him, pointing the end of his pipe at Clavorn.

"Next time we shall be the ones doing the cornering, not him," remarked Clavorn.

The conversation continued for a short while longer before fatigue finally set in and they began to mill out of the ancient willow to their respective quarters. It was still dark out, though dawn was not far off, when the last of them left save for Sefforn who was making no attempt to leave. He sat near Clavorn with his back against the giant tree.

"So what happened? Didn't the stone work?" Clavorn asked, curious as to why their mission had gone awry while he indulged himself a swig of ale from a flask Sefforn handed him.

"No." he answered simply, as he reached for the flask he had handed him.

Clavorn looked at him in surprise. The Stone of Maltak was supposed to be able to be used by a man if that man was deemed loyal to Maltak. That was why he had put the question to all three of them, according to his understanding that should have been enough for Sefforn and company to be able to find Viszerak. In fact, it should have been more than enough. He stared at the fire in front of them as he tried to recall the legend his grandfather had told him about the stone.

He watched the flames as they danced about the logs before him; soon his mind began to drift. Before long he could almost hear his grandfather's voice as his mind transported him back in time to another fire, another woods, another evening after a successful hunt.

The stars were twinkling over head while a young deer roasted over the flames.

"You know, Clavorn," his grandfather had begun, "legend tells of a man brave and pure by the name of Thorlon. You know the story?"

He remembered shaking his head, 'no.'

"Well, we must remedy that," his grandfather had told him as he took out his pipe and began to smoke it. He recalled watching him blow out rings of smoke before he launched himself into the tale.

"A long time ago, in the early days of men and kings there lived a brave hunter named Thorlon. Now, there are many tales of his adventures, but tonight I shall tell you of one adventure in particular."

His grandfather paused to take another puff on his pipe before continuing.

Fires of Life

"This tale begins on day much like ours was today. For on this day he was out hunting. They say that while he was stalking his prey he heard some unusual noises and became curious, so he went in search of their source. As he approached, he discovered that they were the voices of men arguing.

"At first he desired simply to help resolve the quarrel, but as he drew nearer it became clear to him that these were no ordinary men simply disagreeing over ordinary things. So instead of merely waltzing in on them to help settle things, he resolved to take cover in order to discover the true nature of the quarrel. Thorlon, it is said, then hid himself amongst the trees and bushes of the wood. What he saw and heard next shocked him."

"What was it, grandfather? What was it?"

"Well, if you let me continue I will tell you," his grandfather said, looking down at him with a smile in his eyes. He remembered how he had immediately sat quiet so his grandfather would resume his tale.

"Now to go on with our story…Those men had captured a young dragon and were torturing it."

"That's bad," he recalled commenting.

"Yes, yes it is, my young Clavorn. I see you have a good heart much like our good Thorlon. Now at first he could not understand the reason for their torment of the poor beast. Not that it mattered much. He would gladly have jumped in to defend it. Why do you think he waited?"

"To better understand his enemy?"

"Yes, that is precisely the reason. I see you will make a good warrior someday just like your father."

Clavorn remembered having felt proud after his grandfather's comment and wondered what he would think of him now if he could see him.

"As I was saying," his grandfather went on, "as Thorlon watched the reason became clear. For the young dragon was apparently no ordinary dragon, but instead it was one gifted with the rare endowment of breathing elements into the world, and the one element the men seemed particularly obsessed with was gold. This was the apparent object of their disagreement, for neither man was satisfied with his amount. Thorlon then observed the men torture the poor creature into breathing mounds and mounds of the precious element into being, in an ever increasing endeavor to slake their desire. It is said that is how most of our gold came this world."

"Really?" he remembered remarking, wide eyed and full of amazement. He recalled how fascinated he had been as a youth to learn how everything in the world had come into being.

"Yes, so they say, but that is an aside. Shall we continue with my story?"

"Yes, yes, grandfather."

He remembered how his grandfather had laughed, apparently amused by his enthusiasm, before he continued on.

"Well, as I was saying, Thorlon noticed that each time the young dragon created the gold it became weaker and weaker. It is said that, Thorlon became enraged by what he saw. Such was his wrath, they say; that he could no longer remain hidden and burst forth upon the men, demanding that they release the dragon immediately. But the men only laughed at him and offered to cut him in on the deal. Thorlon, legend tells, refused their offer, telling them he would rather die than harm such a creature for gain of any kind.

"The men, however, only laughed at him more. They cared not for the creature, or any creature; life being only there, in their opinion, to plunder, to use, to serve. They only cared for wealth, through which they believed they would gain power. Power and control was their ultimate goal, and to this end their greed would not be satisfied.

"Once again they tried to lure Thorlon with the promise of a share of the profits and the power they hoped to gain. But by now Thorlon had grown quite enraged. Soon a great fight ensued. It is said, that during the course of the struggle, Thorlon released the young dragon from its bonds. In that moment, the dragon transformed before their very eyes into the dragon, Maltak, who then imprisoned the greedy men inside the gold they so coveted by breathing her fire down upon them; essentially emblazoning their essence into the precious yellow metal."

"Really, grandfather, did Maltak really place those men inside the gold?"

"Yes, in a manner of speaking. Legend tells us that, their souls are eternally trapped by that which they coveted so rapaciously. It is for this reason that gold has been forever cursed to cause chaos and sorrow to those who seek it greedily."

"So what happened to Thorlon?"

"Well, they say that Maltak then turned to Thorlon and breathed on him. Her fire being so hot that it transformed the rock around him into Kriac stones of the most perfect sort. Thorlon stood in amazement unable to believe he was still alive and even more astounded at the beauty before him."

"But I thought all the Kriac stones came from the Shardon Lands in a great shower sent by Allethor?"

"They did, but these were special Kriac stones that Maltak herself had created, and one reason why many believe they are so abundant here in Avivron."

"Oh."

"Now to continue," His grandfather remarked, eyes twinkling in the firelight while he elucidated animatedly, "Maltak then reached down and plucked the most unusual Kriac stone from the bunch. It was green, emerald green with a blue heart at its center, and completely flawless. Said to be one of a kind. In return for Thorlon's bravery, loyalty, and purity of heart she gave this Kriac stone to him, telling him that the stone would allow him to call upon a dragon if he ever found himself in need. Legend says that such will be true for any man who, hence forward from that day, was deemed worthy enough."

Clavorn remembered how fascinated he had been by the story and how much he had wished to someday be as worthy as Thorlon of Maltak. He recalled how riveted he had been by his grandfather's telling of the tale and how the stone would glow for those who, it was said, were loyal to Maltak. As far as he could see, from his recollection, the stone should have worked for Sefforn and his two companions who he thought had passed the test, at least to his understanding of it. Unless there was something he was missing.

He tried to remember what his grandfather had said about the stone, but he could not remember anything different than that which he had already explained to the king and court. The evening his grandfather had given him the stone had been much too hectic. Vaulnik's soldiers were everywhere and his grandfather had been concerned about his safety.

He had gone to his grandfather's as soon as Vaulnik had invaded Avivron. Savorn was known to many and Vaulnik's men had already been by inquiring. Clavorn had wanted to take him to safety with him up to Qualtaric's. But Savorn would have none of it. Instead, he gave him the stone, telling him to keep it safe at all costs. Now, it was in the hands of Sevzozak. That failure hit him almost as hard as the news that Sefforn and company had failed to locate the dragon.

I wonder if it was the stone Zarik and company were looking for the night of my father's death?

The question flitted briefly into his mind before returning to the question at hand.

"I don't know Clavorn," Sefforn said, interrupting his thoughts, "Maybe the stone did not deem us worthy enough, or maybe it did not think we were in need enough. I don't know. I just know it didn't work like you said it would. Maybe there is more to it than what you remember. All I know is we were not able to find the dragon, or any dragon for that matter. Not that there is any other dragon to find." He paused a moment taking another sip of ale. Both men were silent.

"Did you ever consider that maybe Viszerak is dead and that's why the stone didn't work," his friend suggested. "From what I've heard, he was pretty beat up at the end of the Battle of Quantaris."

"No!" Clavorn jumped up from his seat. He could not accept that answer. For if that was true, then all hope was lost. "No. I know he is alive," he told his friend emphatically, "I just know it." He could feel it in his bones, as he ran a hand through his hair. Somehow he just knew the dragon still had to be alive. "We must have done something wrong. I'll have to think some more on it," he finished, frustrated by the results and a bit confused.

He passed his hand over his face and paced before his friend. There just had to be another explanation. Then he remembered her words.

'He will fail.'

How had she known? The question plagued his mind. *Who is the one worthy to find the dragon?*

"You know him," had been her answer.

Who is he?

Clavorn's mind was in a whorl. The evening had proved quite interesting and she an even bigger mystery.

How had she known?

The question repeated itself and he could still find no answer. *Who is she?... What is she?*

These questions ran through his mind as he tried to solve the riddle that was her.

Sefforn shook his head and downed the last of his drink. Clavorn glanced over in his friend's direction and continued his inquiry.

"What happened to the others?"

"We lost them in an avalanche near the northern border. A big snow storm had come up and dumped a lot of snow on the mountain, apparently too much. When it stopped and we began again...well let's just say the three of us were lucky enough to be just out of the path of the oncoming snow." He paused, as if recalling that moment,

"If I had known that pass was going to be that treacherous, I would have searched for another way around it, but…"

"Look, there was nothing you could have done. I'm just glad at least you three survived. I was beginning to wonder about you."

"Well, all I know is, any more trips to the north are out," Sefforn noted after a moment of silence, "Sevzozak will be watching for that."

"I know," Clavorn replied simply, his brow furrowed in thought as he stared into the flames before him. It was a terrible loss, the loss of his men. They would be sorely missed. Another great moment of silence passed between them.

"You think he'll try to use the stone?" Sefforn inquired.

"He might, but if it didn't work for you, do you really think it will work for him?"

"No. I was just wondering," his friend replied, leaning back in resignation, the failure of their mission weighing on him. More silence as the two men were lost in their respective thoughts.

"So tell me, how did you come to possess the horn?" Sefforn asked, breaking the dense quiet that hung in the air.

"Oh, uhm…the horn," Clavorn had been too deep in thought when his friend's question came across to him. Now, he was not at all sure how to explain it.

Where do I begin?

He thought a moment.

"Yeah, the horn," Sefforn repeated, lifting his head off the trunk with which he had been resting it on.

Clavorn had no idea how to begin, "This is going to sound a bit strange," *Oh, by Allethor! He is going to think I am crazy…* "but the person who helped me escape from prison gave it to me."

"You mean you had it before I left?!" The inflection in his friend's voice was at once a mixture of surprise, inquiry, and accusation.

Fires of Life

"No," he replied nearly flinching at his friend's accusatory inflection. How did he tell him that she had come to see him and had led him out of camp?

No.

His friend looked at him in confusion. Clavorn paced, running his hand through his hair.

How do I explain this? I guess I just do it.

"They came by the other night and gave it to me," he blurted out, "I know it sounds ridiculous, but that's basically what happened."

Sefforn raised an eyebrow. "Who is this person?" he asked.

"I don't know," Clavorn answered, running a hand once more through his dark hair, "They won't tell me who they are. I only know that they wish to be thought of as a 'ghost.'" he replied.

Images of her visit a few nights ago flood his mind. The cold feel of her blade on his throat, the soft touch of her hand on his mouth, the moonlight caressing her silhouette as they traveled through the woods, it all came back to him. He remembered the morning light in her green eyes as she handed him the horn, and the scarf which so adeptly denied him a glimpse into her identity.

"Here," she had said, "you will need this," as she handed him the beautiful green horn.

He remembered how fascinated he had been by it as it shimmered in an iridescent rainbow of colors as the first rays of sunlight hit it that morning.

"It belonged to Joseavic, the Dragon Caller, your uncle," she had told him, "Wrap it in leather to conceal it and keep it with you at all times."

Clavorn had promised to do so as he placed it within his clothes for safe keeping.

"Keep it safe," she had said as he had moved ahead of her to glance into camp before saying good-bye. But when he went to ask her as to how she had acquired it and when he would see her again, she had once more disappeared just like the early morning mist.

"A 'ghost' ehey," replied Sefforn clearly not sure what to make of Clavorn's answer, "Well, let us hope this 'ghost' continues to be as timely as they have been so far."

Clavorn agreed with him, as he once again he took his place beside his childhood friend. They both sat there for a few more moments taking in what was left of the night. Clavorn offered his friend a bit of ale from his flask and Sefforn took it.

A breeze swayed the tree, its branches billowing and dancing in and out of their space. Outside all was quiet. Only the sound of the occasional man on watch filtered into the old tree. The damp smell of earth, rock, plants, and flowers wafted in on the wind. Spring had long since given way to summer. Evening insects were beginning to give their song away to the birds that had begun to sing their melody while a gentle breeze whispered through the forest.

The two friends sat together passing the flask between them before Sefforn finally rose to leave. Clavorn rose as well and escorted his friend to the edge of the weeping branches. The sun was now just beginning to rise, and with it the camp as well as it began to come alive with activity.

"It looks as if there will be no rest for the weary today," Sefforn commented as he parted the branches.

"I think you might be right, though I would take some time out to rest and recuperate if I were you. You had quite an ordeal back at the castle," Clavorn told him.

He was concerned for his friend. It was clear his stay at the castle had been anything but pleasant. The blood stains on his face and bruises on his body were clearly visible in the light of the early morning dawn.

"Yeah, well, no thanks to a certain friend of mine," Sefforn replied with smile and a pat on Clavorn's shoulder, "but I'll live. Say, tell that 'ghost' of yours 'thanks' the next time you run into him will you," Sefforn told him as he made to leave.

"Sure," Clavorn answered, wondering when the next time would be as he watched his friend leave.

Chapter 17

The sun was just beginning to set over the mountains in the distance as Clavorn made his way up the hillside that led to his grandfather's house. He was enjoying this time with his grandfather. It was his first long-term visit with him by himself. Usually, he and his family just visited on holiday, but this time he got to stay on for a while. His mother and father thought it would be good for him, being almost seven and all. Time he had some time alone, away from them. Time he learned as much as he could from the esteemed old Legend Keeper.

He could see the smoke from his grandfather's chimney as he reached the crest of the hill. As Legend Keeper for the king, he could have lived in a much grander house, but his grandfather would not hear of it. He preferred the simple life of the woods and mountains to the grandeur of the castle, or anything else for that matter. So the king had set him up in a cottage not far from Escadora. Close enough to be easily accessible, yet far enough away to be absent from all the hubbub of the daily goings on of castle, court, and city.

The simple little house lay at the foot of the mountain on a small knoll. A grassy meadow covered the hill leading to his grandfather's house. Flowering bushes of all color were a buzz of activity for all manner of flying insects. The large old oak tree, which stood beside the small cottage, gave it plenty of shade in the midsummer when the sun was at its hottest. But now it was simply a home for several birds and their families. The spring air smelled fresh and fragrant from the late afternoon rain. It was, in short, a perfect evening, Clavorn thought, as he came upon the small house.

Suddenly, from the side of the little cottage he heard his grandfather calling him. Clavorn followed the voice around the side of the house. There he found the white haired elderly man sitting on a log underneath a venerable ancient maple. The giant tree, whose branches rose up high into the sky and spread out towards the small cottage, marked the edge of a forest which began just behind it.

Rings of smoke wafted about him, as he sat puffing on his pipe while the giant tree's branches tree's cascaded about him, sheltering him from the late afternoon sun.

"Come here, my boy," his grandfather said, motioning Clavorn to sit by his side, "come here."

Clavorn did as the old man instructed. He liked his grandfather, and knew he was well respected by the king. It seemed to him that they enjoyed a type of friendship.

"I want to tell you a story," he began as Clavorn sat down beside him, "I want to tell you a story about dragons and witches, about victory and valor, about the time of the first dragons and how they came to be."

Clavorn could hardly wait. He loved the stories his grandfather told, especially about the dragons.

"Do you know the story of creation?" a puff of smoke briefly escaped his grandfather's lips wafting upwards ringing his grandfather's head.

"Well, I know that at first there was only a great powerful light. A light, so bright and wise, as to outshine anything we can imagine."

"This is true, my boy. Go on. What else can you tell me?"

"I know that the Light had no name, for there were no 'others.'"

"Correct. At that time it was only the Light and the Great Void," his grandfather said, puffing on his pipe.

"I imagine it got lonely, being the only one with no-one else to keep you company."

The elderly man chuckled, "I'd imagine you are right. In fact, that is why it is believed that the Light finally divided itself into two, creating Allethor and Thelenor, the Father and Mother of all that is."

"I know."

"Do you now?" his grandfather eyed him down through his bushy white eye brows as he continued to puff on his pipe. "So then a smart lad like you knows about Alhera as well."

"I know some," Clavorn answered, not wanting to give all his knowledge away as he enjoyed his grandfather's stories too well.

Fires of Life

"Hummm," his grandfather eyed him suspiciously, but Clavorn could see the glint in his eye, and the ever so slight upturn to his lips through his bushy white beard and mustache. A beard, which one might say, was as long as his years, for it stretched down long past his navel to somewhere near his feet. "Well, then do you know how dragons came to be?"

Clavorn shook his head 'no,' but he had heard the story a hundred times before.

"I see. Then we must correct this hole in your education," the old Legend Keeper remarked.

Clavorn nodded as his grandfather took in a long deep puff on his pipe, blowing the smoke out in billows, so that it appeared to Clavorn as if his grandfather might even be a descendant of one of the dragons himself, despite the obvious impossibility of that.

"Long ago, before the time of the dragons, when the earth was yet but young, and all the twinkling stars of the Shardon Lands but a gift to please his beloved queen, Thelenor, Allethor and Thelenor had a daughter; Alhera. She was beautiful, smart, and strong with a heart full of courage and love. So Allethor and Thelenor blessed her with the gift of creation, and gave the Earth to her so she could look after it and populate it with all manner of creatures. Which she did, and both Allethor and Thelenor were very proud of her, for the creatures she made were good and beautiful.

"Now, Allethor and Thelenor also had a son. His name was Sespon. He was a handsome prince in the Shardon Lands. Strong, proud, and a bit full of himself if this old storyteller has anything to say," at this his grandfather paused, glancing over to Clavorn before he continued.

"Now Sespon soon grew jealous of his parent's attention and pride in Alhera. Slowly, he grew to despise her creations and hated them for having given her, and not him, this most precious of gifts; creation. Now, both Allethor and Thelenor had given many gifts to Sespon, but creation had not been one of them. For though they loved both their children equally, they thought they deserved different gifts so each could be seen as special and unique."

"That's good isn't it grandfather," Clavorn interjected.

"Yes, my boy it is, but see Sespon did not see it so. His arrogance had grown so that he believed he deserved to have such a gift as well. In fact, his arrogance grew to the point he thought he could rule the Shardon Lands better than both his father and mother. So much so, that he was certain it was his right to rule over all that was, both in the Shardon Lands and beyond. To that end he plotted to over through his parents, but first he needed the power of creation."

"But didn't Allethor and Thelenor see what Sespon was up too?"

"That is a good question, my boy. Some think they let it happen. Others think that they were too kind and giving to see the evil that burned in their son's heart."

"What do you think grandfather?"

"I think they knew of their son's jealousy, but loved him anyway and hoped he would outgrow those feelings."

"So what happened?"

"Well, as you have probably guessed, Sespon complained bitterly to his parents. He wanted the power to create too, and expressed his opinion of how unfair he felt it was that Alhera had this power and not him. He told Allethor and Thelenor that they should have given it to both of them.

At first Allethor and Thelenor refused. In fact, they refused Sespon many times, but then one day, in a moment of weakness, they granted Sespon his wish and gave him the gift of creation too. Sespon thanked them, and immediately went to Earth and created a pestilence to wipe out much of what his sister had created. Outraged by what Sespon had done, Allethor and Thelenor created a new realm and banished their son to it."

"Didn't they take his powers away?"

"No. You see once a power like that is given it cannot be taken away."

"Why not?" Clavorn could not understand why Allethor and Thelenor could not just take that power away. After all, if his parents gave him a sword and he used it badly, he knew his father and mother would take it back.

"Because it was a gift, one does not take back gifts once they are given."

"Why not? My parents would if I used it badly."

"Because it was not that kind of gift. See Clavorn, it was not a thing or an animal. It was an ability, and once a thing like that is given it can never be taken away."

"Oh. But what has this to do with the creation of dragons?"

"Everything," his grandfather went on, taking another long drag on his pipe before he continued. "You see Sespon could have created that realm any way he wished. He could have learned his lesson, and turned his heart to love, and in so doing, chosen to create beauty. But his heart was too consumed with jealousy, hatred, and greed.

"Darkness was all that existed around him, for darkness was all he could tolerate. In place of warmth, cold. A cold so cold it had no equal. Like his heart, the abyss soon reflected only what he carried with in; blackness, and frigid coldness.

"So, while he could have made whatever he liked out of that realm, he chose to create ugliness and evil. The darkness in his heart unable to conceive of anything else and abhorring all others. There, in his hideous realm, he sat on his throne of screaming twisted creatures and pondered, while his hatred of all that was good and beautiful grew, till he vowed to destroy it all one day."

"Yes, he became Zagnor," the old Legend Keeper told him, for he could see the light of realization in his grandson's eyes, "and his realm became known as Zezpok, an evil vile realm full of twisted ugly creatures.

"In the beginning, they preyed upon each other, there being no men for them to torture for their deeds here on earth. See, there was no evil in our world at that time, because Alhera had not created man yet. For as you know, of all the creatures Alhera has created, only men and I mean men in the broadest sense," his grandfather explained gesturing with hands so as to show his meaning to encompass all people, "are capable of evil."

"Why is that grandfather?"

"Good question, my boy. Some say it is because Alhera made us too much like the gods, in form, but lacking in wisdom. This, they claim, makes us vulnerable to Zagnor who seduces us into believing we can be gods."

"How?"

"According to some it varies. They believe that for some he convinces them they are as powerful as the gods. For others, they say, it is by tricking them into believing they own the world and can do with it as they please. Many say it varies from person to person. That Zagnor is always looking to see where we are vulnerable. They believe the easiest place is in our ego. How important we think we are. That is when they believe he can trick us into believing we are above the rest of Alhera's creation, sometimes even above other men, or the gods themselves. It is then, according to them, that we are capable of a great many crimes against Allethor, Thelenor and their daughter, Alhera; crimes of the ugliest and vilest nature."

"What do you believe grandfather?"

"Ahh, now there's a tricky one. I think Alhera did a good job when she created men. Perhaps too good."

"Oh."

"Yes, Clavorn, you see men can do many things. They are capable of great good and great evil. It is up to each of us to decide how we should use these gifts Alhera has given us. Much like Zagnor, we have a choice, and in the end, when our time here is done, it is our choices that will define not just who we are or where we go in the afterlife, but what we leave behind. For you see, my son, our choices ripple through time, affecting this world in ways we can never imagine."

"Really?"

"Yes, really," his grandfather nodded as he removed his pipe from his lips. Smoke escaped his mouth and rose, fading into the evening sky. "So, shall we continue?"

"Yes, yes."

"Okay," his grandfather smiled, "Now Zagnor soon grew tired of sitting on his throne watching his creation squabble amongst themselves while Alhera's creations enjoyed the light and warmth of our world, not to mention the praise of his father and mother. So he hatched a plan; an evil, vile plan to let his creatures loose upon the creations of Alhera here on Earth. One terrible night he opened a door into our world and let his horde loose upon it. Immediately, they began to ravage and consume all life here. Alhera saw this and in her rage she created Maltak, the First Dragon.

"Maltak was a beautiful she dragon with green iridescent scales as hard as Kriac Stones but with the ability to reflect all the colors of the universe. It is said, that this ability allows her to appear to change the colors of her scales to blend into any surrounding, thus making her appear invisible."

"Really?" Clavorn loved the description of Maltak.

"Yes, only her eyes might give her away for they are said to be blood red. To her Alhera gave the gift of restoration, the Fires of Life."

"What are The Fires of Life grandfather?" Clavorn knew. He just wanted to hear about them one more time.

"Well, my boy, it is what the dragons use to renew the earth, to bring life back to a lifeless world, or so it is said. It is a special fire that they breathe onto that which they wish to renew."

"So they cannot create life."

"No. But they can renew it and help it grow."

"That is why the forests look so beautiful isn't it grandfather."

"Yes, Clavorn, that is why the forests look so beautiful. And if you ever see a particularly beautiful forest with ancient trees, and all manner of flora and fauna, it is said that a dragon is sure to live there."

Clavorn smiled. He loved the woods and all the many creatures that called them home.

"So what happened, grandfather?"

Clavorn's grandfather took another puff on his pipe and began again, "Well, according to legend, Alhera rode Maltak to Earth and together they destroyed most of Zagnor's creatures, and drove the remaining back to Zezpok.

"But Zagnor would not be so easily defeated. His heart burned with hatred as he watched Maltak restore what his creatures had so happily destroyed. They say that he sat upon his throne brooding for a very long time afterwards.

"Then one day he rose from his throne and created a great vile gray-green fire. It was out of this fire he created the Vigoths. Horrible gray misty creatures whose sole desire was to absorb all life, all good, all magic and take it into themselves leaving only cold and desolation behind, growing in strength the more they consumed.

"Once again he released these creatures onto our world, but Alhera was ready. She and Maltak soared down from Shardon with Maltak's mate, Altak, who Alhera had created after the great battle. Together they fought off the Vigoths. But it was not an easy match.

"Breathing fire they descended upon the gray misty creatures. The cold emptiness of Zagnor's Vigoths threatened to envelope the dragons as they fought. Maltak and Altak twisted and turned breathing fire in every direction as the Vigoths tried to suck the very life, and magic from their beings.

"The illusive nature of the Vigoths threatened to undo Maltak and her mate, but their hot breath proved to be too much for the creatures in the end. For it was born out of the fires of life itself, born out of the fires of justice and truth, born out of the light of love and eternal goodness, and as such it proved to be too hot for the Vigoths; burning the misty beings just as the sun burns off the fog.

"It is said, that after the Vigoths were defeated Maltak and Altak went around the earth with Alhera. And, being born of life with all

Fires of Life

its magic and mystery, were able to heal the earth; returning flower and fauna to the land with their Fires of Life."

"Is that the end of the story grandfather?" Clavorn asked after a moment of silence.

"I wish it was," his grandfather replied, drawing in the rich tobacco as he sat next to Clavorn before he continued. "Sadly, it is not, for Zagnor would not be undone. His creatures had failed, but we are told that in the battle with the Vigoths the dragon Altak lost one of his blue scales. Zagnor saw this and had one of his demons sent to Earth to retrieve it. With it, so the legend goes, he created a most hideous dragon capable of killing Maltak's children, perhaps even Maltak herself, but that is uncertain.

"This gruesome beast is said to be an evil and vile creature, gray as the storms of the Vilharroon, and capable of bringing with it the same terrible devastation as that of the great tornados. Some say he has even become as black as the black of the darkest cave, absorbing all color, all light, and all life. Its very breath is said to be born of the fires of Zezpok.

"This dragon is called Demonrak, and he is believed to be the vilest creature ever created by Zagnor. He is the champion of greed, and power, hater of all life and love. According to the legends, Zagnor is keeping Demonrak, and his children, in the bowels of Zezpok waiting for the day one of Alhera's children shawl call it forth to destroy the children of Maltak and Altak, raping the land for greed and power."

Silence permeated the night as they sat there on the log together. His grandfather puffing on his pipe as the sounds of nature carried on.

"We are all Alhera's children, right grandfather?"

"Yes, my son. She created us out of the special stones that lined the edged of a small pool."

"The legendary Pool of Life," Clavorn put in excitedly and with an air of pride, but then put a hand to his mouth, had he given himself away, would his grandfather still recount the tale of the Pool of Life?

"Yes," his grandfather remarked clearly impressed by Clavorn, "I see you know more than you let on young Clavorn."

Clavorn shook his head 'no.'

"Tell the truth. I will still tell the tale if you wish."

Clavorn gave in and admitted that he knew, just not how much.

"I thought so," his grandfather remarked with a wiry grin from beneath his bushy white beard, "Shall I continue my story telling with the tale of our creation, or shall we go in for supper?"

"No, no. Tell the story grandfather. Tell it, *please*."

"All right, all right, I'll tell the story."

The sun was nearing the horizon now, her colors beginning their display but only just. A hawk cried out over head as the elderly Legend Keeper began his tale.

"The legendary Pool of Life is said to be the pool from which Alhera created all the life on the earth. It is said, that the stones along its shore hold the magic of life and that they will only glow for Dragon Witches, but I am getting ahead of myself.

"One night, by the light of the full moon, Alhera came to earth to create man and woman."

"Why? Why did she create us?" Clavorn asked.

"Well, that is a good question. One, I think many banter around… I guess perhaps, while she loved all her creations, she may have wanted one that was more like her. Much like we wish to have our own children."

"Oh," Clavorn replied not sure if he totally understood, "go on grandfather."

"Are you sure?"

Clavorn shook his head 'yes' and the old man continued, "Well, on that night she took two multicolored stones out of its waters near the edge, but they were not just any multicolored stones. No. It is said; she needed two very special stones, stones that held within

Fires of Life

them both the magic of the day and the night; one, being the Stone of the Moon, the other, being the Stone of the Sun.

"It took her most of the night to find the first special multicolored Stone of the Moon. The one she was looking for was said to be special, holding within it both the magic of the night and day. Alhera searched and searched the shores, but the pool was large and her stones many.

"Finally, a she panther came to drink by the pool. When she saw Alhera she bowed and cried out. Alhera glanced up from the waters to greet the she panther. As she did so, the light of the moon caught one of the stones just below the surface of the water. In that moment, the stone reflected the colors which were the hallmark of the Stone of the Moon.

"Alhera then thanked the she panther for helping her and blessed her with an ebony coat. In case you don't know that is why all panthers that are blessed with such a coat are considered sacred to Alhera."

"I hope I see one, one day," Clavorn interjected.

"Perhaps you will," his grandfather replied, "That would be a very special day."

Clavorn nodded, his grandfather smiled and continued.

"Alhera waited till dawn. Then, just before the sun rose, she placed the stone down on a bed of soft ferns. As the sun's first rays of light struck the stone, it light up with the Magic of Day; at that moment a hawk cried out and song birds broke into the most beautiful of melodies. Alhera smiled for now she knew she had the stone which would become woman.

"She then searched all the stones of the Pool of Life for the special Stone of the Sun that would hold both the light of day and night. It is said, that while she was searching a lion came to drink by the pool, and as he lapped up the water Alhera could see something reflecting by his paws. When the lion left she went over and, sure enough, there, where the lion had been drinking, was the Stone of the Sun.

"Alhera bent down, and reaching into the water, picked it out from amongst the other stones. Then she searched out the lion and thanked him for his help. To show her appreciation she blessed him with a thick golden mane to frame his handsome face, much like the rays of sunlight frame the sun."

"And that is why lions are so important right grandfather."

"Yes, for they too are blessed by the goddess. Now after this, she then waited till the night and the rising of the full moon. Once more she placed the stone down on a bed of ferns. And like before, as the first light of the rising moon hit the stone it began to glow from deep inside itself with the Magic of Night. At that moment a raven cawed and mice broke into a dance. Now, Alhera knew she had her stone which would become man.

"It was by the light of that full moon that she then began to create man and woman. When the light of the first rays of the sun peeked over the horizon the next morning, the stones were ready. Alhera then breathed on them just as those first rays of sun light struck the stones.

"Suddenly, they began to glow from within. Soon they became so bright that they outshined the sun that morning. Finally, as the sun finished rising, the light from the stones dimmed, and in their place were no longer the stones but the first man and woman."

"Why did she only use two stones?" Clavorn asked.

"Because she only needed two," the old Legend Keeper replied simply as he took another puff from his pipe.

"Oh," Clavorn answered, feeling rather embarrassed by his question.

"You know it was the goddess Alhera that gave the colors their meaning. Do you know what they are?" his grandfather asked after a few moments of silence.

"Yes," Clavorn announced proudly.

"Then tell me, my grandson, what are the meanings of the colors?"

Clavorn looked to the sun as it set over the mountains in the distance, its glorious display of color only deepening the meaning of his words, and his wonderment for the earth and her goddess Alhera.

"Green is for life," his grandfather nodded as he began, "Red for valor, love, and fierceness in regards to protection for all that is living. It has many other meanings but these are the ones the goddess gave it."

"That is quite correct, my boy," his grandfather told him, "Go on."

"Blue for truth, white is the color of peace, harmony, and tranquility."

At each correct answer his grandfather nodded, the smoke from his pipe billowing out and up into the early evening sky.

"Pink is for joy, and laughter, yellow- spirit, happiness, and good will."

"What is purple for?" his grandfather asked.

"That's easy," Clavorn announced, "it's for honor, and fervor; passion but not lust."

"Good! Go on," Savorn waved for his grandson to continue his listing while he continued, puffing on his pipe.

"Orange is for loyalty."

"And gold?"

"That's for justice," Clavorn announced proudly.

"Right! Then silver…"

"Silver is for wisdom, purity, and strength."

"I guess I am now full of strength, wisdom, purity, peace, and tranquility as my head is covered in silver and white hair, ehey boy," his grandfather nudged him playfully and laughed.

Clavorn smiled and nudged him back.

"Carry on. I want to see how much you have learned," the venerable old man said as he waved him on once more while inhaling another puff on his pipe.

"Gray is for death. Brown is the color of the earth and permanence," Clavorn told him.

"And what of black? What does the color black stand for," his grandfather pressed.

Clavorn thought a moment. He had almost forgotten, "mystery, black is the color of mystery and magic. Oh, it's also a color of life, for the richest soil is black."

"And why is it not the color of evil?"

"Because the goddess of life would never give a color such a meaning as all colors are representatives of her generosity to the earth," he announced.

"Good! Tell me why is death itself not an evil?"

"Because without death life could not renew itself, as birth would not be possible, being that all things are limited in this realm. It is unnatural death that is evil, right grandfather?"

"If by 'unnatural' you mean that which is caused out of spite for the living, such as through murder, then yes. Death caused by man's greed, spite, hatred, or other ill desires is an evil," he told Clavorn with another puff on his pipe.

"Zagnor tried to corrupt the meaning of the colors. Did he not grandfather?" Clavorn remarked after a brief pause in their conversation.

"Yes, he did. According to legend, he did not want anyone to see the colors for what they truly meant. That is why the colors now seem to have two meanings, one good, one bad, or as some would say, one light, one dark. But it is only when we see the colors for what they truly mean that they have power."

"What sort of power grandfather?" Clavorn asked.

"All sorts of power, but it is different for each color and some are more powerful than others. See how you can see some colors more vividly in the sunset."

"Yes" Clavorn answered.

"Well, so it is with their powers, but that is a lesson for Dragon Witches not valiant boys," his grandfather told him as he took a puff on his pipe and blew out rings of smoke that seemed to almost encircle what was left of the retreating sun.

Fires of Life

"Why can I not learn the power of the colors grandfather?" Clavorn asked, feeling a bit put off.

"Firstly, because only the Dragon Witches know the power of the colors, and secondly, because I am not a Dragon Witch," he told him as he gathered his staff and rose from the log. "Come. Let us continue this conversation inside. The cold mountain air seeps into this old man's bones and the temperature is falling fast this spring evening."

Clavorn rose with his grandfather and the two of them went into the little cottage. His grandfather lived alone these days, so this visit was a particularly special time for both of them. His grandfather set his staff down and began shuffling around the little kitchen of the cottage to make their dinner. Upon seeing that the fire had died down, Clavorn went immediately back outside and gathered some wood to restart it while his grandfather prepared them a simple meal.

"We'd eat like kings if your grandmother was here, but the gods have seen fit to leave us to suffer my cooking. Here, eat. But do an old man a favor and do not remind him how terrible a cook he is," his grandfather told him, after her had finished preparing their dinner, as he set their plates down in front of them on the wooden table which sat in front of the fireplace.

Clavorn did not care how good or bad his food was. He loved his grandfather and his stories.

"So tell me grandfather, who are the Dragon Witches?" he asked as he sat down and took a bite of his dinner. His grandfather's chair scraped across the wooden floor of the cottage as he pulled it out and sat down.

"Dragon Witches? Well, they're women. That's who they are," his grandfather replied as he swallowed a bite of their supper.

"I know. But *who* are they? You know…tell me."

His grandfather thought a moment as he chewed on a bit of his supper.

"Well, they're women who have been given special powers by the goddess Alhera; powers of the earth, of the colors, and more. They are friends to the dragons, and some say they even have power over the dragons."

"No!" Clavorn exclaimed in astonishment, "No one has power over the dragons," he declared, putting his fork down on the wooden table, "That can't be. Only Alhera has power over the dragons, right grandfather?"

"Well, that's what some *say*. They believe the goddess gave the witches this power so they could be her representatives here on earth, though between you and me I think this is a bit of an overstatement. To have power over a dragon is to have a lot of power. Perhaps it is better said that they have a kinship with the dragons."

"Do they look different than other women?" Clavorn asked after a brief moment of silence as he took a sip of water from the wooden chalice his grandfather had set in front of him.

"Some say they do," his grandfather replied as he too took a sip of water from the wooden goblet before him. "There was a time when their clothing gave them away, but now…" he said, setting his glass back down on the table, "they are said to be stronger and more beautiful than most women. But mostly it is their powers that give them away."

"What sort of powers grandfather?"

"Like the power to heal the wounded or the sick, to grow any sort of plant or tree imaginable. The power to call the dragons, speak to the animals, and some say plants too."

"Really? Can someone really speak to a plant?" Clavorn inquired astonished by this revelation.

"Well, that's what they say. But, as I have never really witnessed it, it is hard for me to say for certain. People do tend to exaggerate sometimes," his grandfather told him, taking another bite of his dinner.

Clavorn looked down at his plate with disappointment. It would be so fascinating to be able to speak to the trees. They were so old. What stories could they tell you?

"They are said to have power over the elements of the earth," his grandfather continued, "Some stones are said to respond to their very touch."

Clavorn took a bite of his food and washed it down with the water his grandfather had placed before him totally enthralled with what the venerable old man was saying. He wondered if he would ever meet a Dragon Witch someday.

"It is from their ranks that the Shaddorak is said to come from," his grandfather announced after a moment of silence.

"Who is the Shaddorak?"

"The Shaddorak is said to be a woman with extraordinary powers. She, it is foretold, will be the only one who can wield both the power of the Kraic stones and the dragons. Only she will be able to call upon the great Maltak."

Clavorn shifted in his sleep. The wind blew gently through the branches of the old weeping willow as an owl hooted out in the distant darkness of the night. A full moon graced the blackness of the sky. Silver blue rays of light seeped into the interior of the tree as he slept. The air was cool as it caressed the skin of his well-muscled torso. Clavorn pulled the thick bearskin up over him and rolled over, immediately falling back to sleep.

The moonlight lit her green eyes. Clavorn could see her holding a Stone of the Moon between the palms of her hands as she lifted them up to her face. Then suddenly the image changed.

He could see her standing naked in the falls, the water caressing her body as she tilted her head back, allowing it to flow over her long dark hair and down her back. Her skin was white against the gray rock of the falls which perfectly accented her magnificent figure. She turned and faced the falls, bringing her hair to her side in order to wring it out, as the water flowed down the front of her. And there they were; the scars, the long scars of what he believe to be Vaulnik's dragon whips.

Once again the scene changed, this time to a garden and a pool by yet another falls. The gentle clear blue green color of its waters reflected in her eyes as she stood before him. Her face shrouded as always, all except her eyes.

Her eyes, her cat like eyes. They mystified him and intrigued him as they began to fade into the background of the clear pool behind her.

Mist filled his dream as horses galloped straight to him through her fading image, and then changed into dragons. In the background stood a fine mountain range and about it flew dragons; lots and lots of dragons. Soon they began to converge and meld together about a single peak until only one image of a dragon remained.

It was the face of Maltak. Her crimson eyes burning, her emerald iridescent scales reflecting every color of light as her image grew and then faded. All that was left was a vision of a mountainside in a forest all a bloom. He stepped towards it. Suddenly, a cave appeared and then disappeared as quickly as it had appeared.

He woke up.

Where have I seen that mountainside?

Chapter 18

The light of the early morning dawn streamed in through the branches of the willow and fell across Clavorn's face as he stared up into its boughs.

Where have I seen that mountainside?

The question would not leave his mind as he racked his brain for the answer. Just then Sefforn entered through the willow branches interrupting his train of thought.

"Cla...Shaltak," Sefforn caught himself, "Vaulnik's army is crossing the border near Festingraw," he announced.

Clavorn sat up quickly, "Say that again,"

"Vaulnik's army is on the move and they are crossing the border near Festingraw," his friend repeated.

"Who else knows about this?" he asked.

"Melkiar and Kevic," Sefforn answered, "It was Alcon who broke the news to us just a few moments ago down by the stream."

"Great! Have him and the others meet me here as soon as they can," he said rising and taking a drink of water from his oil skin bag, "Oh, and Seff..." he continued as Sefforn turned to leave, "Tell Alcon I'm going to want a full report of what he saw, but not to spread it around camp."

"No problem. Melkiar and I already told him not tell anyone until he has spoken with you. I figured you wouldn't want the camp in a stir till you had a plan."

"You figured correctly," Clavorn told him.

Sefforn left him, and Clavorn wondered how he was going to deal with Vaulnik and his men as he went about his business of readying himself for the morning. Running his hand through his hair, he looked about the tree. Not exactly the most ideal place to plan an attack, but it had served him so far. He went outside and down to the stream to wash up.

The ice cold water hit his face, forcing the last remnants of sleep from his body as he splashed it up onto himself. The cold clear water droplets trickled down his tan face and well-muscled chest, while the coolness of the fresh morning air awakened every fiber of his sinewy body. Clavorn looked up. The sun was just making its way over the tops of the trees. Its light dancing and playing upon the crystal clear waters of the little shallow river as it ran, journeying through the willows of Shyloran Forest.

He looked around the camp. There were many new recruits.

Are they ready for an all-out engagement with Vaulnik's troops?

Up till now they had only been fighting Vaulnik's outer forces. Men mainly involved in maintaining order, not in conquering. These soldiers who were on their way were different. As seasoned veterans of Vaulnik's many successful campaigns, they would be unlike any sort of solder these men had faced in the past. Ruthless, fearless, and relentless in a way none of them had seen before.

Now comes the real test. Will they pass?

Only the battle would tell. For now he could only hope that he and his men had taught them well. He splashed some more water on his face and walked back to the tree.

Upon entering it, he noticed some bread from the night before near a makeshift table and went over to help himself. It was stale, but it served its purpose in filling his belli before his men arrived. Ideas raged through his head. Festingraw was a mountain town that used to be quite beautiful, full of trees and wonderful flowering bushes and plants. The people there had been happy once.

Now it was full of despair. Its landscape desolate from the decimation Vaulnik had reeked upon it in his search for the Kraic stones. A city rumored on the edge of existence, its people fighting to hold on as the ground, now scraped free of its precious top soil, struggled to produce any life, let alone crops.

Clavorn wondered what havoc Vaulnik would make of the town on his way into Avivron with his men. He did not have to wonder long as Alcon along with Sefforn, Melkiar, and the other men of his inner council began to enter the tree and take their places. Clavorn took a drink from his oil skin bag and took his place amongst them.

"I suppose you all wonder why I have gathered you here," Clavorn began as he stood in front of them.

"We presume it has something to do with the news Alcon brought this morning," Kevic supplied from his seat nearest the tree trunk.

"Quite right Kevic," Clavorn replied, "Alcon will you please give us your full report and don't leave anything out."

"Are you sure, sir," Alcon began it was clear he was bit anxious about his information.

"Yes, we need to know exactly what is going on," he told him.

"Alright," Alcon continued, "I was patrolling our outer most perimeters on the mountains near Festingraw when I rounded a bend and saw them. At first they appeared as nothing more than a thin black line on the horizon. It was not until I looked through my dragonglass that I could clearly see them. From what I could tell they appeared to be fifteen thousand strong, all marching over the border."

"Had they come upon Festingraw yet?" Thalon asked.

"No. They looked like they were still a few days ride from there. At least that is how it appeared through my dragonglass. From where I was they were on the far outermost edge of the valley just before you enter the mountains on your way to Festingraw," he replied as he stood before them. The sunlight glinted off his blond ruffled hair as it filtered in through the wispy branches of the tree.

"Were they on foot, or on horses?" Clavorn asked as he paced about.

"From what I could see it appeared as if they were mostly on horses, though I did see a few on foot. Sir," Alcon told him as he turned to face Clavorn, "they did appear to be well armed though it was hard to tell for sure exactly how extensive their armament was from my vantage point."

"I think we can safely assume they were well armed. Vaulnik would not send his troops all the way out here unless they were. Go on," Clavorn told him waving him to continue.

"Did they have any Zoths with them," asked Falor before Alcon could open his mouth to resume his report.

"No. At least I didn't see any if they did," he told them.

"Believe me, son; you'd know if you'd seen a Zoth. Big ugly creatures, there's no missing a Zoth," a burly, middle-aged man, with graying dark hair named Yolondon told him from his place by the trunk of the great tree. He would know too. He had been in the Battle of Quantaris. And though he and Clavorn had never met before he joined his army, having fought in one of the other armies present there, he had witnessed firsthand the destructive capability of the Zoths.

"Well, thank the gods for small gifts," remarked Heffron an elderly old warrior, "I'll never forget the sight of those things. Not in all my years have I ever witnessed such ruthless, vile creatures." He too had witnessed the destructive power of the Zoths, for he had been at the Battle of Quantaris as well. So he was quite relieved to hear that, at least for the moment, they were not amongst Vaulnik's contingent. "Just thinking about them gives me a chill."

Both he and Yolondon had been amongst the men who had managed to make it out of Kazengor Castle and join Clavorn's army. Clavorn was glad to have both of them on his counsel. Their experience in The Dragon Wars made them invaluable assets on his council. It made no difference to him that they were not from Avivron. They were all in this war together.

"Yeah, I'll agree with that. Nasty creatures those Zoths. Anything that can decimate nearly the entire dragon population is not something I would want to be going up against, not yet anyway. We have too many new recruits. They'd just wind up as lunch," Clovak commented. The concern in his voice was unmistakable.

"I'll second that," Clavorn responded, "however, we cannot be sure. Could you tell who was leading his army?"

"No. I was too far away, but from what I could see through the dragonglass Vaulnik did not appear to be amongst them."

"Oh?" remarked Sayavic genuinely surprised by Alcon's report, "so you did not see Vaulnik?"

"No." repeated Alcon, "I mean, yes sir. At least as best as I could tell."

"I wonder why not?" Melkiar asked, taking a puff from his pipe as he considered the news.

"Probably because he does not expect us to be difficult to defeat," suggested Koron.

"But it is still possible he was there? You said you could not see who was leading the army," Clavorn inquired, wanting to be sure of his facts.

"Yes, this is true," Alcon replied, "They're still a bit of a ways off."

"Then how can you suggest that Vaulnik is not amongst them?" Sorenavik asked.

"Well, I didn't see his usual accompaniment, so I assumed that meant he was not with them."

Clavorn knew what that meant. Vaulnik was usually in the habit of traveling with several armed guard. They would have been on elaborately decorated war horses carrying his staff of colors, the great flag of black with its blood red dragon in the middle, while he rode in amongst them on his war horse. His men would have been well armed, armed enough to see from almost any distance. All his scouts had been briefed on this.

"For the moment let us assume that he is not with them," Clavorn interrupted, "Chances are he is not if what Alcon says is true. Our biggest real problem is not whether or not he is with them, but how we are going to defeat such a large army with the little amount of men we have. It is clear he thinks he can squash us with this army he has sent."

"And he is probably right," Melkiar put in, taking another puff on his pipe.

"Well, then it is our job to prove him wrong," Clavorn told them, glancing around at all the men seated about him.

"And how exactly are we going to do that with the number of soldiers we have? If you can even call some of them that. I just finished up with the training of many of them. They are still very green," Melkiar replied.

"Aye, I was working with some of them yesterday. They are coming along, but I'm not sure they are ready for this army that is on its way," Yolondon conceded.

"Well, that is what I brought you brilliantly minded men here for, to brainstorm," Clavorn announced with a sideways glance in Melkiar's direction.

"Oh, I was wondering what purpose we all served here," Sefforn put in to his friend, as he crossed his arms and leaned back on his root that was serving as a chair. Clavorn knew his friend well enough to know it was just friendly banter.

"How many days out from Festingraw were they?" Clavorn asked Alcon.

"Not sure, sir. But perhaps about three-four days ride maybe less," Alcon told him.

"Well, shall we get down to it gentlemen," Clavorn remarked, "Thank you, Alcon. You may go now, but stay close by. We may need you to answer some more questions as we go."

"Sure, no problem," he told him as he turned and left the tree but remained waiting as if on guard just outside it.

It was well into the late afternoon when Clavorn and his men finally emerged from the great willow tree. Alcon had been asked to enter the tree several times during the course of their discussion to clarify, or augment his report as they brainstormed over ideas on how best to deal with Vaulnik's invading forces. In the end, Clavorn and his men had to acquiesce to the idea of asking Sevzozak to add his troops to their forces. It appeared to be the only way they would have even a slim chance of defeating Vaulnik's army.

Fires of Life

"You know there is good chance he'll just abandon's us like he did before during the Battle of Salvarrook," Melkiar commented after everyone but Sefforn and he had left.

"Then we will have our betrayal," Clavorn replied simply.

"That is if we survive," Sefforn put in, "Cla... Shaltak, I think I will never get used to this damned name change!"

"I know," Melkiar put in with a puff on his pipe, "took us all a bit to get used to it and just when we do there'll be another I'm sure."

"Come on. Let's stick to the issue," Clavorn protested, as he finally sat down, resting his back against the ancient willow.

"What? You cannot blame us for the inconvenience," Sefforn put in.

"But I can for the sidetracking. Now you were saying..." Clavorn prompted.

"Let me think...Oh, don't you think it is better for us to try and defeat Vaulnik on our own?" asked Sefforn, suddenly serious again.

"Yes, I do, my friend," he answered. He already had the shell of a backup plan in mind, one, if pushed he truly considered his main plan. He doubted very much if Sevzozak would actually commit troops to this battle given his previous performance.

"Don't you think we need a backup plan?" Sefforn commented while Melkiar took another puff on his pipe.

"Yes. Yes I do," was all Clavorn said, as he stared out into the early evening light.

The sun was beginning to set behind the hills and the mountains behind Shyloran Forest. The gray light of twilight was beginning to filter into the ancient tree. Clavorn's voice was distant as he responded to his friends. His mind off wondering, refining what was fast becoming a real alternative. An eagle called out into the early evening sky. Nightfall was approaching.

Chapter 19

"Are you sure this is such a good idea?" Melkiar protested, as he and Clavorn trampled on, leading their horses through the dark densely packed forest, "Ouch! Damned trees! I mean...lovely trees."

Superstition had it that it was bad luck to curse the trees of such a dense old forest. Word was such a forest was usually inhabited by a dragon, and as such a curse upon the trees would, therefore incur the dragon's wrath. And though all but one dragon was rumored to still be alive, the idea of incurring any dragon's wrath still had its hold.

"Couldn't we do this in the daylight? No. Never mind. Don't answer that. That disguise of yours is probably best left for the moonlight."

"True," Clavorn responded, as he pushed back on a branch in front of him. He was not so sure how closely anyone would look at him after the incident in the castle, "And as for this being such a good idea...well I think we'll find that out soon enough, my friend."

"Just as I thought," Melkiar grumbled, "I do hope you have a plan for getting us out of there should this go badly."

"Think positive, my friend," Clavorn told him.

Positive. I'm not sure I can even feel that in this forest.

He hated going through Shaladorn Forest, but it was the best route to take them to where they were going. Shaladorn had been beautiful and lush before Vaulnik had arrived. Now, though while it was still dense, it had taken on a more sinister feel.

Deafeningly quiet. It put both Hawk and Melkiar's horse on high alert, to say nothing about himself, though he had no intention of letting on.

"Didn't I get us out of the castle safely?"

"Yeah, but I hate testing my luck twice," Melkiar replied carefully moving a branch out of his way as they trudged on through the thick forest, "Are we going to mount our horses here soon or are they just along for the ambiance?"

"Patience, my friend, we are just about there," Clavorn told him as a branch snapped under his feet, the sound reverberating throughout the wood.

A flap of wings told him he had scared off some nighttime bird or other. Whispers in the breeze echoed all around them and both men fell silent.

The moon was full as they carried on in silence making their way through the densely packed forest. Despite the moonlight the forest remained quite dark. Only a few brief silver patches could be seen dispersed throughout the heavily wooded terrain.

An owl hooted in the branches above them and then flew off. Here and there small rat-like animals seemed to scurry about the forest floor, but it was the trees that gave the place its real feel. They seemed unhappy, even angry. Their branches more twisted; their poses less artful, more angular. If a forest could be mad, this one was.

Every now and then they startled some small animal or bird. Clavorn was beginning to wonder if he should have taken an alternate route, but then there was none that did not involve the forest.

Rumor had it Shaladorn's dragon had given the trees the power to attack any who strayed there. The further they traveled the more he wondered at the rumor. Even the horses were becoming more edgy and he had to admit to sharing their sentiment.

"Easy boy," he told his horse in soft soothing tones as the animal danced next to him, "we're almost there."

"Are you sure? For I seem to recall hearing those very same words hours ago," Melkiar commented from behind him.

"I know," was all he replied.

However, it was as if the trees knew they were on a mission of some great importance, for they let them pass without incident.

Before long the forest gave way and opened up to reveal a devastating scene. Scattered skeletal remains of tall ancient trees, stumps, dispersed piles of dead branches and debris with barren open land devoid of life between it all greeted their eyes. An empty, cold, grave like atmosphere permeated the landscape which stretched out before them as they came out into the open.

"This is what we needed the horses for," Clavorn told his friend as they stepped out of the woods.

"I see," Melkiar remarked looking over the remains of what had once been a proud and crowded forest.

A brief moment of silence past between the two men as they stood there gazing upon the scene of decimation. Clavorn could feel a heavy weight enter his heart and then slowly begin to burn with rage as he viewed the devastated landscape before him. Every fiber of his being could feel the cry and pain of the forest that had once stood there, and he understood why the trees of Shaladorn were so angry. Hawk tossed his head and blew.

"Easy boy," he told his horse, trying to comfort the beast whose sentiment he could not only feel but understand.

"You know, now that I see this I feel *sooo* much better," Melkiar commented breaking the silence with his note of sarcasm.

"What do you mean?" Clavorn asked thinking he had an idea of what his friend was going to say but wanted to be sure.

"What do I mean? I mean look at this place. Besides the obvious horrific nature of the devastation here, which, that by itself is unnerving, not to mention anything else. We go from so dense we can hardly see, to so barren we are visible to all but the blind. That's what I mean."

"I know but..."

"Don't tell me. But there was no other way."

"Well, there wasn't," Clavorn protested defensively as he mounted his jet black steed with ease while Melkiar murmured some slight grumble and did the same.

The silver light from the full moon cast an eerie glow upon the apparently dead landscape as they traveled on in silence. In places felled remains of ancient trees and long dead trunks were the only sign of the great forest that had once lived there. A cold wind blew through the area so that Clavorn and Melkiar had to pull their cloaks about them. Once again silence was all that passed between them. Speaking seemed almost irreverent here.

Out of the corner of his eye Clavorn caught the shimmer of a lake ahead. The light from the moon sparkled and danced off its surface. A raven called from one of the many tall empty dead trees surrounding it, adding to the eerie grave like nature of the landscape. Suddenly, a cold wind came up driving the raven off his perch, while kicking up dust and debris which only contributed to the feeling of desolation that was inescapable here. Clavorn wondered if life would ever return to this part of the forest.

Down a hill they traveled and around the still and seemingly lifeless lake. Once known as Mirror Lake it had been the jewel in this corner of the land. Full of fish and fauna, its smooth calm waters had reflected the beauty of the land around it.

Now, however, it lay lifeless; its deep waters reflecting only the decimation and sorrow of the land surrounding it. Death Lake was its new name. Clavorn could hardly argue with its new nomenclature. It was said that any man who dared to drink from its waters died a most horrible death. He guessed that applied to any other living creatures as well, given the number of skeletal remains from other animals which littered the area.

A flap of wings was heard as they startled another raven from its perch. Melkiar glanced at Clavorn, but neither of them said a word as they rode on past. Stillness gripped the area. An unnatural tension seemed to surround the place. Clavorn was relieved when they had finally ridden past it, and he could sense that his friend was too.

"How much farther do we have to go?" Melkiar asked after they had traveled a fare distance beyond the lake.

"Not much farther," was all Clavorn answered as once again a mixture of anger and sadness welled up inside him.

Thoughts of the magnificent forest that had once been there filled his head. To him, to think that this land, raped as it now stood, was once a vibrant forest teaming with life pained him to his core. Rage once again began to burn within him; rage towards Vaulnik, rage for the greed of men. He would be glad when they were finally on the other side of this.

Soon they came upon a hillside where trees once again dominated, though not nearly as thickly as they had in the Forest of Shaladorn. However, as they came over the rise they could see there was a wide path cut through it. From its appearance one could tell the area had been deliberately cut. The faint remains of wagon wheel ruts in the now grassy path spoke of its well-traveled past. It did not take long for Melkiar to guess that this had once been a road used to transport the Kriac Stones Vaulnik cherished so much.

"I take it we are to meet them at Kisensgraw," Melkiar commented, quickly deducing where they were now heading.

Clavorn had not wanted to speak of it while they were still at camp, so they had set out without much discussion as to the exact location of the meet.

"Yes," he replied simply.

"I can hardly wait," Melkiar groused a bit sarcastically.

"I know. An abandoned town is not exactly my idea of a good meeting place either," Clavorn replied. He could definitely relate to Melkiar's sentiments.

"Oh really, I was beginning to wonder," Melkiar remarked, "You know it is rumored to be cursed."

"Well, then let us hope it only curses our enemy and not us," Clavorn told him.

He remembered hearing the rumors of a freak illness that had swept through the town killing most of its inhabitance shortly after the harvesting and processing of the Kriac Stones had begun. It was said, that the place had been cursed by the dragons for its disregard of nature, and the goddess Alhera. It was also believed to be the reason why there was still a forest in this area. Apparently, not even Vaulnik's men wanted to cut down the forest for fear of what might happen to them, though it did not seem to stop them from harvesting what Kriac Stones were easy to come by.

To Clavorn, Kisensgraw seemed an odd place for a meeting, but Almaik's messengers had been quite specific. He had hated the idea but had not wanted to tip his hand as to the knowledge of Almaik's previous treachery. After all, Shaltak was not to know of how Clavorn had fallen into his enemy's hands.

"Almaik wanted us to meet where he thought Vaulnik's spies would be less likely to find us," Clavorn went on to explain to his friend.

"Yeah, well the same goes for anyone else," Melkiar commented as they entered the forest.

Trees flanked them on either side as they made their way along the remains of the old road that led to the deserted village. Occasionally, a rustle could be heard in the woods as some animal scurried away frightened by their approach. Clavorn shared his friend's reservations. He knew all too well the trap they could be walking into.

Silence took the men again as they traveled on to Kisensgraw. It was not long before they could just see the outer walls of the once flourishing village through the tops of the trees. After the plague had spread through the town, most of those that had survived left for fear of further retribution from the dragons and the gods. It did not matter that most, if not all, the dragons were believed dead. Their spirits were still alleged to have the power to curse, or so the villagers thought. Vaulnik's men had had to coerce any remaining men to finish processing the Kriac Stones. But in the end it had failed and they had had to finish it themselves.

Suddenly, around a bend, the forest opened up and there, in front of them, stood the gray moss ridden stone wall of the little village of Kisensgraw. It was clear that time was eroding the remains of the abandoned town. A cold gust of wind blew sending a chill through both of them as they exited the wood.

Clavorn and Melkiar caught a glimpse of the village through a broken down section of the wall. Gray moonlight reflected off of the dilapidated hollow empty builds as they stood cold and vacant. Their dark mouths gaping open as if they were crying out to the night. A strange unearthly silence filled the air as they rode past on their horses.

Before long they arrived at the entrance to this apparently cursed village. More of those haunting buildings could be seen through the opening of the decaying wooden gate which at one time would have invited travelers in. Both men looked up as they rode up to the rotting gate of Kisensgraw, its wooden doors held unnaturally open. A raven was perched on the outer wall just above the gate as they pulled their horses up to its entrance.

CAW! CAW!

The two men exchanged glances. A cold breeze suddenly blew through the abandoned town, causing a door to creak and bang from the other side of the wall. The horses tossed their heads and refused to enter as they tried to encourage them forward.

"Easy boy," Clavorn told Hawk as he gave his equine friend a reassuring pat on the neck. He could not blame him for shying. The place was beginning to give him the creeps too.

Another chilly wind blew and sent shivers down his spine. Clavorn glanced up through the gray decrepit doors. Rotting wooden buildings with shudders and doors partially off their hinges greeted his eyes. Inside another raven could be seen perched atop a decaying thatched roof.

Clavorn sat up in his saddle and gently urged Hawk forward. Neither man spoke as they crossed the threshold of the village's gray desiccated gate with its broken dragon carvings staring ominously at them.

Melkiar glanced about warily as another gust of wind blew, sending wooden doors flapping and creaking in its wake. Dust swept up from the ground, swirling and blowing about, adding to the creepy nature of the abandoned empty ruins of this once thriving small village.

Fires of Life

"Cheerful, so when does our host arrive," Melkiar finally inquired as they continued to ride forward.

"How about now," a voice announced from above them in what had been the temple belfries.

Most of the buildings in the small town had been built from wood. The temple was no exception. Usually such a building was made of marble with glorious appointments of statues, silver, and stained glass. But while this had been a thriving village once, it had not been a terribly prosperous one. And though the temple did have some wonderfully carved wooden statues and heavy relief filled double doors to boast about, it was still a simple structure by comparison to those of its kind in more prosperous cities.

Wooden steps led up to a colonnade area where huge tree trunks supported the roof. The tops of the columns were carved so that they resembled heavily foliate trees. A relief carving showing Maltak and Altak returning life to the earth ran across the top of the inner wall of the colonnade where the two huge double doors now stood partially ajar. Large dragon heads adorned the corners of the roof, while their bodies and their wings swept together in an artful dance that formed the roof, and a portion of the pediment, culminating in the bell tower.

A graceful statue of Alhera rested between the dragons on the front of the pediment. Her long hair flowing out behind her while her dress clung to her body as it stood proudly in the face of an imaginary wind. At her feet were the remains of, what must have been, beautifully carved flowers. What had been in her hands was anyone's guess as both had been broken off. Only her elegant face and graceful body, adorned with a soft free flowing garment, remained.

The whole building would have been colorfully painted at one time. One could just imagine how beautiful it must have looked in its day, the center of village pride. However, time and lack of attention now showed vividly in the light of the moon. Its weathered haggard appearance did not escape notice as both Clavorn and Melkiar looked up.

Standing above them was Almaik dressed all in black, darning a heavy black cloak, with the remainder of a large old brass bell behind him. Its cracked and broken appearance seemed only to whisper down to the men below as to the nature of the kingdom they were trying to defend.

There were two other men with him. They stepped around from behind the remains of the bell, there cross bows in hand, the moonlight glinting off the swords at their sides. They too were dressed all in black.

Melkiar glanced at Clavorn and the two men exchanged looks. Clavorn was beginning to wonder if his friend's assessment of their situation might have been correct.

"So I see you have a flare for the dramatic," Clavorn commented as he looked up not wanting to let on to any of his doubts about their safety.

"It is nice to know someone who appreciates it," Almaik replied, "So how can I, or rather your king, be of service to the Great Shaltak?"

"He has need of your, or rather, our king's troops," Clavorn replied matter-of-factly.

"Oh, he does now," Almaik's sarcastic malevolent voice boomed down from the bell tower.

Clavorn wonder what had become of Almaik to turn him so malicious. Or was this his true self and his other nature a ruse? He could not decide as he looked upon the man who had betrayed him.

"But first I am forgetting myself, of whom do I have the pleasure of addressing this evening?"

The wind riffled through Almaik's dark hair as a gust blew through the town once again sending doors creaking, and shudders banging and flapping about. Melkiar's horse started at the sound, and he had to quickly rein him in.

"It is I, Mentak and this is Melkiar, my liege," Clavorn replied as he extended his hand in Melkiar's direction, "I trust you remember us."

"May I see some proof of this," Almaik requested, gesturing to them while he placed one hand on the hilt of his sword.

Clavorn lifted his hood. He had worn a similar cloak and disguise as he had on the night of the party at Escadora Castle, only this time his clothes were toned down, as would be befitting one who is traveling on a clandestine journey through the woods.

As Clavorn lifted his head to look into Almaik's face, the moonlight caught the gruesome puffy flesh. Its silver light reflected off the disgusting sight.

"I see that time has not changed your wounds any, my friend," Almaik commented, his voice undulating with suspicion.

"No, it has not, my liege. Nor is it likely too. I am told," Clavorn replied, hoping his answer would suffice.

The air had turned even colder since their arrival in the abandoned town. Now a chill suddenly threatened to send a shudder down Clavorn's spine. But then burning thoughts of defiance and revenge began to flow through him, and his chill passed relatively unnoticed to him.

"You may call me Almaik. I am satisfied that you are who you say you are. Please, be as you were," Almaik replied as he motioned for them to return to their previous state.

With that Clavorn proceeded to replace his hood as his horse shifted under him.

"Come, let us talk. I will meet you inside this lovely abandoned house of the gods," he told them, the sarcasm dripping noticeably from his voice as he waved his hand about.

Melkiar and Clavorn briefly exchanged glances before dismounting. As much as every fiber of Clavorn's being did not trust Almaik, he had to make it appear as if he did. He could only hope that Almaik would not betray them here. But then that was why he had not come as Shaltak. Instead, he posed only as one of his trusted inner circle, Mentak. As long as Almaik believed that he was Mentak, he believed they stood a chance.

Both Clavorn and Melkiar tied their horses up and began climbing the old steps to the temple. Occasionally, one of the steps would creek echoing throughout the vacant village, but neither of them let on as to the unnerving nature of their surroundings.

A cold breeze blew through the rotting wooden doors as they opened them to enter. Dust blew in from behind them. Cobwebs were everywhere. Both Melkiar and Clavorn had to brush them aside as they entered. Clavorn guessed that Almaik had entered by a back door judging by the undisturbed dust and grit on the wooden floor.

Bats flew about the high ceiling. A crunch of glass sounded beneath their feet as they stepped on the broken shards from the damaged stained glass windows that lined the little temple. Images of the gods peered down on them from what was left of the stain glass.

One image of the goddess Alhera caught Clavorn's eye briefly. Her soft face looked down on him as she rode Maltak through the sky, while her dark hair billowed out behind her as the dragon breathed the Fires of Life onto the earth.

"Welcome gentlemen," Almaik's voice startled Clavorn momentarily as he turned on his heels to face him, "Shall we talk and plan. Sorry about the theatrics, but I figured we would be less likely to be visited by Vaulnik's spies here. Please, sit," Almaik told them as he gestured to the dusty pew before them.

In front of them, at the end of the temple, in the back of the sanctuary, stood the remains of a large wooden statue of the goddess Alhera and her father Allethor and her mother Thelenor. Their flowing garments clinging to their bodies as a fictional wind blew into their faces; furling and undulating their hair. Behind them stood a huge wooden carving of the dragon Maltak, her eyes gouged out, no doubt, by Vaulnik's men. The statues were badly defaced not just from time, but presumably from the soldiers as they left, taking with them what little treasures there were adorning them. Oddly enough, however, there was still a simple elegance about them that neither time nor defacement could take away.

As he briefly stared on, Clavorn could not help but notice how artfully the wings of Maltak blended into the wall of the temple, and helped to support the structure. All while, what once must have been beautifully colored stained glass filled the empty spaces of the wall which the great statue was so cleverly supporting, with its partially outstretched dragon's wings. It pained him as he tried to imagine what the statues must have looked like in their prime.

"So tell me, why does the Great Shaltak need the king's troops, and why has he not come himself?" Almaik began once they were all seated. All that is, except for the two guards Almaik had brought with him. They appeared to be standing watch from the tower above them.

Melkiar glanced up. What was left of the huge bell hung down above them. Occasionally, a bat flew about the rafters. Clavorn guessed he must have more men about outside the city.

"Because, my liege. I mean Almaik," Clavorn corrected himself as he began, trying to refocus his mind away from their surroundings and back to his task at hand, "Vaulnik has invaded Avivron near the border with fifteen thousand soldiers. Shaltak fears he does not have enough men to adequately repel them. He is, therefore, graciously requesting the assistance of our king. I was told to inform you that he would do so in person, but for the need to prepare his troops. He hopes that your highness will forgive him for not coming in person given the circumstances."

"I see. Well, of course, we shall forgive the Great Shaltak," sarcasm dripped once more from Almaik's lips as he spoke. Clearly, Almaik held Shaltak in some distain, "but we would certainly appreciate his appearance sometime, so that we may properly thank him."

"Certainly, my lord," Clavorn responded with deference, knowing full well what kind of gratitude he intended to bestow, "and I can assure you that were it not for the direness of the situation he would have appeared before you himself."

"Can you now. Well then, we shall see won't we," again the sarcasm continuing to ooze fourth from Almaik's lips.

Clavorn wanted to reach for his sword, but he knew he needed him to betray his country before he could openly kill him.

"As for sending troops to assist," Almaik continued, "this does pose a predicament, for you see, if I send the king's troops to help Shaltak defend Avivron who shall protect her king?"

"The king need not send any more troops than he can spare. But any that he can spare would be greatly appreciated by Shaltak, and the people of Avivron," Clavorn told him emphasizing the last portion of his phrase while trying to be as diplomatic as possible. This was proving to be more difficult than it appeared given the fact that every fiber of his being wanted to shout a different response.

"I see. Well, I cannot promise, but I shall see what I can do. However, meet me here in three days' time and you shall have your answer. Come just the two of you as you are tonight so that my men shall know you," Almaik told them offhandedly as he rose and made to leave.

Clavorn and Melkiar rose as well.

"My liege, Almaik, if I may, why can you not give an answer tonight? In three days' time Vaulnik's men will most likely be bearing down on us, and we may not be able to properly defend his majesty's kingdom," Clavorn protested.

He needed him to commit to troops, and he needed him to do it tonight. He had not come all this way for a half answer.

"I see. That would be a problem," Almaik paused, and Clavorn glanced at Melkiar who had taken a seat in a pew in front of his, "But I still need time to discuss this with the king. No. I still stand by the three days." Almaik turned again to leave without waiting for a response.

"My lord," Clavorn implored, raising his voice so as to stop Almaik in his tracks, "then your king risks being perceived as abandoning his people to the fates. Could this not be seen as abdicating his responsibilities?"

Almaik turned on him, "How dare you!" he cried through his teeth as he rushed forward coming face to face with Clavorn.

"It is easy, my lord," Clavorn replied calmly, "Is it not the king's responsibility to defend his people?"

"Yes," replied Almaik as he glared at Clavorn, his apparent agitation subsiding a bit at Clavorn's reply, "However, the king did task Shaltak to do so."

"Pardon me, my lord, for stating this, but it was Clavorn who began this rebellion and Shaltak who has taken up its cause. I understand that now our good king wishes him to finish this task, and he will, my lord, but if the king refuses his request for adequate reinforcements, then it could be seen as an abdication of his responsibility to defend the people of Avivron. And is it not his responsibility to do so to the best of *his* abilities?"

"Yes," again was the answer by Almaik, clearly reluctantly retreating from his hostility.

"Then how can you let your king down by not committing to help Shaltak in this time of his country's most urgent need," Clavorn continued to argue.

Almaik paused as he considered his words.

"Fine," he answered tersely, "you will have your troops, but I will want to know what Shaltak's plans are for retaliation when you return," Almaik informed him.

"My lord?"

"Yes, I cannot send troops in to fight a battle I have not approved the plans for, and besides my generals need to know where they will be deployed," Almaik told him.

"I will inform Shaltak," Clavorn told him, "However, there may not be time for much debate, or approval. Vaulnik's men are moving fast. I know Shaltak was hoping for a response tonight. This will delay his ability to attack. He will need an idea of how many men in order to plan his offensive.

"Nevertheless, if you could give me a rough idea of how many soldiers King Sevzozak might be able to send, then I could inform Shaltak of how many men he might be able to expect. Thus, enabling him to provide you with the information you request. Though I still do not believe there will be time for approval. His majesty may just have to trust in Shaltak's abilities."

"Yes, well..." Clavorn could tell he had clearly unnerved the prince, "I suppose this is a sound argument. Let me think a moment," There was a brief pause as Almaik appeared to reflect on Clavorn's response. Melkiar glanced at him and the two exchanged looks, "I think we could spar two legions."

"Are you sure?" Clavorn replied, "I should think it would not take more than two legions to defend the King's castle. Surely, the King would want to send more troops to defend his people."

He could sense Almaik's anger rising again, and he knew he was unsettling him. Almaik eyed him.

"I see why Shaltak has sent you Mentak," he commented surveying him, "Very well then, as you have so eloquently pointed out, the King would love to send as many of his troops as possible to defend his people. Shall we say five legions then?"

"My lord, your generosity knows no bounds. I am sure Shaltak would be grateful to your liege," Clavorn told him as he bowed his head with apparent gratitude.

"Good. Then till three days, or should I say three night's time then," Almaik replied abruptly, turning once again to leave.

"However, may I entreat your highness to consider a lesser time frame say one night's time," Clavorn called after him.

Almaik turned back clearly annoyed, "Why I would think Shaltak would need more time to consider his options?"

"No, my lord. I know he would want to move fast before Vaulnik can gain much of a foothold on our land," Clavorn responded confidently.

There was a pause as Almaik again eyed Clavorn, then raising one eyebrow he said, "Fine, so be it. But it will be Shaltak's head if

Fires of Life

the king loses his troops to a poorly planned offensive," and with that he turned on his heels and left as a large gust of wind blew outside the temple, throwing open its doors, and sending a shower of debris and leaves inside.

Both Melkiar and Clavorn watched the dark figure of Almaik descend into the murky shadows at the rear of the sanctuary. Clavorn guessed that there must be an opening in the back of building through which their host had availed himself of.

The creepy nature of the small temple had not changed any during their brief conversation with Almaik. If anything it seemed to only have heightened its ominous feeling. Clavorn took a brief glance up before leaving as bats flew about the ceiling with the rush of another gust of wind.

He turned to go. Both he and Melkiar began to make their way out. Suddenly, a loud crash could be heard as the sound of braking glass echoed throughout the temple. Both Clavorn and Melkiar ducked as a shower of broken glass rained down upon them.

Clavorn lifted his head and looked in the direction the fallen shards had come from. He could see the moon shining in through the window above them. It was the window he had seen earlier; the window in which Alhera had been looking down upon them as she rode Maltak. Now, only the moon could be glimpsed shining into the temple where the goddess's face had once been.

Chapter 20

All was quiet in the camp that night when they returned and handed their horses off to one of the young men on duty. The moon's glow still fell across the trees and stream that flowed through the forest, its silver light giving a surreal feeling to the landscape. Melkiar said his goodnights and Clavorn did the same. Back at the tree he removed his disguise, once again letting the horrid flesh which had been attached to his face burn in the remnants of the evening fire.

Dropping the cloth filled with tar from his face in the smoldering fire, he turned and stepped outside. The return journey had taken sometime because they had wanted to be sure Almaik did not have anyone following them. It would not belong before the moon set and the sun rose. With the exception of those on watch all were asleep. Clavorn walked to edge of camp and stood a moment observing; the upcoming battle weighing heavily on his mind.

Suddenly, an arrow crossed his path and lodged itself in a tree next to him. The act snapped him out of his musings as another arrow flew past him and lodged itself squarely in the same place as the first, only this time there was a note attached. Clavorn snatched the note from the arrow and read it.

Find the dragon.

"Great! How am I to find a dragon when I have a war to plan?" Clavorn almost shouted in exasperation.

"Simple, you look for it at night."

Clavorn nearly jumped out of his skin as he whirled around. There facing him was her, dressed as usual. Her eyes the only real thing he could recognize.

"Dragon curses woman! Are you trying to kill me?!"

"No. I am trying to save you and this country," she replied calmly her green catlike eyes staring into his.

"Well, you could have fooled me a moment ago," he told her, "Besides, if I try to find that dragon at night, how am I going to be up for this war. I thought you said I needed to find a 'worthy man?'"

"I did."

"Well, it might save time if you enlightened me as to who the 'worthy' fellow is."

"It might," she replied as she turned and wondered off into the forest.

Exasperated, Clavorn followed her. Twigs snapped under his feet as he tried to keep pace with her.

"So do you mind letting me in on who it is," he inquired of her as trudged on behind her.

"The dragon is close," she told him as she turned briefly to face him before turning once more into the woods.

"Well, if it is so close, why don't *you* find it?" he protested.

"Because I am not the one who has to find it," she told him as she brushed a branch aside which nearly hit him in the face as it swung back when she let go. Catching it, he moved it aside and kept following.

"I know. I know; a 'worthy man.' You mind telling me who it is."

I really don't have time for this.

Suddenly, she stopped, turned, and faced him. "You really don't have a clue do you?"

"No. Not really," he replied as he halted dead in his tracks, "If you haven't noticed, I've been a bit busy fighting a war. And now with Vaulnik's army invading…"

"That is why you need the dragon," she interrupted

"Terrific! But how am I supposed to *do* that when I don't even know who it is you want me to send on this mission. I thought I had already sent them."

He had a feeling the last dragon might be needed in order to win the war, but he had not been sure, not till she confirmed his suspicions. Now, with fifteen thousand of Vaulnik's men on their way, it seemed he had little time for such indulgences.

Doesn't she get it? There is no time.

"What more do you want?"

"You will need the dragon in order to succeed. If you want to win this war, it is your only hope."

"Great!" he exclaimed as ran a hand through his hair in exasperation, "I still need to know who to send."

"Think Clavorn. You know him well," she stared deep into his eyes and for a brief moment he thought he understood.

"No. You cannot mean…"

"Yes, Clavorn, it is you," she told him.

"Why? I thought you said only a 'worthy man' can find it. What makes you think I'm that *worthy* man? Why can't it just as easily be someone else? What is it about *me* that is so special? I refuse to believe I am the only one worthy of the job."

"Because that is the way it must be," she told him "Haven't you figured that out yet? Haven't you had the dream yet?"

He stared at her.

How does she know about that? Could she be…

"No, what dream?" he heard himself say, and decided it was because he did not want to let on that he had.

At his response she waltzed up to him, coming within inches of his face and looked him squarely in the eyes.

"Well, maybe I have, but what does that prove? I still don't understand why it has to be that way. If all we need is the dragon, then what does it matter who finds it?"

"It matters plenty," she told him, "The dragon will not follow just anyone. It can only be someone pure of intention, someone with a worthy heart."

"But how do you know that is me? Couldn't there be someone else, say… you, for example?" he argued. He just could not accept that he was the one who had to find the dragon, least of all because of some dream. Wasn't that for men far worthier than him?

"No!" she turned on him, her eyes intense, "No. If you are to lead these people to victory, then it must be you and only you."

"Question," he asked, relaxing in his posture.

"Yes," she replied as she turned to resume their journey through the forest with him following after her.

"Is it just because you want *me* to lead these people that you are so insistent that I find the dragon? Is that the real reason it must be me?" he inquired of her, feeling as if that had to be the reason she was so intent on him finding the dragon. The other was just far too fantastical to be believable.

"No," she replied, stopping in a small thicket surrounded by dense forest. The light of the moon reflected off her cloak and scarf making it difficult to see her eyes for a moment. "Not anyone can find it." She gestured about her. Her exasperation with him was clear. "The dragon would never reveal itself for Vaulnik, or Sevzozak for instance, these men are not worthy. Not even if they possessed the Stone of Maltak," she continued, "They have no love for the earth. Their only wish is power. Their only desire greed. They care nothing for the land or the living." She came closer to him, her eyes looking deeply into his. "But Clavorn, you do."

"How do you know that?" he asked, searching her eyes, "I may be just like these men once power comes to me. How can you be so sure?"

"I just am," she replied, turning away.

There was a brief pause in the conversation before she abruptly turned back to face him. Clavorn stopped as he came up short in front of her.

"I cannot tell you exactly how I know. I just do. You'll just have to trust me," she told him, pausing for a second before she continued. Her eyes penetrating his soul, "Besides, have no fear. If you turn out to be just like them, I'll run you through."

"Oh, that's comforting," he replied as she turned to leave.

Clavorn eyed her fading form intently, but something in her voice told him she might be right, though his head still refused to totally accept it.

"Okay, let's say for argument sake that I believe you. Which I am not sure I do. How do I go about finding this dragon?"

"You already know where it lives. You've seen it. Search with your heart and you will find it," she told him, turning and coming close to him again.

"But don't I need the Stone of Maltak?" he protested.

"No," she replied.

"Why? No. Wait. Don't answer that. My heart will tell this dragon that I am the one," he replied with a mixture of sarcasm and exasperation as he turned and walked away from her a few steps.

"Yes, but you will need this," and with that he turned to face her. Clavorn looked down as she handed him a small light blue green stone that seemed to glow for a brief moment as she passed it to him.

"What is this?" he asked, looking from it to her.

"It is a small shard found in the very same place in which they discovered the Stone of Maltak. It has been kept though out the ages by the Dragon Witches' Grand Mother, and has been a very guarded secret. Tell no one," she informed him.

"I won't," he replied, staring into her eyes. They were so beautiful, and beguiling, "I was right you know. You are a Dragon Witch," he announced his dark brown eyes dancing.

"No, but I was given this stone by one," she told him.

"The Grand Mother I suppose," he replied. He had caught her. She was as he supposed.

"You read too much into these things," she said, avoiding his eyes, "Now just take it. It will begin to glow when you are close to the dragon."

Clavorn looked down at the stone in his hand. The moonlight seemed to dance inside it as he turned it over in his hands.

"Remember, you cannot win against Vaulnik until you find the dragon," she told him as he continued to gaze at the remarkable little shard in his hand. "Follow your heart."

"Yeah, but..." he looked up and she was gone. Just like mist and smoke there was no sign of her. He turned and searched the area with his eyes, but he knew he would never find her.

Chapter 21

"Great!" he exclaimed, "You know I am really starting to tire of these disappearing acts!" he shouted into the forest. But not a sound was heard in reply. Frustrated and overwhelmed, he started his journey home.

"Must find the dragon. Must find the dragon. But Where?!" he muttered to himself. Then he stopped in his tracks, "The dragon is close she said," he remarked again to himself as he paused in thought.

Clavorn looked down at the stone he held in his hand. The light dancing inside it seemed to hint at the promise of a dragon.

But where?

There had been his dream. If he could just remember where he had seen that mountainside? He stood in thought as he tried desperately to remember where he had seen it. But try as he might its whereabouts still eluded him. Clavorn continued to examine the stone as if by examining it, it would somehow reveal the location of the dragon, the legendary last dragon, Viszerak.

'Follow your heart.'

Her words echoed in his mind. Clavorn closed his eyes and tried to search his heart with every fiber of his being. Her green eyes came clearly into vision as he calmed his mind, and then a picture of a dragon came into view. It appeared to be inside a cave, suddenly his mind switched to the mountainside. He was riding his horse ... darkness, nothing but darkness.

Clavorn opened his eyes. Frustration dominated his thoughts.

Why can I not remember where that mountain side is?

He looked around him for a clue, anything that would trigger a thought, a feeling, a hint as to the direction he needed to go, but nothing came to mind. It all looked the same, dense forest.

"I have no time for a dragon quest now," he muttered in frustration as he trudged off through the woods on his way back to camp. "This could take days. What am I thinking? Need a dragon..."

He pushed a branch out of his way in irritation as he pocketed the little stone. "Well, if I do. It surely won't be found tonight."

Another step, he looked up. He could see the outer reaches of his camp and the sun beginning to rise over the mountains in the distance.

Chapter 22

"So here we are again," Melkiar observed.

Clouds mingled with the wind to add an extra chill to the night air. The little village seemed even less inviting tonight without the glow of the moon; if that was even possible.

"Yes, my friend," he replied as they began to make their way into the small abandoned town.

"And I thought it was cheery the *last* time we were here," Melkiar commented sarcastically as they crossed the threshold into the village.

A gust of wind set the doors and windows creaking and banging as a raven started from its perch, calling out as it did so. The clouds that swirled overhead threatened to poor down upon them. It was easy to envision a curse upon the sad little village.

"I hope that is not a sign," he mumbled under his breath to Clavorn.

"Let us hope that if it is, that it is for them and not us," Clavorn mumbled back.

Leaves and dust blew about as the wind continued to kick up. A door slammed shut and creaked open again. Hawk raised his head.

"Easy boy," he said as he patted his horse on the neck, "It's just the wind."

But as much as Clavorn tried to calm his horse he could tell that the beast just did not believe that everything was fine. He was not sure if he did either.

Other than the wind, and the creaking and banging of windows and doors, the town was eerily quiet. Clavorn and Melkiar exchanged glances as they continued on their way into the village. It felt as if the dead still lingered in amongst the ruins watching, warning. Clouds continued to swirl overhead, a bolt of lightning flashed.

CRACK!

Fires of Life

Thunder crashed overhead. Clavorn and Melkiar exchanged glances once more as they rode forward, their horses clearly nervous about their surroundings.

"I thought you would never arrive," a voice called down to them from the belfries of the little temple.

"Well, here we are," Clavorn announced as he glanced up at Almaik.

As before, Almaik was dressed all in black. His cloak billowing out behind him in the wind as the two guards who were with him once again came from around the damaged bell to stand beside him.

"I see," Almaik remarked, "I do presume I have the same pleasure of addressing Mentak and… Melkiar is it?"

"Yes, my liege. You do," Clavorn responded.

He could tell by the way Melkiar shifted in his saddle that his friend's blood was beginning to boil, Almaik's condescending voice grating at him. He only hoped Melkiar could contain his fiery nature.

"Good, then shall we meet as we did before, inside this quaint little temple," Almaik continued his voice much as it had been the other night, dripping with both sarcasm and hypocrisy as he gestured about him.

"Certainly," Clavorn replied and he began to dismount.

"Always such a jovial fellow of late isn't he?" Melkiar whispered as he came up to stand beside Clavorn, the sarcasm unmistakable in his voice.

"I agree," Clavorn whisper back as he turned to enter the building, "Come on, my friend. We have a date with Zagnor. Remember?"

"How could I forget?" Melkiar replied with continued hushed sarcasm.

Once again the heavy wooden doors creaked open as they pushed them aside to enter. Clavorn could see from the remnants of dust, dirt, and glass on the floor that no one but them had been in the little temple since their last visit. A good sign as far as Clavorn was concerned, but he still did not trust Almaik. In fact, he wondered how he ever had. But back then he had not seemed like the man he presented himself to be today.

"Well, do you have the plans for me?" Almaik asked as he appeared out of the shadows from the rear of the sanctuary.

"I do, my lord," Clavorn replied as both he and Melkiar ventured further in.

"Remember, please do call me Almaik. We are not in a formal setting here. Let us not stand on pretenses shall we." Almaik's voice grated at Clavorn. He was sure the same was true for his companion as well.

"I beg your pardon Almaik," Clavorn replied, wanting to choke on the words as he gave a brief bow of his head, "Here are the plans," he told him as they met up, handing him a dried roll of animal skin neatly tied with a leather string.

"May I?" Almaik asked as he took the scroll.

"Certainly," Clavorn replied and gestured for Almaik to open it.

Almaik untied and unrolled the scroll, reading it quickly. Fortunately, Clavorn had had the presence of mind to have Sefforn write down his attack plans. He did not want to risk Almaik recognizing his handwriting.

"So what do you think?" Clavorn asked after a few moments of silence while the prince read.

"I think it all looks in order. I shall study it further. If there are any changes, I shall send a messenger to inform Shaltak on the field of battle," he replied rolling up the dried animal skin and retying it with the leather tie. "You have served Shaltak well. Tell him my troops will meet up with him at the location designated here, on the time he has requested," he told them. Then eyeing Clavorn, "I would like to offer you a place in my court once this is over."

"Sire?"

"Well, that is provided you live," Almaik replied, returning to his usual doubled edged speech. "Don't worry. I do wish us all the best of luck. May the gods be with us," he remarked as he turned, gesturing about him as if to invoke the gods and goddesses of the humble temple, although it was clearly not meant to be a pious comment, only to appear as one.

"Yes. May Allethor, Thelenor, and Alhera grant us victory," Clavorn replied loudly at Almaik's receding form. His dark figure fading into the shadows like some horrible apparition as it departs into the night.

"Did he just offer you what I think he offered you?" Melkiar asked once it was clear Almaik was gone.

"Yes. I think he did," Clavorn replied slightly surprised, "Guess our little ruse is working so far."

"Umf," Melkiar replied blowing a hair out of his face, "If we can trust what took place here."

"Too true, my friend. Too true."

Once again a cold breeze blew in through the temple doors ushering in a wave of dust and debris. Clavorn glanced about. The stained glass windows were all dark this evening, as were the faces of the statues that remained scattered about. His eyes paused on the face of the statue of Alhera at the front of the temple. Cobwebs billowed in the breeze as bats flew about the belfries.

Do I see sadness in her eyes? No. It's probably just my imagination. A trick of the light.

"Come on," Melkiar urged, "Let's go home."

Clavorn searched the pains for the picture of Alhera and Maltak. But without the moon all the windows remained dark. Despite the obvious hindrance to finding what he was looking for, his eyes continue to search the damaged depictions. Then he remembered that with her face gone, Maltak was all that remained.

He continued to comb the stain glass windows above them. Then, just as he was about to give up, he saw it, the face of Maltak, lit briefly by a flicker of moonlight. Her red dragon eyes stared into his, searing his soul. Then they were gone; darkened once more by the lack of light as clouds smothered the brief sliver of silver light which had given them life.

"I'm with you," Clavorn replied to Melkiar as he turned to leave; leaving behind the darkened image of the dragon Maltak and her faceless goddess Alhera.

The two men walked out of the temple, only glancing back briefly once they had mounted their horses, before departing for their encampment. The breeze blew coolly behind them as leaves, dust, and dirt kicked up into the air. Clouds swirled and thunder cracked in the sky above them while sounds of creaking and banging were heard as they began to put some distance between themselves and the unnatural village.

Chapter 23

Mist and shadow filled his vision as an arrow pierced a tree.

"You must find the dragon," he heard her voice say as an image of her eyes came into view through the fog.

Suddenly, Alhera came riding Maltak through the mist while Maltak breathed fire. Then an image of a larger dark dragon came into view. The two confronted one another fading into the haze. All of sudden the dark dragon flew in front of him breathing fire and flames upon the land. Screams were heard in his head, loud screams. The dragon vanished. Alhera was gone. Maltak was gone and all was quiet. A field lay in front of him. Moans and groans of men filled the air about him.

"You must find the dragon."

Her face with her green eyes came into view once more as the words rung out in his mind, then it changed and all he saw was Alhera. Light shined behind her as she walked the field of battle; horses following her.

Suddenly, Maltak's face crashed through the image, her deep red eyes burning into his soul as she flew through him. He turned and the image changed. A mountainside came into view. The same mountainside he had seen before. At first it was just as before, glorious with flowers everywhere and full of life, then suddenly it changed to charred ruins. As he moved closer, he could smell the putrid scent of burning dragon flesh.

Clavorn woke with a start. She was right. He had to find the dragon, but how? He was leaving for battle in the morning. He sat up and ran his hand through his dark hair. Where had he seen that mountainside? Clavorn rose and went over to his oil skin bag and drank a swig of water. The thought would not leave his mind.

Why could she not just take me to the dragon? Probably because there is some purpose to the actual act of finding the dragon myself.

Though, try as he might the reason for this eluded him.

Grabbing at a pouch about his neck, he stepped outside. He had placed the stone inside the pouch for safe keeping. Now he wanted to reassure himself of its presence.

The moon was still up. He could see it now for the clouds had dissipated from earlier in the evening. By its position he deduced he had little time before dawn. He walked to the edge of camp and paused at the stream that flowed through it. The willow branches swayed in the gentle breeze as Clavorn tried again to remember where he had seen that mountainside.

'Follow your heart.'

He heard her say in his mind's eye as he closed his eyes to splash water on his face.

"Right and how am I supposed to do that?" he spoke out loud to himself in an exasperated tone as he wiped away the icy droplets with his hand.

"How are you supposed to do what?" Sefforn asked as he came up from behind his friend.

"Oh, nothing really. Just trying to find something," he replied a little embarrassed.

"Well, if that something is love, it shouldn't be too hard for a guy like you to find," Sefforn commented with a twinkle in his eye.

"Oh, and exactly how do you propose I do that in a camp like this with no women?"

"Simple," Sefforn replied with a cocky mischievous grin, "We invite them. Now, come on. Let's get some breakfast," he continued, gesturing for Clavorn to follow.

"But..."

"But there are no women up yet," Sefforn remarked jokingly, "Oh, Yeah, in fact there are no women in camp period, as you have already pointed out. Don't worry. I know a good cook. Come on. The sun will be up soon and we'll have to ready the men. You can chase damsels in distress another evening." His friend remarked with an inviting smile, "Besides, I hear the sound of roasting rabbit. Don't you?"

Fires of Life

"No, I have to find...," he could not just tell him.

How do you explain that some strange woman, who broke you out of the tower dungeon, is telling you that you need to find a dragon before going into battle? A battle that you are about to leave for on this very morning.

"Well, I'm sure whatever it is can wait..."

"No, I..."

"Look, I've got roasting rabbit on in my quarters and it is saying you cannot go into battle without a solid meal. Now, come on."

There was no getting around Sefforn once he put his mind to something. Like it or not he was going into battle without the dragon, at least for the moment anyway.

Oh well, perhaps it's just a lot of superstitious nonsense anyway; he rationalized, trying to calm the warning bells that were ringing in his head.

Besides, there is no way I'm going be able to find it before morning, judging by how close it is to dawn anyway.

Another mental placation and he knew it. But in his mind he just could not see how he was going to accomplish both; leading his men into battle and finding an elusive dragon. As a result, leading his men into battle won.

"Alright, you twisted my arm. So where did you say this roasted rabbit was anyway?" he asked, after arriving at what he thought was the best decision given the circumstances.

"At my place, where else," remarked his childhood friend with a huge smile, hands outstretched gesturing to himself like a peacock.

Clavorn smiled, "You are insufferable you know."

"I know. But what would you do without me?"

The two men made their way across camp to Sefforn's tree. Huddled against the back drop of the dark forest stood a robed figure; then it was gone.

Chapter 24

Sunlight rose and the camp was all a buzz. All around men were preparing their horses, preparing themselves, readying their armor, their swords, their bows. The whole place was a stir of activity.

Despite the delicious nature of Sefforn's roasted rabbit, Clavorn could not help but have a conflicted heart as he left his childhood friend's quarters for his own in the great tree. He had failed to acquire the dragon, yet there had been no time. How was he to search for a dragon with Vaulnik's men invading their boarders?

No.

So it was with a heavy heart that he began his preparations that morning, despite his friend's best attempts to cheer him up. There was no one in the tree with him as he entered and set about gathering his provisions. Just the noises from the outside as the men went about readying themselves to leave for battle.

Clavorn went over to the tree trunk and picked up his saddle bags to fill them. Taking them over to a large root that was serving as a sort of makeshift table; he set them down and began to gather his supplies.

"You still need the dragon."

"Yeah, well there's no time. I'll just have to go to battle without it," he heard himself say off handedly as he went about his tasks half feeling as if he was speaking out loud to a voice in his head.

Suddenly, a knife came down between his hands as he was placing a shirt in his bag, logging itself in the root below.

"What the…"

"You will need that dragon," she repeated intensely as his eyes met hers. Fire raged in her green eyes; fire like a dragon.

"Well, there's no time. In case you haven't noticed I have a war to wage and a battle to fight," he replied exasperatedly as he returned to his task at hand.

In his heart he knew she was right. His conscious hammered in his head like a drum that would not stop beating.

"I know. That's why you need the dragon," she told him, dislodging the knife and placing it back in the sheath at her side.

"I have no time for a dragon quest now. Vaulnik's men are bearing down on us as we speak."

"Precisely," she told him. He looked at her, "No time to waste running after Vaulnik's troops who will kill you and your men. You must have the dragon if you are to win."

"I can't just leave them now! They need me," he could not contain himself any longer.

How am I to be in two places at the same time?

"If you don't leave them, they will die and you will fail," she told him. "Better they stay here without you and wait till your return, than be slaughtered on the field of battle. With the dragon you will be in a much better position to fight."

"Provided I find the creature before he wipes out who knows how many villages along the way. No. That is just not acceptable."

"Neither is failure."

He stared at her and for a moment there was a brief pause. Silence gripped the air as the rays of light streamed in through the gently swaying branches of the old tree.

She's right and you know it. No. He has to be stopped. But what if you really do need that dragon? If you fail...

"Then I'm coming with you," she announced, breaking into his thoughts.

"Oh, no you're not," he told her emphatically as he returned to his preparations, "I have enough to worry about without having a *woman* to concern myself with."

"Oh, now I'm a *woman*. Hasn't it occurred to you that I have done quite well on my own? Thank you very much. Besides, *I* am the one who broke *you* out of Vaulnik's dungeon." She paused briefly, "You are going to need me."

"I doubt that," he replied sheathing his sword. His mind did not want to accept what his heart was screaming, "I have fought numerous battles without your help. I can fight this one too."

"Is that so?"

"Yes! Now, if you don't mind, I have preparations to complete, so…"

"Who are you talking to?" Sefforn asked as he entered Clavorn's willow, "or rather should I say arguing with."

Clavorn looked around. She was gone just like always. He was beginning to wonder if he was losing his mind, or if she really was a ghost. But then the stone around his neck suggested her reality.

"Oh, ahh, no one, just myself it seems," he replied awkwardly as he checked his quiver. "So what brings you here?"

"Not much. I was walking past and well…"

He did not need to say anymore for Clavorn to understand why he was there.

"Say, nice job getting job getting Almaik to commit some of the king's men," Sefforn continued after a brief moment of silence.

"Yeah, well I'm not holding my breath," Clavorn told him, "My gut is telling me he has no real intention of coming to our aid."

"Well, still…"

"Still, nothing," he interrupted his friend as he leaned on his bow for a moment, "I know this could be the thing we could use over his head if he fails us. But we have to survive it first. Anyway I've been mulling over a backup up plan should we need it."

"I know. You always have one."

Sefforn's words hung in his mind as he finished assembling his provisions. Still, he could not shake the niggling feeling that she was right. He needed that dragon.

But how?

"You want me to bring Hawk around?" Sefforn asked when he was about finished.

"Sure. Why not? Once he and all the men are ready we will break camp. Spread the word," he told him.

"No problem," Sefforn replied as he turned and left to find Clavorn's mount.

Clavorn glanced about the interior of the tree. The huge spreading branches of the magnificent old giant swayed. Their dangling boughs with their adornment of leaves moved gracefully to rhythm of the gentle breeze. Rays of sunlight passed through them, highlighting the interior. The effect was quiet peaceful which contrasted sharply with the day's task. War was never a pretty sight and her words plagued his thoughts.

Am I rushing into battle? Do I really need that dragon?

The memory of the carnage he had seen in his dream haunted him as he glanced around the tree, but there was no sign of her. A moment later Melkiar entered.

"So, I see you are about ready," he commented.

"Yes. How's morale?" Clavorn inquired, trying to turn his attention away from the woman who had invaded his space.

"High, but uneasy. It was good you brought them news of Sevzozak's men, though I still doubt the truth of their intentions."

"Me too, my friend, me too, but that's what a backup plan is for right?" Clavorn replied as he clamped his hand on his friend's shoulder to reassure him. Or was it himself?

"True," Melkiar remarked, though from the tone of his voice it was clear that it did not seem to totally satisfy his naturally pessimistic friend. And if truth be told, he was not sure it totally satisfied him either.

At that moment Sefforn showed up, holding Hawk on his lead.

"Ahh, Thank you, my friend. That should help expedite things a bit," he told his childhood friend as he took hold of Hawk's lead and began to stroke his forelock. "Are the men about ready to depart?"

"Yes, though the new ones seem a bit nervous," Sefforn replied.

"I should think so," Melkiar comment, "I would not want Vaulnik's men as my first encounter with battle."

"I'd have to agree. Fortunately, they have us seasoned veterans to count on to help them through this," Clavorn told him. "Here, can you hold this?" he asked Melkiar who was standing next to him.

Melkiar took the lead as Clavorn went over to retrieve his saddle bags and paraphernalia.

"We may be a seasoned veterans, but these men are of all ages; some too young, others way too old. I don't know about this battle. I'd feel more comfortable if we had more experienced men, less farmers and field hands, merchants and messengers if you get my meaning."

"I do. But who better than those with the most reason to fight to fight," Clavorn told him, "These men have everything to go into battle for. This is their land, their country. It is their freedom at stake, their families. I know of no other more powerful elixir than this to conquer the fear of such an enemy, or to give the necessary courage with which to wage war. They have the best reason in this conflict- a just cause."

"Well, just causes don't always win wars," Melkiar pointed out, "or battles."

Clavorn knew his friend was right, as he placed his saddle bags on Hawk. The horse shifted and looked back at him.

"Yes, boy, we have another battle to wage." Hawk blew as Clavorn gave him a friendly pat.

He had fought many battles with Hawk and could not imagine going into a major conflict with any steed other than him. He had proven himself time and time again. It was almost as if Hawk was merely an extension of himself, moving with his every thought. His horse always seemed able to sense the enemy. He had been given to him by Qualtaric, his old mentor, as a colt. The two had literally grown up together in a fashion. Training him had been a breeze. It was as if they were of one mind when he rode.

"I know, my friend, but right now it's our best hope," he told Melkiar, returning his thoughts back to their conversation.

"Well, all I'm saying is; that it is not the best state of affairs."

"Perhaps, but it is the only one we have."

Or do we?... Yes. It's our only option. I cannot let Vaulnik ravage this land? But if you need the dragon...We'll just have to manage. We've done it before.

Melkiar grumbled and gave him a look then turned to leave. He could not blame him. He had his own misgivings about the situation, but it could not be helped from his point of view.

"Well, I am off," Melkiar told him as he departed, "I have preparations to finish."

"I'll see you at the designated area," Clavorn shouted after him. Melkiar waved his hand in acknowledgement as he continued on his way.

"I am not surprised by their nervousness," Clavorn told Sefforn as he returned to the business of preparing his horse, "Vaulnik and his men have a bit of an ominous reputation. It'll be a couple days ride from here. Let's hope the time lag doesn't finish scaring them off."

"Aye, the gods know we need every last one of them," Sefforn commented, "Look, don't worry about them I'm sure they'll do fine."

"I hope your right, my friend," Clavorn replied, turning to face him.

"Look, most of the men I talked to are just glad to be fighting with The Great Shaltak," Sefforn told him reassuringly, "They would not leave if the gods came down and asked them too. And as far as how well prepared they are...Well, I think they are better prepared than I was for my first battle."

"Let's hope so," Clavorn commented, "Alright. Meet you on the other side of camp. It's about time we were off."

Sefforn nodded as he left to find his horse.

Clavorn turned to Hawk and finished tying his sword to his saddle.

Clouds were beginning to roll in over the mountains and cover the sun while a slight breeze began to pick up. As he surveyed the area around him, he saw men of all ages and backgrounds busily preparing to break camp. A few of the youths were helping some of his men with their mounts while others were helping to gather supplies.

Weapons readied the night before were being placed on horses or otherwise being readied for transport. It was a sea of purposeful confusion and apparent chaos, though in actuality everyone was quite organized. As he watched, he could see some lining up ready to leave.

Clavorn mounted his horse and glanced about the camp once more. It would be slower going this time as there would be men on foot. Many of whom had come from villages where their horses had been confiscated for the service of transporting Kriac Stone back to Zvegnog. And then there were the youths...and those with too many years, he worried about them. War was never kind to such these.

"Come on Hawk. Time for us to lead this army," he told his trusted equine friend. Hawk blew as he turned him in the direction of the distant mountains.

It was midmorning by the time they set off to intercept Vaulnik's army. Clavorn and Hawk led the way flanked by Sefforn and Melkiar with Thalon, Falor, and Kevic just behind him leading the first three groups of men. The wind blew as the clouds continued to roll in over the mountains.

Chapter 25

It was a whole day earlier than planned when Alcon burst into Clavorn's tent. Night had long since descended on the camp. No fires this night. They did not want their enemy discovering their whereabouts; not yet anyway. Most of the camp was asleep. Not Clavorn though, he was still up mulling over strategy in his mind and going over the plans with Melkiar and Sefforn.

"Shaltak," Alcon said in a low voice as he entered the tent.

"Yes, what is it Alcon? Aren't you supposed to be patrolling the boarders?"

"Yes, but...but Vaulnik's army..."

"Yes?"

"It looks like they will be on us by morning, sir," Alcon told him in a hushed voice.

"What?!" Melkiar remarked rather shocked.

"It looks like..."

"I know what you said," replied Melkiar, "May the curse of the dragons be on you Almaik! Where are those troops he was supposed to send? Any sign of them?"

"No," replied Alcon.

The troops Almaik had promised were supposed to have met up with them the morning before. However, there had been no signs of them, and they had been forced to camp at the meeting site, far too far out and exposed for Clavorn's liking, not to mention for far too long.

Clavorn listened to the report. Somehow there were no real surprises in it. He ran a hand over his face. The only good thing about it was that now they knew they were on their own, and that his men would have to face Vaulnik's army alone and outnumbered.

"Well, it looks as if we are going to have to implement our alternate plan gentlemen," he announced.

"We don't have much time," Sefforn commented.

"I know. We are going to have to modify it," Clavorn told him, "Alcon."

"Yes, sir,"

"Are you sure they were headed in our direction, as in directly towards us or just in this general direction?" Clavorn asked.

"They were clearly head straight for our location, sir. At least that is how it appeared to me through the dragonglass. And sir, it looks like they are in a big hurry to meet up with us."

"How did they find our location? We have not lit any fires despite this blasted weather," Melkiar commented.

It had been cold and dreary ever since they left camp. He had not even lit his pipe so as to keep their location a secret, and it was beginning to show.

"We cannot be sure they know exactly where we are. They could just be headed in this direction because that was their plan all along. After all the mountains in this region don't lend themselves to too many options." Clavorn remarked not wanting to jump to conclusions but wondering the same thing himself.

Was it possible Almaik or the king had tipped them off? The question had to be posed. The answer to which he could easily guess but had no intention of voicing yet.

Melkiar made as if to respond to his comment, but Clavorn raised his hand to stay his friend's remarks for the moment.

"Did you happen to notice what sort of accompaniment they had?" he asked.

"Sir?"

"Yes, was it the usual, or do they have anything different or unusual," Clavorn wanted to avoid any surprises like the one that had taken place at the Battle of Quantaris.

"Ah, no, sir," Alcon replied clearly a bit bewildered by his question, "It does not appear that they have anything out of the ordinary".

Fires of Life

"Thank you Alcon. Good job." Clavorn told him, but inside he could only hope the young man's assessment of their forces was correct. Vaulnik could never be trusted.

Alcon turned to leave.

"Oh, and Alcon, I'll want another report before morning," he told him.

"No problem," he replied as he left the tent, leaving the three men to contemplate what to do next.

Morning arrived and Clavorn could see from the cloud of dust that rose in the distance that Vaulnik's men were not far off. Shortly after Alcon had left his tent, he had finished working out the details of his alternate plan with Melkiar and Sefforn. His men had then slaved away the rest of the night to prepare a little surprise for the oncoming army.

Now all that was left was to pray their new plan would work. Pray that they would survive the day. Pray that perhaps Almaik would come through with his troops. But that was a prayer best left to the wind. If he knew his old friend well, there was very little chance that he ever intended to send his army to assist them at all. In fact, in all likelihood, he had been the one to tip off the enemy. No, this battle was up to them.

From the hilltop on which Clavorn was perched he could clearly see any movement by Vaulnik's men. He turned his gaze to the north. No sign of Almaik, or his men. Five legions, five legions he could desperately use. Now, as things stood, there seemed to be very little real chance of their success. But he had faced such odds before and come out on top. Yet somehow there was this nagging voice in his head that told him this battle was different. He pushed the thought aside and focused on the moment.

The sun was just peering over the horizon and everything was in place. Three thousand men, the estimated number burned in Clavorn's mind. To think that included all his new recruits. Was she right? Would he need that dragon she kept insisting on? He knew he was about to find out.

Clavorn paused in his thoughts. There would be no grand speech this morning. No brave pep talk. No. Only silence. The speech would have to wait. Silence was the name of the game this morning. His talk had come last night just after all his men had been roused and gathered to inform them of what was to be done. No. Now was a time of action.

Stealth was the operative word as his men moved themselves into position. How he wished he had had more time. Time to find the dragon, time to gather more men, time to be better prepared, but battle was upon them now.

Hawk stirred under him, and Clavorn new the moment was close as the first of Vaulnik's men entered the little ravine. The plan was simple. To wait until about half of his men were through and then close it off. If all went as planned, his men would split the enemy's troops in half, making it easier for his men to surround them and take as many down as possible.

A raven cawed from a nearby tree.

"I hope that is not a sign," remarked a young warrior mounted next to him in low voice.

"It is only a sign that someone is going to die today, and that is the only certainty it points to. Who, is anybody guess," remarked Clavorn in a distant yet wise voice. "What matters is how you choose to view that omen."

"Then I choose them," the young man replied again in a low voice.

Clavorn gave the young man a smile and a nod as the tension around him began to rise.

Soon more of Vaulnik's men were through the mountain pass and into the ravine. Some of Clavorn's men, led by Thalon, had spent a good part of the night loosening up some large boulders that flanked the narrow pass. At a signal from him they were to start an avalanche, hopefully cutting Vaulnik's army in half, thereby reducing their numbers, if only for a time.

Clavorn watched as more and more of Vaulnik's men rode through. Finally, he gave the signal. Moments later a great sound was heard on both sides of the ravine as boulders, dirt, and trees tumbled down both sides of the mountain in a great avalanche. Before long Vaulnik's army was cut in two. As the last of boulders fell, the engagement began just as he had planned.

Soon he could see Clovak signal his men to launch a wave of arrows which rained down on Vaulnik's troops while others on foot or on horseback tried to cut them down with swords. Special mounted archers also joined the fray, picking off men that strayed from the encirclement. So far the plan was working. Vaulnik's men were caught off guard by the avalanche and the surprise had temporarily given his men the advantage. Clavorn watched as his men were successfully able to surround this portion of Vaulnik's army. Now, if they just had enough time.

But then it came, the signal from a watchman indicating that the rest of Vaulnik's army had found a way around the escarpment and was on the move. Clavorn ordered his men to fall back, and like a bad storm they dispersed into the trees leaving Vaulnik's men to try and follow them.

Soon a raging river of Vaulnik's men came charging over the mountainside. Clavorn's men continued to fall back. Trees had been strategically cut in the night, and as the men retreated, others of Clavorn's army, led by Falor, finished felling them. Now, he could see Vaulnik's men falter as scores of their horses started at the sudden fallen trees and ensuing commotion. Many of the enemy lost their mounts and were picked off by his archers, but others were soon using cross bows to pick off Clavorn's men. Before long the casualties began to mount for Clavorn as many of his men lost their way in the confusion of the retreat.

The plan had been to fall back to a small valley and retreat into the forest, allowing Vaulnik's men to enter the vale where they would try to surround them again. But it was quickly becoming clear to Clavorn that such a strategy was never going to work. Too many of his men were disoriented in the unfamiliar territory. Too many were dying.

He spurred Hawk into the fray, wielding two swords he began to take down the enemy left and right. It was a valiant charge, but one he knew he could not keep up. His best hope was to distract them long enough to give his men time to escape into the woods and regroup.

He turned Hawk again and again moving him with the flow of his enemy. The horse instinctively felt Clavorn's wishes as they telegraphed through his body down to him, all while Clavorn slashed and cut down those of his enemy closest to him. Out of the corner of his eye, he spied Sorenavik wielding his sword as he cut down one of the enemy's men.

Dust and dirt flew everywhere as the chaos of battle continued. Once more he found himself giving the order to retreat while he desperately tried to give his men cover. However, Vaulnik's men were too numerous. It was just a matter of time before he too would be forced to retreat.

Suddenly, from the east, over a ridge, there came a sound like distant thunder, shaking the earth. Horses reared unseating their riders, arrows stopped flying, and there was a general pause in the chaos of the battle as the sound drew closer and closer, becoming louder and louder with each passing moment.

For a minute, Clavorn thought a dragon might appear, as he paused to see what was causing the break in the battle. But instead of a dragon, out of the forest came hundreds, perhaps thousands, of horses all charging head long into the battlefield, straight through the line where Vaulnik's army met his, trampling under hoof hundreds of Vaulnik's men that had been unseated from their mounts; their horses joining the crushing horde. Others who managed to keep their mounts were soon overrun as the horses kept galloping across their

Fires of Life

path, pulling many along with them any who dared stray into their wake.

Clavorn turned his horse and watched in utter dismay at the sight before him. Many of Vaulnik's men did the same as the ground shook and shuddered under their feet, causing a temporary pause in the battle.

At the head of this advancing horde of equines was a woman mounted on a white horse. Her hair trailing after her like an extension of the great mane of the horse she was riding.

Clavorn could only make out her silhouette from his position due to the arrangement of the sun. Some of Vaulnik's men began to flee in fear, some in confusion, others in sheer panic as their superiors shouted curses and orders for them to go on with the fighting. But to no avail. The herd of horses just kept coming for several minutes. Then, just when it appeared to be dissipating, it turned and came charging straight for Vaulnik's advancing forces, forcing them to turn tail and run while untold numbers of them were trampled.

Clavorn watched, mesmerized by the scene created by the woman who led the horde of horses. Arrows flew at her and the horses, but with no effect, their tips missing their mark every time. Then like smoke and mist they were gone over the mountainside, leaving Vaulnik's army scattered and shaken, retreating back in the direction from which they had come. Clavorn looked on for a moment more then turned Hawk to regroup with his men.

Chapter 26

The sight that awaited Clavorn when he arrived at their new makeshift camp both shocked and saddened him, bodies were strewn everywhere. The number of dead and wounded worried him. Young men, old men, men with families, anger began to mix itself with his sadness as he somberly rode through the sobering sight before him. This was what he hated about war. It seemed an unfortunate fact that there were times in history when such carnage was necessary to through off the yoke of oppression and injustice, but he still disliked it.

However, he abhorred even more those who would force war on others with their greed and lust for power, their desire for dominance, for control. Vaulnik was the embodiment of such men, the culmination of generations of such vile desires. Now, the carnage before him was just the beginning, if such as he were to succeed.

Suddenly, Sefforn strode up, "Oh, thank the gods. We all began to worry about you when you got cut off from us by the heard of horses. Did you see that woman leading them?" Clavorn nodded but said nothing, his mind still in shock at the sight before him. "It was as if she knew just when to intervene."

"Were any of the men injured by the herd?" Clavorn asked, suddenly aware that many of the men there could have been trampled by her horses.

"No. It appears as if our men were all spared her wrath," Sefforn told him.

Clavorn glanced down with inquiring eyes.

"We were about to be surrounded. Most of these men had been shot, some with poison tipped arrows. Anyway they were closing in on us when we heard the thunder and felt the ground shaking. It stopped Vaulnik's men in their tracks, all of us really. Some men took advantage of the situation to flee deep into the woods here. Others backed off fast as the herd came over the horizon.

Fires of Life

Then we saw her riding the lead horse. Some of the men are saying she was a Dragon Witch come to save us. While some say she was Alhera. Others don't know what to make of the vision. A few think she was just an illusion of the mind. The only thing they know is that without those horses, or this woman, if there was one, they would be dead." Sefforn finished as Clavorn dismounted.

"Well, it's good to know someone is on our side, witch, or otherwise," he commented as a young boy came up to take Hawk's reins. His clothes tattered and his body soiled, obviously from the battle of the day, but otherwise well enough. Clavorn was glad to see at least some had fared well.

"He needs…"

"Don't worry, sir. I know what he needs. I'll take good care of him for you," the boy said with a smile.

"Thank you," Clavorn replied, "What's your name son?"

"My name?"

Clavorn nodded. The young blond boy smiled broadly, proud that he had been noticed by The Great Shaltak.

"My name is Feorn," he announced proudly.

"Well, Feorn, I see Hawk is in good hands and I am glad that such a fine young man as yourself fared so well today," Clavorn told him.

"Yes sir. I mean…thank you, sir," the young boy replied as he took Hawk off to care for him.

Clavorn returned his attention to Sefforn as they walked the camp. Sunlight streamed in through the trees of the forest, spotlighting and shadowing the carnage, which only seemed to add to the feel of desolation and defeat. Sefforn led him in the direction of a small dear skin tent that had been set up for them at the far end amidst a stand of large deciduous trees.

"So how many men do we have left?" Clavorn asked as they continued their trek to the tent. He still could not get over the number of wounded. Sure they had been severely outnumbered, and he was expecting wounded, but this. Only the battle of Quantaris rivaled the sight before him. Memories from the long ago battle filled his mind and his heart was heavy with sorrow.

"Numbers vary as some continue to trickle in, but the estimates are about twelve hundred, give or take a few," Sefforn told him, "That includes most of the wounded you see before you."

Clavorn was silent for a moment as he looked about the scene in front of him; a mixture of feelings flooding his heart.

"None of these men here are going to be fit for duty any time soon," he finally remarked as they passed rows and rows of wounded men, many of them still with arrows protruding.

"True, but at least they survived. We survived," Sefforn replied, "Though unfortunately we lost Koron."

Clavorn was saddened by this news, "Well, at least now he can rest in peace with his family," he told Sefforn, "But he will be sorely missed."

Clavorn recalled the day he had waltzed into his camp determined to become a warrior and avenge his family's death. He felt sad at the loss of such a brave man and that he did not live to see his country free, but at least now he would be with his family in Shardon.

They walked on in silence. Finally, they arrived at the tent they had set up for him. Sefforn lifted the flap for Clavorn to enter.

"And what of Melkiar?" Clavorn asked as he ducked to enter.

"What of him?" a familiar gruff voice asked from within as he entered.

"Melkiar!" Clavorn exclaimed as the two men embraced, "I see you too survived to fight another day."

"Yes, unless there is another witch who can appear as me," Melkiar commented as he blew out a puff of smoke from his pipe. The men chuckled briefly as a wave of mutual relief and gratitude washed over them.

"But seriously, who was that?" Melkiar asked, "We could sure use more of her help."

"We will be just fine," Clavorn insisted, "with, or without her help." He had a feeling who she was, and was not so sure they

Fires of Life

should count on it, given her propensity for unexpected arrivals and departures.

"Are you so certain of that?" Sefforn commented, "If it hadn't been for her…"

"I know. You told me. But seriously, when did we forget that we have won fights like this before," Clavorn remarked, trying to be optimistic.

"Cla…Shaltak" Sefforn replied frustrated, "when have we ever been so seriously outnumbered? Come on. Did you see the way those arrows missed their marks as she passed? Surely, you have to admit such help could be advantageous."

"Sefforn's right," Melkiar interjected, taking a puff of his pipe. "There has been no sign of Almaik. Vaulnik's men are going to slaughter us tomorrow unless we can think of something and fast."

"We have too many wounded to move from here," Sefforn put in, "That is if many of them survive the night."

"So what exactly are you proposing," Clavorn asked, lifting his oil skin bag for a drink.

Sefforn and Melkiar looked from one to another. Finally, Sefforn announced after a brief moment of silence, "We think you should try to find her."

Clavorn nearly spat out his ale in the midst of taking a sip.

"Look, what makes you think I even know this woman, or whatever she is. Provided she even exists." he remarked as he finished wiping the spit from his face and taking a large swig of ale.

Melkiar and Sefforn exchanged glances again, "Come on. Don't pretend you haven't been visited by a wo…someone. We know you too well." Sefforn whispered in his ear.

Clavorn halted in his drink and turned to look at him; his eyes wide with surprise. At that point he would have to agree with him. There was no hiding anything from his friends, apparently. And as much as he had tried to hide the identity of his 'ghost,' they had somehow managed to figure it out, at least as much as he knew.

"I know. That's not hard. I told you about the 'ghost'," he replied, trying to recover his composure.

"Yes, but I am pretty sure your 'ghost' is a woman," Sefforn remarked.

"Oh, how so?" He had to know. No one had seen them come and go. Or had they? No. She would not have been that careless.

"Let's just say some of your actions of late were a dead giveaway." Sefforn told him.

Clavorn thought a moment.

Was that possible? Obviously, though I would not have thought so.

"Alright, for argument sake, let's say I know this woman, which I am not sure that I do. Your conjecture presupposes that the woman who led those horses today is the same one who helped me escape," an idea which he was not yet ready to admit to. There was always the chance that this woman was just an apparition, or someone else entirely different from her. "How do you propose I contact her when I don't even know where to begin to look for her?"

"We don't know," Melkiar shrugged as he took another puff on his pipe, "but perhaps it's about time you figured it out."

Clavorn raised an eye brow and looked from one of his friends to another, "Are you both mad?"

"Not as mad as you if you try to go through with this campaign alone," Sefforn remarked, taking a swig of ale himself.

Mutiny! His friends were mutinying on him and all because potentially she, his 'ghost,' had saved their hides, or so it seemed. Clavorn could hardly believe his ears. If it was her, she would be right again! It looked like he was going to need her after all, if for no other reason than to appease his friends. He took another swig of ale and wiped his mouth.

"Alright, if there is any way of contacting this woman, or if she contacts me, I agree we'll bring her on board on one condition."

"What?" they both chimed in.

"That you never speak of this to anyone. I…"

Fires of Life

"… Don't worry. Our lips are sealed. Besides, it's not like she's an ordinary woman you know," Sefforn remarked as he slapped Clavorn on the shoulder. He stared at his friend.

"Yeah, I know. Sometimes, Seff, I swear…"

"You swear what?" Sefforn interrupted.

"Oh, never mind," Clavorn replied, taking another swig from his oil skin bag, "We still need a plan for the morning. These men cannot stay out there. There is no guarantee about this woman, or whatever she is. It may just be a onetime deal. We need to move, or we really will be slaughtered by nightfall tomorrow."

"Probably a whole lot sooner," Sefforn commented.

Clavorn had to agree with his friend's assessment. If Almaik did not show by morning, which signs were doubtful, chances were most, if not all of them, would be dead by noon tomorrow and the rebellion along with them.

"So, what do you propose?" Melkiar inquired, puffing on his pipe as he sat down.

All three men set themselves down and began brainstorming over the issue. But before they could really sink their teeth into the problem, a great commotion began to stir outside their tent.

"What's that?" Clavorn asked as Sefforn rose to see what was going on.

"I don't know. I cannot see. But whatever it is has got the whole camp in a stir," he informed them after taking a glance outside the tent.

Both Clavorn and Melkiar rose to their feet and joined Sefforn as he stepped outside to see what all the fuss was. Sure enough none of them could see over the crowd that was gathering on the edge of camp. So they began to fall in line with rest of the curious men, when suddenly the crowd began to part and the three of them stopped dead in their tracks.

Clavorn strained his eyes to see what was going on. As the last man parted the way, he saw her walking towards them. The most beautiful woman any of them had seen in a long time, if ever. Her long dark black flowing hair billowed out behind her. Only animal skins concealed her svelte sinewy body. At her side, a wild mountain lion walked in stride with her while a hawk perched itself on her shoulder. She wore a long sword strapped to her belt and a dagger in her boot. Slung across her back was a long bow and quiver, but it was her eyes that Clavorn noticed. Her green catlike eyes, the eyes that had haunted him since the first day they met. They were the only part of her that he could focus on now. They caught his attention and held him fixated as she continued to walk towards them.

"I take it you know her," Sefforn remarked to him in a low tone.

"Yes. She's the woman we are looking for."

Chapter 27

The men all stood around her including Clavorn, Melkiar, and Sefforn. The big cat stopped walking forward when she did. Now they all stood facing each other. Clavorn's thoughts were in a whirl.

By Allethor! She is beautiful. But why is she here? Why is she not hiding her face? Will she finally tell me who she is?

"I assume we have you to thank for our good fortune on the battle field today?" he began.

"You assume correctly. But I did not come here to seek your thanks. I came here to help," she announced, "You have wounded. I can help if you will let me."

Clavorn thought for a moment recalling his recent conversation in the tent just prior to her arrival. "Yes, yes, we could use your help if you think you can? But first introductions, this is…"

"Sefforn and Melkiar, yes, I am familiar with them. Can you show me where I may prepare what I need?" she asked as she interrupted Clavorn. His attempt to acquire her name adeptly foiled.

"This way," Sefforn replied before he could get a chance to interrogate her any further.

Sefforn stepped back and motioned her to the tent they had just come from. Suddenly, a voice from the crowd shouted.

"Hey! I know you! You're…"

Instantly, instinctively, she turned to face him, the hawk immediately flying off her shoulder. While simultaneously, she drew two arrows from her quiver and let them fly from her bow as the last words were uttered from his mouth. The man froze as the arrows pinned him squarely to the tree behind him, one landing just above his head and the other just below his groin.

"You were about to say?" she inquired calmly and surely as she held her bow in her hand.

The big cat at her side stared at the man such that all the words went out of him and all he could do was shake his head 'no.' A brief moment of hushed silence filled the air.

"That's what I thought," she remarked as she relaxed out, dropping her bow to her side. "Now let me be clear," she continued, raising her voice for all to hear. "Who I am matters little. I am simply here to help you. Call me a ghost. Call me a witch. Call me anything you like, but do not read too much into these events. Know only this. The forest is my home, and when I am done that is where I will return," and with that she turned around and continued on her way to the tent Sefforn had indicated.

All three men, Clavorn, Melkiar, and Sefforn, exchanged glances before following her and the catamount in. The camp was dead quiet, save for the sounds of the wounded, as the men stared after her. No one daring to say another word least an arrow catch them and pin them where they stood.

"Okay, now that you have frightened all of my men, would you mind telling me what this is all about," Clavorn announced as he entered the tent behind her and her puma, while the hawk alighted in a tree just above them outside, appearing to take the stance of a feathered sentry.

"I already told you what this is all about. I am here to offer my help, and from what I can see you are going to need me. Those wounded out there don't have much time."

"And you can heal them?" he remarked questioningly as he gestured towards them.

Moans from the wounded filtered into the tent and mixed with the low murmur of conversation outside as his men began to relax and discus what had just taken place. It was clear from his tone of voice that he doubted very much if anyone could heal their wounds. Most were so badly injured he felt it would be a miracle if they survived till morning.

"Yes," she replied simply as she quickly surveyed the space then turned to face him.

Sefforn came around Clavorn and gave him a dirty look. Clearly, his friend did not feel as he did, and considered his question an offense towards their benefactor.

Fires of Life

"I am sorry about him. Is there anything we can get you?" he asked her now standing slightly in front of him.

"Yes, I am going to need a kettle and a small bowl for mixing," she replied, "Oh, and plenty of clean water."

"Yes, I will see that you have these," Sefforn told her turning around and glaring at Clavorn once more.

Melkiar raised one eye brow, puffing on his pipe as he looked from Clavorn to Sefforn and back again.

"I will see if I can expedite things," he said as he followed Sefforn out of the tent leaving Clavorn alone with the mystery woman.

"What was that stunt out there? And why have you decided not to hide your face anymore?" he asked in a low but harsh tone once Melkiar and Sefforn had left; the frustration in his voice unmistakably audible.

"I can clearly see that you did not appreciate what I did this afternoon by saving you and your men from certain annihilation. Shall I leave?" she remarked her green eyes glaring into his.

"No, no, forgive me," he did not mean to give her the impression he did not appreciate what she had done, "It's just… it's just I am confused. You fail to show yourself to me. Your identity some sort of big mystery, and then here you are all out in the open, sort to speak," he finished, gesturing so as to emphasize her current state of being with his hands before running one through his hair in frustration, "It's just hard to imagine that's all. And then that final thing you did, pinning one of my men to a tree like that."

"I had to," she told him softening her voice.

"What do you mean, 'you had to?' Unless of course you were afraid he'd recognized you," Clavorn remarked, looking her dead in the eyes.

"Don't be ridiculous," she countered, still avoiding the subject.

Clavorn doubted it was ridiculous. The man could have recognized her. What bothered him the most was her insistence in keeping her identity to herself. Why was that so all important?

"Am I?" He stared at her. A brief moment of silence passed between them before he went on, "Look, you want to keep your identity to yourself I'll accept that, for now. Just help my men."

"Oh, I will and I intend to do a lot more than that. You'll see," she told him as Sefforn and Melkiar entered bearing the items she had requested, and leaving Clavorn to wonder about her final words.

"Thank you so much. Now, if you gentlemen don't mind, I will need this place to myself for a while. I will call you when I am ready to begin treatment," she told them as she all but shushed them out of the tent.

"Well, did she tell you anything?" Melkiar asked once they were out of earshot of the tent.

"Nothing we didn't already know," Clavorn replied clearly disappointed that he was not able to worm any further enlightenment from her lips.

"Well, all I care about is that she is able to help us in some way, any way, so that we can stay alive long enough to be able to defeat Vaulnik," Sefforn remarked as he sat down on a large felled tree trunk not far from the tent.

Melkiar puffed on his pipe and joined Sefforn. Clavorn remained standing as he stared off into the distant setting sun while they awaited her next instructions. The men who had been standing around earlier when she arrived had now all disbursed. A few were grouped together here and there. One could easily imagine what their topic of conversation was. In the distance Clavorn could see Thalon and Falor as they came up to meet them.

"Who is that?" Thalon asked before any of the other three could remark on their good fortune of having survived the battle relatively unscathed.

"We don't know," Sefforn replied before Clavorn could answer.

"Oh?" remarked Falor, "Didn't she say anything to you?"

"Yes," Clavorn told him, "She said she was here to help."

Fires of Life

"But that is no different from what she told all of us before she went into the tent with you. She didn't give you any more information than that?" Thalon exclaimed clearly just as mystified as all of them.

"That is correct," Melkiar chimed in, "Though she seems…"

"…quite insistent that she can heal our men," Clavorn interrupted his pipe smoking friend who he was sure was about to reveal his association with their mystery guest, and he was not so sure he wanted to go into a big discussion on that.

"Well, there is no doubt we could use that," Thalon replied, "Our numbers are severely drained."

"Have you seen the others?" Clavorn asked.

"No. Though I did see Clovak. He's over there tending to a boy who he just brought in," Falor told him pointing to a tree on the far side of camp where many of the wound lay.

"I should go check on him," Clavorn told them as he began to stride off in the direction Falor had pointed out.

"No. Wait!" Falor exclaimed, grasping his arm.

Clavorn turned and looked at him with questioning eyes.

"I think the boy is close to death," Falor told him.

At this news Clavorn halted his exit to Clovak. He understood what Falor was telling him. It was not the right time.

Silence overcame the men at the solemnness of the situation and no further discussion took place between them as they waited to hear from her.

They did not have to wait long. Soon she appeared waving them into the tent.

"I need several able bodied men, boys…persons, to help me give this to the injured," she informed them.

"What is it?" Clavorn asked, wrinkling his nose at the smell of the bubbling mixture above a small fire in the center of the tent.

"It's a tea."

"A tea?" Melkiar remarked raising his one eye brow, "And who are we going to get to drink this?"

Clearly, he felt the smell of the bubbling brew to be far too much of a deterrent for anyone to desire to drink it.

"Oh, never mind him," Sefforn told her, glaring at Melkiar this time, "Come on Melkiar, let's go find some able bodied persons, who can't smell, to help us to dole this out," and with that Sefforn practically grabbed Melkiar by the ear as he dragged him out of the tent. Thalon and Falor followed suit.

Once again Clavorn found himself alone with her; her green eyes captivating him, her body entrancing. He wanted to say something, but found that no words would come to his usually quick witted mouth.

"This *is* going to help them?" he finally managed to inquire after a moment of silence. He still found it hard to believe that such a foul smelling substance could cure anything except congested sinuses.

"Yes, it speeds up the healing process. If all goes well, most of your men should be fit for battle tomorrow."

Clavorn raised one eye brow, "And you still claim you're not a Dragon Witch." he commented feeling that that could be the only explanation for everything.

"Yes," she replied as she stroked and scratched her cougar with familiar ease while they awaited the return of his men.

A low throaty rumble began to emanate from the big cat while the small fire in the center of the tent crackled and popped. Sparks periodically spewed up and out from the small conflagration as it continued to heat the repulsive smelling tea.

As he stood there watching her while they waited for his friends' return, Clavorn could still not imagine how she could be anything else except a Dragon Witch. Everything she had done so far seemed to point to that.

"Here you are," Sefforn announced as he reentered the tent, jolting Clavorn out of his thoughts, "We found you several of our finest young men."

Clavorn glanced outside. Several, was an understatement. He must have found every abled body young man and boy in camp.

Sefforn motioned them to enter the tent and all of them began to file in one by one each expressing, in his own way, his repulsion to the awful smelling contents boiling in the kettle before them.

"Thank you Sefforn," she replied gracefully, "Now, I want each of you to grab a cup and fill it with the liquid in the kettle," she continued as she address the young men and boys who had entered the tent. It was clear from some of their expressions that many of them felt the same way about the smell of the mixture as Clavorn and his friends. "Then I want you to start giving it to the wounded. Make sure they all receive some and don't let them say 'no' just because it smells bad. Tell them a bad smell for a moment is better than a long and painful death."

"You sure that is going work?" Clavorn whispered into her ear as he went to stand behind her.

"No, but it's worth a try," she replied in a low voice and for a moment he saw her as human, but then he glanced down by the fire and noticed all the cups. There appeared as if there were just enough for all the boys and young men to each have one. When he had glanced that way earlier there had only been a couple of them there at best.

Now as he watched the boys and young men fill their cups he noticed not only were there enough for each of them, but also that the kettle never seemed to empty. Calling again into question any idea of her simple humanity.

Chapter 28

When all the boys and young men had finished filing out the tent with their cups full of the precious, yet smelly, healing draught, Clavorn and the woman stepped outside. Sefforn and Melkiar had gone on with the troop of young would be medicine dispensers while Thalon and Falor had each taken cups of their own and were off doing their own dispensing of the fowl smelling liquid. This left Clavorn alone with her once more.

The sun was beginning to set. A chill was starting to settle in about the camp. As he glanced around, Clavorn could see the boys and young men were having trouble giving her tea to the injured. It seemed no one wanted to taste the nasty smelling brew. Complaints were many while the moans and groans of the wounded continued to overlay any other sounds of the forest.

"I don't think your drought is much of a hit," Clavorn commented.

"The evening is yet but young," was all she said, sounding, he noted, all too much like his mentor Qualtaric.

Suddenly, he could see a little ways off, a soldier coming up from the throng of men sprawled across the field and forest of wounded. At first glance Clavorn thought it was Sefforn who was coming to see them. However, upon closer examination he could see it was not his old friend but rather another man, about his friend's build, only older.

He was carrying a young boy of about thirteen years of age. The boy would have been one of Clavorn's youngest to fight in the battle. Unfortunately, with their numbers so low even the very young had been asked to fight along with the very seasoned. It was not a choice Clavorn was fond of making. As the man strode up, it was easy to see that the boy he was carrying was his son. The tears in the man's eyes were unmistakable.

"Please," he implored as he came up, looking straight at her, "If there is anything you can do?"

Fires of Life

The man held out the boy to her. Anyone could easily see that the boy had been badly injured. His blood stained broken body nearly brought tears to Clavorn's own eyes.

By the position of the arrow that was protruding from the child, one could easily guess that he was mortally wounded, if not already dead. From the looks of the dirt, debris, and other injures he appeared to have been trampled as well. Whether that had been from fleeing soldiers or horses was difficult to tell, though Clavorn guessed it was more from fleeing men than any horse.

The mysterious woman looked down on the man with tender eyes, and then examined the boy.

"I am sorry, he is gone," she informed him in a gentle tone.

"Please," the man begged, "He is my only child. My wife is dead. If there is anything, anything..."

The man's desperate eyes looked up into hers, pleading. She looked back at the boy and felt his body one more time.

"He is still warm. Maybe there is still hope," she told him. The man smiled up at her. "I cannot promise that I can bring your son back," she continued, clearly not want to raise the man's hopes.

"It is enough to know that someone has tried," he replied gratitude written unmistakably on his face.

Bending down and reaching out, she gently took the boy in her arms and walked with him back to Clavorn's tent. Clavorn turned and followed her, after giving the man a reassuring squeeze on his arm before he left.

As he neared the tent, she turned on him.

"No!" she ordered, "I must work alone. Wait out here and pray. Pray that Alhera will bring this boy back to his father." With that she and the boy entered the tent as the deer skin flap closed down behind them.

Clavorn turned, his eyes searching, and found the boy's father just where he had left him. He went down to the man and joined him.

"What is the boy's name?" he asked kindly.

"Meshron," the man answered.

"Come. Let us pray together," Clavorn told him as he motioned the man over to a log not far from them. The man nodded, and the two sat together and prayed.

Time passed and the sky was now turning dark. The first few stars were just visible in the night sky. Clavorn could tell the boy's father was starting to lose hope. The light from the fire inside the tent glowed, but there were no telltale signs of what was taking place inside.

"Why don't you tell me about your son?" he suggested, trying to take the man's mind off the time.

The man was just about to speak when a huge gust of wind blew up, shaking the trees violently. Then all was quiet. A few moments later the flap of deer skin opened and out walked a shaky Meshron with her at his side.

The man jumped up from Clavorn's side and ran to his son with tears of joy in his eyes.

"Thank you! Thank you," he repeated as he hugged his son close to him.

"It was the will of Alhera and the dragon," she replied as she bent down close to the man and his son with one hand on each of their shoulders. The man nodded with a smile as he cried tears of happiness.

Clavorn stood where he was rooted, amazed at what he had just witnessed.

And she still claims she is no Dragon Witch?

The question of her identity still gnawing on his mind, and like the others of his camp, his speculations ranged.

Word spread quickly of the miracle that had just taken place. Soon the wounded started to take the bad smelling drink, and a lightness began to take hold around the camp. Where there had once been the heavy feel of defeat now began to be replaced with hope.

Fires of Life

Chapter 29

Whispers and rumors abounded about the camp. Some said she was a valhera sent by the gods in their hour of need. Others called her a Dragon Witch, and still others thought her to be the daughter of Alhera. No one, to Clavorn's mind had any real idea of who she was, except perhaps the unlucky fellow who had spoken up earlier that afternoon. Now, as he watched her nurse his men, it was hard to see as her anything but a beautiful woman, inside and out.

"So, who's our mystery woman?" Kevic inquired as he came upon Clavorn who was sitting on the fallen log just outside his tent watching her treat the wounded. He had just finished a planning session with Melkiar and Sefforn and was taking a moment for himself before joining in on helping with the wounded.

"Anybody's guess if you believe half the rumors circulating around camp," Clavorn replied as he made room for his elderly friend.

"Well, I'm not going to question the will of the gods," Kevic remarked as he sat down next to Clavorn.

"Oh, don't you want to know who she is my old friend?"

"No. Not really. I find its best not to look too closely at a miracle least you find a flaw."

"Sound advice, but still…"

"Come, come, some things are best left in the hands of the gods, or fate if you're an old man like myself."

Clavorn smiled and the two watched as she pulled an arrow out from Alcon's shoulder.

"Ahh!" he cried, but then marveled at how quickly it seemed to feel better once he had mustered up the courage to sip her tea.

"I think they will all do well," Kevic observed after a brief moment of silence.

"So do I," remarked Clavorn taking a swig of ale from a flask he had brought outside with him.

"Well, I am going to turn in. You let me know what the plan is tomorrow."

"Of course," replied Clavorn with a smile, "Don't I always."

The old man nodded, and he watched as the elderly gentleman rose from the log and disappeared amongst the men, trees, and shadows of the camp; the moonlight glinting off his silvery white hair. As Clavorn observed the scene before him, he noticed that the commotion of the day had died down. Now the only dominate sounds were the cries from his men as arrows were removed or bones were set, and then the complaints for the smell or taste of the tea, followed by praise for how it made them feel once they drank it. It was an amazing ending to a long and arduous day.

Clavorn stood up and walked over to where a young boy was helping her with a feisty warrior who had a particularly bad wound. An arrow had pierced his side and had penetrated deeply, while two others had found their marks by lodging themselves one in his shoulder and the other in his thigh.

"Shaltak, will you tell this woman... ahh, that it is better to just kill me now... rather than let me suffer here. ...By morning we will all be slaughtered anyway," he told him in an angry labored voice as Clavorn came by.

"No." Clavorn replied. The warrior looked at him. His matted dark hair was stained with blood and dirt. "I will not have you kill yourself while help stands next to you. I trust her. It is my understanding that if you drink that draught she has that you will be better by morning," he told him.

"No tea can do that! Ahh!" he spat as a spasm of pain wrenched his broken body. It was easy to see that the man had lost a lot of blood. His clothes were nearly soaked in it.

"And we were all supposed to be dead," Clavorn remarked, "including that young boy over there." The man looked up at him, his eyes questioning, "Yes. That's the boy who was supposed to be dead."

Fires of Life

Clavorn pointed off in the direction of Meshron, the youth she had just brought back to life. He was standing with his father by the side of another young boy who had been injured in the fight. All were smiling as the other young boy had apparently taken the drink and was now on his way to feeling better.

"Oh, dragon's dung!" the man exclaimed, "You don't expect me to believe that boy was dead do you?"

"Well, as matter-of-fact I do, because he was." Clavorn paused to let his words sink in. "But if that is not enough for you, how about the fact that we should have all been wiped out by an invading army that severely outnumbered us. Yet here we are, alive, with a chance to fight another day. Now drink, my friend, and dare to live. Dare to fight another day," he told him as he bent down close to him.

Clavorn then took the cup from her with her special brew in it as she watched. He lifted the man's head to help him drink.

The warrior hesitated, making a face at the smell and looked up at Clavorn. Clavorn nodded for him to drink. Finally, he quickly slurped a sip from the cup.

"Ahh! Yuck! What is that awful stuff?!" he exclaimed.

"Here drink again," Clavorn encouraged.

"No way! I ... I think I'd rather die. Wait a minute," the man looked down. His wounds had started to heal, and the bleeding had stopped. Suddenly, she reached over and pushed part of the mortally wounding arrow through the man.

"Ahh!" he cried as the arrow pierced his flesh and came out the other side. Then reaching under him she broke off the tip. Once again the man cried out, but before he could protest what she was doing, she immediately pulled out the remainder of the arrow that was lodged in the man's side.

"Ahh!" he cried out once more. At first it bled and then it stopped, healing before their eyes.

Clavorn looked over at her as she proceeded to do the same with the other arrows, obtaining the same results. He marveled at what he was witnessing.

"Shaltak," the man exclaimed as he reached over and grabbed his arm, "I do believe you are right."

"Oh?"

"I *will* fight another day!"

Clavorn smiled and the warrior smiled back, "What is your name?" he asked.

"Bennethor," he replied.

"Well, then Bennethor, I expect to have you fighting by my side tomorrow," he told him.

"I will, and we will give them something to remember Avivron by," Bennethor told him as the two men clasped hands.

"Now recover well, my friend," Clavorn told him as he rose.

"Thank you," the man said to her, "Please forgive an ignorant warrior who is too used to fighting."

"You are forgiven," she told him as she took the cup from Clavorn, "Now drink again."

The man did as he was instructed, and Clavorn could see that she had the situation more than under control. He walked off to see how the rest of the men were fairing.

As he strode amongst them, he could see that a good number of them were in various stages of recovery. Some were even trying to get up and walk, as he witnessed Heffron help Yolondon try to stand up. A smile came to his face when he saw the old survivor take his first steps. Again he marveled at her skills. Still there were many more left to treat, but the night was young.

As he walked amongst them, he spied another young boy helping to administer the draught to another injured warrior. From the looks of things the boy was clearly in need of relief himself. Clavorn walked over to the boy and touched him on his shoulder.

"I'll take over from here. You've done a great job. Why don't you go get some rest. We have a big day tomorrow," he told the boy.

"Oh, ah… are you sure, sir?" the boy remarked a bit surprised.

"Yes. Now hand me that cup."

"Sure sir, thank you, sir," the boy replied, standing up and handing the cup to Clavorn, "Oh, sir, something you ought to know about that cup."

"Oh?"

"Yeah, it doesn't empty."

Clavorn smiled, "Well, at least that cuts down on trips to refill it."

The boy smiled and left as Clavorn turned and bent down to help another injured warrior.

Chapter 30

It was well into the night by the time they finished. Clavorn entered his tent. There was a soft glow of embers from the fire she had started earlier to brew her draught. Its light was a warm and pleasant sight after the long day, so much so that he could not resist sitting down near the inviting glow.

For several minutes Clavorn stared into the light of the glowing embers before it dawned on him that no one had been in his tent to stoke the fire. In a normal fire the light from the embers, and their soft flickering flames, would have long since died in the span of time it was left unattended. But not these, they were still burning just as they had been when he had left hours ago.

Suddenly, he heard a loud rasping sound, and began glancing around to see if he could find its source. It did not take long as his eyes followed his ears to the back of the tent. There, stretched out upon the ground, was the large mountain lion licking and bathing itself in the warmth of the fire. He was about to start when she came in.

"Don't let Salhera scare you. She is really just a big kitten."

"Ah, who said I was scared? I was just going to get myself some ale. You want some?"

"No thanks. I'm just going to have some water," she replied as she came further in and reached for her oil skin bag near the fire. Taking a swig she sat down by it. The light from the embers and gently flickering flames only seemed to add to the mystery that surrounded her. Clavorn could not resist asking her about it as he sat down with his ale across from her.

"So, *now* are you going to tell me your story? I promise I won't tell a soul if you don't want me to," he told her gently, "I would just like to know more about you. Zezpok! You've saved my life a number of times and now the lives of my men. You can't expect me not to be curious."

He paused and waited for her to speak. The glow from the slow burning embers lit her eyes, and they seemed to dance with the firelight as she stared into it. But her eyes were not seeing the glow of the embers or the dance of the small flames. No. They were looking into some far off distant place, her mind oceans away from the little tent in the forest where outside recovering men were sleeping.

Her mind's eye could perceive it all. Being who she was now she could see and feel, even hear the thoughts of all involved, as if she were one of the gods witnessing it from the Shardon Lands. Clavorn could see she was worlds away from him viewing something only she knew.

Large heavy ornate doors that led to the king's inner sanctum opened and in entered a guard. Heavy armored boots pounded and echoed off the stone floor. The clang of his sword and the ching of his mail rung out in the silence of the large cold room as he purposefully strode across the chamber to where a tall slender dark haired man, with just a touch of gray in his sideburns, was standing beside a long tall window overseeing his land.

The man's robes, his crown, and his stance were a clear indication that he was in charge of this land. No one was to question that. No one was to challenge him. He would rule it all if he could. If he could just find the Shaddorak, the prophesized woman who held the key to the power of the dragons and the Kriac Stones. The woman who would hold the power of world in the palm of her hands. He had to find her. He had to possess her.

As she looked up, she could see into the chamber. Her eyes watched as the head guard removed his helmet and began to speak to the king. On the gray stone walls of the chamber before her hung huge tapestries most of which appeared to depict scenes from the history of this land, Ishalhan, or rather, Zvegnog, as it was now called.

Odd that some of those tapestries from the Before Days should still be up. She would have thought he would have had them removed. But as she looked harder at them she could tell they had been altered, altered to reflect a new history. A history more to Vaulnik's liking and one which clearly emphasized his role. Her eyes searched the walls for any clue as to the king's origin, but there were none. The tapestry which hung just opposite of her, however, spoke to her in a way the others could not, for it depicted the legendary clash between Maltak and the Vigoths.

Her eyes scanned the ancient textile depicting the well-known scene in which The Great Green Dragon, and her mate, Altak, defeated the dark gray misty creatures of Zagnor. An unforeseen pride welled up within her as she viewed the tapestry even as the humiliation of her capture still burned in her heart. But as she continued to scan the tapestry it became all too clear that Vaulnik had altered this story as well, giving it an entirely different ending. She blew hair out of her face in degust.

Just like an egomaniac to alter the truth.

She tugged on her arms trying once more to free herself, but her captors held her fast. Till today she had prided herself in her abilities to move as one unseen, and they had served her well, until the unthinkable had happened. Now she was here. Her mission an apparent failure, but it was not over yet.

"My Lord Vaulnik, we found this woman sneaking around the Dragon Chamber," she heard the head guard say as he stopped in front of the king, gesturing with his hand to the open doors in her direction. The tall dark haired man surveyed the entrance.

Humm.

He eyed the woman held by his two guards. His mind immediately drawing conclusions it hoped were true. Then he nodded abruptly to the guard, for he did not need to speak. A look was a good as a command to those he placed in positions of power. Flavious was his most decorated guardsman. The feathers on his helmet and the red carnelian dragon clipped to his black cape over his left shoulder were only part of the hardware that demonstrated the man's loyalty. He knew this one understood his every movement.

Immediately, Flavious beckoned her captors to bring her in. The two guards at her side dragged her struggling into the chamber. Her long dark hair partially obscured her face as they gruffly positioned her before Vaulnik. The scar which crossed his right eye loomed ominously before her as he scanned her appearance from his place near the window.

Now, she could clearly see the gold crown upon his head. It was encrusted with all manner of precious gems. At its center was a large ruby dragon cut and carved from one very large stone, its eyes a blaze with fiery diamonds. In its talons it held one large Kriac Stone, she presumed, to demonstrate his power and dominance over all things, including those given by the gods.

His dark robes and black fur trimmed cape were elegantly adorned so that there was no question as to his rank. A huge gold and blood red dragon clasp made of rubies was fastened over his left shoulder from which hung his fur trimmed cape. Its eyes were studded with diamonds as well, and in its mouth was also a single Kriac Stone.

By contrast she stood before him in peasant clothes. Clothes she had stolen along the way.

"We found these on her as well, sire," the guard named Flavious told him as he held out an ornate sword and dagger they had confiscated from her to show him.

Vaulnik walked over from the window, a sinister smile beginning to grow on his face. He descended the steps and took the sword from Flavious's hand.

Can it be? Have my men found the woman of my dreams? The woman who holds the key to my obtaining ultimate power.

He turned it over in his hand. On its hilt was the design of a dragon with a ruby in its mouth. His lips began to turn up as he glanced from the blade to her in a most unnerving and menacing fashion.

Dragon curses! I knew I should not have brought that sword. But what choice did I have?

The sword had been the only thing she had from her past. Would it reveal too much?

"Well, well, well, what do we have here? A woman of noble birth, an Avivronian I think, or a thief, maybe both," he paused a moment as he paced around her. She could sense his eyes on her, penetrating, probing, unsettling. "Or perhaps a Dragon Witch," he announced as he paced behind her, "or better still the fabled Shaddorak." His voice dripped with malice as he uttered the last word in her ear before facing her.

"You wish!" she spat, flipping hair out of her face as she stood proudly before him. Her green catlike eyes burning with the fire of defiance as the guards held her fast.

SMACK!

Insolent bitch!

The blow came hard across her face as Vaulnik hit her with the hilt of her sword. She could feel the blood beginning to drip from where it had struck.

"Your insolence will not be tolerated! Now tell me who you are," he rebuked.

"I will tell you nothing!" She fired back, raising her head from his blow, blood dripping from her lips.

Power hungry, murdering, sadistic creep! You will get nothing from me.

"Oh, to the contrary woman," he told her as he circled her again, this time in the other direction. The sound of his boots on the stone floor echoed eerily about the room, "You *will* tell me everything I want to know. If you are who I suspect you are, then it is a good thing we did not kill off that last dragon." He stopped in front of her his icy blue eyes peering deep into hers. "Take her to the dungeon," he ordered to the guards holding her as he went abruptly back up the

Fires of Life

steps and sat down upon his thrown. His fur trimmed cape furling out as he seated himself on his gaudy seat of sovereignty made from the remains of slaughtered dragons and conquered enemies.

Behind him stood a large looming sculpture of a violent dragon carved from red granite. In the talons of its left paw it held a single Kriac Stone, and under its belly, crushed by its right leg, were the sculpted remains of a Dragon of the Earth.

She hated the imagery, though it suited Vaulnik's egocentric, sadistic nature. The great wings of the creature unfurled up and out behind it so as to serve as a sort of frame for the overbearing ruler of the land. The long, elongated windows from which Vaulnik had previously been standing, rose up on either side of the great beast, and cast an eerie light upon the staged spectacle before her.

"You won't get away with this! Alhera will see to it!" she yelled as they began to haul her off.

"I think not, my dear," his voice silkily calm and malicious, "Haven't you heard? The gods are dead. I killed them. I killed your precious Maltak too," he spat the last sentence out with complete distain. He hated the gods. Hated them for denying him the power he so desperately craved, "Now take her away!" he ordered again waving her off with his right hand.

*I have you now. You are **mine**.*

The two guards who had brought her before him resumed their task as she struggled to free herself.

"That's it, my dear," his sinuous voice came from across the room, and she halted dead in her tracks. "Please continue to struggle. It will only weaken you and make you all the more vulnerable to me when we speak again."

His words shuddered through her body like evil baritones.

*Speak to me again indeed! Coerce more like. Well, you will get no such satisfaction from me. I will tell you **nothing**!*

She stood up tall and walked proudly out with the two guards at her side.

Pride, ehey. Well, we'll see how much of that she has left after I'm done with her.

"Would you like us to prepare her for you, sire," asked Flavious with his helmet still clutched at his side. He had not moved from his position since he had given him her sword and dagger.

"No, I think I shall enjoy this one myself," he replied, an evil, malicious smile gracing his face as he stroked his chin with his right hand. Pleasurable, vile thoughts ran through his mind as he envisioned himself interrogating her.

Flavious nodded abruptly, turned, and left, placing his helmet upon his head as he marched out of the room. Vaulnik rose from his thrown and returned to looking out his chamber window. Success now seemed emanate as he gloated over the thought of interrogating her. He was sure she was the one he was searching for.

Looking down, he inspected her sword and dagger. As he turned the sword over in his hands, the glint from the ruby at the end of its hilt caught and refracted the rays of sunlight almost as if to hail this glorious moment. He smiled wirily.

Now to bend her to my will.

The scene changed in her mind, and now she was seeing something different. It was a prison cell, her cell, below in the bowels of the castle.

It was dark, the only light coming from the torch just outside the cold stony chamber of her confinement. The air about her was thick with putrid smells. The chains around her writs chafed. She had failed the dragon. In her mind she could still see him chained down in a cave on the castle grounds. A place they called The Dragon Chamber.

Large painful gashes along his sides were kept open by the guards as they periodically reinjured him. His wounds were not enough to kill him, just enough to hurt him, to weaken him. For some strange reason she could feel it every time they reopened them. She did not

Fires of Life

know why, but somehow she and the dragon were connected. Perhaps because it was the last of its kind, perhaps it was something more. She did not know. But it was this connection that had brought her to the castle, to the dragon. It was also what had helped to give her away.

Sneaking into the castle had been easy. Dressed as peasant girl, wearing a cloak, she had barely been given a second glance. When it came to finding the dragon, well that had proved a bit trickier, but still nothing that she could not handle. Listening in and sneaking around, she had found out where he was; in The Dragon Chamber. Skulking quietly, she had followed a guard to the chamber.

That was when she had caught her first real look at the dragon. He was in a sad condition. Huge gashes along his side appeared to keep him in a weakened state. His body weight and mass for a dragon his size were way under what they should have been. Pain and anguish were clearly visible in his eyes. She had known some of that before she arrived, but nothing could have prepared her for the reality of it.

However, it had not taken her away from her focus at the time; only deepened her resolve. Quietly, she had snuck up on one of the guards near him and used one of her specially tipped blow darts. The dart, along with others she had on her, had been dipped in a concoction designed to instantly knock anyone out who was even so much as scratched with it. Once she had neutralized him, she had immediately gone on to two others who were on the same side. Everything was going down as planned.

Her trouble began when one of the guards on the opposite side of the dragon suddenly, and without warning, stabbed the dragon with a huge lance in one of the open wounds, causing both her and the dragon to cry out. At the sound of her outcry the remaining guards had immediately rushed upon her.

Wasting no time, she had brandished her sword from behind her back, under her cloak, and immediately began to fight them off, wounding two of them. The dragon had lashed out at his captors in an effort to assist her, but they had countered with their own weapon designed specifically to subdue dragons, and it had all been over for her.

The pain from the weapon used on the dragon caused her to double over and trip. When she did, the sword fell from her hand and flew across the floor. In an effort to defend herself she had reached for the dagger in her boot and thrown it; killing the guard who was about to kill her. However, an astute guard had noticed the correlation between the wounding of the dragon and her fall, and had stopped the next guard from killing her. Instead, they had merely captured her and brought her before Vaulnik.

Now she was imprisoned in this cold hard cell, and to make matters worse Vaulnik had her sword and dagger. That sword and dagger had belonged to her father's, father's grandfather. Her father had not been interested in history, preferring the new to the old, so the old Legend Keeper had seen to it that they were given to her. She could hear his words now.

"It is called Shevardon," he had said, handing her the beautiful blade, "The Sword of Justice and this is its companion Galhidor, The Dagger of Truth. Be careful with them. They belonged to your father's, father's grandfather and were used during The Time of Great Sorrows. They brought much victory and eventual peace, but at a terrific price. You must keep them safe. Never ever let them fall into enemy hands."

Great! I have failed there too. I can only hope he does not know more about them than I. Perhaps he will just dismiss them. One can only hope.

But thoughts of the sword and dagger in Vaulnik's hands did not comfort her.

*I have got to get out of here. I **must** get out. I have to free that dragon. But how and how do I retrieve my sword and dagger? Those may be lost for now. The dragon takes priority. But how am I going to free him?*

Fires of Life

Frustrated, she pulled on the chains which held her shackled to the stone wall of her prison cell. The cold unforgiving metal refused to give in to her will. There clanging echoed throughout the tiny icy hollow space that was her prison. Frustration rose within her.

Outside the bars of her stony confinement she could hear the sounds of other prisoners. Their agony and cries of discomfort reverberated into her small confines. She searched about for anything she could use to free herself, but there was nothing except for a small rat sniffing the far corner of her cell, searching, she presumed, for some tiny morsel in which to nourish itself.

Voices from the cells outside hers continued to reverberate off the walls. The rat in the corner now scurried along the wall making its way for the door. She watched its gray furry form move along the wall and doubled back on itself after reaching its apparent destination. Apparently, the door had offered nothing it wanted. Suddenly, it stopped, stood on its hind legs and sniffed the air, its tiny nose twitching, searching, for exactly what one could only guess. Then it dropped to all fours, and continued back along the wall the way it had entered, through a hole in the corner of her cell.

She shifted positions. The sound of her chains as she repositioned her body echoed off the stone walls which imprisoned her. Frustrated, her mind wandered to the question of her connection to the dragon.

Can I be the Shaddorak spoken about in the legends of old? No, surely not. But what about all those visions that came from the dragon and the incident in the Dragon Chamber? Odd, yes, but be the Shaddorak?

The question had never entered her mind before. But now that Vaulnik had proposed the idea, she could not but wonder if there was any shred of truth to it.

She stared down at the chains about her writs, but her eyes did not see them as she desperately searched her mind for an explanation, a clue, anything. The night she had awoken in the middle of the Forest of Herlona with Salcon, her beautiful gray stallion, standing over her, his white muzzle nuzzling her to wake her up, had been quite traumatic.

As she stared down at the chains which bound her, her mind drifted back to that horrible night. She could see it now, how dazed she had been as she sat up trying to recall why she was there. Then it had hit her, the memory of The Great Battle. How she had woken up from what she had thought was a bad dream only to have it turn out not to be one.

Her mind traveled back in time as she sought to review that night. Its events had been so pivotal to her life; surely there must be some meaning there.

It had all started in the wee hours of the morning, way before the sun had risen. Everyone in the castle was asleep save for the guards on duty. All was quiet when what she thought was a dream had begun. Dark images, pain, and confusion she could feel it, see it almost as if she was living it in that moment so long ago.

Dragons, lots, and lots of dragons, she could feel their rage, sense their anticipation of an impending battle in the predawn darkness. Scenes of a mountain top covered with row upon row of angry dragons ready to fight an, as yet, unseen enemy. Clouds, smoke, men on horses battle ready, their steeds pawing at the ground, throwing up their heads in anticipation, the enemy a black line in the distance.

Tossing and turning she woke up only to discover it was no dream for the images never left her mind. Fumbling and staggering, she moved about her room. Thoughts and images crowded her mind as she found her dressing robe, but then the scenes before her eyes would not leave. She stumbled about her room groping, knocking over objects in her attempt to find her way. Her eyes wide and wild as the images crowded before them, a sense that she must leave, must find this battle flooding her soul.

To that end she fumbled and floundered about her room trying to reach her wardrobe. She reeled as the images kept coming. In a far

Fires of Life

off distance she could see the enemy. Dark horses, large war machines, hordes of soldiers, and on the mountains and in the air dragons, their anticipation continuing to flood her veins.

Finally, her hand felt the handle of her wardrobe, and immediately she turned it to open its door. Groping once more, she searched as if she was a blind person hunting for her garments, the visions continuing to cloud her eyes.

At last she had found them, her hunting clothes. Desperately, she placed them on as the images kept coming. She felt once more for the sword and dagger which the old Legend Keeper had given her. Fumbling and scrabbling around her wardrobe, she had finally managed to grasp them. Immediately, she adorned herself with all that she had just retrieved.

Awkwardly, she opened the door to her room. Down the hall, to the stairs she had all but stumbled. Concentrating, she pushed through the images in order to negotiate the stairs. Onward she traveled through the castle till she came upon the stable.

All the horses... I must focus...must focus. I have to find Salcon.

Concentrating, trying to see past the images to what was before her with all her might she finally spied him. Fumbling a bit for his saddle, and praying she did not attract the attention of the guards outside, she managed to make her way over to him. He danced and paced in his stall, unnerved by her state of mind.

"Easy boy, easy," she told him in hushed tones, her hands groping for him, hoping against hope that she could calm him. "We just need to hurry. I have to get to this battle." Salcon stopped and stood, blowing with defiance at the unseen enemy in her mind.

"I know. It's okay," she cooed as she saddled him up, his white fur reflecting and contrasting vividly in the dark surroundings. The smell of horse, hay, and damp earth dominated the air around her. The moonlight streaming in through a broken slat in his stall provided the perfect light with which to see by as she attached her sword to his saddled. Slowly, quietly she snuck out of the stable as the images of the impending battle continued to flood her mind.

Slipping past the castle guard was not going to be easy. Nearing the gate she searched the ground; a stone. She reached for it.
NO!
Dragons, men, swords, battle.

CLANG! CLANG!

Fog, blur, haze, smoke, the images flooded her mind, throwing her back against the stone wall of the castle.
Concentrate!
Confusion, chaos blurred her vision, forcing her to focus, to drive it all to a place in her mind where she could still see.
Fire, pain, wings, talons, faces, she needed to push them back. More smoke, arrows flying…
Concentrate!
She closed her eyes and forced herself to calm her mind, to see past it all. Dragons, fire, teeth, smoke…
Focus!...Breath!...Success!
She opened her eyes.
Now to reach for the stone.
She reached for the stone, picked it up, and flung it to distract the men on watch. Their backs turned to see what had made the noise. Carefully, she walked herself and Salcon out past them despite the images that still threatened to overload her mind. Somehow she was managing to achieve a level of control over them.

Once out of sight of the castle gate she up and mounted Salcon, riding hard towards the battle in her mind, driven for some unknown reason to join the fray. She could feel Salcon under her as they rode through the city of Escadora. His hooves echoing off the silent cobble stone streets. The guards at the main city gate briefly stepped out in front of them only to quickly step back as she and Salcon flew past.

On they rode. She could feel the power of his hooves as he tore up the ground under them. Tearing over hill and vale, they

Fires of Life

eventually left the road and entered the Forest of Herlona; dodging trees and jumping logs. Before long she could see the sun as it began to shine through the canopy above despite the horrid images of battle she was witnessing through the eyes of the dragons.

Suddenly, it hit; a jolt of tearing, ripping pain like she had never felt before.

"AHH!" she screamed as the pain forced her to double over in the saddle.

Salcon sensing her distress galloped harder into the wood and hills to meet the offending foe. Through the images another sudden bought of pain hit her so hard that she could no longer see where they were going.

BAM "UHH!"

THUD "AHH!"

A tree branch collided with her as Salcon galloped easily under it knocking her from him, smacking her forcefully against the hard earth as she fell. The pain from hitting the branch and ground felt like nothing compared to the pain she felt at that precise moment as yet another bought of tremendous agony ripped through her body.

There she lay staring up into the canopy rolling, writhing in horrible pain while twisted images of battle danced before her eyes. Something was causing the dragons' tremendous pain. Something was hurting, wounding them.

What is it?

Pain, anger, she could feel it all. Suddenly, she could see the offending foe; other dragons, their talons, their teeth ripping and tearing into the flesh of the dragons in her mind. They had appeared seemingly out of nowhere. Dark, shaggy, twisted versions of the dragons she knew, but she could feel them as well as dragon fought dragon.

On and on she writhed in pain and disorientation while the horrible twisted visions kept coming, invading her mind.

Through the fog of pain came the vague distant sound of hooves coming to a halt but never seen. No. In her mind all she saw was the far distant battle that raged on, never ceasing. Then, as she rolled and tried to focus on where she was, came the clouded, distant, but hazy over lapping image of one hoof, and then another as Salcon came and stood over her while she grabbed and tore at the earth in agony, uprooting grass and flower.

The day went on about her, but she saw none of it. Only the visions of the long distant battle, a battle she could never get to. Soon the sun set, stars came out and stared down at her from the lofty Shardon Lands above the tree tops, but in her mind all she saw were the horrible twisted, terrifying, gruesome images of dragon fighting dragon.

Dragon should never be pit against dragon. The emotions, the blasphemy, the agony; she could feel it all. Finally, as if it could not become any worse, she was flooded with the thoughts, feelings, and pain of the last surviving dragon as it witnessed the death of its beloved mate. Then the world went dark.

The first thing she saw when she finally woke up was the muzzle of her gray horse as he nuzzled her face and hair, the light of the full moon behind him glistening off his white coat, silhouetting his face.

"It's okay, boy," she told him in a weakened voice as she gently stroked his face to reassure her loyal friend, "I'm alright now." His big brown soft eyes stared down upon her with curious concern.

Slowly, she dragged herself to her feet. Then up onto his back and rode off into the woods; some feeling deep inside her telling her not to return to the castle. Rationally, she knew she should. They would be looking for her. But some unknown force was telling her she should not return. Things were going to be different now, now that the dragons were gone.

The evil forces she had just witnessed would have very little to stop them. Part of her wanted to return to the castle to fight them off, yet every time she set off in that direction she was flooded with the terrible sensation that that was not the right choice. Even Salcon seemed reluctant to return home.

So she journeyed into the woods, letting Salcon lead the way. Once more day blended into night and the dawn of yet another morning, and still she had no idea where would be a safe place for her to rest and collect her thoughts. Suddenly, through the forest she spied the calm of an inviting pool. Branches cracked under Salcon's hooves as they approached. Birds sang while a gentle breeze blew through the trees. To her left she could see a high cascading waterfall. She dismounted and went for a drink near the edge of the pool.

Crystalline waters sparkled and danced in the light of the morning sun. Salcon immediately began to enjoy the grass near the water's edge. Suddenly, there was a quick flash in the water. She paused, searching. Then there it was again. Fish, the water was teaming with them. Hungry, she went in search of something with which she could use to catch the potentially tasty creatures. Back towards the waterfall there were some great looking bushes which she thought just might have what she was looking for.

Eagerly, she searched around the area when suddenly, just as she was about to reach for what she thought was a perfect implement for her fishing needs, she spied it; a cave. A small dry cave hidden behind the bushes and cascading falls. It was perfect, just the place to hide and think. The more she investigated the space the more she knew this was the right choice.

It was there she had remained till now, living off skills which she had learned at first as lessons given to her by the old Legend Keeper, then as those taught by others. She had been different from most royal princesses of the past, in that she had desired to not only learn the ways of hunting and survival but of warfare too. To that end, she had listened in surreptitiously on all the lessons of strategy and war that were given to her bother, and another. One she presumed her father thought would make a good companion for him.

She remembered coaxing her brother's Swords Master into teaching her the art of sword play. It had not been easy. Her father did not approve of the teaching of such skills to women, but she had found an ally in the old Legend Keeper, and so her education in the art of swordsmanship had been done in secret.

That was how she had come by the sword and dagger. They had been a gift once she had achieved the degree of proficiency both the old Legend Keeper and her Swords Master deemed worthy of the noble weapons. All of what she had learned in those days had kept her alive, been honed with time and practice, practice which included living as one who does not wish to be found.

However, none of it seemed to explain whether, or not she was the Shaddorak. Yes, it was foretold that the Shaddorak would see as the dragon sees, but it said nothing about feeling as the dragon felt. The Shaddorak was supposed to be able to wield the power of the goddess Alhera. She certainly had no such grandiose powers, though occasionally some stones would glow for her. But that was not particularly unusual. Many women who eventually went on to be Dragon Witches had such powers. It did not prove she was the Shaddorak, for she was no Dragon Witch. It was from their ranks that the Shaddorak was supposed to come.

No. He is just a madman. I came here because of the visions of this dragon, but they did not start till after the invasion, and those were mainly dreams, dreams of his captivity. Why? If the dragon has been here since The Great Battle, then why have I not felt him till now?

The question gnawed at her mind.

Did the dragon have anything to do with it? Maybe, but I'll never know the answer to that. I don't even know why I felt them that day of The Great Battle. This has to do with something else, for if I had the power of the goddess I would have freed that dragon and we would both be far, far away from here by now.

She puzzled over it.

Proximity? Is that the answer to the shared pain? No. That would not explain The Great Battle. But it would explain the chamber. Maybe sheer numbers explain The Great Battle and the real answer is intensity. Perhaps. Still that does not answer the ultimate question.

Her mind continued to ponder.

Oh, who knows if the Shaddorak has even been born yet?

She blew a hair out of her eyes.

Once again she glanced around her cell. No sign of the rat, just dust and cold hard stones. She sat back against the wall. Her mind spent. Gradually it began to wander. A vision of a beautiful spring day from sometime during her early childhood floated into view.

The air was warm. Trees and flowers were in full bloom as she frolicked outside somewhere. A feeling of childish mischief came over her as she snuck out from the safety of those in charge to see the beauty of the woods. As she reached their edge, she felt a strange pull to enter. Into the forest she traveled following the feeling in her heart. Giggling and laughing, she journeyed through the wood not caring if she was damaging the beautiful silk of her tiny blue dress as she pushed past branches, stepped over logs, and traversed through underbrush while making her way deeper into its heart.

Suddenly, all the feelings of childish wonder filled her as she push back the branch of a hawthorn tree, fully laden with flowers, and stepped into a thicket bursting with all sorts of flora. It was a riot of color and light. The sun's rays twinkled in through the canopy, her eyes following their light as it fell on a magnificent female dragon. Her beautiful green scales glistened in the sun, radiating a multitude of tiny rainbows throughout the thicket in which she was resting.

She gasped in wonder and delight, standing transfixed by the spectacle before her. The dragon lifted its magnificent head and stared at her. It felt friendly, and she was about to step towards it when she heard her mother calling and had to run off. But not before taking one last look at the marvelous creature.

She remembered how wonderful that day had been. It had been her private secret.

But that still does not answer the question. Oh, does it matter if I am the Shaddorak or not? Unless I suddenly grow some mystical powers, it looks as if this is where both the dragon and I will die. I have got to get out, but how?

She searched the space again for any sign of something she could use to her advantage, but nothing. She leaned her back against the stone wall again, her mind temporarily blank.

Am I the Shaddorak?

The question once again returned to her mind, gnawing on it, yet her search for the answer remained as elusive as ever.

Why am I bothering? The idea is just the ravings of a mad man, a lunatic who is obsessed with power! What I really need is a way out of here.

Once more she tugged on the chains, crying out in frustration at the captivity in which she found herself. Trapped, ineffective, she needed to free herself. Free she was sure she could release the dragon from his captivity. She knew her mistake, and for now it seemed they were leaving the dragon alone.

But I have no weapons. That can be remedied. But how do I control the pain if they should return to hurting it?

Try as she might she still did not have an answer for that.

Oh, Alhera help me! I must free that dragon! He is the last of his kind. The world needs him.

Nothing.

She looked up at the ceiling. The cold impassive stones of which it consisted offered no insights. As she stared across the confines of her cell, all her mind could see was Vaulnik's dragons as they flew over her cave in the woods.

It was a beautiful fall morning as she knelt by the pool gathering water. The sunlight dancing through the canopy of oranges, reds, and various shades of yellow, the air crisp and fresh, then suddenly, like an ugly knife, his dragons came, their flight darkening the ground near her cave. She looked up only to catch a glance of their shaggy gray forms. Their horrid cries echoing across the land.

Almost immediately she could smell their fires burning in the distance. It was not long before she heard the cries and screams of villagers. Quickly, she went into her cave and grabbed her bow and sword, then ran out just as Salcon was about to run off in fear. But she ran in front of him, grasping his reins and hoisting herself on his back. Off they rode following the cries and screams.

Through the forest they went as fast as they could towards the burning conflagration. Over logs, under branches, and then suddenly they found it. She pulled up short, bringing Salcon to an abrupt halt. Flames were licking the outer walls of the village. Through the gates she could see Vaulnik's men as they raped and pillaged the small town. Smoke and flames swirled about her and Salcon.

She notched a few arrows in her bow and let them fly. They found their marks easy enough. As she drew her sword, and was about to attack, a great wall of flames suddenly welled up, blocking her path. Salcon reared and she was forced to retreat. The heat and smoke interfering with her sight as the flames threatened to engulf both her and her horse.

She tried circling the inferno to find an opening, but to no avail. Every time she tried to move in close it seemed the flames threatened to engulf them. Finally, she was forced to watch from a distance as his army marched across the land, invading Avivron. Sorrow and rage took her as she rode to her home in the woods. There was nothing more she could do.

But then the dreams had come, and she could no longer remain in hiding. She had to seek it out. She had to find the dragon. To free it at all cost.

A clanging of keys startled her out of her reverie. The sound coming closer as a guard and his footsteps neared her cell. She looked up. The sentry was now opening the door to her chamber, and with him was Vaulnik.

The guard was about even in height with Vaulnik, though significantly more well-built. His hair was black and greasy, his beard stubbly. Obviously, he spent way too much time in the dungeon. Both men were dressed in black, but Vaulnik's clothes were considerably more refined, as was his appearance.

"Get up!" the guard ordered, his sword clanging against his mail as he came over and stopped in front of her.

Good for nothing bitch! Another dead end treat for our good king.

She spat on him as he tried to haul her to her feet.

A hard smack came across her face as he hit her for her insolence.

Feisty one. He'll have fun with you!

"The king is here to question you," he informed her as he finished dragging her to her feet.

"So the rumors *are* true. He does like to get his hands dirty, or is it that I am that important," she remarked her eyes on fire.

Another smack came across her face, this time harder than the last. She could feel the area swell where he hit her, its sting reverberating across her face.

"Don't think to flatter yourself," the guard told her gruffly.

Bitch!

"Oh, then the king *is* in the habit of getting his hands dirty," she replied sarcastically. The guard made as if to strike her again but Vaulnik stopped him, catching his hand before it struck.

"Come now, Varthrak, we don't want our guest *too* manhandled; yet," Vaulnik's voice was sinisterly sweet, "Now unchain her and

Fires of Life

bring her to The Chamber," he ordered brusquely as he left the cell, the sound of his diminishing footsteps echoing throughout the small space.

"Make one wrong move and I'll have no problem running you through," Varthrak told her in a hushed tone once the king was out of ear shot, his dark eyes menacing, penetrating.

"No, *you* might not, but my guess is your king would have a problem with you running me through," she replied impudently, refusing to be impressed by his show of intimidation.

Another smack came down across her face as he then grabbed her by the neck and shoved her up against the hard stone wall behind her.

"Have no fear," he told her in a muted angry voice. "If you try to run, I *will* kill you. It's my job to protect the king, and from where I stand you are just a threat to him no matter what he wishes," Varthrak finished through his teeth.

"Varth! What's taking so long?" The king asked from the corridor of the dungeon.

"Better hurry," she told him her eyes flaming, "Your master is calling."

Varthrak glared at her a moment before he released his grip. "Nothing!" he shouted over his shoulder in reply to Vaulnik. Then he gruffly unchained her.

She rubbed her writs. Red, angry, raw marks looked up at her from where the chains had been.

"Come on bitch! Your new master wants to speak with you," he told her as he grabbed her by the arm and shoved her along in front of him, all the while keeping one hand squarely on the hilt of his sword.

The clink of his armor echoed in the stony hollow of her cell as once more he shoved her forward and out past its entrance, into a corridor which led down a hall of prison cells. The awful sights and sounds coming from the other prisoners as they traveled to their destination reflected and reverberated in her mind.

Groping hands reached out through cell bars with crowded conditions. Unsavory smells filled the air, the stench nearly causing her to vomit. A few solitary cells with victims hanging from chains dotted their path. Dim torch light flickered and danced along the images of these tortured souls as they passed by while their moans of pain filled her ears. How she wished there was something she could do.

Soon they stopped in front of a large heavy metal door. A loud authoritative knock by Vaulnik brought its guard on the other side to attention, and a brief exchange of entry dialogue took place. Arms groped towards her from behind bars as prisoners begged Vaulnik for mercy. The man in front of her, dressed in his fine robes, stood stoic and unmoving. Apparently, undisturbed by the cries and pleas of those imprisoned around him while the guard on the other side opened the metal door before them.

Vaulnik arrogantly stepped through. The guard who had opened it gave a half bow, but the tyrant in black gave no notice as he passed. Varthrak shoved her through the metal entrance that led to a set of narrow winding stone stairs. She nearly tripped on the first step as once again he shoved her forward.

Vaulnik was well ahead of them. The light from the torches that lined the narrow stony staircase flickered and danced off the walls. Their steps echoed up and down the tiny space as they went. On and on it seemed to ascend till finally they stopped. Keys chinked and clanked as another guard, who had apparently been waiting for them, unlocked a large wooden door which creaked as it opened.

"Ah, our destination at last," Vaulnik commented once the door was opened. "You may leave us," he barked to the guard who had opened the door. The guard nodded quickly and left, the sound of his receding foots steps echoing as he went.

"Come now, my dear, it is time for us to have a little chat," Vaulnik stood in the entry and gestured for her to enter. She stood solid, refusing to move. Varthrak shoved her forward and through the doorway which led into The Chamber.

Fires of Life

There were no windows in The Chamber. Only the light of torches lit the circular room. A pair of chains dangled down from the ceiling in the center while various torture devices hung along the wall on one side of the circular chamber. Defiance was the only emotion that gripped her heart as she was shoved through its entrance. Fear had long since left her. In a situation such as this there was no room for fear, only defiance. He would get no satisfaction from her.

"Chain her up," ordered Vaulnik as he stepped in behind them while the guard did as he was instructed, shoving her along in front of him.

She wanted to resist, to fight. He turned her to face him; the entrance open behind him, his sword unattended. Quickly, she reached for it, grabbing at its hilt, raising it out of its sheath, and making to strike Varthrak. Then all of a suddenly she felt him grab her hair and shove her violently around, a hand to her throat. He squeezed her neck so that her eyes began to darken and stars formed in front of her. She could hear the sound of metal meeting the floor as she was forced to drop the blade.

Good. Defiance, fight, it will be delicious to break her.

Vaulnik's thoughts churned as he witnessed her attempt at escape.

"Careful Varth I still need her alive."

Vaulnik's voice sounded distant in her ears. Then she felt the guard release his grip on her neck. She gasped for breath.

"Try that again…" he told her through his teeth still clutching her hair, holding her against his chest.

"Varth! Chain her up!"

He released her hair, and gruffly grabbed her arm to comply with Vaulnik's request. Soon she hung nearly suspended by her arms in the center of the chamber. Her feet flat on the ground, the torchlight flickering sinisterly about the walls of the circular enclosure.

"Now I want you to leave us," the king ordered. "Go and inform the dragon keepers that I wish them to harm the beast."

At this her eyes burned with rage.

NOOO!

She struggled against the chains in vain to free herself.

Good. Just as I thought, empathy for the creature. Let us see if we feel his pain too.

"Tell them not so much as to kill the poor creature," he continued, "No. I simply want them to hurt it."

Varthrak looked puzzled as he nodded, glancing back at her just before he left the room. A loud bang of the door as it closed echoed within the chamber followed shortly by the telltale chink and click of a key turning. They were sealed in, her chance of escape gone; for the moment.

"I see my orders to hurt the dragon upset you, my dear," Vaulnik said to her once the guard had left them, his voice oozing with sickly sweet malice.

No words left her lips. She refused. Silence was all she was going to give him.

"Oh, come now, we both know you have a special interest in this dragon of mine. Otherwise why would they have found you in the Dragon Chamber?" a pause, "You know silence will get you nowhere, my dear."

He stepped around her, removing the whip from the wall. The whip made from descaled dragon's skin which he knew would inflict tremendous pain, pain that would last long after its initial bite.

"Now I ask you again, who are you?"

Silence.

"Defy me all you like, my dear. One way, or another I will have my answer."

Suddenly, she felt a great stabbing pain in her side, "AHH!" she cried unable to stop herself.

"Ah, I see my orders arrived swifter than I thought. They have begun to torture the dragon."

I have you now. I know who you are.

Again she felt another stab, this time on her other side. Her face twisted as she tried desperately to control the pain.

Fires of Life

"The longer you refuse to help me the worse it will be for your pet. See, my guess was right." A pause, "I know who you are," he whispered sinuously into her ear as he walked around her, letting his words sink in, "You are the Shaddorak," he continued now in her other ear.

She glared at him.

I am no such person!

"The one who feels what the dragon feels….The one who holds their power," he went on, standing in front of her, "The one who can control the fate of the world." He spread his hands out to indicate the world.

"You're wrong!" she shouted through the pain of another stab, breaking her personal vow of silence, so outraged she was by his suggestion, though doubt niggled at the back of her mind. She pushed it out.

"*I* am wrong?" he remarked sinisterly, "See how you writhe in pain as the dragon is injured. I think not my dear. How else would you explain your current condition? There is no one else here to torture you."

"I am **not** the Shaddorak!" she shouted through her teeth defiantly.

How can I be? I have no real power… or do I? The stones…

Pain seared through her body once more, this time a picture entered her mind, a picture through the dragon's eyes of his attackers as they wounded and taunted him once more.

"Oh, but I believe you *are*. And you *will* help me," he insisted as he waltzed around her.

"I am not!" she told him defiant through her teeth, "I …"

"You what?"

"I am **not** what you seek. And even if I were. I would **never** help you!"

"Oh, I think you will," he mocked from behind her. "By the end of the day you *will* know you are indeed the Shaddorak and you **will** help me."

"I think not!" she fired back with all her might, but another stab of pain from where they were hurting the dragon shot through her body, preventing any other thought or vocalization to leave her lips.

"See my dear, you *are* the Shaddorak," he whispered silkily in her ear, "Accept it. There is no point in denying your destiny."

"You're crazy!" she shouted through her pain.

Megalomaniac!

"Am I? Are you sure?" The questions seemed to slither from his lips. He paused for effect before stepping back behind her, "But enough of this. We are wasting time. Time I am sure your dragon does not have." At that moment he drew out the whip, cracking it in air, allowing its sound to reverberate off the walls of the chamber. "Let's begin shall we," he announced as in one violent motion he lashed at her with it.

The sound of the whip echoed throughout the chamber again, and shuddered through her body as it inflicted its burning, tearing pain.

"AHH!" she screamed feeling the whip's hot searing pain right down through the reaches of her flesh as it tore open her skin.

"Now help me!" he shouted through his teeth. The venom and frustration in his voice resonated about the chamber, giving her pause to wonder if it had been designed to do just that.

"Help me!" he shouted again.

"Never!" She would never give in no matter how much he hurt her.

CRACK!

"AHH!" she cried out again as another strike of the whip met its mark and burned deep within her flesh. This time she could feel her blood as it oozed down her back.

"Again I ask you, or shall I have your precious dragon killed!"

"NOOO!" She cried.

He cannot kill that dragon. I came here to save it. It's the last of its kind.

"Then help me," he hissed as he gruffly turned her to face him, the chains clanging as he did so and echoing throughout the chamber. His face was close to hers, so close she could smell his breath, the horrid jagged scar across his right eye glaring at her. Another stab of pain shuddered through her side as they injured the dragon once more. Her eyes rolled back as she connected to the great beast, their minds mingling briefly.

He shook her.

"Help me," he hissed again as her consciousness returned back to him; his voice sounding much like that of a venomous snake. "Help me and I'll spare your precious beast. Help me control the world and I'll give you a place of honor at my side."

Her consciousness burned with rage.

"Never!" she shouted through her teeth and pain, glaring at him straight in the eyes.

In your dreams you son of Zagnor!

There was no way she was going to help this monster take power, take control of the world.

"Very well then," he announced, letting go of her so that the chains righted her, returning her so that her back once again faced him, "Have it your way. But by the end of today you *will* help me, or you and your dragon will die."

CRACK!

"AHH!" she cried out again as the pain seared her body.

On and on it went, again and again Vaulnik unleashed his whip. Blood splattered the walls, and delirium threatened to take hold of her mind till suddenly a great jolt of pain ripped through her body and the entire world went dark.

At that precise moment all the torches went out in the chamber as if they had been blown out by a great force or wind. Vaulnik searched around the room, but no light was to be had. He stood there, in the darkness, alone. Silence permeated throughout the chamber. Only the occasional ting of the chains as she hung suspended in the room could be heard.

Suddenly, from outside came the sound of footsteps rushing his way. Cling, chink the door opened and the light of a torch flickered in the darkness.

"Sire, Sire, the dragon is dead!"

It was strange how she could now see what went on after her world went dark, but then not much fazed her anymore. The images of her past kept flooding her mind as she sat staring into the gently flickering flames. Clavorn remained quiet as he sat watching her from across the warm glow of the slow burning fire, wondering what sights were passing through her mind. All she could see was The Chamber with its flickering dim torchlight, and Vaulnik's ugly scarred face.

"NOOO!" he screamed angrily at the news of the dragon's death. He needed that dragon. He had captured that dragon at the battle of Quantaris, kept it alive just for this. No! He needed it to be her dragon. He never intended the dragon to die. That had merely been an idle threat. One meant to coerce her into cooperation.

"Who killed the beast? Tell me. I want his **head**!" Vaulnik grabbed at the guard, rage spilling forth.

"No one, sire," the guard replied fear written clearly in his eyes.

"WHAT?!"

Liar!

"That's just it, sire," the guard tried to explain, "The beast just died. No one was even close to it. No one was even touching it."

"That's impossible! Someone must have struck the final blow." Vaulnik refused to accept that the dragon just died. That just could not be.

"No, sire, no one did," the guard replied, fear and nervousness clearly present in his voice.

Fires of Life

Vaulnik could see from the guard's expression that he was telling the truth and was just as perplexed as himself. He released the guard and paced the floor in front of him. Eerie shadows danced upon the walls of the blood splattered chamber.

"Sire!" the guard exclaimed as he held the lit torch and pointed over Vaulnik's shoulder.

Vaulnik turned around. Darkness and shadows flickered about the room, but the light from the torch clearly lit the sight in the center of it. There, lit by the wavering light of the torch, hung her lifeless body suspended by the chains. Vaulnik went over and felt her pulse, but there was none.

"CURSE THE DRAGONS!" he exclaimed.

So close and now this!

"Remove her body and have them both destroyed. I want no evidence of their existence. Do you understand me?! NONE!"

"Yes, your highness, but…but how?"

"Don't ask! Just do it!" he demanded as he stormed out of The Chamber.

Anger and frustration clutched at his heart. Now he would never be able to complete his plan. Thoughts whirled through his mind. The Dragon Witch had said he needed the Shaddorak. That he needed at least one dragon alive from their world otherwise, she had warned, the Shaddorak would be useless to him.

He flew up the stairs, rage pulsing through his veins. Suddenly, at the top of the stairs his heart stopped. There at the top of the staircase was an ancient mural. Or would he? He paused a moment in his trek, gazing at the scene before him as a new thought entered his deviant mind. A smile began to briefly form on his face before he continued down the dark and dismal hall back to his chambers.

She could see the mural in her mind, and felt the importance of the dragon she needed Clavorn to find grow within her. The scene changed yet again as her mind shifted through the history of her past, and once more she was plunged into the sea of memory.

Suddenly, she felt herself gasp for breath as she awoke to a great wall of fire. Choking, she could feel the heat from the burning flames nearly scorch her body. Only the dragon's tail protected her. As she tried to gaze through the smoke and fire, she could just make out Vaulnik's men standing outside the blaze, watching while the conflagration licked and scorched the earth, burning the pyre they had built to destroy their bodies. Only for some reason they were not burning.

All of a sudden a great wave of anger flew through her. And for some inexplicable reason she lifted her head to the sky as a huge outpouring of energy was expelled from her body, squelching the flames, and knocking all the guards unconscious.

When she opened her eyes she could see it was night. A clear sky shined down upon them. Stars and moonlight flooded the area with light, casting an eerie glow upon the scene. As she glanced about, she noticed that the guards were all out cold, and both she and the dragon were healed. Although there were clearly scars on the dragon, and she assumed on herself as well, from where they had been tortured by Vaulnik and his men.

"Now what, my friend?" she exclaimed as she stepped away from the dragon to view the scene.

The dragon's blue scales glistened in the moonlight.

What beautiful creatures they are. It would be nice if he had a surviving mate. Perhaps then there would be a chance for more of them, so that one day they might rule the skies again.

"Nice thought...But now we must leave," sounded a voice in her head.

She nearly jumped out of her skin. "What? Who said that?"

Her mind raced as she tried to figure out the source of the voice she had just heard.

"*I did,*" replied the voice in her head.

Instinctively, she looked up into the face of the only other conscious creature nearby.

"You can speak to me?!" she exclaimed surprise clearly audible in her voice.

"*Now I can. But we have no time for this at the moment. We must leave here at once. Jump on my back. It is best if Vaulnik believes we are dead and our bodies nothing but smoldering ash,*" the dragon informed her, his voice in her head sounding as familiar as an old friend.

Without any hesitation she climbed onto the dragon's back. Before she knew it he had spread his great wings. With one powerful thrust downward they were off the ground. One more beat of his great wings, and they were high above the site of their supposed disposal. Suddenly, the dragon breathed fire down upon the very spot they had been and scorched the earth.

"*Now they will believe they have done their job,*" the dragon remarked.

"But there won't be any remains of our bodies," she commented.

"*True, but wasn't that his instructions?*"

"How do you know that?"

"*Magic is a powerful thing, and you are in the thick of it my dear. Come, let us hide ourselves till the time is right, and I will teach you all that you need to know.*"

"Then I *am* the Shaddorak," she exclaimed surprised by her own revelation, the suspicion that had been introduced during her interrogation now taking its full fruition.

"*Yes, Alethea, you are,*" the dragon replied simply.

"That is not my name," she remarked.

"*Yes, Alethea, that is your true name,*" the dragon told her as he banked over a mountain ridge. Alethea held on tight as she felt the force of the dragon's motion.

My true name. What does that mean?...Alethea.

She mulled the name over in her head trying to recall if she had ever heard it used before. Try as she might she could find no recollection of it having ever been used to refer to her.

"Wait a minute you said 'true name.' What about my other name?" she asked of the dragon.

"That is part of your past now. That part of you is dead. You are Alethea, the Shaddorak now," the dragon finished simply.

She wanted to ask more. To inquire as to 'why,' but then she remembered that she was in the thick of magic now, the magic of the gods.

The cool evening wind blew through her hair. She settled in on the dragon's back, his huge blue body shimmering in the night sky as they flew above the trees to some unknown destination. Somehow she felt strangely comfortable in the knowledge that she was the Shaddorak, almost as if some part of her had always known.

She relaxed and connected her mind to his. Soon she could feel his joy of flight, of freedom, of life. The more she connected with him, the more she too felt those feelings and began to revel in them. She closed her eyes and lifted her face into the wind.

Her green eyes starred into the flames as the visions of the past faded. The fire of the embers burned in her emerald catlike eyes as she lifted them to meet his.

"My name is Alethea."

Chapter 31

"So, you have a name," he commented, "Is there a story to go with this name?"

He really wanted to know more about her. The mystery that surrounded her haunted his mind, teasing him like an unsolved puzzle.

"You now know who I am. I do not need to explain anything else," she replied clearly agitated.

He was about to object when she threw a log on the fire.

"You know I could use your refusal to tell me who you are as a reason to bar you from battle," he told her as he watched the flames flare and being to lick the virgin wood.

"You would regret it," she replied matter-of-factly as she flicked the hair from her eyes.

The lioness rose and came to sit by her. Alethea stroked the big cat as she looked off in the distance. Soon a low rumbling sound permeated throughout the little tent as the big cat purred, clearly enjoying her attention.

"I believe you are right though," he replied.

At his remark she suddenly turned her face to his.

Is that surprise I see in her eyes?

"So I will agree to have you help, however you deem fitting," he finished, looking into her green eyes.

For a moment the two remained staring into one another's eyes before she broke their gaze. Silence took hold between the two as she took her sword out and began sharpening it. Salhera stretched out and started to groom herself again.

"You will still need to find the dragon," she told him, breaking the stillness between them while she continued to sharpen her sword.

"Why?"

"You know why," she replied, putting down her sword abruptly, briefly startling the catamount.

"Then give me time," he urged her, "I cannot find the dragon with the enemy breathing down my throat," his frustration clearly evident in his voice.

"Sefforn can lead your men as needed while you go off and find the dragon."

"But the men expect me to fight *with* them," he protested.

Doesn't she understand the subtleties of leading men into battle?

"I have promised many of them they could fight at my side tomorrow. What do you suggest I tell them? That I have a dragon quest to go to? That I have matters of greater urgency than their survival?"

"No, that would not do," she replied.

"There! You see," he remarked almost in triumph though the frustration was still evident in his voice.

"No, you fight tomorrow if you must, but then let Sefforn take over and lead your men. You must find the dragon."

"Alright, I will agree to leave the day after tomorrow, but I need more information about the dragon's whereabouts."

"I am afraid I have given you all I can," she told him, peering deeply into his eyes.

The fire in her eyes penetrated his soul.

"Just follow your heart. You know where it is. Listen with your soul, and you will find the dragon."

Suddenly, the tent went dark. Clavorn looked around, but there was no sign of her anywhere, or the mountain lion. He stood up and went outside. The cold mountain air bit into his flesh, but he did not feel it. His heart burned with frustration and vexation. She had done it again! She had slipped away into the night, disappearing without a trace.

He glanced about the camp and woodland. Silver moonlight streamed downward from the Shardon Lands, reflecting off the resting men and forest floor. The only sounds he could here was that of the occasional owl crying in the night. A gentle breeze came up and riffled through his thick dark hair.

Where is she?

His dark eyes penetrated the night, but to no avail. He had little doubt he would see her, but a part of him hoped he would.

Who is she?

All he knew for sure was her name. There was more to her story, he could feel it. He ran a hand through his hair, her final request to find the dragon weighing on his mind. Turning, he drew the deer skin flap that severed as the entrance to his tent back and reentered.

On the ground he could just make out the hint of his sleeping role, the thick furs inviting him in. Suddenly, he was overcome with the need to sleep.

Rest, the idea sounded so good in his mind. The questions that had threatened to override his brain and keep him up slipping into the farthest reaches of his consciousness. All he felt now was the overwhelming desire to sleep.

He walked over to his role and lay down, stretching out on the floor as he drew up the bear skin. Oh, how it felt good to lay down, the smell of the earth, the stillness of the night…

Before long Clavorn was resting peacefully, the events of the day gone from his mind. In the distant reaches of the woods an owl hooted and flew off.

Chapter 32

Sunlight filtered through the mist of the forest. The air smelled of damp earth as if just after a rain. Clavorn moved through the forest, pushing back branches as he stepped along. Wildflowers dotted the floor of the woodland, their perfume filling the misty air.

All of a sudden, the mist began to thicken so that he could travel no further. Soon all he could make out were a few tall tree trunks near him. Streams of sunlight filtered in through the canopy. Out of the mist a mountain lion padded towards him. Clavorn watched as it came up to him, and then in one bound, leapt over him. As he turned to follow where the big cat had gone, the forest turned dark and a great ravine opened up near his feet. The figure of the catamount disappeared into the image of a burning village where Kriac Stones were being harvested.

Suddenly, a huge dragon came over the horizon; dark and menacing, breathing fire upon the land and destroying the forest where he stood. As the dragon turned for another pass, its red eyes glaring, its black body blending into the night sky, its face changed to that of Vaulnik. His icy blue malicious eyes staring into his. The scar across his right eye giving his face an even more sinister appearance as it melted into the form of Zagnor; his laugh echoing throughout the woods and valley.

All around Clavorn the smell of smoke, ash, and burning flesh filled the air as the sound of Zagnor's laughter reverberated in his ears. Faces of his men dead bled through the image of Zagnor's face as it closed in on him, enlarging as it came closer. Their broken bodies strewn across a field of battle, while all around him the land burned and life withered.

Then a voice called to him in the woods. It was a familiar voice, soft, almost lyrical. Flowers sprung up about his feet, and all around him the forest was filled with their glorious colors as her voice enveloped him. Once again sunlight filtered in through the tree tops and mist of the woods.

Fires of Life

Clavorn found himself turning in circles as her voice repeated.

"Find the dragon. Find the dragon. Find the dragon."

Suddenly, she was standing in front of him. Clad just as she had been when she had arrived in his camp. Her dark hair billowing out behind her, her emerald green eyes staring into his, burning his soul while the animal skins she wore accented her svelte figure.

"Find the dragon!" her image ordered.

Clavorn woke with a start as he put his hand up to shield himself from the light of the full moon. The moonlight was streaming into his tent, and onto his face through a small opening in the flap that served as a door. The images of his dream still haunted his awareness as the memory of her final words to him reverberated in his mind. He lay there staring at the ceiling of his tent going over his last conversation with her before he had fallen asleep.

'Listen with your soul.'

Those words burned in his mind as he lay on his sleeping role, the fur skins soft against his flesh. It was clear what he had to do. The only question now was how best to execute it.

The moon was beginning to set over the tops of the trees as he opened the flap of deer skin that served as the door to his tent. The sun would be up soon, but he had to find Sefforn. He stepped outside. Most of the camp was sleeping peacefully now, except for the occasional watchman circling the perimeter. Clavorn glanced around and soon found his friend pacing about on night watch. It was not long before Sefforn caught sight of him and came over.

"So what has you up so early," he inquired as he came up to him.

"Seff, I want you to assemble the men. I wish to speak to them," Clavorn told him simply.

"Alright," Sefforn remarked a bit puzzled.

The directness and finality of Clavorn's request meant there was no time for questions. That whatever his reason, he had made up his mind. Now, the only thing that was required was action. Sefforn turned and began to carry out Clavorn's instructions.

A few minutes later Sefforn came into Clavorn's tent and announced to him that the men were assembled and awaiting him. Clavorn exited the tent with Sefforn right behind him.

The sky was just beginning to lighten as he stood before them. Their faces staring into his, questioning, puzzled, eager. A hawk cried out over head as he began his speech.

"I know you were all looking forward to fighting Vaulnik's men today, but I have decided that it is best if we retreat for now."

Great groans went up from the crowd of men assembled as they expressed their disappointment at not having a second chance to fight Vaulnik's army. Clavorn raised his hands to quiet them before continuing.

"I know, I know, you are disappointed, but do not think of this as a retreat, think of it as a regrouping. It is my firm belief, that if we are to win this war, and win we must, then we are going to need the dragon; the Last Dragon, Viszerak. When we are settled safe in the mountains I will leave you to find this dragon."

"But Shaltak, won't that mean that Vaulnik's army will be able to overrun this land while you are gone?" a man from the crowd asked. Clavorn recognized him as one of the men he had promised would fight beside him. The man called Bennethor.

"Yes, it is true they will make progress," he replied.

"Then why don't you let us raid them, slow them down…" Bennethor continued. Nods and voices of agreement rippled through the crowd of men.

"No. You must remain hidden. Let the enemy believe he has defeated us, that we are scattered to the wind. Strengthen your numbers secretly. Strengthen yourselves, so that when I return with the dragon, we may rise again like the great phoenix and defeat this vile scourge which threatens this land."

"But what of the woman?" another man from the crowd shouted.

"Valheras, ghosts, Dragon Witches, do we want it said that Avivron won her freedom because of these? Or do we want it said that Avivron won her freedom because of the valiant, brave men of

Fires of Life

this land? No. We shall take back this land for our families, for the dragon, for the life that dwells within its borders, for all free creatures everywhere." Clavorn paused. He could tell his words had met their mark.

"I do not know how long I will be gone, but do not despair or grow impatient. I will return, and I will return with the dragon."

His final words were uttered with the emphasis of his determination. He hoped they would heed his message, and wait, wait till he returned. Their success depended upon it.

Clavorn turned and left the throng of men. The sun was now peeking over the horizon. In the background he could hear Melkiar issuing orders for the men to break camp, and to be ready to leave as soon as the sun was up. He strode over to his tent and went in.

"Are you mad?!" Sefforn exclaimed as he entered behind him, "You can't just leave these men now? Where will we go? How will I keep them lying low till you return? You know there will be those who will feel they must go out with a fight even if they die and will not have the patience to wait."

Clavorn could think of several men who fit that description, himself included if he were to have to stay behind.

"I know," he replied, acknowledging the truth of Sefforn's words, "But you must do what you can to stop them. We must remain a united front. Our strength is in our unity. I will leave as soon as I know you are all safe," Clavorn told him as he began packing up.

"But what of Sevzozak's men? They could be here any day?"

"Are you sure? What do the scouts say?" Clavorn countered. He had serious doubts about the promises Almaik had made in the temple.

"They have not seen any sign of them as yet," Sefforn replied, "But that does not mean they are not on their way."

Clavorn paused in what he was doing and turned, looking his friend straight in the eyes with one raised eyebrow.

"Alright, maybe it does. But what if they show up expecting us to be here?"

"Then let them fight. It is about time they got the taste of war, but something tells me they will never show," Clavorn told his friend as he returned to his packing.

"Okay, let's say you are right. How will you find the dragon?" Sefforn pressed, "Is she going to help you?"

"No."

"Then how will you find the dragon?"

"I just will. I must!" Clavorn snapped, turning to face his friend, exasperation and frustration getting the better of him. He ran a hand through his hair. How could he make his friend understand, "Without the dragon we don't stand a chance."

"And if you don't?"

"I will!" he exclaimed, fierce determination emanating from his voice.

"Then at least let me come with you," his friend pleaded.

"No, Seff. I need you here." Clavorn told him, placing a hand on his friend's shoulder, his voice suddenly soft and urgent, "The men need you here. You must be my voice in my absence. If anyone can keep them together, it is you."

"But what about Melkiar or Thalon," Sefforn countered.

Clavorn took his hand from Sefforn's shoulder.

"I like them both, but they are not you. Look, we've known each other since childhood. You're the only one I trust with this job." Clavorn reached out and clasped his friend's arm, looking him straight in the eye, "I'm counting on you. Now, I must go as soon as I have located a safe campsite for you, but I will return, and I will return with the dragon. You can mark my words."

"Then we will look for your return," his friend replied finally acquiescing to Clavorn's argument. The two men clasped hands in a gesture of camaraderie, "Good Luck!"

"Same to you, my friend. Same to you," Clavorn told him.

After a brief moment, the two men released their hold of each other. A few seconds later Sefforn turned and left the tent, leaving Clavorn to finish with his packing.

Before long Clavorn was ready and mounted upon his horse. As he rode up through the remnants of what had been their camp, the first rays of light came over the mountain, clearing the tops of the trees, and casting a golden violet hue to the landscape before him. Clavorn and Hawk rounded a small hill that was covered with tall trees. From there he could see that his men were ready sooner than he expected. He made his way to the head of the formation, and with a nod gave the signal for them to move out.

Melkiar, Sefforn, Thalon, and now Bennethor joined him in the lead. Before long a scout rode up informing him that Vaulnik's army was on the move, and that they were just clearing the hillside that formed the ravine in which they had spent the night. His fears were coming into reality.

Are we going to have time to escape a battle, or are we going to be forced to face Vaulnik anyway?

He wondered at the wisdom of his decision.

Quickly, he searched the horizon for a suitable place to mount a defense.

"To the ridge!" he yelled, pointing his sword in the direction of the geographic formation he thought suitable as he spurred Hawk into action.

When he finally came over a rise where he felt it was safe to look back, he could see smoke coming from the place of their encampment. Clavorn watched for Vaulnik's army expecting to see them coming over the hill at any moment. He and Hawk stood searching the scene while he simultaneously encouraged his men to hurry past him and take their places along the ridge.

Suddenly, inexplicably, a wind came up; kicking up the fires Vaulnik's men had started, driving the smoke and flames right into them. Immediately, they began to retreat from the fierceness of the firestorm that was set upon them. At that very moment a great sound was heard from the north as a huge horde of ravens flew in over the mountains, their numbers forming a giant black cloud with a definite mind of its own.

Clavorn watched as the birds drew closer and closer like a massive winged storm. As soon as they reached the place where Vaulnik's soldiers were, they began circling and diving, attacking them in relentless waves of winged confusion.

Soon he could see Vaulnik's army fleeing, retreating back over the hillside which they had come, and into the land beyond as the flock of ravens continued to pursue them. The cries of the birds rose above the sound of the flames, and echoed throughout the land as their voices reverberated off the mountains. Clavorn smiled to himself as he turned Hawk and galloped off to join his men. She was giving him more time.

Fires of Life

Chapter 33

 Days went by as Clavorn lead his men back over the mountains and deep into the forest, back towards the valley of the willows, towards Shyloran Forest, where they had been safe before. Something in his gut told him that area seemed to be highly favored by the gods and would be just the sort of place they needed. However, they had already stayed quite a long time in Shyloran Forest with its meandering stream and ancient trees. He did not want to place it any further jeopardy than he already had, so he decided to search the mountains near there for a new location which might provide similar safety and secrecy. Clavorn rounded the mountain that encircled the ancient forest of willows, and rode straight along its spine. Then down over it and up onto a new mountain ridge.

 This territory, he was fairly certain, was pretty much unexplored; being that it was particularly rough going with its rocky outcroppings, sheer cliffs, and thick forests. Known as the Dragon's Lair, it was said to be in habited by an Ornskyterrak. Half eagle, half dragon, with just enough panther in it to make it an extremely dangerous creature even at night. No one had ever been able to lay eyes on one and live.

 Very territorial, and fiercely protective, it was not a foe anyone dare cross. Said to possess many powers none the least of which was the ability to see into a man's soul. Like dragons, they were considered sacred. This territory would then be considered hallowed as well, and off limits for habitation and exploration, but not for those seeking sanctuary; making it the perfect place for them to hang out. Provided Vaulnik had not already desecrated the area in his relentless search for Kriac stones, or the Ornskyterrak did not want them on his territory. A big gamble, but one he felt the situation warranted.

 He urged Hawk forward.

 "We're not going in there?" Bennethor commented.

"You're new with us aren't you," Melkiar remarked, moving his horse alongside the dark haired warrior.

"Well, I guess you could say that," he replied.

"Then you should know that when it comes to it. All of us close to Shaltak have learned to trust in his crazy ideas. Right Seff," Melkiar informed him.

"Right," Sefforn replied, affirming Melkiar's statement about his old friend.

"But there is an Ornskyterrak in there," protested the sturdy warrior.

"Yeah, probably why he's going in there," Thalon put in, riding up to join in the conversation, "I know I would. Look at this area. It's probably remained this untouched just because of it."

"Not afraid of it are you?" Clavorn asked over his shoulder.

"*No*," the rugged tough warrior replied, "I just thought…"

"You just thought someplace safe meant someplace other than a place said to be inhabited by an Ornskyterrak," Thalon finished for him.

"Well…ah, yeah, I mean no. I mean…"

"Ha, ha, ha," Clavorn and company started to laugh.

"It's alright Bennethor, they're just messing with you," Clavorn told his newest member of his inner circle.

"Yeah. Tf truth be told," Sefforn added, "We all have our misgivings about this path."

"This is true. I was just about to ask him that very same question myself," Melkiar told him. "In fact, I thought I was the only one who was wondering what we were doing going this way, but…"

"So what happened to all that bit about trust?"

"Oh, it's still there. I just wanted to know if you had gone *Dragon Crazed*, or not, yet," Melkiar told Clavorn.

"No. No Dragon Crazies yet, my friend. Just if you want to stay safe, sometimes it is best go where your enemy fears to tread."

"See. What did I tell you?" Sefforn commented, "He always has a reason. No matter how insane it may appear."

"I just hope that creature is either the stuff of legends, or truly sees us as a group of men on a noble mission," Melkiar remarked as they continued to follow Clavorn up over the hill and into the ominous woods.

Silence once again settled over the men as they entered the legendary forest. Every man was on edge and on the lookout for the legendary beast. Secretly, Clavorn was hoping the creature would just leave them be and let his men stay, but in his heart he could not help feeling that an encounter with the creature was sure to happen. His only hope was that he could convince it of their need.

Before long they were deep within the new forest riding through the mountains of the Dragon's Lair. The tension in air was thick. Tall dense trees and lush landscape filled the ominous forest. Every foot fall seemed an intrusion into this untouched land. Every unnatural sound an alarm for such a guardian, and yet it did not show itself.

Before long some of them began to relax. Short comments began to be whispered amongst them. Clavorn, however, remained ever vigilant. Creatures such as the Ornskyterrak were rarely lax in their duties.

Suddenly, as they made their way through the dense woodland and rolling rocky landscape of the mountain, the forest opened up allowing him to see down across a meadow and over into the areas beyond. That was when he spied it. The place he had seen in him mind's eye, the place that would keep his men safe while he journeyed off to find the dragon. He drove Hawk hard down into the tall grassy valley, and up towards the place he felt certain was the one he was looking for.

Here he entered a forest once more. Tall trees reached high into the sky for several dragon lengths. Once again the land here took on its rolling and rocky nature. Falls could be heard in the distance. Shorter trees dotted the landscape along with many fir, and pine. Sunshine filtered in through the canopy above, spotlighting the forest floor which contained many a fern and flower.

Suddenly, he slowed his horse. Here the forest thickened, if that was even possible, but what caught his eye was the fast flowing mountain stream flanked by a stand of ancient willows that appeared even more ancient than the ones at their old campsite.

The mountain stream which fed these great trees rushed and flowed down through the rocky terrain creating miniature waterfalls here and there. Pine and hawthorn grew thick amongst the willows along with various other deciduous trees. Long strands of moss grew down from the tall branches as ferns and bromeliads took up residence high in the canopy. Up on the hill giant oak trees artfully spread their branches amongst maple, wild apple, and more. Flowering vines of all colors decorated the oaks while a variety of rushes grew in clumps along the sides of the fast flowing stream.

Interspersed amid the rocks and trees were tall grasses, and the most gorgeous carpet of wildflowers imaginable. Every color in the rainbow seemed to be sprinkled about the forest floor. From tall fuchsia foxglove to blue delphinium, pink dragon's breath and purple violets, yellow buttercups to red paintbrushes the colors abounded. Bumble bees and yellow swallowtail butterflies danced around large purple thistle while honey bees busied themselves amongst the variety that was set before them. Other insects could be seen partaking in the bounty as hummingbirds, and a host of other butterflies flitted about. Songs of birds of all sorts could be heard wafting in the air.

He pulled Hawk up a moment as he took in the scenery before him. Then his eyes spied them, white wild roses growing near the rocks of the small river. The delicate white flowers were rare, and according to legend were the flowers of Alhera.

Allethor, her father, was said to have given the white wild roses to her for her birthday. The goddess was then said to have used them to bless the earth. It was believed they were supposed to denote the goddess's presence and protection.

"This is it," Clavorn announced more to himself than to anyone else, "This is the place."

"What?" Sefforn inquired as he pulled up his horse beside him.

"This is it!" he repeated more loudly to his friend, "This is the place where you will be the safest."

"How can you be so certain?" asked Bennethor, pulling his horse up between the two of them.

"Just look at it. Look at these trees, the denseness of the wood, and the beauty of those willows, and the hawthorn. They're old, very old, and all those wild flowers, and the roses. The gods favor this land. You will be safe here."

"Well, let's hope they favor us as much as this land," Melkiar commented, pulling up his horse, and signaling for all the men behind him to do the same. "Oh, and did I forget to mention the Ornskyterrak? Yes. I hope it doesn't mind us treading on this land."

Thalon rode his horse up to join them. "By Allethor!" he exclaimed before Clavorn could respond to Melkiar's concerns, "Would you look at this place. The gods must have been keeping it secrete from our enemy. It is gorgeous and rich with life."

"Yeah," exclaimed Sayavic as his horse stopped just short of the rest of them, "The only explanation I can see for this place is everyone's fear of the Ornskyterrak."

"The question then is, why has that creature not shown up yet?" Melkiar pointed out.

"It has to be the will of the gods," Falor put in as he too rode up and joined them just as Melkiar was finishing his query.

"Ummm," was all Melkiar uttered as others rode up to join them. Always a sceptic. He preferred it, if the beast were going to show up, to just get it over with. He hated wondering, trusting to fate, and 'the will of the gods.' Though he had seen that strategy play out fairly well before, it was still not a part of who he was.

Sefforn and Clavorn nodded then turned their horses to ride further into the forest to have a look around just to be sure. Bennethor rode along beside them. Before long Sayavic, Clovak, and Sorenavik came up to join them.

"It is as if the fairies live here and man forgot this place," Sorenavik commented.

"I'll second that," remarked Sayavic as they continued to ride along side.

"Or the dragons never left," Kevic added, coming up beside them. Both Clovak and Sorenavik agreed with him.

"More like their fear never let them get this far," Melkiar mumbled under his breath, being always quick to point out a more reasonable explanation, at least from his point of view.

Yolondon and Heffron rode up to join them making the same comments as all the others before them. Melkiar just rolled his eyes and kept his comments to himself.

Sunlight streamed in through the canopy above them as they continue to ride forward, adding to the wonder of the place as it cast various spotlights on the forest floor, illuminating the tall grasses and colorful wildflowers.

"The power of the dragon is strong here." Clavorn remarked seemingly more to himself than to those accompanying him. "This is definitely the spot," he continued now more loudly, "This is where you will be safe."

It was as if all his intuition told him this was it. The power of life was intense here. He could feel it vibrating all around him. His grandfather told him that such places held the magic of the dragon, and were highly favored by the gods. He could not imagine a safer place for his men.

"Well I don't know about protecting us, but feeding us is definitely not going to be a problem," Bennethor remarked as a group of deer pranced off into the woods at their approach, and a flock of song birds rose high into the sky. As Clavorn glanced about, a rabbit suddenly darted off into the bushes to reveal a patch of wild raspberries.

"Look there! Are those wild apples?" Sefforn exclaimed, pointing to a tree alighted in the distance.

Fires of Life

"Yes, I think so," Clavorn replied with a smile as Hawk danced under him.

"Well, then I do believe you have found us at least a suitable spot to stay while you go off on this quest of yours," Melkiar commented. "Provided that beast doesn't show up and toast all of us for trespassing on its turf."

"I think, if it were going to show up, it would have by now," Thalon put in.

Clavorn made no comment. One could never be certain when it came to magical beasts, especially those entrusted as guardians.

"Alright then. Give the order. Everybody dismount and make camp," he announced in a friendly tone.

Melkiar turned and immediately began barking orders to those behind him. Clavorn rode Hawk a little further in to scout out a place which would serve as their main command center and temporary resting quarters for him before dismounting.

Near the stream there were several old willows. As he glanced about, one seemed to catch his eye. Light from the sun streamed down through a few scatterings of clouds, shining and drawing attention to its huge magnificent form, giving it an almost ethereal appearance as its weeping branches swayed ever so gently in the soft breeze. Butterflies danced about it while honey bees carried on their work amongst the flowers along the banks of the small river. He could almost hear her voice in his head.

'*Listen to your heart.*'

As he looked on at the ancient willow before him, he now knew for certain he had found the right campsite for his men, and the tree which would be the heart of their operations here.

That night passed uneventfully as his men settled in. The full moon over head graced their new home with silver light while most slept peacefully under its watchful eye.

Chapter 34

When Clavorn opened his eyes the next morning he saw beautiful soft streams of golden sunlight filtering in through the wispy branches of the ancient willow he had chosen for himself. A gentle breeze flowed through the tree causing its branches to sway in a kind of lyrical dance. Outside the sound of the rushing stream could be heard as it flowed on past the great tree. Its delightful music had lulled him into a deep sleep the night before. Now it served as a wonderful backdrop to the songs of birds that filled the air.

He stretched his lean muscular body and felt the furs of his sleeping roll softly about him. Images and reflections from the night before of his men and him enjoying the comforts of this small peaceful forest flooded his mind. It had been good to see them having fun after the hardships and harshness of the previous days.

It had taken them several days to arrive here. Morale had been low after the sting of their last battle. The men had wanted to stand and fight, but he had felt it was better for them to regroup while he went off in search of the dragon. Last night it had been good to see them resting and enjoying themselves. Here was a safe place, a place where his men could rest and recover.

It will be good for them.

A warm and pleasant feeling filled his heart as he sat up to greet the new day.

He felt strangely refreshed as he parted the delicate weeping branches and stepped outside. The air here was fresh and clean. Tiny insects and butterflies could be seen resuming their days work. Clavorn walked over to the stream and began to wash up.

As he splashed the cold crisp water on his face, he wished that he was here under different circumstances. For finding this place meant now it was time for him to leave his men and journey to recover the dragon. He looked about him.

The question is which direction do I go from here?

Fires of Life

Locating this place had been relatively easy by comparison. He had known their previous campsite amongst the willows had been safe, so he had just set off in that direction and let his instincts take it from there.

He stepped into the rushing stream, then taking a deep breath; he dunked his whole body into the icy frigid mountain water. Its coldness hit his skin, shocking every nerve into awareness. He paused for moment under its surface, letting the water rush over him.

'*Listen to your soul.*'

Her words came back to him as he broke through the surface, taking in a huge gulp of air.

Clavorn glanced about him, sweeping his dark hair back with his powerful hands. Behind him Hawk was busy nibbling on the tall grasses near the stream. In the distance he could see his men awakening, and going about the business of settling in. He stared in front of him. The sun was streaming down on the little thicket just in front of him, highlighting its tall grasses.

As he looked on, out of the bushes a huge buck stepped into his line of vision. It turned its great majestic head and peered around the tiny meadow. The large rack of antlers it held upon its head denoted its place as king amongst its kind. Proudly, it stepped into the light of the morning sun that shown down upon a patch of grass on the other side of the small river. Clavorn watched almost mesmerized by its presence. He observed it as it began to nibble the grass before him. Then it looked up and stared straight at him.

Surely it will flee.

But it merely stood up proudly and wondered off up the mountainside, following the rushing stream, and yet climbing slightly to the northwest of it.

Within a moment the buck was gone. Suddenly, from high above him came the distinct cry of a hawk. Looking up, Clavorn could see he was right. It called out again, and then flew off in the same direction as the buck.

Could it be? No.

He shook his head and dunked it in the icy river one more time. Surely he was losing his mind. He came up and shook the water from his face, throwing his hair back.

Clear cold drops of water flew about him reassuring him of the reality of the moment. Every fiber of his being was alive and awake now as he felt the contrasting heat of the sun on his flesh, yet his mind was full of questions as he considered the possibility of the fleeting thought that had briefly entered it.

"Well, that's certainly one way to wake up."

Jolted from his thoughts, Clavorn turned in the direction of the familiar voice. The tall lean blond figure of Sefforn smiled down at him from the bank near the ancient willow that had been his home for the evening.

"Yeah. Well, what about you?"

"You know me," Sefforn said from the riverside, "Nothing like a hearty breakfast to bring a body to life. Care for some hunting?"

He produced a bow, and as Clavorn began to make his way out of the fast moving stream, it occurred to him that a good hunt might be just the thing to clear his head.

"Sounds like a great idea," he replied as he made his way up on the bank, "Just let me get my bow."

Clavorn strode past his friend and entered the willow. A few moments later he emerged, bow in hand, dressed in dry clothes.

"So you have any ideas of where to begin," he asked.

"Well, I should think in this place it really hardly matters," Sefforn commented.

Suddenly, a shock wave reverberated through his being at Sefforn's remark.

"Actually it does," he told him.

Something that he remembered from long ago, something his grandfather had taught him suddenly echoed through his mind across the ages of time.

"What? How so?" Sefforn asked clearly confused by his friend's statement, "The prey is everywhere."

Fires of Life

"That's just it," Clavorn replied, running his hand over his face as he tried to recall the exact words his grandfather had used. Right now it was more of a feeling than anything else. "This place is favored by the gods, more specifically, Alhera." He motioned about him, "Look at all this life. It's everywhere. It's everywhere for a reason. My instincts tell me that we should not hunt here. Not on the campsite or anywhere close to it."

"You mean hunting is forbidden here?" Sefforn said a bit befuddled and put off.

"Yeah, you could say that. In any event, I would not recommend hunting here. From what I remember my grandfather telling me, we could invite not only the wrath of the gods and Alhera, but also the Ornskyterrak. Spread the word. Tell the men to hunt off site."

"Ah, you tell them. I want no part of that news. Many of them have already gone off to hunt."

"Then we have to stop them, Seff. Come on!" Clavorn felt a sudden urgency about it.

Sefforn shook his head and followed. The two men jogged off. Clavorn paused in the middle of camp and looked around. Most of the men were still just waking up, but it was clear a few had already wondered off.

Sefforn came up to him a bit out of breath, "So what do you propose now?"

Clavorn spied Melkiar and motioned him over.

"How many are out hunting?"

"Not many," Melkiar told him as he stopped in front of him.

"Who's out?" Clavorn continued.

"Bennethor, and a couple of others. Why?" Melkiar inquired.

"Because we need to stop them before they make a kill. Do you know what direction they went in?" Clavorn asked.

"Yeah, that way," Melkiar pointed off to the south and into the woods, "Someone spied some deer off in that direction. Mind telling me what's going on. Why can't we hunt here? I thought part of the appeal of this place was that it was teaming with prey."

"No time for explanations, but thanks," Clavorn told him as he patted him on the arm before jogging off in the direction he had given him.

Using his tracking skills he began to scour the area for Bennethor's trail. Sefforn came up beside him and together they combed the forest. It was not long before they picked up their trail. Sure enough they were headed south and deep into the forest. Both men moved quickly, picking up on the signs and following them. Suddenly, as they rounded a stand of trees Clavorn spied him with a couple of others. As he looked, he could see they had their bows trained on the very buck he had seen that morning.

How? How did he get over here?

The question flew threw his mind. He could tell it was the same one by its distinctively large rack of antlers. Only this was quite a distance from where he had last seen him. Seemingly too far for the buck to have traveled in such short a time.

Quick, he had to think fast. He had to stop the kill, especially of that buck. He searched the forest floor and found exactly what he was looking for, a decent size stick. Swiftly, he picked it up and threw it in the direction of the buck, scaring it just as Bennethor's arrow flew in its direction. Another arrow was off, but the buck had turned just in time to miss it. A sigh of relief escaped Clavorn as Sefforn came up beside him.

"What was that about?" Bennethor protested as he made his way towards Clavorn with the others following suit, "I had that buck. We would have been enjoying a nice venison breakfast this morning."

"I know, but that buck, this land…"

"Is sacred," Sefforn finished for him.

"I thought that was the idea. That was why we would be safe," replied one of the men who were with Bennethor.

"Yes, but I just remembered something this morning my grandfather mentioned about never killing in such a place, not even to feed yourself."

"You're joking, right?" Bennethor replied, looking bewildered and perplexed.

"No, really, he isn't," Sefforn told him, looking as if he could empathize with Bennethor and company.

Bennethor looked from Sefforn to Clavorn.

"Look. This land, it is full of life," Clavorn began.

How am I going to explain this? I just know we can't hunt here. But how do I explain this to him and everyone else? Especially since it's more a feeling and word of mouth than anything tangible like hunger.

"Yeah, that's what makes it great hunting ground," Bennethor commented obviously confused and frustrated.

"True, but it is also what makes it sacred and off limits. It has been blessed and made a sanctuary by Alhera. Those roses over there, see the white ones?"

"Yeah," Bennethor replied.

"Well, they belong to Alhera. According to legend the goddess places those on the lands she has specially blessed. They are what indicate this place as a type of sanctuary. If we hunt on it, especially where it is the strongest, like here, we will defile it and it will no longer be a sanctuary for life." There he said it, but he could tell it was like saying that the moon was somehow going to fall out of the sky if they danced under it, judging by the looks on Bennethor's and his companions faces.

"Are you sure?" he asked, "Because it seems to me that the gods allow for creatures to hunt and be hunted."

"Yes, but not here," Clavorn told him, "Look around you. Do you see any signs of any hunting here? And I mean even by the animals themselves."

Come to think of it none of them had.

"Now that you mention it, no," Bennethor replied obviously amazed by his own answer. "I thought that was unusual, but I just dismissed it as part of our good fortune."

"Precisely, so did I till Seff asked me to go hunting. It was then that I recalled what my grandfather had taught me a long time ago. Now let's go back and tell the others."

"Alright, but where *can* we go hunting?" Bennethor inquired.

"Outside this land," Clavorn replied simply, "Probably just beyond those foothills over there," he said point over their shoulder, behind them.

"You mean we need to travel outside this sanctuary to hunt?" Sefforn stopped dead in his tracks. Apparently, it had not really sunk in what he meant by they could not hunt here.

"Well, yes, but you'll still be safe as long as you keep close to its borders."

Sefforn and Bennethor exchanged glances with each other as did the other two men who were with Bennethor.

"Look, I know it sound a bit superstitious…"

"We didn't say that…Just it is a bit to swallow. We need to eat. All creatures do. The deer eat the grass. Why can't we eat the deer?" Bennethor inquired.

Clavorn ran a hand though his hair. He knew he was right, but he also knew that it was not worth the risk of destroying the nature of the place simply for their sake.

How do I get this across?

"Regardless and irrespective of 'the will of the gods' this place is special," he explained. "It has been kept secret and safe for millennia. That is obvious," he continued, "Our treading here is a great disturbance. We need to leave it much as we have found it. Hunting will change the nature of this place. It will encourage the animals to go elsewhere. We will have introduced fear in a place where there is none. As a result, we will have changed their behavior which will affect the forest. There is no getting around that. It is not fair that for our own selfish reasons we irrevocably change the nature of this forest."

"Well, now that you put it that way I see your point," Sefforn told him, "I hadn't thought of it like that."

"No. We are too used to seeing things only from the perspective of our own needs. I think that is why a lot of the time things are told to us as the 'will of the gods,' whether they actually are or not is unimportant. The gods will always be on the side of what is best for creation, and while we are a part of that, we are not the whole. Hence, why somethings are deemed sacred and off limits for us. It seems easier for us to understand that. Perhaps we are more like children, no matter how old we are, than we'd like to think."

Sefforn nodded and he could see he had made his point with the others as well.

"Now to explain it to the rest."

"This should be fun," Sefforn commented as he followed Clavorn back to camp.

Bennethor and company turned and marched off in the direction he had pointed out to find some suitable prey.

Sure enough the men groaned when Clavorn informed them of the situation regarding hunting on the land they now occupied. But after much discussion most were either understanding or just did not want to take the chance of having the land, or themselves, be cursed by the gods or ravaged by the Ornskyterrrak.

"Well, that went better than expected," Sefforn commented from behind him as the men disbanded.

"Yeah, thank the gods," Clavorn replied relieved that he had temporarily adverted disaster.

"So, anything else I should know before you go off on this quest of yours," he inquired. Clavorn thought a moment.

"No, not that I can think of, but if I should recall anything I promise I will let you know before I leave."

"Good, because I'd hate to be responsible for upsetting the gods."

"No, that's my job," Clavorn joked.

"So, are you still up for that hunt?"

"Sure. Why not? Can't leave for a good quest on an empty stomach," replied Clavorn, slapping his friend on the back.

It was not long before they were back out amongst the woodland trudging through the thick vegetation. Finally, it began to thin. The sun was now higher in the sky, and Clavorn hoped it would not be too much longer before they found their quarry, especially now that they were out of the area that appeared to be part of the sanctuary. His stomach was seriously starting to complain. If it became much louder, he feared it might jeopardize their hunt.

Suddenly, Clavorn caught sight of some movement in the bushes off to his right and began stalking in that direction. Slowly, he crept so as not to scare the beast into full flight. He reached back quietly with one hand and found an arrow from his quiver. With slow, but even movement he notched his bow; readying it for the kill should a suitable beast appear.

Down he crouched into the bushes with his back against a tree. He listened. Sefforn was close beside him. As he listened he could hear the beast's movements, step, blow, step... pause. Clavorn ventured a look through the bushes. What he saw amazed him. There, not more than ten paces away from him, was the same buck he had first seen that morning. His distinctive rack leaving no doubt it was the one and the same animal.

Clavorn lowered his bow, motioning Sefforn to do the same. Sefforn gave him a puzzled look. Clavorn motioned him to glance over in the direction of the buck. Sefforn lowered his bow at the sight of the huge male deer with the distinctive rack of antlers. From the look his friend gave him it was clear he found the stags appearance here just as perplexing.

"You go on and see what you can find," whispered Clavorn, "I am going to stay with this one and see where he takes me."

Sefforn nodded. He had known his friend long enough to trust his odd inclinations. Quietly, he turned and backed off from Clavorn, being careful not to startle the creature, and went off in search of new prey.

Meanwhile Clavorn returned his attention to the magnificent buck with the glorious rack of antlers. As he peered through the bushes, the creature suddenly stopped and stared straight at him, lifting his wonderful head. The sunlight streaming through the trees spotlighted him perfectly as he stood there before Clavorn. It was truly a wondrous sight.

A sound from the trees caught Clavorn's attention and drew it away from the buck for a second. When he returned his gaze the buck was gone. Clavorn stood up quickly, placing his arrow back in his quiver and his bow over his shoulder. Looking around he could see no trace of the male deer, then, out of the corner of his eye, he spotted it. It was heading in the same direction as it had earlier that morning. Clavorn followed it sensing that there was some importance to this stag.

Suddenly, it sprang off, leaping gracefully through the woods. He followed it breaking into a run, pushing branches out of his way, leaping logs, and plowing through vegetation till suddenly he stopped, nearly falling into a precipice below. As he looked down, he could see a river raging over large boulders, and feel the spray coming off a waterfall that was rushing down into it not more than a dragon's head from his face.

Clavorn looked up. He could see its source, though he could barely make it out due to all the undergrowth and trees that lined the hillside. His eyes scanned upward. High above him was a jut in the mountainside. It was over that jut that the waterfall was pouring straight down nearly a ten dragon lengths to the river below.

Clavorn steadied himself as he gazed out over the river to the hills and mountains beyond. That was when he discovered it. There on the edge of that cliff. The cliff which he was led to by the stag with the glorious rack of antlers is where he finally saw it, the mountain from his dream. The mountain which he was sure contained the dragon.

It was in that moment that he realized the place he had seen that mountain before was in a dream from long ago, a dream from his boyhood. Now, as gazed upon the mountain, everything about the moment appeared the same as had in his dream all those years ago, the cliff, the river, the time day, everything. It was called Dragon Seeing, rare but not unheard of. He remembered his mother speaking of it occasionally. Now, he was experiencing it as he gazed upon the mountain before him.

Low clouds adorned its base as the sun hit its eastern face. From his vantage point it was difficult to tell how far out it was. The rough and rugged nature of the land in between made gaging the duration of a journey there difficult.

Clavorn made a mental note of his bearings before he turned and started back to camp. Not, however before giving the mountain one last good look. It was beautiful, just as in his dream. The area leading to it appeared devoid of human habitation, but thick with every other form of life. Even the trees appeared to grow tall there. A hawk swooped down from over his head crying out, and then continued on in the direction of the mountain. He smiled to himself as he turned to leave. Now he had his destination.

Chapter 35

When he arrived back at camp the men had already started a roaring fire over which a young deer was turning on a spit. He could see Bennethor checking on its condition while his friend, Sefforn, stood over it working his magic. Sefforn was the best cook in camp. Melkiar was seated on a rock near the fire smoking his pipe while overseeing the whole process. The other men in camp were engaged in various activities. Some were finishing settling in. Others were sharpening their swords, or washing up while still others were sitting round telling jokes, laughing, and enjoying the respite.

"I see you brought us a pheasant to add to our feast," Melkiar shouted from his place near the fire.

"Yes, well I couldn't very well come home empty handed now could I," he replied as he strode up.

"No. That would not have done at all, now would it Seff?" Melkiar shouted over his shoulder.

"No. It would not," Sefforn replied in a loud voice as he cut a slice from the succulent beast to test how it was coming.

"Well, then it is good I did not," Clavorn told them as he continued on his way towards them.

Clavorn stopped in front of them and handed the pheasant off to Meshron who had just come running up asking if he could take it for him and dress it. He thanked the boy who immediately left with it to fix it for cooking. One would never know that just a few days ago the boy had been dead, so full of life he was now. He smiled as he watched the boy run off with his catch.

"So, will you be leaving us soon?" Bennethor inquired as Clavorn scanned the area for a convenient place to sit.

"Yes," he replied simply he not wanting to elaborate further yet.

"So, you figured out a direction," Sefforn asked as he sprinkled some herbs over the creature roasting before him.

Clavorn was about to open his mouth to respond to his friend, when out of the north came a sound like no other.

EEEEAWWWW HAWWWW!!!!

Flames crossed the sky. A great storm of wind and wings shook the trees, blowing out the fire before them, and scattering virtually all of his men to the safety of the forest as the great creature landed before him.

EEEEAWWWW HAWWWW!!!!

Again it cried out as it blew flames in the air and pawed at the earth. It was an Ornskyterrak. The brown feathers of its proud head ruffled in the breeze as it set its great golden wings down upon its back. Its beautifully colored body resembled that of a golden panther while its powerful front paws clearly denoted its kinship with the great cat. Defensive and angry, there was no doubt it was upset about something.

"Shaltak, what do we do?!" Bennethor yelled.

Clavorn raised his hand to stay their actions while he calmly kept his gaze on the angry beast.

Once more it cried out and pawed the earth. The long claws of its powerful front paw dug deep into the earth. He knew they must have done something to upset the creature. The trick now was to figure out what. Calmly, he bowed to it and stood up. The creature cried out and pawed at the ground once more. Clavorn could feel the heat from its flames as they shot up in the air not far from him.

"You will not be able to calm him that way," a voice said in his head.

For a minute Clavorn thought it was her, but then a woman dressed in a soft flowing green robe strode out from behind the beast. Her long red hair fell gracefully about her shoulders, and stretched nearly down to the ground like a flaming red river. The deep blue of her eyes rivaled that of any sea. While the fairness of her skin could only be compared to that of the softest white rose.

Bennethor nearly tripped on himself as he rose. The same was true for Melkiar and Sefforn.

"I am Shalmaray, leader of the Kalmak. You are trespassing on our lands," her voice persisted in his head as she continued to come forward, raising her right hand to stay the beast.

"We meant you no disrespect. We had no idea these were your lands," he told her gesturing to their surroundings.

"We are its keepers actually."

"We? Where are the rest of your people? I have never heard of the Kal…"

"Silence! I can hear your thoughts in my head. It is better if we speak this way."

Clavorn was puzzled, but decided to honor her request.

"Alright then. Who are your people?"

"We are Dragon Witches. More specifically we are a special sect. Our main charge is as keepers and protectors of this land, and other sacred grounds like it throughout our world. We watch over them, and keep them safe from the world of men," she answered as she came to stand in front of him.

Now Clavorn could clearly see the silver diadem she wore around her head with its silver leaves in the form of oak, and a single Kriac stone in its center. Two sapphires flanked the beautiful green center stone. Both of which nearly matched the color of her eyes. Around her waist was a belt of silver rope.

"Skytak alerted us to your presence and has been watching you."

"Why did you not come forward sooner?"

"We have been assessing you and your people. We know of your need and needed to determine if you were worthy of our protection."

"And what have you found?"

"Most of your men are good people, but there is one amongst you who harbors much ill will, Clavorn, son of Remmaik."

"Who is he that I might send him away."

"Unfortunately, that is for you to discover. This is just a warning. You and your men are welcome to stay. But know this, that whoever

he is, he has already been cursed. His fate sealed. There is nothing you can do to change that. I am merely informing you of his presence and warning you and your men to be careful. He intends to do great harm."

"*Is there any way you can tell me who he is?"*

"*No. But you must not let your guard down, Clavorn, son of Remmaik. You have a mission. I suggest you fulfill it soon."*

With those last words came a swift single beat of the beast's wings and she was gone. Then, with one last cry, the Ornskyterrak leapt into the air and flew off.

"What was that all about?" Sefforn asked as soon as the great creature was out of sight.

"Yeah, and who was she?" Melkiar added, refilling his pipe.

"A Dragon Witch," Clavorn replied simply still looking in the direction she and the Ornskyterrak had just been.

"So. What did she say?" Bennethor asked.

"She said we could stay," he answered succinctly as he turned to face them.

"That's it? I thought there would be more with as long as you took," Melkiar commented a bit put off by the shortness of his answer.

"I'll second that," added Thalon as he came up to join them.

"Really there was not much more. Introductions and so on," he told them. He did not want to go into it.

"Oh, would you look at what that beast did to our dinner," Sefforn exclaimed. He could tell when his friend was purposefully concealing things, and distracting the others with a comment on dinner was his way of diverting their attention.

"What do you mean?" Bennethor asked.

"I mean look at it. Not only did that Ornskyterrak put out our fire, but he got dirt and soot all over it. Now, I'll have to see what can be done to salvage it, and it'll never taste as good."

"Oh, I don't know about that," Clavorn told his friend, "With you cooking, I am sure it will still taste excellent." His friend gave him a look. "Well, at least far better than it would in any of our hands."

"No one can doubt that," Thalon put in, "Come on. I'll help you, and before you know it this deer will be no different than it was before that creature arrived."

"Well, I am not so sure about that, but I'll take the help," Sefforn replied.

"Say, who was that and what did she want?" Sayavic inquired as he strode up to join the group.

"A Dragon Witch," both Melkiar and Bennethor replied simultaneously.

"All she apparently wanted was to inform us that it's was okay for us to stay here," finished Bennethor.

"With all that fuss, I would have thought she had found some reason to kick us out," Thalon replied.

"Yeah, well join the club," Melkiar told him, "but our fearless leader here says that was it."

"Oh?" replied Yolondon with one raise eye brow, his expression one of pure befuddlement. He had just strode up to see what all the fuss was with the Ornskyterrak and the woman, when he overheard their conversation. Sayavic said nothing, but it was clear from his expression that he felt the same.

"Well, there really is not much more to tell," Clavorn insisted.

"If you say so," Sefforn put in, "Say Thalon, I'll take that help now."

"Sure." and with that the two men went to work on cleaning up their soon to be dinner so that it could finish being cooked.

"Say you want some more help with that?" Sayavic put in after seeing what Sefforn and Thalon were up too.

"Certainly, extra hands are always welcome," Sefforn told him.

Yolondon turned and joined in too. Soon there were more than enough hands cleaning up and readying their dinner.

Meantime, Melkiar set about restarting the fire and his pipe while Bennethor wandered off; apparently to spread the word to the others around camp who were now returning from their retreat into the woods. Clavorn went over to help Melkiar with the fire.

"So, what did she really have to say?" he asked in a low voice.

"Not much more than what I told you."

"Alright, but I still think there is more you are not tell us," Melkiar told him as he poked the fire with a long stick to heat it up.

Clavorn wanted to say more, but felt better of it for the moment. Something told him there was a reason she had only shared the information with him.

Chapter 36

"Do you have any idea where you'll start looking?" Sefforn questioned him as he packed for his journey. He could tell his friend wanted to ask more but was respecting his silence.

The wind gently blew through the willow, swaying its long thin branches as the early morning light filtered in. Outside the songs of birds could be heard as they flitted amongst the trees. Clavorn felt a mixture of both optimism and apprehension as he packed for his journey. The stag had given him a renewed sense of confidence and hope while the Dragon Witch, Shalmaray, had given him a cause for concern.

Finding that dragon was their best hope for success, and after his conversation with the Dragon Witch he was even more convinced of his mission. As far as he could tell, Sevzozak's troops had never arrived, and, from what he knew of the good king, he was almost positive he probably never intended them to be sent in the first place. Add to that the fact that Vaulnik's troops out numbered them so dramatically, and it was pretty easy to see that the dragon was their only hope. But the idea of a traitor amongst them worried him.

Who is it?

"Yes," he replied, not looking up, he was anxious to be on his way. Time was of the essence. Both Alethea and Shalmaray had made that plainly clear.

"Well, this sounds promising," Melkiar commented, puffing on his pipe as he sat seated on a large old root watching him prepare to leave, "Are you sure you do not want any of us to join you on this little escaped of yours?"

"Absolutely," Clavorn replied, looking up for a moment from his task. "I need you both here to look after the men and keep them from doing anything rash."

"We know. But still it will be dangerous out there for you, and we need you to return in one piece," Sefforn told him as he lean against the great willow's large trunk.

"I *will*," he replied emphatically. "Look, I know you are both concerned about my wellbeing, but I tell you I'll be fine. With any luck I will find the dragon and return before the next full moon."

"Isn't that a bit ambitious," Melkiar remarked as a whiff of smoke encircled his head.

"Actually, I am counting on finding him well before then, my friend, but I don't want to place your hopes too high," Clavorn told him as he patted him on the shoulder while he stepped past him to retrieve his sword.

"Well, at least no one can say that he does not have any optimism, ehay, Melkiar," Sefforn commented in jest.

"No, I should think they would say quite the opposite. That he is completely *mad*," Melkiar replied to Sefforn.

"Come now you two. You would think I was going off to my doom or something. I'm just going off to find the dragon and bring him back. I'll be fine."

"Oh, would you listen to him," Melkiar remarked to Sefforn as he removed his pipe from between his teeth while smoke billowed out his mouth. "'I'm just going off to find the dragon.' Look man. It's not your lost boot you're going off to find, you know," he continued now turning his attention to Clavorn, "It's common knowledge Viszerak can be a rather cantankerous dragon. Not to mention difficult to locate. Or did you forget that we no longer have the Stone of Maltak. Which, need I remind you, is safely in the hands of… Oh, help me Seff."

"King Sevzozak," Sefforn interjected.

"Oh, yes, our dear friend and ally King Sevzozak. Have I missed anything Sefforn?"

"No." he replied his arms folded as he continued to lean against the trunk of the ancient tree.

"Come on you two. Have a little faith. It's hard enough going on a dragon quest without your friends adding to the air of gloom." Clavorn turned to face them, "Yesterday morning when I woke up I had no idea which direction I was going to start off on. Sheer

Fires of Life

numbers will tell you that my choices were quite limitless. But now I have a direction *and* a general destination."

"Given to you by a stag," Melkiar pointed out. Melkiar was not given to intuitions and dreams. He put very little stock in such things, and as such was more than a little skeptical of Clavorn's revelation. "Who, I might mention, nearly led you over a cliff."

"Yes, I know how it looks, but Seff you tell him," Clavorn turned back to his packing.

"Melkiar, I think Cla… Shaltak is quite aware of the gravity of the situation. Come. Let us let him finish in peace, my friend. We are obviously out voted, and have done all that we can to pound any ounce of sense into him. Soon he will be in the hands of the gods, and so will our fate as well. Though in my experience that is not as bad as it sounds. For some reason, which I have yet to fathom, the gods seem to favor him. So with any luck, they will favor us too and aid him on his quest. Come now. Let us leave this stubborn mule to his task." And with that Sefforn winked at Melkiar and motioned him to follow him out of the tree.

"Stubborn mule…Well…." They were long gone by the time Clavorn looked up. He stopped in mid-sentence as he was not able to counter his friends, "Well, we'll see about that when I return with the dragon in a few days' time," he muttered to himself as he finished sheathing his dagger and strapping it to his waist.

Clavorn stepped outside the willow. Hawk was not far off, grazing on the grasses across the stream. He whistled for him. Hawk lifted his handsome black head and came trotting through the river over to where he was standing.

"Good boy," he told him as he stroked the forehead of his faithful equine companion, "Come, my friend, we have a journey to ready ourselves for."

Clavorn turned and lifted his saddle onto his great steed. Hawk stood while he continued to ready him for their adventure. His head up and ears twitching, alert to his surroundings in anticipation of what was to come.

"May I accompany you?" he heard a voice from behind him ask. He turned his head to see it was Bennethor.

"No. I want you to stay here with the men in case they are attacked. They will need all the good warriors they can spare."

"Sir, aren't we supposed to be safe here?"

"Yes, but one never knows for certain."

Especially with a traitor amongst us.

"Look, if you leave me here, I am likely to go crazy. I will feel like an old woman watching over the grandchildren. I am afraid I will do something totally mad or start a fight just to end the pain of waiting for one. Besides, you might need me."

Clavorn looked into the man's eyes and saw that he was right, "Okay, but when I tell you to let me go on alone you must. I and I alone must face this dragon do you understand?"

"Yes, I think."

Clavorn wanted no confusion of intention when he faced the dragon. He wanted it to see the clarity of their need. More than one mind, his mentor used to tell him when discussing the subject of speaking with dragons, was often a recipe for disaster.

"And if it comes to a fight or a test, I must do so alone. Do you understand?"

"Yes, but…"

"No buts. Do we have an agreement?" Clavorn stopped what he was doing and looked him straight in the eyes.

"Yes."

"Then you may come," he told him as he went back to his work.

"May I ask one more question?" Bennethor continued as he stood beside him.

"Certainly."

"Why must you face the dragon alone?"

"Somehow I thought you were going to ask that question," Clavorn remarked as he pulled down on the cinch. "The short answer is just because. The longer answer is that dragons are known to be particular about who they align themselves with. If I am worthy,

Fires of Life

then we will have a great ally. If not..." he lifted his travel bags on to Hawk and slapped them in place, leaving the outcome of failure to Bennethor's imagination. "I can only hope that the dragon finds me worthy."

"I see," was all Bennethor replied. "Well, I'll be off then," he told him after a couple moments of silence.

"Yes, meet me on the northwest corner of camp. We'll make our start from there." Clavorn informed him over his shoulder as he tied his sword to his saddle.

"Sure, I'll meet you there." Bennethor replied as he strode off to ready his things.

Soon there was a throng of men at the northwest corner of camp. They had all gathered to see Clavorn off. The sea of well-wishers parted as Clavorn strode through the middle with Hawk in tow. At the end of the line was Bennethor already mounted and ready for their journey. Sefforn and Melkiar along with Kevic, and the others who were close to him, were also waiting for him at the end of the line, though clearly planted on the ground as they were staying behind. As Clavorn approached with his trusty steed, Sefforn came up to meet him before he reached the end.

"I thought you didn't want anyone along on the journey," he whispered in his ear.

"Very true. Especially when it comes to you and Melkiar," Clavorn replied with a smile as he paused on his way through the crowd, "See, I need you here."

"And him," Sefforn inquired in a low tone, gesturing discreetly towards Bennethor with his head.

"Well, I did you a favor. He was going to be trouble for you," Clavorn told him under his breath as he smiled to the crowd around them, trying to appear natural.

"That's good. Now he will be trouble for you."

"I wouldn't be so sure. Besides, nothing I can't handle," he tried to reassure his friend.

"I hope you are right," Sefforn warned, and for a split second the words of the Dragon Witch passed through his mind but were immediately dismissed.

What trouble could he be? Too overly zealous.

"You know what I think," Clavorn commented, walking away from the crowd for a moment, "I think you are jealous."

"No. But now that you mention it, yes. I would rather be coming with you. I hate administrative jobs. You know that."

Clavorn smiled to the men gathered and looked back at Sefforn.

"Look Seff, I could see in his eyes he would never be satisfied with just sitting put. This way he is doing something. I did you a favor," he told him, slapping him on the shoulder as he walked past to rejoin the crowd, not giving his friend time to respond.

Sefforn took a moment to regain his composure before turning to join him on his way to meet up with the person of controversy.

Before long they had reached the end. Sefforn glanced up at Bennethor before joining Melkiar and the men in the sendoff.

Upon reaching his point of departure, Clavorn turned, and raised his hand to the men who were gathered, "I want to thank you all for this sendoff." Cheers went up from the crowd. "With any luck we will be back soon, and with the dragon."

Another round of cheers went up from the men gathered there. Suddenly, a voice was heard in the crowd.

"Why does he get to come with you," a boy of about fourteen shouted.

"Because he asked first," Clavorn answered with a smile above the din of excitement. Not entirely a true answer, but one he figured the boy would accept. Then he turned and mounted Hawk.

Sefforn came up to Clavorn's horse as he mounted, with Melkiar not far behind. "Good luck out there," he told him extending his hand to Clavorn.

As Clavorn looked into his friend's eyes, he could tell he still held some reservations and wished he could be joining him on his quest. He tried to reassure his friend silently as he bent down to clasp his hand in friendship and good will.

"The same goes for me," Melkiar interjected, "Be back soon!"

"I will, my friends, I will." Clavorn told them. Before letting go of his friend's hand he added in a near whisper, "Be careful. There may be a traitor amongst us."

Sefforn was about to ask more, but Clavorn let go of his hand as his horse shifted in anticipation, forcing him to gathered up his reins to steady him. Then he turned Hawk to the crowd, and waved to the men before he turned him again and rode off up the mountain to the northwest with Bennethor and his horse in tow.

The sun was just beginning to rise above the horizon as they departed up the hillside. On a large pine perched a hawk, his gaze following the tiny band of two as they made their way through the forest.

Chapter 37

They were three days in. It was late afternoon and their trek to the mountain was beginning to wear on them. Thin rays of sunlight streamed in through the canopy of leaves high above them. Down where they were the vegetation was lush and thick. Songs of bird and insects filled the air. Toad stools, moss, and fern decorated the trunks of the giant trees. Great flowering vines wove their way amongst the trees and verdure of the forest.

Finally, it became so thick that they had had to give up riding through it and walk with their horses tagging along beside them.

"Say, you think this wood will ever lighten up before we're through?" Bennethor commented, obviously becoming tired of trudging their way through the dense forest. "At this rate the war will be over before we get to the mountain, let alone find the dragon."

"I agree with you. This place is beautiful, but not exactly adventurer friendly."

"You think we should let the horses go? I'm sure they could find their way back to camp. It seems to me it would make slogging through this place easier."

"Maybe. I still believe we'll need the horses. When it does thin we'll make up the time then."

"If it thins you mean," Bennethor mumbled.

"Hi there!" a high nasally voice said as they rounded a large tree.

Both Clavorn and Bennethor nearly jumped out of their skins as they searched the area for the being associated with the voice they just heard. Finally, they looked down to see a very short, slightly pudgy little creature. At first glance one might have mistaken him for a dwarf only with rather elongated pointed ears and no beard. However, his very small stature, being only about two dragon's claws high, was enough to rule that out. He had a small tuft of long fire red hair, which grew up from his head more like a patch of grass than a lock of hair, and quite large intensely blue eyes. Neither Clavorn nor Bennethor had any idea of what he was.

Fires of Life

"We don't get many travelers through the forest. If fact, we don't get any travelers through the forest," the creature lamented, shaking his head. "My name is Skibjak. I tend these woods."

At that Clavorn noticed tiny branches, of what appeared like a tree, growing out of his arms through his tunic. He wore short trousers which revealed patches of bark on his legs. His feet were bare, with tufts of red hair on his toes much like the one upon his head.

"Who are you all?"

"I'm Shaltak, and this is Bennethor. We are on a quest…"

"Quest? What quest? Tell Skibjak. Skibjak never goes on quests," the creature commented, looking down mournfully, "Too much to do. Too much to look after… Do they have names?" he asked, referring to the horses as he turned his attention back to them, "Oh, never mind, I'll just ask them myself. Tall folk never know the names of their animals."

"What?!" Bennethor exclaimed indignantly, "I most certainly know the name of this horse. It's…"

"Nahahhan," the creature finished for him.

"Na…What?" Bennethor remarked, nearly tripping over himself verbally.

"Nahahhan. He's tired…" the little creature remarked as he stroked the nose of the curious horse. "Want to come to my place?" he asked, pausing and looking up at the men before him, "Yes, yes, I think you come to Skibjak's home. He likes company. Don't get much company," he said, looking down. "But I like company," he told them, looking up with a smile. "Yes, yes, you come. Stay, rest, I fix you grand dinner." He spread his arms wide, becoming quite animated. "You will like. You will see. Your friends are tired," he said returning his attention to the horses. "They need rest. Come. Come," the odd little being beckoned, turning into the forest.

Clavorn and Bennethor glanced at one another.

"We have a quest of most urgency. I am afraid we cannot…"

"NO!" the creature named Skibjak interjected turning back abruptly to face them, "Your animals need rest." he continued more softly, "You need rest. It is just a short distance to Skibjak's home. Come. I not accept no. Skibjak likes company. Yes, yes, they will have much fresh grass. Come," he beckoned again, "Skibjak not keep you long."

Both Clavorn and Bennethor were surprised by the creature's ferocious refusal to accept their declination of its invitation. However, Clavorn could see no real harm in having a nice dinner with the well-meaning lonely creature, so he agreed to follow him back to his humble abode.

Deep into the forest they trekked. Both Clavorn and Bennethor marvel at the way the trees and bushes seemed to part for the creature to make room for them to pass. Branches lifted or curved away. Bushes moved back, vines curled or lifted up, and flowers bowed. It was amazing to watch the way the forest reacted to Skibjak's appearance. Birds and butterflies flitted about his head and he appeared to nod occasionally to them as if he were having some sort of deep conversation with them.

"Here we are," he announced as they arrived at a small thicket in the forest. Deer looked up at their arrival and then went back to eating. There was a small pond around which willows and other trees grew. Tall rushes, cattail, and waterlily were abundant. One could hear the croaking of frogs and toads that undoubtedly lived in its waters.

At first glance Clavorn could not see any home nearby. The trees on the edge of the little glade were thick, but there appeared to be no home to speak of. Initially, he thought that perhaps the little creature simply lived in the thicket. Trees could make a good shelter as he and his men had proved, except in a serious down poor of course, so it was not a surprising thought.

However, upon closer inspection he could just make out the faint outline of a hut which appeared to be constructed from a combination of trees and bushes, or rather by them, for as they approached the bushes extended their ceiling and the trees parted so as to allow for their size.

"See, Skibjak, has nice home. Good for tall folk," he said with a smile as the branches of a flowering jasmine parted to allow them to enter.

Clavorn and Bennethor looked at one another.

"They will be fine," the creature told them, referring to the horses, "They will not leave. They like you too much, especially you," he remarked pointing to Clavorn. Clavorn raised an eyebrow.

Shortly thereafter he turned Hawk loose and Bennethor followed suit. Soon their horses were happily grazing outside Skibjak's humble home.

"Come. Come. I show you my home. It is good. It is dry. You see. I make great dinner."

Again Clavorn and Bennethor glanced at one another before entering the unusual abode.

Inside, the place was warm and inviting. Windows, archways, and partitions were all made, it appeared, from the living bushes and trees of the forest. Upon Skibjak's entry they moved and changed form, seemingly to conform to whatever need he had.

Flowers from the bushes or vines of the wood which constructed his house bloomed profusely. Their perfume wafted through the air while butterflies danced and bees busied themselves amongst their bounty. Tree branches dangled down as hooks, knots doubled as cubbies, the trees adjusting their size and number to fit his needs. Their roots appeared to respond to his wants as well, such as for seating and tables.

It was amazing to watch the plants and trees respond to Skibjak's requests. The animals too he seemed to be able to communicate with, no matter what the species. Spiders were allowed; it seemed, but their webs they kept neat and tucked out of the way. In one corner was a honey bee hive. But the bees never seemed to bother him, keeping to their business of making honey.

"Here. Sit. I make dinner. You tell Skibjak what you quest."

"First, pardon an old warrior," Bennethor began, "but what are you?"

"*Wha*t?! *What* am I? I am not a thing, sir," the creature replied indignantly, "Warrior or not! It is rude. I am a being. Just like you," he said, pointing his chubby little finger at Bennethor.

"I am sorry," Clavorn interjected, "My friend here has little experience with beings outside his home. What he means is that we have never met anyone like you before and would like to know more about you," he told the creature named Skibjak while giving Bennethor a look.

"Humm, tall ones always think the know everything. Seen everything. There are many mysteries to the forest and many a creature like me," he paused as a branch moved and a squirrel entered. "Skibjak is a whimpernickle, to answer your inquiry," he continued allowing the squirrel to crawl on his arm and sit on his shoulder, "I tend the woods and her creatures. So do others like me. We usually like company, but we don't like to feel like a *thing*," he emphasized, "I am not a rock," he announced proudly, then more to himself, "though rocks have feelings too. You tall folk too dense," he remarked turning his attention back to them, "Too concerned with yourselves." Skibjak shook his head with his last remark. There was a pause in the conversation as neither man knew what to say next.

"Pardon my denseness but how old are you? I mean if you tend the forest…" Clavorn asked awkwardly trying to break the silence.

"Whimpernickles never give out their age," the creature told him a bit piqued, "We are as old as the wood. If you must know," he continued. "You are as young as newly sprouted saplings, so we will forgive your questions. Here, sit," he all but commanded as he pointed to two roots which came up out of the ground to form seats in front of them around another very large one which Clavorn presumed was to serve as a table. "Tell us tales while we make dinner."

Clavorn was not sure what meant by 'we' until he witnessed the whimpernickle as it went about fixing their meal. As he watched, he

Fires of Life

noticed mice, birds, bees and other creatures of the forest as they assisted Skibjak in the preparation of their food. It was amazing to watch. He began to assume the 'we' referred to them, for he saw no other whimpernickles.

Not far from the root which had appeared as a table there was a little hearth made from stones which he presumed were provided by the woods. He noticed, uncannily as the whimpernickle placed a rather large caldron in the hearth, that the stones from which it was constructed appeared to move to accommodate its size, and, for a moment, it seemed that their feel even changed. Meaning, if it were possible, the stones seemed lighter, perhaps even happier in their hosts presence than not.

"Come. Speak. What do you seek?" Skibjak asked as he set a drink down in front of them.

"We seek a dragon," Clavorn told him simply as he took a sip of whatever drink it was Skibjak served.

It was unusual; sweet, yet green and plant tasting, if a drink could taste like a color, but in a good way. Clavorn found it strangely refreshing.

"Dragon?" their host replied. "Dragons are great creatures. Old creatures they are. Skibjak like dragons…"

And from there the whimpernickle launched into a long dissertation about dragons; the extensive list of those who were his friends, stories about their doings together, and much, much more. Clavorn could see his new friend and travel companion was becoming somewhat bored with the whimpernickle's tales. However, he did not want to appear rude by interrupting the obviously lonely creature and risk upsetting him again. After all they could both endure a little boredom for an evening, and if it brought the creature some happiness, so much the better.

So dinner came and went. The sumptuous meal was quite good despite the obvious vegetarian nature of it. Even Bennethor commented on the deliciousness of it. Desert arrived with a lavish helping of honey drizzled about on some sort of pastry type dish while Skibjak continued to regale them about his adventures amongst the creatures of the wood.

After a time Clavorn rose.

"Well, it is probably time we were on our way, my friend. We would like to thank you for your hospitality…"

"No. No. You mustn't leave now. Skibjak has yet to hear your tales and it is late. You need sleep. Rest. You stay the night. Skibjak has soft beds. You see. Stay. I take care of your four hoofed friends. They will be fine. You see."

Not wanting to hurt their host's feelings, Clavorn agreed to stay the night. There was no more traveling they could do now anyway, for it was well into the evening by the time they finished up with dinner.

The beds, which were remarkably provided by the bushes and trees of Skibjak's home, were surprisingly comfortable just as he had said. When Bennethor and he awoke the next morning, they found themselves to be very refreshed indeed. Nevertheless, when they went to leave their host protested once more, insisting they stay for breakfast. Once again Clavorn agreed to stay and have breakfast with the whimpernickle. After all they did need to eat.

"Now, my friend, I am afraid that we really do need to be on our way. Our quest awaits," Clavorn told their little host.

"Nonsense. You cannot go on a good quest without a nutritious lunch. I fix. You see. Tell Skibjak of your home."

"No. I am sorry, but we really must be going," Clavorn tried to insist.

"NO! Skibjak says you *must* stay. Skibjak like company."

"We like you too, but…"

"NO! Skibjak say you stay!"

And with that said the 'door' to his home closed shut by the bushes which comprised it and they were sealed in. Clavorn tried to appeal to the creature, but he would not hear of it. He wanted company. He missed company and he would hear of nothing to the contrary.

For what felt like days Clavorn and Bennethor tried to appease the whimpernickle by regaling him with stories about their home and Vaulnik. Even telling him about the war and their battles, but every time Clavorn tried to impress upon him their need to leave the creature would just insist even harder that they stay.

"It safe here," he would argue.

"But it won't be if Vaulnik is not stopped," Clavorn would counter. "We need the dragon."

But no matter how hard he tried to get Skibjak to understand, the whimpernickle would just not budge.

"We could chop a hole in this thing," Bennethor proposed one night after Skibjak had gone to sleep.

"No. That would not do, my friend," Clavorn answered in a hushed tone.

"Why not?"

"Because we would make an enemy of a very old, well-meaning creature, who has the entire forest as his ally, for starters. How far do you actually think we'll get?"

"You have a point." Bennethor replied. "Still…"

"No. This calls for delicacy and patience. I am sure a solution will present itself."

"Well, let's hope it is before the war is over and Vaulnik is in charge."

Clavorn could not help but share his sentiment.

One morning, after breakfast, Clavorn was once again making his case for Skibjak to let them leave when a raven alighted on the windowsill.

CAW! CAW!

Skibjak turned and gave the bird his full attention.

CAW! CAW!

The bird cried out again as an apparent conversation ensued between their host and the large black bird.

"Really," Skibjak said to the raven, "We see... No. Skibjak had no idea."

A few more moments passed as the whimpernickle continued with what appeared to be a deep conversation with the bird. Clavorn and Bennethor exchanged looks, but remained silent, not wanting to interfere with what was taking place between the fine feathery creature and their host. Finally, the Skibjak turned and faced them with a very sheepish look on his face.

"It seems Skibjak has been wrong and selfish in keeping you here. He sorry and hopes tall folk will forgive."

"No problem, my friend," Clavorn told him graciously.

He understood the creature was simply lonely and was just glad the bird, or whoever, had intervened on their behalf.

"I take you to edge of forest. It will be faster. The trees, they listen to Skibjak. Skibjak sorry. He is very lonely. Don't get visitors much. I make up. You see. Come. Come."

With that the little whimpernickle motioned them to follow him outside.

Once outside Clavorn could see Hawk and his traveling companion's horse had fared well despite his and Bennethor's internment.

"Here. You ride. I will lead. Skibjak take you to border. Make up time. You see."

Bennethor looked to Clavorn with one eyebrow raised but said nothing.

"Thank you, my friend. We would appreciate that."

The little whimpernickle smiled and clapped his hands. At that the horses' gear magically found its way to its proper place upon their horses and within seconds they were ready to ride.

Then out of the woods appeared a stag with a large rack of antlers. Before their eyes the great deer knelt down so the little whimpernickle could get on. Skibjak smiled at them once he was mounted, then, in short order, the stag was up and prancing off as the woods before them began to part. Sure enough, like Skibjak had said, the trees and verdure of the forest cleared a path for them at, what appeared to be, his request. Within no time they were galloping on their way through woods.

In less than a days' time they had reach their destination at the edge of the forest, nearest the mountain.

"Here Skibjak leave you. I hope you forgive."

"All is forgiven, my friend."

The little whimpernickle smiled a big broad smile, and Clavorn thought the little branches that protruded from his arms looked perkier and sported a couple extra leaves.

Chapter 38

The forest near the base of the mountain was different from the one in which they had just left. Tall silver barked trees made up this wood. Their white paper like bark dominated the landscape. The heart shaped leaves which adorned their canopy shimmered in the wind.

It was high noon when Skibjak had said his good-byes and they had parted ways with the little whimpernickle. Now, the sun had long since set and a full moon graced the night. As they rode on, the landscape shifted again. Tall cypress like trees grew up out of what appeared to be a large lake in front of them. The full moon reflected off its surface as a fog began to roll in.

"Terrific! Just what we need to help us on our quest," Bennethor exclaimed.

"Well, we are near a dragon's lair. At least I hope, so not entirely unexpected."

Before long they were near the would-be lake. Both men remained mounted as they took their horses over to have a drink of water. All was calm. The night was eerily silent. Only the sound of summer night insects filled the air.

"This place gives me the creeps," Bennethor commented.

Clavorn thought it unusual, but said nothing as he scanned the area with his eyes. Suddenly, Hawk lifted his head and snorted; his ears perked forward, alert. Bennethor's horse shied away from the lake while Hawk stood fast smelling the air through his large nostrils.

"What is it boy?" Clavorn asked as his eyes searched the darkness.

Then suddenly he did not need to ask that question as a large creature, with an alligator like head and dragon like body, lunged at them; the frills about its head unfurled, its teeth bared. Instinctually, the horses turned and took off. Clavorn could feel the heat on his back as the creature blew hot flames in their direction.

Fires of Life

It was a Hindolin. One could think of them as a cousin to the dragon; part alligator, part dragon, with a pack mentality a kin to a wolf. They inhabited the swamps and bogs of various forests. Incapable of flight, they were known to be able to reach speeds that rivalled the fastest creatures on land or in the water. Where there was one there was usually more.

Sure enough, suddenly their appeared another one. Before Hawk could swerve out of its way it cut in front of their path. Both Clavorn and Bennethor pulled their horses up short and changed direction, but another one came and cut off their path. Soon they were surrounded by giant mouths with rows of angry sharp teeth.

Hawk reared. Bennethor's horse shook his head and backed up. "What do we do now?!"

Quick, Clavorn searched his mind for the answer. His grandfather had spoken of such creatures; if he could just remember. He unsheathed his sword. Bennethor did the same.

"Calm your horse!" Clavorn shouted above the snarls and the flames.

"Right!" Bennethor fired back, the sarcasm clearly audible in his voice.

"If you want to live, calm yourself and your horse," Clavorn told him again.

The creatures pawed the earth and inched their way closer. Clavorn squelched his fear and felt Hawk begin to calm down. With his sword in hand he encourage Hawk forward straight for the one he perceived to be the alpha. It blew flames across their path. Hawk shook his head, but Clavorn remained calm as he halted his horse.

The beasts took a step closer. Bennethor remained where he was.

"I am Shaltak, Slayer of Dragon Killers and I have come in peace to find the dragon!"

The alpha beast blinked and eyed Clavorn.

"What are you doing?!" Bennethor asked, "It's a beast. It can't understand you!"

"Who is he?" the alpha said in a loud rumbling voice, eyeing his companion.

"It speaks!" Bennethor remarked clearly in shock.

Both the Hindolin and Clavorn ignored his remark, although for entirely different reasons.

"He travels with me," Clavorn told the creature.

"He is not like you. He fears us. I can *smell* it."

The Hindolin inhaled deeply and eyed Bennethor with a look that could only be described as a combination of disdain and disgust.

"I am the one who seeks the dragon," Clavorn remarked, "He travels with me."

"Why do you seek the dragon?" the beast inquired turning his head to face Clavorn with narrow eyes as suspicion dripped from his voice.

"We seek its help to defeat an enemy who has defiled Maltak's children."

The beast raised an eyebrow in surprise.

"You would defend Maltak's children?"

"Yes, I am Shaltak, Slayer of Dragon Killers, Defender of …"

"…Maltak. You are not unknown here," the alpha told him, "We are grateful to you. But he is different," the creature replied, motioning his head towards Bennethor.

Bennethor shift in his saddle.

"He does not know of you. Forgive his fear."

The Hindolin snorted and smelled Bennethor. Bennethor stood his ground.

"Still, why do you seek the dragon? Your kind rarely cares about creature other than themselves," the alpha replied, turning his attention back to Clavorn.

"You are right. But if we fail, all life will be at stake."

The alpha considered his words.

"You are different. We know of you, we know you care for more than yourself. But we do not know him."

Fires of Life

Here the creature paused, blew, and smelled Bennethor once more. Bennethor's horse tossed its head and backed up. The alpha eyed his companion with apparent suspicion as he appeared to consider his worthiness.

"I will vouch for him," Clavorn told him.

Once more the Hindolin rose, what could only be described as, an eyebrow. Again, it appeared to be considering his words and the character of the man who traveled with him, as it turned its attention back to Bennethor.

Moments passed in silence as the alpha peered down at his companion, apparently examining him. Bennethor glanced in Clavorn's direction, but held fast, following his example.

After several minutes more the Hindolin finally replied, "Since he travels with you we will let him pass, but not without our reservations."

"I am grateful that you should let us pass," Clavorn replied.

"Know this," the alpha continued, "If the dragon deems you worthy, then we will fight with you. We know the foe you seek. We wish to end his rein."

"We would be very grateful to have your assistance," Clavorn told him.

The alpha bowed his head. Clavorn nodded.

"Before we go, what is your name?" Clavorn asked.

"I am Ferrterrak, Leader of the Hindolin," he replied.

"It is good to know you, Ferrterrak. May we meet again on the field of battle."

"May it be so," Ferrterrak told him as he stepped aside to let them pass.

With that Clavorn and Bennethor passed the great creatures and continued on their way up the mountain.

Chapter 39

Clavorn was not sure how much time had passed since their journey began. Skibjak had them all but encased and sequestered in his home, so that the passage of time was difficult to tell. The encounter with the Hindolin proved to be a fortuitous one, though it could have turned out very differently. Hindolin were known for eating anything that strayed into their territory, including men and horses. Now, they were a few days out from their encounter with the beasts and still no sign of the mountainside from his dream.

Bennethor, however, was proving himself to be a good hunter and companion on their journey. Clavorn was glad that he had agreed to let him come along. Alone would have been fine, but the company was very much welcome.

The morning sun was just peeking around the edge of the mountain as they mounted their horses after finishing off a bit of bread and cheese Skibjak had given them for their journey just before he left them. He had used his magic to fill their saddle bags with food for their journey saying, 'It was the least Skibjak can do.' Then he and the stag had sprung off back into the woods. Now, both men were in relatively good spirits as they began their continued ascent up the mountain

"Do you think we'll find that mountainside of yours today?" Bennethor asked.

"To be honest I have no idea, though I am hopeful that we will find it soon." Clavorn told him as they rounded a side of the mountain.

On they traveled, the terrain becoming rockier as they continued to climb higher. A few hours later an eerie fog began to set in. The farther on they traveled the thicker it seemed to become. Now, they could barely make out those trees that were within a few dragon claws in front of them.

"I wonder if this fog is natural to this mountain." Bennethor remarked.

Fires of Life

"I was just wondering the same thing myself, but it's hard to tell. Maybe it has something to do with the dragon."

"Well, dragon or not, natural or not, I've never navigated a fog this thick before. How are we supposed to know where we are going? For all we know we could be traveling away from the mountain."

"Not likely as we keep going up."

"True. But that's the other thing I am afraid of," Bennethor said.

"What do you mean?"

"I mean…well; here we are traveling along, basically blinder than newly hatched chicks. What happens, when trudging forward as we are through this mucky mist, and there's a precipice or something? It seems to me we'd be very likely to just step off and... well…splat."

"I see. So what you are saying is that because of this mist we might say…stop for a while till it lifts."

"Something like that," Bennethor told him.

"And if it doesn't?"

"I guess we try it your way."

"Well, we could do that," Clavorn told him, "only we have people back home who are depending on us and we have already lost too much time. As such, time is now a luxury we cannot afford to waste. War is upon us. Every day that we spend out here is another day Vaulnik has to wreak his vengeance on Avivron. No. I am afraid we have no other choice than to keep moving."

With that said, Bennethor relented in his attempt to persuade Clavorn to stop till it cleared. However, by noon Clavorn was wondering if he should have heeded Bennethor's advice. For instead of the fog lifting, like one would expect it to as the sun rose and the day warmed, it only seemed to become thicker. In fact, to Clavorn it appeared as if it was getting denser the further up the mountain they traveled.

Mist swirled about them. Here and there they heard the occasional flapping of a bird's wings as it flew off. Silence seemed to permeate the woods in which they traveled. Clavorn could sense his companion's uneasiness. Every sound seemed accentuated in the quietness of their misty surroundings. Twigs snapped under their horses' hooves as they slowly navigated their way up the mountain, sounding louder in the silent stillness of the foggy forest.

Suddenly, in the distance Clavorn could hear the distinct sound of an animal in distress. As if it was trying to free itself from something.

"Did you hear that?"

"Did I hear what?"

"That sound in the distance. Almost like an animal struggling, or something."

"No. I haven't heard a thing. Except the sound of our horses' hooves as we trudge through this misty murky mess," Bennethor told him clearly unhappy about their current state of affairs.

Clavorn halted his horse. Bennethor did the same as his horse came up beside him. He was about to speak when Clavorn held up his hand to stay his words. Through the mist and fog Clavorn strained his eyes and ears for the sound he had heard. Eerie silence seemed to dominate the landscape. Then he heard it again. Only this time it was more distinct.

"Hear that?"

"Hear what?"

"There, there it is again. It sounds like a horse's whinny," Clavorn told him, "Don't you hear it?"

"I don't hear a thing," replied Bennethor.

"No. I clearly heard it," Clavorn told him as he strained his ears one more time.

Bennethor sighed, clearly frustrated by the situation. Suddenly, out of the misty white fog Clavorn heard it again. This time it was much clearer, and more distinct. Quickly, he turned Hawk, and led them off in the direction of the frantic sound.

As they rode on through the woods, Clavorn continued to listen for the noises of the animal he felt sure was in trouble. They were his only guide to the poor beast. Bennethor followed reluctantly behind.

Fires of Life

"Couldn't this be a trap?" he pointed out." You know, all this; the mist, the sounds of distress, and everything. Couldn't it be an elaborate way for someone, or something, to lure us in and have us for lunch, or take us prisoner?"

"Yes. I suppose so, but then it could just be exactly as it sounds."

"I don't know. I still think this is a bad idea," Bennethor told him as he shook his head.

On they travelled. The further they went towards the sounds the clearer and more distinct they became. Then suddenly in the distance, through the fog, Clavorn began to see a shape take form. From what he could make out, from his current position as he gazed through the mist, was the apparent form of a white horse that was somehow caught in something. Cautiously, he nudged Hawk forward, for he did not want his equine friend to become trapped like the poor beast in front of him.

All of a sudden Hawk came to an abrupt halt. Clavorn was about to encourage him to move forward when he happened to glance down. Immediately, he raised his hand to stay Bennethor's advance. As he looked down, he could see what had trapped the unsuspecting beast.

"Why are we stopped?" Bennethor inquired.

"Quicksand," Clavorn replied, "The beast is trapped in quicksand."

NAAAY!

The horse called out again as it struggled to free itself.

"Well, that does it. There is not much more we can do for it," Bennethor remarked, "Best if we finish it off, and let the sand take it than to allow it to continue to suffer."

"NO! Wait!" Clavorn exclaimed as he raised his hand to stop Bennethor who had already taken out his bow and was notching an arrow. "I have rope. I could lasso it around its neck. Then Hawk and I could pull it out."

"Are you nuts?! It's more likely to drag you in."

"Possibly, but I'd like to try first. If there is no other way, then we'll do it your way."

"Okay, but I still think this is a waste of time. Time, which you so avidly pointed out we don't have lots of," he told him, placing the arrow back in his quiver. His bow, however, he kept handy.

"We have time for this," Clavorn replied calmly with a mixture of determination and compassion in his voice. Then he took out his rope and began to form a lasso. Twirling it above his head, he took aim and let it fly. The horse pulled its head back away from the rope and struggled harder, whinnying as it did so. Clavorn's lasso ended up in the mucky mess of the quicksand, totally missing its mark.

"I'm telling you this is a waste of time," Bennethor commented as he sat on his horse in frustration.

Clavorn made no comment as he reeled in his rope for another try. Again he twirled the rope above his head and let it fly, but poor visibility conditions made gauging the distance, and anticipating the beast's movements rather challenging. Once more the horse reeled backwards, this time lurching itself part way out of the quicksand, only to sink further in.

"It is only going to keep sinking," Bennethor insisted.

"Perhaps," Clavorn replied somewhat absentmindedly as he readied himself for another try.

SWOOSH! SWOOSH! WAAAH!

Clavorn let the lasso fly. This time it caught around the beast's neck as it jerked its head up in fear. Immediately, he braced for its struggle and began to urge Hawk backwards as he wrapped the end of the rope around the horn of his saddle. At first their efforts appeared in vain. The harder they tried to pull the creature out, the harder it seemed to struggle against them. But then suddenly it lurched and gradually began to struggle forward out of the sinking sand and mud.

Bennethor watched as Clavorn and Hawk pulled the beast through the mist and muck to safety. As it neared them, its figure began to become clearer.

"By Allethor! That's no horse!" Bennethor exclaimed.

"What do you mean it's no horse?" Clavorn asked as he turned his head to face forward. He had been looking behind him to be sure Hawk did not run into any difficulties himself as they pulled the creature forward.

"By the gods!" Clavorn exclaimed in shock, a bit awe struck, as what was emerging from the icky quagmire was none other than an exquisite white unicorn, with its long pearly white horn protruding elegantly and unmistakably from its noble head.

Hawk continued to move backwards, pulling the magical creature through the muck. Finally, the beast tossed its head, and lurched forward one more time before it fully emerged from the deadly throws of the sinking sand. Once free of the quicksand the unicorn shook itself, sending a spray of sand and mud out from itself.

"Oh, nice!" Bennethor remarked as some of the mucky mess found its way to him. "Thank you!" he yelled to the unicorn.

Clavorn laughed, "Well now you can say you've been blessed with unicorn mud."

"Terrific!" he groused as he took out a handkerchief and began wiping the mess from himself. "And I suppose I am supposed to be grateful too."

Clavorn shook his head and turned his attention to the beast he and Hawk had just freed. Now the creature stood before them in all its glory, its thick white mane rippling in the gentle breeze.

Bennethor stopped his doings, and both men sat silently upon their horses as the grand creature made its way towards Clavorn. Clavorn gazed on in wonder as the beast walked over to him and nodded its noble head in apparent thanks. No words came out of either man's mouth as they sat on their steeds in awe of the magnificent creature.

After a couple of minutes Clavorn finally regained his composure and urged Hawk slowly forward, closer to the unicorn. To his surprise the beast remained calm as he and Hawk finally came to stand beside it. Slowly, he offered his hand to the creature. He could feel its labored breath against the back of his hand as it blew and took in his scent. Gently, he moved his hand to stroke the unicorn's soft neck.

Bennethor watched in silence as Clavorn then removed the lasso from around the majestic creature's neck. The unicorn could have taken off into the woods after that, disappearing into the thick mist, but instead it stayed and bowed its elegant head to Clavorn.

Clavorn gently rubbed the beast behind its ears and on its forelock. Time seemed to stop for that brief moment as he took in the grandeur of the magical creature before him. Then suddenly, the unicorn stepped back, reared up, and took off up the mountain, disappearing into the fog.

"So, was that so bad my friend?" Clavorn inquired of his travelling partner once the unicorn was out of site.

"Speak for yourself," he replied as he brushed another bit of mud from his clothes, "I would have thought the creature could have shown a bit more gratitude by lifting this worthless mist from Zezpok."

"Somehow I don't think that is exactly how unicorn magic works, my friend. Besides, the point of removing him from the muck was to save him, not incur favors."

"Well, I still think it could have shown some semblance of gratitude."

"It did, my friend. It did."

Clavorn turned Hawk away from the sinking sand, and began once more to pick their way through the mist and up the mountain.

Chapter 40

They traveled on with Clavorn in the lead as always. The fog continued to become thicker the farther they journeyed up the mountain. Soon it was so thick that they could hardly see where they were going. Clavorn could feel Bennethor becoming increasingly nervous behind him. Hawk slipped on a rock, sending it rolling down the mountainside into an abyss of white. A not so subtle reminder of the dangerous path they were taking.

Lack of visibility caused them to travel at what felt like a snail's pace. In fact, there were moments in which Clavorn felt sure that he had seen the tiny earth bound creatures traverse across plants and rocks faster than the pace they were being forced to keep. Finally, he pulled his horse up, and stopped. All he could see around him was a sea of white intermingled with the occasional trunk of a tree, or smattering of a bush.

"Now what?" Bennethor inquired as he pulled his horse up to Clavorn's.

"Now I need a moment." All the white everywhere was becoming rather dizzying. He needed a few seconds to clear his head and sense their way before he continued, "I'll need you to be quiet."

"Aren't I always?"

"Yes, but...but this is no ordinary fog," he told him as he searched the ghostly forest for answers.

"How can you be sure it is unnatural? Not that the thought hasn't crossed my mind."

"How many normal foggy days last all day long?"

"You have a point there," Bennethor replied, becoming silent so Clavorn could decipher their next move. After a few moments Clavorn slowly edged his horse forward and Bennethor followed.

Clavorn felt like a blind man feeling his way for the first time in a strange house. The deeper they went the thicker the fog continued to become.

"Are you sure we would not be better off just waiting to see if it lifted?" his travelling companion asked.

"Yeah. But I don't see any convenient campsites do you?"

"No. Out in the open in this stuff is just suicide. Anything could decide to take us, and we wouldn't see them till it was too late."

"Precisely, hence the need for motion," Clavorn told him.

"Right."

On they traveled up the mountainside with only their horses and their instincts to guide them. It was tedious, time consuming, and exhausting. Still, the two men continued to plod and pick their way through the misty murky wood.

"Do you suppose this is some kind of test?" Bennethor finally asked after several hours of silent travel.

"The thought had crossed my mind."

"I wonder how we will know if we've passed?"

"It will clear," Clavorn replied simply.

"More likely we'll step off a cliff to our deaths," Bennethor mumble under his breath.

"Always a possibility," Clavorn replied, startling Bennethor into silence once more.

Time passed, and now the fog was so thick that they could barely make out the horses underneath them.

Where exactly are we?

Obviously, he knew he was on the mountain, but where and how far up were the real questions in regards to that. Hawk plodded on forward as he ducked to avoid a low lying tree branch. Not a sound was heard coming from the forest around them. The still fog was unnerving. Every hoof fall of their horses sounded like an intrusion into the misty cloud like word around them

How am I going to know when I've found the right mountainside if I cannot even see a few inches in front of me?

The question plagued his mind as they trekked on through the thick white haze.

Doubt niggled in the back of his head, but his instincts told him to stay his course and continue moving up the mountainside. However, by now he was relying almost exclusively on Hawk to keep them from stepping off a precipice. Clavorn was painfully aware of the precarious nature of their situation.

The light was growing dim now. He guessed that the sun was beginning to set. Soon they would have to stop. A night in a foggy forest with no knowledge of the lay of the land, to say nothing of its local inhabitants, was not something he was looking forward to. His only hope now was for them to find a cave in which to spend the night.

Suddenly, as if the forest had read his thoughts, the fog cleared in front of them revealing a wondrous sight.

"Look!" Bennethor shouted, "A cave!"

Chapter 41

Sure enough out of the haze loomed a cave. The gray rock surrounding it gave it an almost ominous appearance as swirls of mist and fog danced in front of it. Clavorn and Bennethor walked their horses slowly up to the entrance. Hawk snorted as they came upon the opening which led inside.

"We should be careful," Clavorn cautioned as he peered into the darkness of the cavern from atop of Hawk, "You never know what has been living here."

Bennethor nodded in agreement, "I'll have a look if you like," he offered.

"Well, it may not be as ominous as it appears. Look," Clavorn glanced down at Hawk who was now busy making short work of the grass near the entrance to the cave.

"Well, bless the dragons!" Bennethor exclaimed. Soon his horse was also busy devouring the grass. The calm nature of the horses led them both to believe there was no apparent danger.

"Still, I'll have a look around the inside just to be sure," Clavorn told him, "Now I think it's time to dismount and relax for the evening, but I would be sure to tie the horses tonight. We don't need them wondering off in this fog. We'll never find them."

"Yeah, no problem," Bennethor replied as he dismounted, "I was just thinking the same thing."

Clavorn gave him a brief nod. "Keep them close though. If this fog decides to thicken..."

"...don't worry. I got the idea. In this wood its best to act as if you don't expect to see your hands let alone anything else."

Clavorn smiled as he dismounted and walked up to the opening of the cave. The walls were different from most other caves he had been in. Huge hexagonal quartz like formations comprised the interior walls of the cavern almost as if it was some giant geode. The light, what little there was, seemed to reflect off their surface. Their color appeared to be gray, but Clavorn could not tell if that was because they were truly gray, or because they were merely reflecting the color of their surroundings.

He examined the floor now looking for any signs that another creature lived or had recently been in the cave, but there was no scat or paw prints of any kind. As far as he could tell, there was no indication that any creature, other than themselves, had been there recently. Still he drew his sword before continuing with a deeper inspection of the cavern before him.

Slowly, he advanced to the back of the cave. The deep darkness at the end of the cavern gave no hints at to what might lay beyond it. Once again he crouched down to examine the floor of the cave.

Dust and dirt covered the rocky ground, but as before there was no sign that any creature had been in the cave recently or otherwise. Something he found a bit curious, but was not going to look too closely at given their current predicament. As he stood up, he took in the scent of the cavern trying to discern any unusual odors, but as there were none he sheathed his sword and went back to join Bennethor.

"It looks good," he shouted out to him, "Why don't you see if there is any dry firewood about. I'll do the same while we have this break in the fog."

Bennethor nodded as he finished tying up the horses. He then grabbed a rope from his saddle, tied one end around the tree he had tied the horses to, and the other around a convenient rock near the entrance of the cave. This way they would always be able to make their way back to them no matter what the visibility conditions were.

Finally, he set about gathering firewood. Fortunately, the mist and fog had parted enough to create a small clear area in front of the cavern that was sufficient for what they needed. Before long they had gathered enough wood to be enjoying a nice warm fire near the cave entrance. Darkness was settling in about them as night began to fall.

"What else do you suppose lives in a forest like this?" Bennethor inquired as he tossed another log onto the fire.

"Hard to say. If we're near the dragon's lair, then it will only be whatever creatures the dragon deems best."

"You mean to say if he doesn't like us he will drive us away or… or kill us?"

"Yeah, like I told you, you might have been better off staying behind and 'babysitting' instead of coming along with me."

Bennethor straightened up where he sat.

"Nonsense, no matter what happens anything is better than babysitting a bunch of warriors itching for a fight."

The two men laughed, and enjoyed a bit of rabbit from one which had strayed too close the cavern while they were gathering wood. Bennethor had thrown his knife and killed it before the poor creature had even noticed they were there. Now, the succulent smell of it roasting over their open fire only served to remind Clavorn of his childhood friend, Sefforn.

He remembered how his friend loved rabbit. He missed his cooking. Only Sefforn could roast the best rabbit in camp, but, for the moment, this one was just fine. Both men were starving after the long day of navigating through the misty murky wood.

Night finished its fall, and once again a dense haze cloaked the land. While they had been eating the fog had seen fit to close in around them. Clavorn had watched as the mist had gradually swallowed up the horses, obscuring them from view. Now, he could not make out a single star in the sky nor the moon above them. It was as if they and their cave were the only things in the world, and the rest was all fog, haze, and swirling mist.

This must be what it would be like to live in a cloud.

Looking out from the cavern entrance to the world beyond, he saw only the orange glow of the fire as its light reflected in the mist. Bored by the uniformity before him, he turned his attention to Bennethor who was just reaching for the last bit of their roasted rabbit, which was also beginning to be swallowed up by the fog.

Fires of Life

"I'll take the first watch while you get some rest," he told him as he finished his last bite, discarding the bone in the fire before them. Sparks flew and a little sizzle escaped the burning embers where the small bone had landed.

"Are you sure?"

"Definitely. I need to think anyway, and this will give me some time to do just that," Clavorn told him as he rose and went to stand closer to the entrance, leaving Bennethor near the fire.

"Okay," Bennethor yawned, throwing down his last bit of bone as well. "Suits me fine. I'm exhausted."

Bennethor found himself a comfortable spot on the stone floor near the fire. Then unrolled his sleeping roll and began settling himself in, using his satchel as a pillow.

It was not too long before Clavorn heard the now all too familiar snoring of his new friend and travelling companion. He looked out over the hazy landscape. The horses had long since faded into the scenery. All he could hear was their occasional but gentle blowing. He peered out into the mist.

It's like I am alone in the world...If it weren't for Bennethor's snoring.

He set himself down on a large rock near the entrance of the cave and began to sharpen his dagger. The gray crystalline walls were now black except for the area near the fire. There the dim light of the glowing embers and small dancing flames reflected off the surface of the hexagonal crystals as if they were made of water and not rock. The culminating effect, he observed, was a wonderful warm animated display. Clavorn turned his head away from the mesmerizing sight, and peered out into the foggy mist, his thoughts returning once more to the task at hand.

Where would the dragon be?

He moved his sharpening stone across the polished surface of his blade and looked up. Now the fog had enveloped the interior of the cavern, filling the entire space with a cloudy hazy mist. All he could see were the stones near his feet that marked its entrance, and the soft glow from the fire as its light reflected in the misty murky fog. Clavorn shook his head. This was surely a strange land.

He continued to sharpen his dagger. The night seemed to pass slowly as he had no way to mark the passage of time. Gradually, his eyes began to become heavy. He tried to fight it, but before he knew it he had dropped his dagger, finally succumbing to the pull of the night.

A sudden sound startled Clavorn out of his sleep. He opened his eyes. What he saw brought him to an immediate upright position, for instead of being at the entrance to a large cave, both he and Bennethor were inside some huge cavernous chamber. Immediately, he drew his sword and stood up. This was not the place he and Bennethor had supped at earlier in the evening.

Where are we?

His eyes narrowed searching the space for any clue as to where they were, or who had brought them there.

Who did this?

Who indeed? For whoever it was had left him his weapons, an odd thing to do if your intentions are hostile. Still, he was not going to take any chances.

As Clavorn's eyes combed the area, he could see they were in a cavernous room of ginormous proportions. Its walls rose to a height of nearly five dragon lengths, or more. Giant columns of quartz like crystals seemed to hold up the ceiling above them. The entire space, which Clavorn estimated was large enough to house several full grown dragons with room to spar, was bathed in a golden glow, as if some giant fire were dancing inside the walls and reflecting outwardly into the chamber.

"Bennethor!" he exclaimed with hushed urgency, but Bennethor remained asleep.

Again he called out his traveling companion's name, but to no avail as he continued to remain asleep. Clavorn was about to call his

Fires of Life

name out one more time, when all of a sudden an old woman appeared from across the cavern and began to walk towards him.

He blinked and rubbed his eyes, for she seemed to have come straight out of the rock before him. Her hair was long and white as new fallen snow. The gown she wore was also long and flowing, the same color as her hair. The only thing she seemed to be carrying with her was a long white staff. At this distance he could not make out the form of the figure carved about its top.

Clavorn eyed her approach with caution as she continued to amble her way over towards him, traversing the cavernous space in a relatively short period of time. He stood, sword ready.

"Sit down, my child," she told him kindly upon seeing him, "I mean you no harm."

"Where am I?" he asked as he continued to stand, not quite ready to sit.

"You are where I am," she replied simply, a warm smile gracing her face as she continued to walk towards him.

Clavorn gave her a puzzled look, and the old woman chuckled.

"What is this place? Who are you? And why is my friend still asleep?"

"My, my, my so many questions, my dear boy," she chuckled again as she came nearer to him.

Now that she was closer to him, he could easily identify the carving atop her snow white staff as that of a dragon, a green dragon, he presumed to be the image of Maltak, carved from a single Kriac stone with blood red rubies for its eyes. Its head formed the very top of her staff while its wings, body, and tail stretched down about the length of it, almost as if the creature were flying to the Shardon Lands. Around her waist she wore a sliver belt fashioned in the shape of a dragon with outstretched wings. Upon her feet were silver sandals. Each adorned with a single Kriac stone atop the front. About her head was a simply designed silver diadem with the head of a dragon at its center, whose outstretched wings gracefully curved around to form the rest of it.

As she neared a column, not more than a few paces in front of him, there appeared, as if from nowhere, a beautifully carved crystalline chair in the form of a dragon. The top of the high backed, throne like chair was formed by the head and neck of a sculpted dragon, with a wonderfully carved benevolent expression on its noble face. Its wings swept downward to form the armrests almost as if it were going to embrace its occupant. Finally, its feet formed the front and rear legs of the chair, with its tail melding in to form the column from which it had come. The seat itself was where the belli of the beast would be if it were a living creature. Clavorn notice when she sat down that the entire chair, and everything which comprised it, glowed from the inside outward, giving it an almost lifelike appearance.

"Are you a Dragon Witch?"

"Another question. Do be seated." She smiled warmly to him and gestured for him to sit. Her kindly face looked into his as he stood refusing to be seated.

"There is no place for me to sit unless you are referring to the floor, in which case, I prefer to stand."

"Look again. Are you sure there is no place for you to sit?"

Clavorn was about to answer 'yes' when he glanced over to his left and saw another beautiful crystal chair. Not at all like the one she was sitting in. No. This was simply a chair, but exquisite in its own right, carved with a definite dragon motif.

"I'd still prefer to stand for the moment. If you don't mind," he replied, for he did not as yet feel comfortable enough to sit.

"Suit yourself, but I think you will want to. Please, at least sheath your sword. I mean you no harm, and if I did that sword would hardly do you much good."

Clavorn paused before sheathing his sword, satisfied for the moment that her intensions did not appear to pose a threat, though he was still a bit wary.

"As to your questions, well let me see...What do *you* think?"

What is she playing at? If I knew the answer to those questions, I would not be asking her. On the other hand if she is anything like Qualtaric, then perhaps this is some sort of test.

"My instincts say that you are a Dragon Witch," he answered boldly.

"Well done," she replied, "but that was an easy one. Can you deduce the answers to any of your other questions?"

"Hmm, since you are a witch you must be responsible for my friend's inability to awaken," he told her.

"True, but then he could just simply be a heavy sleeper. How do you know it is me?"

He eyed her across the space. "For one thing, I have been traveling with him for days now, and he has yet to have been this difficult to awaken, therefore there must be some other explanation."

"And naturally I am the likely suspect, but couldn't there perhaps be another explanation?"

Her answer was puzzling and he felt a bit confused.

What other explanation could there be?

"But on to your other questions. What do you think about where you are?"

"As to where I am, I am at a loss. Except that we are in some sort of cavern. As to how we arrived here, I can only assume you are responsible for that as well."

"You are correct, though I had a little help."

Clavorn could only wonder who that 'help' might be.

"To give you a partial answer to the, 'where you are question,' you are deep within the bowels of the mountain you were on. And if you haven't figured it out yet, I am Eshnara, Grand Mother of all Dragon Witches."

"Then you know where the last dragon is. You know where I can find Viszerak." Hope glimmered for a moment in his heart.

"Yes, to both questions," she put her hand up to stay his next inquiry, "But it is not for me to tell you the answers to these questions." Clavorn's heart fell, "It is for you to find the answers to those questions."

"Then why am I here? Why did you bring both of us here?" he asked confused by her answer.

"Both to test you, and to show you something," she replied "Maybe even to give you something."

Now Clavorn's look of puzzlement grew as he raised one eyebrow.

Give me what? And what could she want to show me if it is not where to find the dragon?

"Come here, Clavorn Remmaik, son of Favorn," she commanded.

Clavorn went to stand in front of her.

"Kneel."

He did as she commanded, kneeling down on one knee before her and bowing his head reverently before The Great Witch, then lifting his head his eyes met hers. There within her ancient face he saw a pair of deep blue eyes. They were the blue of a midwinter's sky. Not the faded blue of age but the bright blue of youth.

"That's it, my boy, look deep within my eyes," she told him. Clavorn found himself looking even deeper into her eyes.

Suddenly, he was transported to a mountaintop. It was snowing and bitterly cold. He felt himself shiver as he stood while the wind whipped around his body.

"Tell me, boy, where is there life?"

He turned around, and there she was standing a few paces behind him, her staff in her hand, but she was not shivering. No. There was no sign that she was even affected by their apparent surroundings.

"Here, on this mountaintop?" he replied as billows of vapor escaped his mouth. He could feel his teeth begin to chatter as he wrapped his arms about him to keep warm, pulling at the cloth of his tunic. It was late summer back home, and he was in no way dressed for these surroundings.

"Yes," she replied calmly coming to stand closer to him, "But more specifically."

Fires of Life

Clavorn thought as he fought to think through the freezing cold. The wind whipped his hair and bit into his flesh as he glanced around to see if there was any life on the apparently lifeless mountaintop, but all he could see were barren rocks and snow. The whole area appeared empty and devoid of anything that even remotely resembled any form of life, save for himself and Eshnara. He paused a moment.

Then he remembered what Skibjak had said about the rocks and 'tall folks.' He recalled how even they had moved for the little creature, and even appeared to feel 'happy' by his presence.

"All around us," he answered still shivering, "There is life all around us."

"Very good," she told him, "Now look deep into my eyes again."

Once again Clavorn did as the old sorceress requested.

All of a sudden he found himself deep within the bowels of the earth at the heart of a great volcano. The heat was intense, searing his flesh, causing him to perspire, but for some reason he did not burn despite the obvious high temperatures. Not far below the small jetty they were stand on, molten rock swirled about like a great ocean churning, and twisting.

"Tell me, my boy, is there life here?"

He thought a moment, "Yes."

"Where?"

He thought again upon his visit with the whimpernickle.

"Everywhere," he replied now more confidently.

"Good. Now where is there power?"

Her question took him by surprise. Power appeared to be ubiquitously around him. The great molten waves turned the heavy red melted rock like water. The heat seemed as if it was everywhere, emanating its great energy, its great power, yet he had a feeling this was not the answer.

"Well, there is obviously power everywhere here, but I believe the power you are referring to is the one which dwells within us," he replied.

"Correct. But why is that?"

"Because, while there is obvious power here, the power within us is the one which can be used for the greatest good or the greatest ill, giving it a more precarious nature which is different from that of this molten rock, primarily because it is the one which is under our control."

"I see you do see," she replied, "Now look into my eyes once more."

As all the previous times before, he gazed into her eyes, only this time he found himself back in the cavern exactly where he had begun the journey.

"Can you guess why I asked you those questions?"

Again Clavorn thought. "Because within each of us lies a great power, a power for good or ill, but the power of life is the greatest power of all, for it binds all living beings together, and crashes through all sorts of barriers to survive. Now I must use the power of life within me to crash through the barriers that stand before us to defeat Vaulnik and find the dragon."

She smiled, "You understand much, Clavorn Remmaik, son of Favorn. Tell me the answer to one more question. Why did you answer that there was life all around us when we were on the mountain and within the volcano?"

He paused a moment before answering, "Because of a recent encounter with a little friend, who opened my eyes to possibility that life exists in more places than most of us are taught to believe."

"I see," she answered, "I assume this 'little friend' you are referring to is the whimpernickle who tends the forest at the base of this mountain."

"Yes. But I do admit rocks are difficult to see as 'living.' Understanding that they have life on them is easy, but in them? Well…" he stammered, looking for the right words, "I mean, I know about the power they carry in them, the Effora. But being beings themselves? That I think I still struggle with. Though I must admit

Fires of Life

seeing them behave the way they did for him does make me wonder."

"Not all life is as we understand it," the old Dragon Witch replied. "The Effora, as you mentioned, is only one aspect of this. That is why all creation is important. Now rise, my son."

She lifted her right hand as she said it in demonstration.

Clavorn rose.

"Go and wake your friend. It is time for a toast."

Without hesitation Clavorn went over and woke Bennethor.

"What? Huh, where are we Shaltak?"

"I see your friend is in need of some introductions," she remarked calmly, but with a subtle edge, so that he could not tell if she was just referring to herself or to him as well, given the fact that Bennethor did not, as yet, know his true name.

"Who is there Shaltak, and what is she talking about? I see no one. Is it the mysterious woman from the battle?" It was clear Bennethor was confused and not totally awake yet.

"No, my friend, it is not," he wondered why his friend could not see the old sorceress. "Tell me, what do you see?"

"I see darkness and shadows. I can barely make out your face. Shaltak, what is going on?"

"I don't know, but I am about to find out."

Suddenly, Clavorn grabbed his sword, and unsheathing it, pointed it at the old woman.

"What kind of trick is this? Why can't my friend see you, see us? What kind of game are you playing at?"

"Remember, my son, I said was going to test you, and then I was going to show you something."

"Yes, I remember," he replied. His eyes narrowing as he edged the blade closer to her. But she remained calm.

"The question now remains, who will you believe?"

"What?" He inquired confused.

"Yes. Who will you believe? Me or your supposed friend."

"What do you mean my 'supposed' friend? Of course he is my friend. He has fought beside me in battle, and now travels with me to find the dragon that will save this land from Vaulnik and his vile Zoths."

"Has he done all that now," her voice had changed. It was now clearly tinged with sarcasm. "Well, then it seems there is no point to my next question, but let us see if he can pass the last test."

She clapped her hands, and Bennethor jumped to his feet apparently able to see where he was, and more importantly, who else was in the room with them. Clavorn kept his sword trained on the old woman.

"Who is she Shaltak?" he asked with a puzzled expression on his face.

"Yes, tell him who I am," she told Clavorn with a wave of her hand.

"She is, Eshnara, Grand Mother of the Dragon Witches," he informed Bennethor.

Is that a flash of terror in his eyes?

But then it disappeared almost as quickly as it had appeared, and Clavorn thought he must have just been seeing things.

"What is it my friend? Do you not see a kindly old woman in the room with us?"

"Yes, yes, I do, but…"

"…but what Bennethor," she inquired of him as she looked down upon him from her throne like chair.

At that particular moment, Clavorn noted, it had somehow managed to appear even grander, giving her an increasingly imposing presence. The eyes on the carved dragon's head atop her throne glowed even brighter as she spoke. Clavorn noticed its intimidating effect on his friend and travelling companion.

"Nothing, nothing," Bennethor replied as he stood up tall shaking himself, "I was merely disoriented that was all."

"Good," she replied, "Shall we toast then?"

Fires of Life

Clavorn looked at her as if she were mad. There was no wine anywhere, or much else for that matter, then, as if from nowhere, a silver carafe appeared by his feet with three similarly arrayed goblets.

"Come now, my boy, pour the wine for us and let us toast."

Clavorn still did not wish to lower his sword.

"Oh really, don't be silly. You can see he is unharmed. Lower your sword." Clavorn hesitated, "I could force you, but I would rather you did it yourself," she told him.

Tentatively, Clavorn lowered his sword and sheathed it before bending down and reaching for the ornately decorated carafe. As he picked it up, he could see there were scenes depicting the gods and dragons on it. Scenes from the legends of old clearly embossed about its surface. He then bent down and picked up a similarly styled goblet, and poured the wine, handing the first to Eshnara, the second to Bennethor, and the last to himself before setting down the fine carafe. Finally, the two men stood before Eshnara with the wine in their hands waiting for whatever was to come next.

"Good. Let us toast to the worthy. May they pass here unharmed," she announced as she lifted her chalice.

An odd toast.

He lifted his goblet in kind.

Both of the men waited for her to drink first before venturing a sip. A moment later she drank from her goblet, and watched while both the men before her did the same. Suddenly, Bennethor could no longer breathe. Clavorn unsheathed his sword, and put it to the old woman's throat again.

"What magic is this? Release him! He is a good warrior!"

"Are you sure?" She questioned him.

For a split second Shalmaray's warning about a traitor flashed into his mind, but he once more dismissed it based on Bennethor's actions.

Bennethor was turning red.

"Release him, or I'll gut you where you sit!"

"Fine sentiment, but I doubt he feels the same," Clavorn looked at her and narrowed his eyes. "Look in his satchel." She ordered. Clavorn hesitated, "Look!" she commanded her voice booming across the chamber and echoing off the walls.

Sheathing his sword Clavorn reached over and grabbed Bennethor's bag.

"Now open it," she ordered.

Bennethor was turning blue; soon it would be too late.

"You are delaying this, old woman. I know your game."

"Open it!" She commanded again, fire blazing in her blue eyes while her voice once more echoed off the cavern walls. The eyes in the dragon's head above her glowed even more intensely as if they mirrored her emotions.

Clavorn opened the bag.

"Now empty its contents."

He did as she told him, quickly turning it over, spilling out what was inside. At first, all he saw were all the usual things one expects to find when one is traveling, but suddenly, in the bottom of the bag, something strange dropped out. Whatever it was it was wrapped in a skin and tied with a leather tie. He picked it up.

"Unwrap it!" She ordered tersely.

"But he will die soon," Clavorn protested.

"Not if he is as good a warrior as you say," she told him calmly.

Fear showed in Bennethor's eyes as he continued to struggle for breath, finally falling to the ground, writhing on the floor, desperately trying to gasp for air.

Quickly, Clavorn cut the package open with his dagger. Shock showed on his face as he viewed what was before him.

Suddenly, Bennethor writhed and convulsed for the last time, expiring before him.

Clavorn looked up confused.

"What is this trickery?" he remarked in confusion turning over the horrid object in his hands.

Fires of Life

"It is not trickery, my son," she told him. Her voice once again soft and full of knowledge, "that dagger you are holding is, Zvullungol, The Dragon's Bane Dagger."

Clavorn was stunned. He had heard of, The Dragon's Bane Dagger, but had never believed it actually existed. His mind reeled.

How had Bennethor come to possess this?

He turned the dagger over in his hand once more. Its hideous golden hilt glistened in the glow of the room. Gaudi ugly images of vile dragons and creatures that could only live in Zezpok adorned the hilt of the loathsome blade. Its black ominous tip was unlike any dagger in history. Made from what appeared to be a dragon's claw, it was said to be sharper, and more deadly than any dagger known to man.

"See now who is worthy," the old sorceress said.

Clavorn could see why she was the, Grand Mother of all the Dragon Witches.

"The Dragon's Bane Dagger," she went on "was made from the claw of a dragon, as I am sure you have deduced. But not just any dragon, an evil dragon, sacrificed in a ritual killing designed for one purpose and one purpose only, so that its blood and claw could be harvested and used to kill another dragon."

"It is said," she continued as she rose and stepped down from her throne to meet him, "that the blood of this sacrificed vile dragon was placed in the hilt, so that upon the claw's penetration the blood would be released directly into the dragon's wound, killing it in a most horrible and agonizing manner." She was standing next to him now, her hand outstretched, so as to receive the menacing weapon. Still stunned, Clavorn placed it in her hands.

"I see you are a bit confused," she commented as she turned away and walked back to her seat.

"How can I be sure your story is true, and not one designed to explain why you killed a good a warrior? For all I know you placed it in his satchel."

"Think, my son," her voice was calm and gentle as she spoke to him from her throne, "why would I kill your friend and not you? Clearly, it would be more advantageous to kill you."

"I guess, but…"

"You still find this all hard to believe."

"Yes, I trusted him," he replied, looking down upon the body of his now deceased travelling companion.

"You have a good heart, Clavorn Remmaik, son of Favorn, but you need a gift that you are missing. Can you guess what that is?"

He thought on his past, on similar situations, and he knew the answer, "The ability to see into a man's heart."

"Yes. You use your intuition for so many things, and it servers you well, but in this you seem blind. The gods have given you too good a heart I fear. Trust is a good thing, but not all are worthy. Though I cannot totally fault you, many men are quite good at hiding their true intensions. Such was the case with your friend here." She paused a moment looking down on Bennethor's body. "Here drink from my cup and have your eyes opened."

After what Clavorn had just witnessed he hesitated.

"I see you are learning, but too much distrust can be just as harmful, if not more so, than too much trust. Many atrocities have been committed by men who fear other men, and so distrust them. Come," she motioned him over, "come and partake in the truth of life. I promise that all you will see is what is true in a man's word."

"This is what you had to show me. This is what I was to learn," he replied in a hollow voice as one does in a time of shock.

"Yes, Clavorn, I am sorry, but it is important if you are to succeed in freeing this land."

He looked at her and suddenly he understood. With an outstretched hand she beckoned him to come to her. As he did, he stared into her youthful blue eyes and wondered at the knowledge stored there. Reaching out, he took the goblet she held in her hand in his hands and drank.

Fires of Life

The red wine tasted good to his lips. At first there was nothing only the taste of the fruity wine. He swallowed and took another swig. Suddenly, a torrent of images flashed through his mind. Images from his past and others he could not quite make out. Fog, mist, fire, dragons twisting, churning, stars, light, bright light. More images, faster they came. Snapshots he could not make out. They burned in his brain as they flooded it with information. The pain of it was so intense that he dropped the chalice, spilling its remaining contents on the floor of the cave.

His eyes rolled back, more images; fire, flowers, life, green, water, smoke, blackness. Searing heat and intense pain simultaneously flooded his mind, and spilled over into his body as he placed his hands about his head to try and stop the pain. Then the world went dark.

When it was over he found that he was on the floor with his head cradled in her arms. He had no idea how he had arrived in such a position, all he knew was that life still flowed in his veins.

"I see you have passed through, The Eye of the Dragon, and come out on the other side," she remarked, gently wiping his forehead with a soft cloth.

"What do you mean?" he inquired, attempting to sit up. His head ached and he felt dizzy.

"I would not attempt to sit right now," she told him gently, "Lay back down, rest."

Clavorn did as she suggested; his body clearly in no shape to argue.

"What was that that you gave me to drink?" he asked his head still reeling.

"The Tears of Maltak," she replied simply, "I placed a drop in my goblet so that your eyes might be opened from now on to the truth in a man's heart."

"But what about all the images I saw?"

"Many are from your past, but others are part of the future, some part of the dragon, and still others that are part of a collective from an ancient time, a time before men. It is all part of what happens as one passes through what we call, 'The Eye of the Dragon.'"

Clavorn was still a little dazed and confused. The pounding in his head felt as if a million boulders had just been dropped on it, but at least he was alive, unlike his traveling companion. He tried to stand up, but found that his legs would not stay under him.

"I think it is still a bit soon for that, my son," she told him as she helped him back to the ground.

"Somehow I think you are right," he relented, glancing over at Bennethor's lifeless body. He still could not believe that he was somehow a traitor. He had seemed like such a good man, but then being a good warrior does not necessarily make one a good person. That is a thing much deeper than hunting skills, bravery, or congeniality.

"You want to know his story don't you," she said almost begging him to ask. He nodded unable to speak for the pain of the moment, "Alright. I will tell you," she told him. "His name is Vorig, son of Zvelgog."

Clavorn looked at her, surprised by her announcement.

"Yes, I see you recognize the name. Yes, he is Zarik's brother and the last of the Darzors. He was commissioned by Vaulnik to infiltrate your ranks and kill any dragon left in Avivron."

That is what Shalmaray must have meant when she said the traitor intended to do 'great harm.'

But why had she healed him? Why not just let him die?.

His head hurt and pounded with every movement, yet as she spoke he knew the old Dragon Witch told the truth. Shalmaray had warned him, but he had not seen it. Blinded by his skill and apparent interest in his cause, he had dismissed any signs to the contrary. Now he understood why the Hindolin had sensed he was different.

But why hadn't she?

"You wonder why she did not warn you. Why Alethea healed the man who could destroy The Dragon?"

"Yes. Yes, I do. She could have at warned me. If he harbored such evil, why heal him?"

"To give him a choice," the Grand Mother of Dragon Witches told him. "It was for his sake, not yours. To give him a chance to be more than what he was."

"Then why did you kill him. He could still have change."

"Could he now? He continued to carry Zvullungol, instead of disposing of it. If he had any hope of changing, of choosing a different path he would not have expired by the drink in his goblet. However, he did. That was the nature of that toast and the reason for it. To discern his true heart."

"I see," he replied simply.

He glanced over at the lifeless body of the man he had known as Bennethor. Images of him and Zarik came to his mind. He saw Vaulnik hand him the dagger. The dagger, he had to know more about the dagger.

"But the dagger…" a knife like pain shot through his head as he tried to sit up again.

"Lay back, the pain will go in a couple of hours." Clavorn lay back sensing the truth of her words, finally acquiescing to his predicament.

"The dagger is dark magic," she continued, "from a time before men. This is the work of Zagnor. You must find the dragon, Clavorn Remmaik, son of Favorn, or our world as we know it is doomed."

Suddenly, the cavern went dark, and she was gone.

Do all Dragon Witches have to make such dramatic exits?

Once again he tried to sit up. The sides of his head pounded, and he was forced to lie back down again. Sleep called to him. He tried to fight it; however, its pull was so strong that no matter how much he fought it he was destined to fail, and fail he did, falling into a deep and peaceful slumber.

Chapter 42

The sunlight streamed in through the cave entrance hitting Clavorn square in the face. It's blinding light nearly burning his eyes as he tried to open them. He sat up and looked about him. The memory of the past night flooded into his mind like a bad dream. Vorig's body was nowhere to be seen, but all of his travel items, save for the dagger, were strewn about the floor of the cave near where the fire had been. Clavorn thought on the man whom he had helped, and who had been his travel companion all these many days. It was still hard to believe he was Zarik's brother, let-alone a Darzor bent on destroying their only hope of success.

As he glanced out over to where the horses were, he could see they were both tied up by a tree not far from the cavern. It took him a moment, but then he it hit him. He could see. The fog was lifted. The mist burned off. It was a clear, crisp morning, perfect for travel. Not far from the cave entrance, past the horses, he could just make out the silver ribbon of a stream.

He smiled to himself.

And you thought last night was a dream.

It was quite clear to him now that the fog had all been due to some form of magic. Whether it was from Eshnara or from the Kalmak's curse mattered little. He rose and stretched.

Time to complete this quest...Time.

The word hung in his mind.

What is it about time that seems to speed up, slow down, or altogether stop depending on the situation?

Sometimes he had the feeling that time was almost an entity all to itself. At present, though, the only thing about time that really concerned him was his need for more of it.

He went down to the horses and greeted both of them. They nuzzled and nudged,

"No, sorry fella's I have no great carrots with me this morning."

Fires of Life

Then suddenly, one of his pockets felt full. He padded it, and found that it did indeed contain something. He reached inside and sure enough...

"Well, bless the dragons!" he exclaimed, smiling to himself as he thought of the kindly old woman whom he had met the night before, "Looks as if you two are in luck," he remarked as he pulled out a carrot for each of them.

After some loving on both the horses he strode on down to the stream below. The crystal clear waters looked inviting after his ordeal that evening. He bent down and splashed his face with its icy waters. The feel was at once refreshing and exhilarating.

Clavorn took a few sips of the deliciously cool clear water before he stood up and glanced around. His dilemma was much as it had been a few days ago, which way to go from here. This morning, however, no signs seemed willing to point out the direction necessary for his quest. He walked back up to the cavern and began to pack up his things.

It did not take him long to ready his belongings. Soon he was mounted on Hawk ready to break camp. Vorig's horse he tethered to his. Normally, he would have just turned it loose, but they were short war horses, so he was going to do his best to see to it that this one made it back with him.

Breakfast had been easy this morning as it turned out the tree Vorig had tethered the horses too was a wild apple tree. Its succulent fruit had been just the thing to start the day. Though reaching them had been interesting since the horses had apparently availed themselves of all those within easy pickings.

Now, as he looked back over at the cave, he could not help but think back on all that had transpired there. Hawk shifted under him, and he spurred him gently to move forward.

After much thought Clavorn had decided that the best direction to travel in was to continue winding his way along the side of the mountain. He had a feeling that around one of the bends he would stumble onto the mountainside he had seen in his dreams.

The going was much faster now that the fog had lifted. Before long he realized he was more than half way up the mountain.

It has to be around here somewhere.

He could feel it. The dense forest, the wildflowers everything was starting to look familiar.

Clavorn pulled Hawk up and glanced about his surroundings.

Where is the dragon?

Then he remembered the stone she had given him, the stone that had been found near the Stone of Maltak. He reached up and felt for the little pouch around his neck. Upon finding it, he opened it and took out the small rock Alethea had given him. He could still remember her green catlike eyes as she had given it to him that night.

Who is she? Certainly no ghost. Dragon Witch? Maybe. Woman? Definitely.

He recalled how she had looked as she had waltzed boldly into his camp, the catamount padding along beside her, and the hawk perched on her shoulder. He could see it all, the wind as it gently blew through her dark hair furling and unfurling it out behind her. Her svelte figure covered so perfectly by the animal skins she wore. But the one feature he could never seem to get out of his mind was her eyes, so green, so mysterious. They captivated his soul. Caught by them since the first day he had gazed into them.

Clavorn shook himself as he gazed down upon the little stone. Green, like the Stone of Maltak, it glistened with the light of day, its blue green heart clearly discernable. Once again the stone seemed to have a life of its own as the sunlight danced inside it. He held it, remembering how it had seemed to glow in her hands momentarily while she passed it to him.

Where is she?

Only now did he realize he had not seen her since that night of the last battle, the night she had spoken her name to him. Alethea, the name itself seemed almost magical.

Fires of Life

As he held the stone he began to realize that it was starting to glow with a faint light from within. Not the light of the sun but another entirely different light. Hope began to burn in his heart. Perhaps he really would find the dragon.

He placed the stone back in its pouch and gently urged Hawk forward. Up ahead was a bend in the terrain. As he came upon it, the land opened up. There before him was the hillside in his dreams just as he had dreamt it.

He rode over to it and stopped before it, once again removing the stone from its pouch. Suddenly, it began to glow with a light of its own, brighter now, and more intense than before. Clavorn searched around. There must be an entrance, a way into the dragon's lair.

Clutching the stone, his heart began to sink as he realized there was no apparent way in. The hillside was just that, a hillside. After several minutes of a frantic searching, he placed the stone back in its home, and sat mounted on Hawk thinking. He went over in his mind what she had told him. Perhaps there was a clue anything that would help him to discover the dragon in the words she had spoken that night.

'Listen with your heart.'

He recalled.

Is that it?

He had tried listening with his soul, it had led him this far, but what of his heart? He had always thought of them as one and the same, but now, as he sat perched on Hawk, he wondered.

Perhaps they are not the same.

Clavorn closed his eyes and tried to listen with his heart.

At first all he could here were the songs of birds as they called out to one another. Then it was the sound of the wind as it filtered through the trees. He calmed his mind, trying to empty it of all thought. Next, his mind found the sounds of the horses as they shifted and moved. He could hear their breathing, feel their life force. Gradually, he began to become aware of the other life forces around him, the trees, the birds, the insects, and finally himself.

Clavorn listened as he heard the sound of his own breathing, felt the pounding of his own heart. His heart, his mind reached out and touched it, delving deep within it. Suddenly, feelings and images began to appear, the face of Maltak, of Alhera in the stain glass, of her, Alethea, till at last he saw a dragon, green and shimmering in the sunlight, its red eyes flaming down upon him. His heart felt warm as it touched and merged with the life force of the dragon.

All of a sudden the ground began to shake around them. Hawk reared, and Vorig's horse nearly pulled Clavorn's saddle off as the land opened up before them. Clavorn grabbed Hawk's mane, surprised out of the trance. He watched in awe as rising out of the ground was the largest and most beautiful dragon he had ever seen, her green iridescent scales shimmering in the light of the sun, casting tiny rainbows of light throughout the hillside and surrounding forest.

As she rose The Great Dragon spread her wings causing near hurricane force winds to blow down the mountainside. Clavorn had to steady both himself and his horse as the great beast flew up, and landed not far from them, alighting just outside the huge cavern of earth it had just released its self from. Settling her wings into a resting position, her great long tail stretching out behind her, the she dragon looked down upon him with her ruby red eyes.

Hawk danced under him, and it took everything he could think of to convince him to stand before the great beast. Vorig's horse pulled and tugged on the line that held him tethered to Clavorn's saddle. Suddenly, the line slipped. Clavorn tried to hang on to it, but Vorig's horse was too scared and frantic. Finally, he was forced to let it go or risk being pulled off Hawk and drug down the mountain. Immediately, Vorig's horse took off, galloping in fear into the woods and down the mountainside.

Once he was free of his dead companion's horse, however, it did not take much to calm his. When Hawk was settled he took out the stone Alethea had given him. It shined a new with a light like he had never seen, brighter than the sun.

Fires of Life

The dragon's eyes flamed as it looked down upon the man and the stone. Suddenly, a great burst of flames spewed forth from its mouth, up into the sky.

Clavorn had no idea what to do next. He closed his hand and placed the stone back in its pouch. Clumsily, he tried to speak to the magnificent dragon before him.

"I...I am Clavorn, son of..."

"I know who you are," a voice spoke in his mind. *"Our minds have touched. Our hearts have joined. You are the one worthy of my awakening, Clavorn Remmaik, son of Favorn. Together we shall call forth the Shaddorak, and defeat this scourge that threatens not just your land, but the entire world."*

For a moment Clavorn was speechless, "Who are you? You cannot be the Last Dragon, Viszerak?" he ventured tentatively not want to upset the dragon least it change its mind and return to the earth from whence it rose.

"Correct Clavorn," the words gentle in his head, *"I am Maltak, The First Dragon; Friend to Alhera, Breather of Life and Mother of the First Dragons."*

Clavorn could hardly believe what the dragon was saying. All this time he thought his mission was to find the last dragon, then he remember her words.

'Find the dragon.'

So simple, so honest, so true that he had never thought she meant to find *The* Dragon, Maltak.

"Forgive me, Maltak, for not recognizing you," he exclaimed as he bowed his head before the great legendary beast.

"There is nothing to forgive, Clavorn Remmaik," she remarked.

Clavorn lifted his head and looked up at her. Her magnificently arched neck looked down on him with a noble almost regal air.

"It is time to call forth the Shaddorak," she proclaimed her voice booming about inside his head.

"Excuse me, Maltak, but how do we call forth the Shaddorak?"

"The same way you called me out, with your heart," the Great Mother of All Dragons replied simply.

"But I do not know the Shaddorak," he protested, "How…?"

"Search with your heart Clavorn," Maltak spoke gently in his mind, *"You know more than you think."*

Confused Clavorn closed his eyes, and began searching with his heart just as he had done to find the dragon. Maltak closed her eyes, and together he could feel their minds blend, their hearts becoming as one voice combing the world for the one woman upon whom its fate rested, the Shaddorak.

Time seemed to stand still as their spirits melded, reaching out into the world. In his mind's eye now, all that Clavorn could see were her eyes, her green catlike eyes. Try as he might to change the vision, all his heart could do was fall back to her.

"Stop fighting it!" Maltak's voice sounded in his head.

Clavorn could not understand. Surely he had to be doing something wrong.

"You cannot direct the vision," he heard Maltak say, *"Let it flow."*

Unsure, but trusting in the wisdom of the legendary beast, he tried again. Following Maltak's advice Clavorn let the vision go. Before long his feelings began to overpower him as a strong burning sensation consumed his heart, his mind, his body, his soul.

Suddenly, a great wind appeared out of nowhere, and Clavorn opened his eyes. There flying above him was a huge blue dragon. He would have nearly missed seeing it except for, in the angle it was at, the sunlight was shimmering off its scales producing a similar effect as Maltak's.

The huge blue beast alighted down not far from Maltak. Off its back she came. Her dark hair flowing out behind her, her green catlike eyes burning into his as she waltzed over to meet him.

"So, you're the Shaddorak," he said surprised. Hawk shifted under him as she walked over to where they were.

"And he is Viszerak, The Dragon of the North," she announced calmly, her voice smooth as silk.

Now the pieces of the puzzle were finally beginning to come together. Her powers, the dragon, why she needed to keep her identity hidden; it was all beginning to make sense. The one piece he did not have was the explanation for were the scars on her back, but then he did not need an explanation. The only thing he did know was that he was in love with her, whether she was the Shaddorak, or not.

Chapter 43

"I do have a few questions," he managed to say after he recovered his composure.

"I should think so," she replied, gazing up at him, "but you might want to get down off your horse to ask them."

"Oh, yeah... right," Clavorn felt ridiculous, but he had forgotten entirely about Hawk as he sat mesmerized by the revelations before him.

Clavorn dismounted, and stepped around Hawk to Alethea. Hawk stood his ground, and eventually began to graze nearby while he met up with her. He could not help but notice how the armor she now wore suited her. It was blue green like her dragon, fashioned from a sort of unusual metal. He could tell it had been uniquely crafted to camouflage her presence as she rode the dragon. In fact, he observed, it would camouflage her no matter which dragon she rode.

"Alright," he began once he had finished dismounting Hawk, "why me, why was I chosen to find Maltak, and don't just answer, 'because you are worthy?'"

"Well, it is very difficult to answer such a question when you are insistent upon denying the answer," she told him, then she raised her hand, gently touching his lips to stay his next words, "But I cannot fault you, most good people have a hard time believing they are chosen for anything important. They find it difficult to fathom that it is somehow their fate, their destiny, to fulfill some task, some role decided for them by the gods. It seems, however, that it is this humility which is one of the reasons, one of the qualities the gods are looking for," she paused, "The universe is a mysterious place, Clavorn, and her reasons, like the gods', are not always clear."

"Then why do you, or the gods even need me? You have the power to stop this. You are the Shaddorak," he remarked. Her eyes looked deep into his, penetrating his soul with their gentleness, their understanding. He had only had glimpses of this side of her before today.

Fires of Life

"Some things must be fought for," she answered him, "freedom, and the right to live, while granted without strings by the gods, are not by men. It seems here good and evil are pitted against each other to sort out the destiny of mankind. Will a man live free, or will he die a slave; a slave to another man, a slave to his fears, a slave to his desires, a slave to his quest for power? Will a man live, or will he perish for his lack of love, passion, or appreciation for life, all life? Those are the real questions that seem to be destined to play out here."

"So what you're saying is we must fight for our freedom, for the right to live."

"What I am saying is, in this realm, where good and evil share this domain, man must choose to live. He must choose to be free, and then, if necessary, he must fight for his choices." She paused a moment to let her words sink in, "I cannot fight this war for you, nor can the gods decide its fate. That is something you must choose."

"Then I choose freedom. I choose life," he told her emphatically. The choice seemed so clear to him he could scarcely imagine another. "But that still does not answer the question, 'why me?'"

"You are the champion of men. Chosen to be so because of who are. It is your heart, your love and appreciation for *all* life that sets you apart. It is why only you could be the one to find and awaken Maltak."

"But why would a man choose slavery, or death?"

"Some men are seduced into believing that if they serve evil, or themselves, then they will have the power of life and death, that they will have the sole proprietorship of liberty. Through their greed, greed for gold, for lust, for whatever they believe will bring them power and dominance. It is through this that they then feel they have the right to decide the fate of others. But they are wrong. Soon they become a slave to evil, to themselves, to their greed, and the life they felt within them dies. So they become nothing more than empty, hollow individuals pulsing with the essence of life, but dead to its reality; forever searching for that which they themselves killed. Never realizing what they have done till it is too late."

Clavorn thought on her words, and the truth of them spoke clearly to his heart. He could see them take shape in the form of Vaulnik and Sevzozak, even Almaik, and in so many others.

"The dagger then, Zvullungol, the Dragon's Bane Dagger," As he uttered the name of the vile weapon, Maltak stamped the ground with her huge foot, clawing at the earth and breathing fire in anger.

*"That dagger is an **abomination!**"* the legendary creature shouted in his head.

"Yes," he told her as he turned to the outraged dragon before him, "Thankfully that dagger is no longer in the hands of the enemy." At his final words Maltak seemed to settle back down, but clearly just the name was disturbing to her.

"That dagger is the only weapon in this world capable of killing, not just any dragon of Alhera's, but Maltak herself," Alethea explained. "That dagger was responsible for the death of Altak," she finished gently.

Now all the pieces of the puzzle were starting to fit together, and the picture of everything that had transpired up till now was becoming clear to him.

"Well, then what are we waiting for?" he announced, "We have a war to fight."

"No, we are not finished yet," Maltak announced, *"Alethea must receive her full powers."*

"But I thought she was the Shaddorak, that …"

"…I already had all my power." Alethea finished for him. "No, it doesn't work that way. Maltak must empower me with the last and greatest of my powers." Clavorn looked puzzled, "Even a Shaddorak must be worthy," she informed him with a smile.

Then turning she walked up the mountainside to where Maltak was waiting, and went and stood in front of her. Clavorn watched on in amazement as he witnessed one of the rarest sights ever; the Final Empowerment of the Shaddorak.

Alethea knelt in deference to Maltak, The First Dragon, Friend of Alhera, Breather of Life, and Mother to the First Dragons of Old, and thereby Mother of All Dragons. Then she unsheathed her sword, the glint of its sharp blade and the sparkle of its ruby pommel catching the light of the sun as she placed it before her, an offering to the dragon.

Clavorn caught a glimpse of the sword as the light of the sun glinted off the ruby pommel. It appeared old, its craftsmanship from another time. It was clear to him that this was no ordinary sword. Next, she did the same with her dagger. Clearly, they were no ordinary weapons. Their decorations suggested that they were important somehow, but how he could only guess at. Of one thing only could he be certain, these were not the weapons she had brought with her into the camp that day.

"Do you have the stone, Daughter of Alhera," Maltak asked formally, proudly arching her neck.

"Yes, Great Mother of All Dragons," Alethea responded, bowing her head.

"Then place it before me," Maltak commanded.

It was then that Clavorn noticed the satchel she was carrying with her. As she brought it forward and open it, out came the most beautiful of all Kriac Stones he had ever seen. From where he was standing it appeared to be a perfect specimen. Crystal clear and the largest of its quality he had ever known to exist.

"I see you have past the tests. You have found The Stone of Alhera, and retrieved Shevardon, the Sword of Justice and its companion Galhidor, the Dagger of Truth." Maltak continued in her formal tone. Clavorn could hear it all perfectly in his head as she spoke, *"Now, are you prepared to receive the powers of the goddess?"*

"Yes."

"Do you swear to only use them as the goddess commands upon pain of your destruction should you violate them?"

"Yes," Alethea replied her head still bowed in deference.

"Do you understand that they are not for your personal use, or the use of any man, but solely for the purpose of carrying out the will of the goddess?"

"Yes."

"Then Alethea, Daughter of Alhera, I claim you as the Shaddorak. Receive your powers and fulfill your destiny."

With that Maltak lifted her great head to the sky, her eyes flaming. At that moment it appeared to Clavorn as if the light of the sun intensified, causing the dragon's scales to shin so brightly that he had to shield his eyes with his arms. Then Maltak breathed fire into the Shardon Lands. The flames soared high above the mountain almost as if they were going to reach up and touch the gods. Finally, she turned her head and breathed down on Alethea.

Clavorn stood in shock at what he saw. His heart lurched, and it took all his will not to rush up the mountainside. He knew this was some sort of ritual, but still it was difficult for him to resist the urge to run to her, to protect her from the flames of the dragon. Time seemed to slow as he watched the dragon's flames engulf her. Clavorn felt his feet begin to move.

"Do not interfere," he heard a voice say in his head. But he could still feel himself inching forward. *"Clavorn, son of Favorn, stand your ground,"* the voice ordered. It was a stern male voice and though every fiber of his being wanted to intervene, he did as it commanded.

Just when he thought he could not take it a second more Maltak stopped. The fire was gone and amazingly there was Alethea, still kneeling before the dragon, her hair flowing out behind her. The ground around her was totally scorched, leaving no doubt about what he had just witnessed. Yet somehow she and the objects before her were unharmed, just changed. He could tell; something in her demeanor. He questioned himself; or was it something else, some intangible something that he sensed.

"Now, Alethea, Daughter of Alhera, receive the Stone of Alhera. Use it well," Maltak announced.

Fires of Life

Alethea took the stone before her and held it in her hands. As she did so, the stone began to glow with a light unlike any Clavorn had seen before. It was as if the light of Shardon itself was shining through it. Alethea stood up and lifted the stone to the Shardon Lands. As he watched, the stone grew brighter and brighter until finally its luminosity blinded him, and he could no longer gaze upon the sight before him.

Then almost as suddenly as it had started to glow it ceased. Alethea reverently replaced the stone in her satchel as she turned and faced Maltak.

"Alethea, Daughter of Alhera, receive Shallahona, Sword of Life, and Alsenar, Dagger of Truth, Alhera's weapons. Use them wisely. Use them justly. Use them with honor," Maltak told her.

"I will," Alethea replied as she reverently bent down, taking the sword in her hands, and once again offering it up to the sky.

It was then that Clavorn noticed her sword had been transformed, for it too began to glow, growing brighter and brighter, and then it stopped just as before. As she sheathed it, he could see that it had been changed somehow by the fires of the dragon. For it was no longer made of metal but appeared to be formed out of Kriac Stone, the hardest substance known to man, though how that was possible remained a mystery to him.

Legend had it that a Kriac Stone tempered by a dragon's breath was impossible to break and any edges on it would become unbelievably sharp. He could only imagine the might of this sword.

As she sheathed it, Clavorn noticed that not only had the sword's make up changed but so too had its shape. From what he could see from his vantage point, the sword now appeared to be in the shape of a dragon with its head and breath comprising the sword itself, its body making up the hilt, its wings the cross guards, and the end of its tail creating an equally dangerous end for the pommel.

Alethea performed the same ritual with her dagger as she had with her sword, offering it once more to the goddess. As before it shined brightly as she lifted it skyward, then ceasing. She sheathed it and placed it in her boot. Like the sword it too appeared to have been transformed into Kriac Stone, and shaped into the form of a dragon only with its wings folded. The head and body once more comprising the hilt with the blade manifested as the fires of the dragon.

"Now you are truly, The Daughter of Alhera, and her warrior on earth. Go and fulfill her commands. Complete your destiny." Maltak proclaimed and with that Alethea bowed to her. Maltak tipped her head in acknowledgement.

Then Alethea turned and began to walk over to him, the ceremony complete. But as she walked a great gathering of song birds began to flit about her singing and dancing in flight. Butterflies too fluttered around her. With each step she took the grass began to grow and wildflowers sprung up at her feet.

Suddenly, Salhera padded over the summit of the mountain to meet her while a golden eagle cried from overhead. Alethea paused raising her arm to it. Clavorn watched as the most beautiful golden eagle he had ever seen flew down and alighted on her arm. From a distant pine a hawk cried out as it sat perched observing the whole affair. She was truly magical to watch, her hair flowing out behind her as she came down the side of the mountain to meet him, her catlike eyes staring into his.

Clavorn did not know if he should bow or what as she came up to him, her emerald green eyes staring, continuing to burn into his. Suddenly, the eagle flew off as she met up with him. She stopped and stood so close he could sense her power, smell her perfume; feel her essence. Then suddenly, without realizing it, he found himself bending down to kiss her. Her lips folded into his. Her body melting in his arms as his passion grew. Then she pulled away slightly.

"It is time Alethea," Maltak announced interrupting the moment.

"I know," she replied not taking her eyes off of his.

"I love you," he found himself saying.

"I know," she replied, her eyes beckoning him to kiss her again, and he found himself giving in to her, his passion no longer being contained as she reciprocated his feelings. They stood thusly reposed for several minutes before Maltak once again interrupted.

"It is time for us to go," the dragon declared this time more sternly.

"Yes," they both replied simultaneously and then laughed as they broke their embrace.

"I believe we have a battle to fight," he said with a smile.

"I believe you are right," she replied, straightening herself up, "so what are we waiting for? Let's go."

Chapter 44

Clavorn began to turn back towards Hawk, but Alethea caught his arm, "Not so fast," she told him, "There's a quicker way."

He looked past her following her thoughts and recalled how she had arrived at the mountainside.

"You mean..." Her eyes spoke volumes. "But what about Hawk?"

"He'll be fine Clavorn," he heard Maltak say.

He gazed up at Maltak. The expression on her face was soft and reassuring.

"Alright, but how? I've never ridden a dragon before," he asked as a sudden excitement began to course through his veins.

"You ride horses bare back don't you?" Alethea teased, her green eyes dancing.

"Yes, but..."

"You'll see," Maltak interjected, *"I promise, you'll be a natural."*

Clavorn was skeptical. Still, to ride a dragon, just the idea of it was thrilling to his mind.

"Oh," Alethea caught his arm again as he began to move in the direction of The Great Dragon, "I won't be going back to camp with you."

"Why?" he asked confused by her announcement, turning once more to face her.

"It is best if the enemy does not know about me yet."

"But how will he know?"

"Only the Shaddorak rides Maltak," Viszerak told him.

The sudden interjection of the male dragon's voice stood out in sharp contrast to Maltak's, and he found it momentarily disconcerting.

"I guess you will choose the timing of your entrance," he said to her searching her eyes, her face for any clue while burning the memory of that moment in his mind forever.

Fires of Life

"Yes," she replied, "Now it is time for Maltak and I to go, but I will be with you when the time is right."

He nodded and embraced her, their lips folding into one another one last time.

"Take care of yourself," he told her as they parted.

"Haven't I been?" she replied with a smile then turning, she strode off up the mountainside to Maltak, Salhera following along beside her.

Clavorn could not help but be concerned for her, despite knowing who she was, as he watched her leave for The Great Dragon. His love for her would not let him simply pass off the danger they were about to face. War and battle were unpredictable things.

He watched as the mountain lion sat down and observed her mount the dragon. Alethea glanced down at him. Then Maltak raised herself and spread her huge wings. The big cat braved the sight as the enormous dragon made the first downward thrust with its wings. The wind whipped the catamount's coat, swayed trees, and nearly bowled him over as it lifted its tremendous mass off the ground. The mountain lion then let out a huge roar as Alethea and Maltak rose and took flight.

Clavorn steadied himself as he watched her and Maltak fly off over the mountain ridge before turning his attention to Viszerak. Hawk whinnied as he strode off in the direction of the great male dragon.

"It's alright boy," Clavorn told to his equine friend and turned to head back in Hawk's direction, "Go back to camp!"

The horse whinnied again and reared. Clavorn paused a moment as the horse trotted up to meet him. His soft brown eyes quizzical as Clavorn stroked his forelock.

"It's alright boy," he told his trusted equine friend again, "I need to go with them. You need to head back to camp. We'll see each other there."

The horse nickered. Clavorn stroked his long dark neck and rubbed his forelock. He would miss him just as he knew his horse would miss him, but this was best. He knew it. Time was of the essence, and dragon flight was, after all, much faster.

"Go on boy. I'll meet you there. Go, go on," he told him as he stepped back.

Hawk stood his ground a moment, nodding his noble head and pawed at the earth.

"I know this is a first, but I need you to meet me at camp. Go, go on."

The horse bobbed his head one more time.

"Go!" he shouted finally and sent him off with big smack on his hind end. Hawk immediately took off. He was a smart horse. Still, he could not help but feel a pang in his heart as he watched his loyal friend take off. Then, just as Hawk reached the edge of the hill, he stopped, turned, and reared once more.

As his hooves found the ground again, Clavorn shouted, "Go on!"

The horse tossed his head, and then tore off down the mountain. Hawk's backside galloping off was the last thing he saw of his trusted steed before he turned his attention back to the dragon before him.

He could feel his excitement build as he walked over to the large male dragon. His handsome blue body rippled and undulated as he repositioned himself to accept a rider. That was when he noticed them, scars, deep long gashes that ran along the body of the great beast. He paused.

"War wounds," the dragon volunteered.

Clavorn felt slightly ashamed for he knew Viszerak had been injured in the Battle of Quantaris. Just seeing them this close was a painful reminder of that horrible day.

"I am sorry, my friend," he told the dragon.

"No need for apologies, Clavorn Remmaik, son of Favorn. There was nothing that you could do to stop it."

Still, the dragon's words did little to squelch the feelings of remorse and regret over the outcome of that day.

"Come, climb up and let us be off. There is a new battle to wage, and time is of the essence."

"Yes, yes, you are quite right, my friend," Clavorn replied as he snapped himself back into the present.

Reaching for the huge limb before him he took hold and climbed up the dragon's enormous leg, hoisting himself up onto his back. It was easy to see how he was to ride him now that he was on him. Viszerak's enormous spines gave one plenty of places from which to hold on and brace. While the scales behind his neck served as the perfect place to sit. Clavorn settled himself up by his neck between his wings just as if he were a horse.

"Ready?"

"Ready, my friend," Clavorn told him.

All of a sudden Viszerak opened his great wings and began to take off. Clavorn could feel his powerful muscles under him as he thrust his wings downward for lift. The wind they created under them swayed trees and broke branches. Fortunately, it only took two such downward thrusts before they were high off the ground.

Clavorn looked down over Viszerak's shoulder and saw the forest far below. He could see the mountain lion standing now, staring up at them. It called out as he and Viszerak turned and soared off.

The strength of Viszerak's wings meant he could glide much like an eagle. He marveled at how easily such an enormous creature could maneuver in the skies. Soon they were flying high above the clouds and the mountains. He glanced behind them and caught a brief glimpse of Maltak and Alethea as they disappeared over the distant mountains to the north.

He turned his head back and faced the wind. The feel of it on his face was so exhilarating. Every fiber of his being felt the glory of being alive as the wind rushed past him and flowed over his body, rippling and furling his clothes. He closed his eyes to drink in the moment, the freedom, the excitement and he cried out for the sheer joy of it.

Suddenly, Viszerak swooped down and turned. Clavorn opened his eyes and hung on, startled by the abruptness of the motion. The speed at which the dragon dove was unbelievable. Viszerak banked hard between two mountain ridges. He could feel the force of the turn. It was fantastic!

Soon he spotted his campsite. The area was not hard to miss from the air, the ancient willows serving as a distinctive marker.

"There!" Clavorn shouted.

"You needn't yell," the great dragon told him. *"I can hear your thoughts just as well as you can hear mine."*

"Oh," Clavorn thought surprised by this revelation.

As Viszerak circled the encampment, Clavorn could clearly see the tall ancient willows with their great weeping branches, and his men as they paused in their work, eyes aloft, as well as the stream, and waterfall that were all a part of the landscape there. Viszerak alighted down on top of a grassy knoll on the mountainside nearest the encampment. Several of the men, who had spotted the dragon upon their approach, came running up the mountainside first, with the whole camp following behind them to greet the great dragon and himself.

Viszerak's landing blew the trees, and caused his men to stop and stare. The force of the wind created by the dragon whipped their hair, forcing many of them to shield their eyes from the debris kicked up. Sounds of awe struck voices filled the air as the great beast settled itself. Clavorn climbed down and dismounted to a throng of cheers.

"Well, it looks like you managed to find the dragon after all. And before the coming of the next age." Sefforn announced as he greeted him with a smile and a friendly embrace.

"That was the plan," he told him in jest.

"You'll have to tell me all about it later," Sefforn told him in his ear as Melkiar came up to them.

"Well, I never thought you'd actually find the dragon, but I guess congratulations are in order. Say, where's Ben…"

Fires of Life

"It's a long story," Clavorn told Melkiar over the din of the excitement.

Then he turned and addressed the crowd.

"As you can see, I brought back the Last Dragon, Viszerak," a roar of approval and joy went up. Viszerak sat nobly in the background while Clavorn waited for the exuberance of the men to die down bit, "He has agreed to fight with us."

Another great ovation went up, nearly deafening Clavorn and his friends. Once more he waited for them to quiet down.

"Now it is time to take this fight to them," he shouted as more shouts of approval rose up, drowning out any other sound.

Clavorn smiled as he put his hands up to quiet the crowd.

"It is time for us to take back this land, take back our freedom, and take back our lives. Not just for ourselves, but for all life everywhere."

Another round of cheers went up, and he could tell it was going to be a night for great celebration.

"Tonight we celebrate, but tomorrow we take this war to Vaulnik!"

A huge roar went up as the men lifted their arms to the sky.

Chapter 45

Clavorn's mood was sober as he gazed out over the horizon through a small clearing in the trees. Sounds of the celebration continued on behind him. All was dark save for the few stars that were out and the glow of their camp fire. The moon would not rise for several more hours. On the horizon he could see a distant low-lying cloud. But it was not the cloud of weather, for beneath it lay the telltale glow of a raging fire. Then he glimpsed them, the unmistakable flickers that were the breaths of dragons, dragons clearly in the act of destruction. The Zoths were doing Vaulnik's dirty work, destroying the land and leaving nothing but devastation and sorrow in their wake.

"You do know there's a celebration going on in your honor, don't you," he heard his friend say from behind him.

Sefforn sauntered up to Clavorn who was standing away from the festivities, glancing out over the horizon.

"Oh, I see you noticed," Sefforn remarked as he came to stand by him. "Yes, Vaulnik's been busy while you were away."

"Tell me," he inquired. His eyes remaining fixed on the distant glow. He needed to know, though he already had a pretty good idea.

"Well, he's been burning everything he can as he enters this land, villages, farms, whole forests. It's like he has something against anything that's living." Sefforn shook his head, "I tell you it's a mystery to me as to why. It doesn't make any sense. A kingdom's worth is more than a lump of rock."

"I agree," Clavorn acknowledged a bit mystified himself, though, knowing Vaulnik, he had to have a reason, and he could only wonder at the last words the Grand Mother of Dragon Witches, Eshnara had told him.

Was this the work of Zagnor like she said? Was Vaulnik in league with him?

He was not sure, but something in the pit of his stomach told him she might be right.

Fires of Life

"What do you suppose he hopes to gain?"

"I'm not sure, but it won't matter much longer," he told his friend not wanting to voice what Eshnara had told him.

Clavorn turned away from the sight. He had seen enough.

"How can you say that?" Sefforn asked, "The battle is not won yet, and one dragon hardly makes up for the sheer numbers of men he has, to say nothing of the Zoths."

"Because one way, or another it will be over soon, and all of this will be history. Have any of the scouts been able to give us a report."

"No, not until recently. Mostly we've been able to deduce what's going on by watching the horizon and from reports by villagers as they flee his path. I tell you it's not good. Vaulnik is enslaving, or destroying all he can."

"How so?"

"It seems that after everything that transpired during our last encounter they fled back and regrouped. This time they brought the Zoths. Reports are inconsistent as to actual numbers, but everyone agrees there's more than one of those things, and that the amount of men he has is great."

Clavorn recalled his dream and wondered.

"Do you have any reports regarding Sevzozak?"

"Only that he is amassing his men near the castle. It seems he wants them to guard himself and the nobles while Avivron burns."

"Not much of a surprise there, though I would have hoped for something more," Clavorn told his friend. "We need a way to kill to those Zoths, or at the very least neutralize them," he continued thinking aloud.

"Yeah, tell me about it. If only that dragon of yours could talk."

"Wait a minute. That's it!" Clavorn exclaimed, "Why didn't I think of it earlier? Seff you're a genius," he announced, patting him on shoulder before turning to leave.

"Are you going somewhere?" Sefforn shouted after him clearly bewildered by his friend's behavior.

"Yes," he shouted back over his shoulder while he continued rushing off for the forest. Leaving Sefforn to wonder what he could possibly be up to.

A short while later Clavorn found himself pushing his way through the last of the forest that stood between him and Viszerak. Breathless, he broke through the final vestiges of vegetation and ran up the mountainside to where the dragon was sitting, looking out over the horizon.

"The enemy is burning your land," the dragon told him without looking down.

"Yes," Clavorn replied out of breath, "I know. That's why I am here."

The dragon turned his head and look down at him.

Fires of Life

Chapter 46

Clavorn made his way back to camp, and immediately went to find Sefforn. "Seff, I need you to round up a few men you can trust to keep a secret and have them meet me in the clearing as soon as possible. We don't have much time, so we need to work fast."

"Ahh, you do know there's a celebration going on. You know… festivities. Something you should be participating in."

"Yes, but the war is not won yet. I need a few men for a special job. Unfortunately, it cannot wait. Our enemy is closing in, and tomorrow we set out to engage him. I don't have time for celebrations, Seff."

"Alright," Sefforn acquiesced, "Mind telling me what all the mystery is about then."

"Later. I can tell you it has to do with those Zoths."

"Oh?"

"Yeah. Get some men together and meet me here as soon as you can."

"How many do you want?" Sefforn called after him as he had already started to leave.

"Oh, about a quarter to half a dragon's jaw, no more," Clavorn replied as he dashed off towards the woods again. Leaving Sefforn to wonder what could be of such extreme urgency that he would leave a celebration in his own honor.

He shook his head. It was not going to be easy convincing this crowd to leave the celebration, but he had a few ideas of who to tap first. Sefforn turned and set off to find the men his friend requested.

Meanwhile, Clavorn had his own questing to do. He stopped just briefly at his willow for a satchel in which to put his findings before setting off in search of what he needed. Frantically, he scoured the forest floor for what Viszerak had told him he would need.

Fortunately, the moon, which had finally risen, was full, allowing him good visibility. It did not take long before he found what he needed. Taking out his satchel he gathered just the appropriate specimens. Then closed the bag and headed back to camp.

Once there he found Sefforn, and a small group of rather disgruntled men standing around in the middle of camp. Kevic, Clovak, Sayavic, Sorenavik, Falor, and Thalon were amongst them with Melkiar, and his ever present pipe. Sounds of merriment continued on in the background as he came up to the band of men assembled. Just then Yolondon and Heffron came jogging up to join them.

"I think I speak for all of us when I say, I hope this is good," Melkiar remarked his pipe making rings of smoke about his head.

"You most certainly can, but I believe you will all soon see the importance of why you have been dragged away from the celebration," Clavorn told them as he met up with them.

"Speaking of which shouldn't you be enjoying yourself rather than finding more things to do?" Melkiar commented,

"My friend, when have you ever known me to enjoy myself before a battle?"

Melkiar raised an eyebrow and grunted in defeat. He knew he was right. Clavorn never relaxed before an engagement, too much to consider, too many plans and angles to contemplate.

"Now, I need you to organize in groups. Here is how this is going to work..." and he began explaining his plan to the men gathered there.

"Okay any questions?" he inquired when he was done. "No. Good. Let's split up as planned, and meet here in few hours, or as soon as you're done." The men all nodded in agreement and spread out in their various groups as Clavorn had ordered.

"Melkiar, my friend, what is it?" Clavorn asked as he noticed him waiting to leave.

"I have just one question," the stout, bearded, brown haired man said as he removed his pipe from his mouth. A whiff of smoke escaped his lips and lifted up into the cool night air.

"What?" Clavorn inquired.

Fires of Life

"Are you sure this is going to work?" he asked, blowing out another bit of smoke from his pipe.

"Well, I have it from a good source," Clavorn replied.

"I hope you are right," Melkiar grumbled.

"Haven't I been so far?"

"Yes, but … oh never mind, it seems you have the gods on your side. Let's just hope they stay that way," he muttered as he acquiesced to Clavorn.

"I'll agree with that," Clavorn said, slapping him on the back. "See you back here soon," he told him before rushing off to do his own task.

"Where are you going?" Melkiar asked curious.

"Off to finish my end of this scheme," Clavorn told him as he continued to dash off.

Chapter 47

"Will these do?" Sefforn asked as he entered Clavorn's willow. A small fire was burning in the center space. Clavorn stepped away from a kettle that was bubbling and boiling above the flames, and walked over to meet his friend to check the contents of the satchel he was carrying.

"Yes. That's perfect," Clavorn told him after finishing his inspection, "How is the rest of the project coming?"

"Not bad, though finding some of what you requested has been difficult. But I think we should have it all together before morning."

"Good," Clavorn replied as he turned back and walked over to the bubbling kettle.

"You know, it was a good thing your new friend gave you that tool, or we would never have been able to accomplish the task you gave us," Sefforn commented.

"I know. Only a dragon hardened Kraic stone can cut or shape a Kraic stone," Clavorn replied simply, his back to his friend as he continued with his task at hand which, for the moment, involved stirring the boiling contents.

"Cooking?" Sefforn inquired, coming to stand around in front of him, "I thought you were never hungry before battle."

"Not unless it's yours."

"Then what, may I ask, are you brewing," Sefforn inquired, walking over to the pot that was bubbling above the small fire.

Clavorn stopped stirring, leaving the spoon he was using in the pot and looked up at his friend.

"Something special."

"Oh, may I...?" Sefforn asked as he took hold of the spoon he had left in the pot and filled it with a sampling.

Clavorn grabbed a hold of his friend's hand just before he was about to take a taste of the contents.

"That is not for us, my friend. Now, why don't you see what the others are up to while I finish with this."

Fires of Life

"Sure. No problem," Sefforn replied, replacing the spoon he had in his hand back into the kettle. "Any chance you'll tell me what this is all about."

"Well, you already know part of it. The rest will become clear soon, my friend," he answered, and Sefforn left shaking his head.

Once the sticky brew was done Clavorn covered it and left, placing it off to the side with a pile of furs over it. Then he grabbed his satchel, filed it with the objects Sefforn had brought him and made for the woods.

The moon was beginning to set as he trampled his way through the dense forest. A rabbit scurried off out of his path as twigs snapped beneath his feet. Normally, he would have taken his time and been quieter, but tonight he was in a hurry. He needed to finish his task before morning.

Soon he could hear the sounds of the waterfall as he neared the top of the hill which opened up to the grassy knoll, where he and Viszerak had alighted just that afternoon. As Clavorn pushed a branch aside, there lay the dragon partially curled up; his blue scales shimmering in the light of the full moon.

He marveled at the magnificence of the creature as he came up to him. The dragon's scales just seemed to melt into the night's sky as he approached.

"I brought you what you requested," he told Viszerak upon his arrival.

"Place them on the ground before me," the dragon told Clavorn as he sat up.

Clavorn did as the dragon asked, and carefully laid out the contents of the bag before him.

"Now stand back," the dragon ordered rising up on his haunches.

Clavorn took several paces back and moved off out of the way. Then he watched as the dragon breathed down heavy flames upon the objects before him. Several minutes later glistening items lay before the dragon's feet ready for Clavorn to collect them.

"Thank you, my friend," he told the dragon as he busily placed the objects back in his bag.

"It always seems odd to me that sometimes in order to save a life one must take a life," the dragon commented as Clavorn placed the last item in his satchel.

His hand paused briefly before closing his bag.

"I agree with you there. I hate that sometimes there are those individuals who believe they have the right to take life or enslave it. It seems the worst of them will stop at nothing to accomplish their vile goal. Unfortunately, that leaves their victims no other choice but to defend themselves, however necessary, in order to survive or be free, which, as much as I hate it, often means killing. Men like Vaulnik just run over the peaceful. He cares nothing for life. Regrettably, neither do his Zoths."

He shook his head.

"War is always messy," he went on, "and not always about such lofty ideals as the preservation of life or freedom, but this one is, and I am afraid this is one of those times."

"Such a waist. There should be another way," remarked Viszerak as he looked down on Clavorn.

"I agree," Clavorn replied as much of warrior as he was he hated killing, but he hated watching the suffering of innocents even more. "If you should ever find a better solution, let me know," he told Viszerak.

The dragon looked down on him ruefully and shook his great head.

"No. I am afraid in this case our adversary leaves us no choice, and neither do his minions. I was just musing on the subject. Now I best not keep you from your task. Morning will be upon us soon, and there is still much to be done."

Clavorn nodded as he went off to finish his mission.

Chapter 48

The sun was just climbing over the mountains as Clavorn finished with the last of his preparations. He had been to see Viszerak several more times before the evening was through and was now satisfied that he had enough of what he needed, or at least so he hoped. Sefforn and Melkiar had both come to see him earlier, before the sun rose, to report that their tasks were also completed.

Smoke poured forth on the distant horizon producing a dense orange haze on the edge of the far off vista. Clavorn could just make out Vaulnik's Zoths as they scorched the earth in the distance. As he glanced about camp, the men were busy readying themselves for war. He turned and entered the enormous ancient willow.

It was his turn to ready himself for battle. This would be his first battle without Hawk. He wondered where he was and if he would ever see him again. It seemed odd going into battle without him. They had been through so much together. He hoped his trusted equine friend would make it back fine.

Sunlight streamed in through the branches of the magnificent old willow, while song birds flitted about its boughs. Clavorn sheathed his sword and darned it shaking his head, marveling at how easily nature continued about its business despite the looming danger on the horizon.

Before long all were ready. It would be a good day's ride by horse before they intercepted Vaulnik's army. Clavorn had already discussed with Sefforn the plan for the day. Sefforn and his men would travel on ahead, while Clavorn and Viszerak would meet up with them that night. If all went according to plan, they would attack Vaulnik's army that evening. He could only trust that Alethea would arrive as promised.

"The men are ready to break camp," Sefforn announced as he entered from behind him.

"Good." Clavorn replied as he turned to face his friend.

"You really think this plan can work?"

Clavorn thought a moment. He hated such questions.

No one can ever be truly certain, but doubts never severed anyone well.

"Yes," he answered simply.

"I hope you are right," Sefforn replied.

"How are the men feeling?" he asked trying to change the subject.

"Their spirits are high now that we have the dragon. However, I fear as we approach the scene of Vaulnik's destruction, it may all become too real for them, and their current optimism could fade. Our numbers are so few by comparison. Do you really believe we stand a chance?"

Clavorn paused a moment. There was that question again, "Yes," he answered briefly.

There were always doubts. War was such a messy business, with its outcome never truly certain. The trick, he found, was not to dwell on the uncertainty but to see it as successful and focus on the moment; being that, the only thing one could be certain of in war was one's will to win and the reality of the immediate.

"But how can you?"

Clavorn turned to his friend and patted him on the shoulder. He could not fault him. Not after their experience during their last engagement with Vaulnik's army.

"Sometimes you just have to have a little faith, my friend."

"But…" Sefforn tried to protest. It was clear to Clavorn that the difference in their numbers, and the outcome of their last engagement was undermining his friend's confidence.

"Look, if everything goes as planned, and even if it doesn't, tomorrow will be a day to remember."

"If we're all still here to remember it," Melkiar put in. He had just arrived behind them, and had come in time to overhear Clavorn's last comment.

"Ah, my ever present optimist," Clavorn remarked with an edge of friendly sarcasm, "It wouldn't be a proper send off without you," he turned to face him.

Fires of Life

"Well, someone has to be the voice of reason around here," Melkiar replied.

"Reason, true, but this is war, and there is very little that is reasonable about it, my friend. Just have faith. Have the gods not come through for us so far," Clavorn was trying to sound reassuring.

"True," Melkiar replied, raising an eye brow.

"Trust me. We will defeat this scourge, and send his vile Zoths back to Zezpok," Clavorn told them emphatically.

"That sounds like a speech to rally the troops," Sefforn told him.

"Well, you are part of them," Clavorn told him as he patted him on the shoulder, "Look. I need the men to see you both as strong and positive until I join you. Keep their spirits up. I have faith we will win."

If truth be told, he was anything but sure of success. However, he did not want to further undermine their confidence by appearing doubtful, and then there was Alethea. Her words came back to his mind.

'I will be with you when the time is right.'

"Why is it I get the feeling you are not telling us the whole story," Sefforn commented clearly suspicious that there was more to the battle plans than Clavorn was telling them.

"I don't know. But I can tell you that our chances are not as bleak as they might seem. Now go. I will be out there shortly."

"Is she fighting with us," Melkiar asked.

"Well, if you are referring to who I think you are, then the answer is uncertain. The one thing that is certain is that this battle is ours to win, or ours to lose. The fate of our freedom and our world rests with us. But I have faith that we can win this battle," he replied.

Alethea had not said when she would join them or exactly how. However, just the idea of her presence gave him added hope. Hope that he was sure his friends were picking up on.

"Besides, I don't hear any better plans from either of you." He continued trying to divert the conversation away from her.

"True," Melkiar nodded.

"Well, if I was going to play Zagnor's advocate here, I'd have to say that we could always ask Sevzozak for reinforcements, but," Sefforn raised his hand to stay his friend's words, "I know we should sooner wait for icicles to form in summer than to count on him coming to our aid. So I will stay my words. Shall we be off?" he finished looking straight at Melkiar.

There was no more point to any further discussion. The sun was rising, and time was of the essence now. Battle would soon be upon them, and he knew Clavorn was right, belief was sometimes just as important as ability, if not more so.

Both Sefforn and Melkiar turned and left the ancient willow, leaving Clavorn to collect his thoughts before speaking with the men.

Clavorn walked up the hill past the throng of men who were waiting to hear him speak. Each was battle ready, each was eager, and yet somber. The day's task not yet won and the fate of the world resting on their shoulders. Clavorn could sense their anticipation as he took his place in front of them, the sun at his back. He could only hope his words would be enough to see them through the day. The men greeted him with cheers and eagerness. This gave him hope as he began his speech.

"Yes, yes, it is a good day," he began trying to quiet them down. "The sun smiles on us," More cheers went up, and he waited for them to die down. "Today, my friends, we battle not just for the fate of Avivron, but for all. As you leave here and travel on your way to meet our enemy, you will see much that may discourage you. Fear may grip your now optimistic hearts, and despair threaten to overtake you. But remember The Dragon, remember Avivron, remember that you are more than this. For we are Avivronians! We dare fear and challenge evil!"

Cheers rose up from the men and he waited for them to die down.

"Today, we are fighting not just for our liberty, but for the liberty of all creatures everywhere."

More cheers and shouts rose up from his men.

"This is the day a new chapter in the legends will be added; our chapter. A chapter that says, that men will **not** succumb to evil, a chapter, which when the dust and smoke of battle clears, will find life as the victor, and men her champion. So go, my friends, into the smoke and fray of battle, hearts lifted, for The Dragon flies with us, and we **will** see the dawn of tomorrow!"

Huge cheers went up at the end of Clavorn's speech, and he knew he had struck the right chord.

Chapter 49

Clavorn watched the men leave. His speech had been well received. Lots of cheering and hollering had gone up at his mention of the dragon and victory. For the moment, everyone seemed in high spirits as the horses and men began to move out. He could only hope that they remained so as they neared the field of battle.

A horse pulling a cart laden with a large object passed by in front of him. The object was covered with a heavy leather tarp, and strapped down with a thick rope. Clavorn watched as it passed him. His small group had labored most of the night to build three such objects. Now, with any luck, the contraption underneath it would prove to be one of their most useful weapons.

As the last of his men disappeared into the woodland, Clavorn turned, and went back into the giant willow he was using as a temporary shelter and base of operations. The swaying of the giant tree's graceful weeping branches seemed to belie the ominous affair that was about to take place. Sunlight filtered in, and the songs of birds could once again be heard as they flitted about its upper branches and throughout the surrounding forest. Everything was ready. All he could do now was wait. Wait until the cover of darkness.

Darkness arrived as soon as the sun set, but it did not come with a clear sky. Thick clouds covered the moon and stars while a dense fog had settled in about the forest. It seemed to Clavorn, as he sat sharpening his sword by the light of some fading embers, that even the animals of the wood now sensed a growing danger on the horizon. He put down his sword and listened.

The old willow was unusually still. Its branches enveloped his space like a giant curtain of unwavering calm as he sat enclosed by its grandeur, listening, sensing the night. An ominous tension seemed to have infiltrated the forest. The usual noises of the night

Fires of Life

were eerily quiet, and he wondered, just briefly, if he had been too optimistic in his prediction of victory.

He rose and swept aside the weeping branches of the ancient tree as he stepped outside. The acrid smell of Vaulnik's fires could now be scented on the wind. His army was closing fast, and Clavorn wondered if his men were already engaged in battle. He strained his eyes to search the horizon for any signs of an ongoing battle. But all he could make out through the dense fog were the evil vile breaths of Vaulnik's Zoths.

Twisted creations, which only vaguely resembled their more honorable counter parts, Zoths were merciless when it came to their brand of destruction. Nothing was ever left alive in their wake. This is what led many to believe that only Zagnor himself could have helped bring them into existence. As he watched their vile flames scorch the earth he could only hope that his men were not engaged with the horrid creatures.

Silently, he stood for a moment watching, listening. Stillness continued to penetrate the forest. He strained his ears, and thought one might just be able to make out the drumbeats of Vaulnik's army as it marched in behind the terrible Zoths. Clavorn questioned their chances of victory as he once again witnessed their cold hearted destruction. Memories of the Battle of Quantaris filled his head, visions of his dream passed through his mind.

Must shake them. We have the dragon and her. Still nothing is for certain. War is an unpredictable game.

He turned away from the scene and reentered the ancient willow. With one swift motion he picked up his sword and sheathed it at his side. Then he turned, grabbing his bow and quiver that were resting against the magnificent tree's trunk and left. Once outside he began to make his way into the wood and up the hill to Viszerak.

As he moved aside the last of the branches that stood between him and the dragon he could not help but notice how noble and proud a creature Viszerak was. With his long arched neck so proudly held, his wings folded behind him, and his blue scales which aptly camouflaged him as he sat gazing out over the distant horizon. He was truly a magnificent beast.

Clavorn stepped out of the forest and onto the grassy hillside.

"We need to hurry," Viszerak announced glancing down at Clavorn as he approached. The words pierced his mind like great baritones ringing out an urgent warning.

"Yes, but surely…"

"No! Get on my back at once. Your men are about to be attacked."

There was no mistaking the earnestness in the dragon's voice, and Clavorn immediately did as Viszerak ordered.

Dragons were known for their keen sight and intuition, so he did not need to question Viszerak's order. Without hesitation the dragon lifted them off into the night sky. Clavorn could feel the dragon's powerful muscles as they worked to gain as much speed as possible. Moments later they were flying over the scene of conflict that would decide the fate of their world.

"Hold on!" Viszerak shouted back to him, his voice echoing in his mind.

Clavorn held on as the dragon banked hard to the right. Suddenly, he could see the field of battle below. Scorched earth was everywhere. Fires still burned the ground in patches where charred earth had not finished being consumed. As he glanced about, his eyes suddenly caught sight of movement, there, right in the middle of all the decimation, were his men. He could see them charging Vaulnik's army on horseback, their swords glinting in the light of the fires. Smoke filled the air.

"Time to join the party," Clavorn told the dragon.

"I agree."

Suddenly, Viszerak banked again and Clavorn was made aware that they were not alone any more, nor were his men the only ones about to be attacked. For out of the clouds came a dark ominous shape flying straight for them.

Fires of Life

He could clearly see the creature's dark gray scales, shaggy ragged edged wings, and hideous face as it dove straight for them, breathing fire, and reaching out for Viszerak with its long dark talons. The great blue dragon breathed flames back at his assailant just as another flew in for an assault.

Viszerak banked hard and dove. Clavorn held on tight as the dragon dodged and weaved his way around their attackers. Finally, he leveled himself off and came hard about to face the vile creatures.

Quickly, Clavorn readied his bow. He had modified his arrows just for this evening's battle. They had been specially tipped with heads of tempered Kriac stones, curtsey of Viszerak, and then dipped in a special poison that the dragon had told him how to make. And while the amount of poison his arrows had might not be enough to actually kill one, he was betting it would at least weaken it. It was one of the things he had been working on with Viszerak the night before, now to test out their effectiveness.

Flying straight at their attackers, Clavorn drew the string of his bow back, but just as he was about to fire his arrow Viszerak was forced to turn and dive to avoid the assault of yet another oncoming Zoth. In the process, Clavorn lost the arrow he was about to let loose, as he was forced to suddenly grab on to the great dragon as it twisted and turned in the night sky, breathing fire on their attackers. It was all he could do to just hold on and wait for an opening in which he could attack.

Finally, on one pass Viszerak turned and dove under one of the assailing Zoths, narrowly missing it, yet simultaneously exposing its underbelly to Clavorn. At once Clavorn drew his sword and stabbed it directly into the abdomen of the assaulting beast. While the creature's scales prevented his sword from delving any sort of mortal blow they did not, however, keep it from going totally unscathed. Immediately, the horrid creature wrenched and pulled away, breathing fire at him, nearly scorching both of them as it reeled away from the unexpected pain.

Clavorn could sense Viszerak's pleasure and momentary relief at his successful thrust, but there was little time to dwell on it for within seconds another Zoth dove at them. He quickly sheathed his sword and readied his bow. Not more than a few seconds later he fired, his arrow landing squarely at the base of the oncoming Zoth's neck, piercing its scaly armor. The creature flinched and roared with furry as it continued its dive with even more intense zeal.

"*Hang on!*" Viszerak ordered.

Clavorn grabbed on to him as the dragon turned over and locked talons with the Zoth, biting at it and breathing fire as they twisted and twirled, seemingly out of control, while they rapidly descended to earth. Clavorn had seen eagles perform this maneuver before but never dragons. He thought for sure this would be their end when suddenly he heard a loud whizzing sound, and then…

THWACK!

The vile dragon who had been attacking them suddenly released his hold as a large arrow pierced its armor like scales, sending it reeling off, crashing to the earth below.

Viszerak righted himself, and Clavorn was able to catch a glimpse of the contraption he and his men had worked so hard on the night before. Now, as he looked down, he could clearly see Kevic and a group of his men reloading the large crossbow, readying it to take aim at another vile dragon. None too soon, he thought, for just as he looked up another Zoth was making a dive for them. But just as it was about to release its terrible flames upon them, a large arrow found its mark, driving the beast temporarily into the night sky, only to descend into a heap in the middle of Vaulnik's army.

A great cheer went up from his men at the sight of the fallen beast and confused enemy, but their victory was short lived as more of Vaulnik's great horde poured forth from around the creature's lifeless mass. Infuriated and enraged, they made their way toward Clavorn's men, their horses being spurred into action. Clavorn motioned to Viszerak and he nodded, just ducking and dodging another Zoth.

This time Clavorn unsheathed his sword and skillfully thrust out with it as the attacking Zoth passed by. Once again he found his mark, sending the opposing beast reeling away from them. But his small victory was short lived as the creature turned on them with a new sense of purpose. Clavorn readied his bow, but the creature was too fast. Viszerak banked hard to the left, and he was forced forget his shot and hang on.

Soaring down, heavy wind in his face, he could feel Viszerak's dive, and then his deep rise to the sky.

"Hold on tighter!"

Clavorn hardly had time to think before the dragon quickly turned to face the oncoming Zoth.

THRUMP!!!

He felt the force of the two dragons colliding, jolting him hard forward, and nearly sending him over the great blue dragon's head, as Viszerak deliberately smashed into the opposing Zoth with his talons outstretched.

The two great beasts swirled and tossed as they blew fire, and bit at one another. On it went, twisting and churning, the huge beasts locked in mortal combat. Clavorn readied his sword, waiting for an opening in which to strike. Then suddenly the Zoth opened his great mouth, and was about to close his teeth down on Viszerak's left wing when he struck out at the creature with his sword, wounding it on its less armored snout.

The creature reeled back and let go. He readied his bow and quickly let an arrow fly. It found its mark in the beasts mouth. Within moments he could see the beast shake its great head and fall back, dazed and confused. At that moment, Viszerak turned, striking the Zoth with his great tail, causing it to hurl to the earth while he dove straight for Vaulnik's line of attack.

Now, they were finally able to let loose an offensive on the opposing army below. Flames scorched the earth as horses and riders went reeling off in retreat at Viszerak's attack. Out of the corner of his eye Clavorn could see Melkiar and his men charge the retreating army, while Viszerak sent another burst of flames into the heart of the offending forces before banking upwards into the night sky.

Again they turned and aimed their assault on the forces descending upon his troops. Viszerak dove hard and fast. On the edge of his vision he spotted movement as a Zoth suddenly turned, taking aim to intercept them.

EEEEAWWWW HAWWWW!!!!

A burst of flames shot past Viszerak and him as Skytak shot past them with Shalmaray on his back. The Ornskyterrak was fast and agile as it tore into the Zoth who was about to assault them. Clavorn watched as the protective beast ripped open a sizable gash in the side of the vile creature. He almost wished, as he watched, that they had had one of them on their side during The Battle of Quantaris. Maybe more of the dragons would have survived, or maybe they would be lost to history as well.

On the ground he could see what he guessed were more of the Kalmak as they rode in on unicorns and joined up with Thalon, and his men, to fend off Vaulnik's troops. Though their numbers were not substantial, Clavorn was grateful for their assistance as Viszerak let loose another burst of flames on Vaulnik's men.

On and on it went. Casualties mounted on both sides as the chaos of battle raged on. He notched his bow, and let an arrow fly; striking its mark in the wing as it suddenly paused in midflight to avoid their attack. Then it turned and dove straight towards them. Viszerak breathed flames onto the oncoming Zoth while he reached for it with his long sharp talons.

THRUMP!!!

Fires of Life

Once more he felt the force of two large creatures crashing into one another as Viszerak engaged the terrible beast from Zezpok. Fire blew past him, nearly burning his hair, as he braced himself from the impact.

Teeth and talon; roar and fire, tossing and tumbling in the air the violent dance raged as dragon and Zoth battled. Suddenly, the Zoth bit down on Viszerak's neck. Viszerak roared in pain and anger. Clavorn reached back, took an arrow from his quiver and quickly stabbed the beast in the eye, causing it to release its hold of the great blue dragon.

"Are you alright?!" Clavorn shouted to Viszerak.

"I am fine. It will take more than a bite like that to kill me," the great dragon replied.

But he was not so sure, as blood flowed from the place where the Zoth had bit him. Clavorn searched the sky for the offending foe, but he could not see him. Then suddenly, he spied it as Viszerak banked again, affording him a bird's eye view of the ground below. Now he could see that not only had his arrow effectively driven the beast off of Viszerak, but its poison had had some effect, for the vile creature lay in a heap on the ground below. He doubted if he had killed it, but at least it was successfully neutralized for the moment.

Suddenly, out of nowhere flames shot past them again as another Zoth attacked. Viszerak dove and twirled then evened out only to suddenly rise to avoid a mountainside. The zealous Zoth who was in vigorous pursuit, however, was not so lucky, and slammed head long into the mountainside, snapping its great neck instantly.

Glancing back down to the field of battle, Clavorn could see Thalon as he struck down one of Vaulnik's men who was riding a creature he had never seen before. The creature appeared much like a wild boar only bigger, and shaggier, with large fangs. A further look around the battle scene revealed more of the creatures and their riders who rode straight into his men. Clearly, Vaulnik was leaving nothing to chance this time.

EEEEAWWWW HAWWWW!!!!

The sound echoed through the sky, breaking into his mind, as several more Ornskyterraks with their riders joined the fight. Clavorn observed briefly how the smaller more agile creatures moved and fought the vicious Zoths. Unfortunately, he also had the misfortune of witnessing the death of one as a Zoth maliciously bit down on its head and ate it, sending its body and rider crashing to the earth below.

That was when he saw them, the Hindolin, come racing onto the field of battle. The smaller cousins of The Great Dragons charged forward to meet Vaulnik's army. He watched as a group of them took down, in pack fashion, one of the large boar like creatures Vaulnik had set loose on his men. The warrior riding the awful beast was then ripped to shreds before the pack moved on.

It appeared to be going well at first, but then a group Zoths attacked several of Hindolin he had been watching. He saw, momentarily, as some of them were torn apart by the vile beasts. Fire raged forth from the surviving pack as they tried to mount an attack on the offending Zoths, but the beasts had the advantage of flight.

"There!"

"I see them!"

Viszerak dove hard and Clavorn readied himself for the attack. He could see it was not looking good for his new friends, the Hindolin. Then an a large arrow pierced the pack of attacking Zoths and their attention was momentarily diverted. However, Clavorn and Viszerak continued on in their assault as Viszerak blew flames, and he let loose his arrows upon the offending beasts. However, they were soon drawn away as a couple of the vile beasts turned on them.

Viszerak rose and dove again. However, from opposing sides two Ornskyterraks descended with great speed upon the Zoths who were trying to engage them. With tremendous speed and force they hit one of the creatures, stunning it and sending it hurtling to the ground

Fires of Life

below where a pair of waiting Hindolin finished making short work of the beast.

Clavorn and Viszerak banked and came about. At that exact moment another of the large arrows went zooming past just missing its mark as the great shaggy beast rolled and banked. Viszerak dove down, the beast followed, but from the side two more Ornskyterraks came out nowhere and struck the beast, killing it instantly.

Once more Clavorn and Viszerak were able to attack Vaulnik's army. This time Clavorn caught sight of Vaulnik. He was mounted on a big black steed. Gold encrusted the edges of his armor and helmet. The huge red dragon emblazoned in the center of his chest seemed to dance eerily to the orange glow of the flames that were scattered about the field of battle. With sword raised Vaulnik led a charge straight for his men. He could see Sefforn and Sayavic as they plunged head long at Vaulnik, spurring their horses into heated action. A volley of arrows rose up behind them to shower Vaulnik's men as they charged towards them.

A great anger welled up inside him as he watched Vaulnik charge his men. More than anything he wanted to end his rein; to kill the man who was the source of such great suffering on his people, their land, their country, their world.

"There's our mark!" he shouted to Viszerak in his head.

"I see him," Viszerak told him as he dove sharply towards their quarry.

Suddenly, Viszerak let loose a huge flame into the oncoming army, straight at Vaulnik and his charging company, then pulled up into the sky just narrowly missing another of the evil Zoths.

Clavorn glanced back so see if Viszerak had managed to kill Vaulnik, but to no avail. Somehow he was still alive, though those of his men closest to him had clearly been killed by the flames Viszerak had spilled forth on them. How Vaulnik had managed to be unscathed by Viszerak's assault Clavorn did not know, but dark magic was the top of his list of explanations.

However, he did not have time to contemplate the events before him as Viszerak banked and swooped to avoid the assault of an opposing dragon. On and on it continued. Clavorn alternated between bow and sword to battle the opposing forces both in the air and on the ground, always with an eye out for Vaulnik. If he could just slay him, if he could just end him, then he could end this horrid engagement, and set the world right once more.

But the chaos of such a battle on two fronts was making accomplishing this task all the more difficult. Viszerak would maneuver them in close to the scene of battle on the ground, only to have to engage a Zoth which threatened to obliterate them from the sky. It was an odd dance fighting foes that were both in the air and on the ground simultaneously.

Still, somehow he and Viszerak were managing to successfully kill off many of the enemy forces. By this time, the bite in the great dragon's neck had mysteriously healed. Giving Clavorn only a momentary pause to wonder, how, before the chaos of battle demanded his attention yet again.

From time to time he could hear the sound of the large arrows as they whizzed past them in the night sky to find their mark. Zoth after evil Zoth fell victim to his terrible machine. By now, there were only two of his great weapons left. On one pass over the field of battle he had spied the broken remains of the one Yolondon had been in charge of. He hoped he had fair better than the mechanism he was using.

As he watched the carnage mount on the ground below, a part of him regretted the awful nature of the huge crossbow, but then this was war. There was nothing pretty or kind about it. Still, he had been brought up to revere the dragon, and this seemed almost a sacrilege. The fact that these were twisted evil versions of the ones he had been taught to respect only seemed to add to the sad state of affairs. He feared that one day such a machine could be used on dragons such as Viszerak.

Fires of Life

However, the battle of the day did not allow much time for such musings as he carried on with the chaos of a war being waged both in the air and on the ground. With each successive pass Clavorn kept an eye out for Vaulnik. He desperately wanted his head, or at the very least his life.

His experience told him that if Vaulnik were dead then the war would end, the enemy's men having no more need to carry on such a battle. Yet frustration gripped him as each time he came close something, some Zoth, some soldier, some anything seemed to interfere with his intent. It was as if dark magic were at work keeping him from Vaulnik, and protecting his enemy. Not even Viszerak's flames seemed to be able to scorch him. Viszerak turned and readied them for another assault.

Suddenly, in the midst of this mêlée came a sound like Clavorn had never heard before; an evil sound from the belly of the earth. It crept out and spread over the land nearly deafening all those who heard it. There was a brief pause in the conflict. Then from near the edge of the southern horizon the ground shook and shuddered. Trees fell as the earth opened up a giant fissure, and a huge dark dragon, the likes of which none had ever seen before, came rising out from the center of it.

Its enormous dark black form took immediately to the sky. With ragged wings it flew straight into the scene of the battle. Fire blew out form its mouth in great jets as its flaming red eyes pierced the smoky darkness of the night.

Viszerak paused in his flight as the great beast drew near. Clavorn glanced down briefly. He could see his men falter and shudder at the sight of the awesome creature whose great mass dwarfed that of Viszerak. In that moment, he witnessed the Hindolin stop and look up, while the Ornskyterraks paused briefly in their flight. Then, before he could react, Vaulnik's men cut down several of his with a barrage of arrows that came just at that moment. The scene did not look good, even as he glanced over at Kevic who was ordering his men to load the large crossbow with three of the oversized specially tipped arrows. The huge demon dragon flew at his army spouting forth gigantic flames.

"Intercept him!" Clavorn ordered.

He had to stop that dragon, that demon from the deep. He had to intercept it no matter what. Smoke and flames immediately obscured the scene below as the menacing creature reeked forth its vengeance.

Suddenly, Viszerak drew back and flew high into the sky, into the cover of the mist, smoke, and clouds.

"What are you doing? We need to engage that dragon! It is going to slaughter them!" he yelled at the great beast beneath him.

"Have a little faith!" the dragon yelled back into his mind as it pierced through the clouds, and flew into the clearness of the evening sky.

Viszerak paused. Then, just as suddenly as he had retreated from the ensuing battle, he raised his great head and breathed flames into the empty stillness of their space.

The moon was full and the stars bright. Clavorn looked around searching for the reason of their sudden arrival in this portion of the sky. Nothing could he see except for the clouds and smoke below them. The rest of the sky was clear and devoid of motion. Frustration threatened to grip his heart as Viszerak hovered there, suspending them in space while a battle raged below them.

He was about to comment on the situation when all of a sudden, from high above them, there unexpectedly appeared an unusual light in the sky. Clavorn looked up to witness the light join with the moon. As he watched, the moon then appeared to grow larger and larger, brighter and brighter, until from deep within the light he began to see the dark silhouette of…*could it be*…he paused in his thinking as he continued to strain his eyes to see…*yes!* Finally, his vision confirmed his suspicions, it was a dragon! It was Maltak! Her green scales glistened in the overwhelming radiance of the moon, and on her back rode Alethea, her amour shining in the brightness of the light.

Suddenly, the clouds beneath him parted as the great light pierced down through to the surface below. Not far behind flew Maltak and Alethea, their brightness nearly blinding him as they flew past. Viszerak dove into the sea of battle right behind them. Clavorn raised his sword, ready for combat.

Chapter 50

In one blinding flash they broke through the clouds and back into the chaos of battle. Smoke and ash littered the air below the clouds making visibility difficult. Only a strange orange glow from the fires on the ground lit the smoggy soup before him. Spirts of flames periodically flashed amongst the sooty cloud where he presumed the Zoths were unleashing their vile wrath or the Hindolin countering their attack. In front of him Clavorn could barely make out the figures of Alethea and Maltak.

Suddenly, he was jerked forward nearly impaling himself on one of the dragon's spines as they came to an abrupt halt just as a large burst of flames crossed their path in the direction of Maltak. From high above them the enormous demon dragon flew straight down, apparently towards them. Viszerak quickly maneuvered out of its way as it continued on past them in a blur of darkness and malevolence.

However, before either he or Viszerak could collect themselves, Maltak turned and flew at the great beast; her crimson eyes burning as she soared straight at the creature from Zezpok. Viszerak and Clavorn froze momentarily as the clash of the Great Dragons took place before them.

From their position Clavorn watched as Maltak breathed hot flames that crossed the sky, and lashed out at the demon dragon with her long powerful claws.

"Correct me if I'm wrong, but that's Demonrak."

"*You would be correct,*" Viszerak told him.

"*How was that thing able to leave Zezpok?*"

"*Vaulnik,*" the dragon answered simply.

Clavorn guessed the arrogant vile ruler had called the demon dragon out of Zezpok. Used the legends of old to call upon Zagnor to release the malevolent creature, and now here it was, but then so was Maltak.

Fires of Life

Now, the two of them hovered in the sky, momentarily mesmerized by the display before them, and watched as Great Dragon met Great Dragon in a classic struggle of good and evil.

But they were unable to remain there long as out of the smoke flew a Zoth heading straight for them. Viszerak rotated and dove into the smoggy soup before them. Clavorn grabbed his spines and hung on as the great dragon suddenly turned hard and flew back up into the sky. The dark creature pursuing them shot hot flames at them as they rose. Clavorn turned and used his bow, but his arrow missed its mark as the creature easily moved to avoid it.

Viszerak turned and flew hard to the left, but the creature remained with them, turning as they turned despite the seemingly poor visibility.

"How's he still with us? I can't see a thing!"

"Dragons can naturally navigate smoke."

"Of course."

"Hold on!" the dragon yelled in his head.

Clavorn held tight as Viszerak dove and flipped catching their pursuer by his claws. Now, the two dragons were locked in mortal combat, spiraling downward towards the earth as they bit and blew hot flames at one another.

The speed of their spiral prevented him from aiding the great blue dragon. The Zoth roared and hot flames flew past him. Viszerak bit down on the beast, but the creature countered with its tail, forcing him to release his jaws. It was all Clavorn could do to hold on. On and on it went as they spiraled to the ground below.

Finally, in a gallant effort, Viszerak surged upward and rolled the unsuspecting challenger so that now it was beneath them, then almost as quickly Clavorn felt a serious jolt as they and the Zoth impacted the earth. However, Viszerak had anticipated this, and released his hold of the vile creature just as it hit the ground. At that moment, using his powerful wings, he countered the force of the impact and lifted them safely into the sky. The same could not be said of their pursuer.

Clavorn glanced in the direction of where the battle on the ground was being fought. Clouds of smoke and flames shrouded the battlefield. Visibility was all but impossible. Suddenly, he saw one of the Zoths swoop down and dive straight for his men as a break in the great cloud of smoke afforded him a brief window into the battle below.

"There!" he shouted involuntarily.

"I'm on it!" the dragon told him.

Viszerak dove with tremendous speed straight for the awful creature, pouring fourth flames in its direction as he neared. The beast turned, but not in time as Viszerak's claws slammed into the beast's neck. The combined force of the blow along with their great speed killed the vile dragon almost instantly.

"Great work!" Clavorn shouted.

"Thanks! Behind you!" Viszerak exclaimed in his mind.

Clavorn turned slashing out with his sword just in time to cleave an opposing spear before it struck him. Viszerak banked, and up they flew barely missing the breath of another Zoth. Clavorn glanced in Alethea's direction. Maltak and her were still locked in mortal combat with Demonrak. The vile dragon blew flames at Maltak, but she maneuvered quickly, flipping under the demon beast, and slashing at him with her great claws.

Clavorn looked back down at his men, but they were hard to see for all the smoke and flames as the great clash of legendary dragons came to be fought just above the battle below.

"We're cut off."

"I know, but so are they," Viszerak told him, referring to the Zoths, as they came to a brief stop in the sky above the field of battle.

For the moment all they could do was watch as the two legendary dragons battled it out, their conflict so dominating the sky that even the Zoths had to cease their attack.

Smoke, flames, and fire poured forth into the sky as the two great creatures fought. From time to time Clavorn caught a glimpse of

Fires of Life

Alethea as she slashed out at the enormous beast with her sword. Once he actual witnessed her magnificent blade as it found its mark, opening a huge wound in Demonrak's side. What looked like blood spilled forth, but, in a rare moment of clarity, he watched as it landed on the ground below, sizzling and eroding the earth, killing any living thing it managed to touch.

On it went, a blur of dragon flesh, fire, flames, and smoke. He watched as the two great beasts bit and tore at one another. Suddenly, he saw Demonrak curve his great body and bite down on the back of Maltak's neck. Maltak reeled back breathing flames and lashing out at the demon creature with her great claws. Fear and tension rose inside Clavorn as he witnessed the event.

He could see Alethea as she shot an arrow from her bow in response to the evil creature's attack. The first one missed as Demonrak jolted quickly out of its way while still holding onto Maltak. Maltak, however, twisted and turned such that Alethea was afforded another clean shot. She took it. This time her arrow found its mark, sending the vile beast reeling in pain, releasing its hold on Maltak.

But this did not last long as the creature turned and flew hard at them, breathing horrible, intense flames. Maltak dodged the flames, turned and came hard about, flying straight for the demon creature with her claws out stretched. Within seconds the two great dragons were locked once more in battle, and Clavorn could see nothing more through the smoke and flames.

For several minutes, all he could see was the intense smoke with its bursts of flames as the two dragons fought. Roars, cries, and sounds of chaotic wing beats emanated from the twisting froth of smoggy soup before him. Alethea had disappeared from his vision along with Maltak as they battled the great creature from Zezpok. Tension seemed to fill the air as he looked on. Concern rising within him as the minutes passed.

All of a sudden, there was a massive burst of light from the cloud of smog that encompassed the two great ancient enemies who were locked in mortal combat before him. The immense outpouring of light was such that it was as if every color of the rainbow suddenly decided to shine simultaneously in all their greatest intensity.

The evil Demonrak roared out in pain as he reeled back from the light. The sound grated at Clavorn's ears. All the Zoths that were left also cried out and wheeled off, apparently unable to stand the intensity of the pure light before them. And for a moment the sky was empty except for the ancient mother dragon and her rider. The light faded and Clavorn breathed a sigh of relief.

But it proved to be short lived. Strange movement below caught his eye. It was then that he noticed the flames on the ground. They appeared to be growing in intensity, but that was not what had caught his eye. It was that they also seemed to be moving, moving unnaturally. He looked about him, but Demonrak was nowhere in sight.

It was not long before his men and those fighting with them were forced to retreat from the center of the battlefield where the inferno had begun to grow. As he looked on, the flames continued to increase and began to dance, rising from the earth as they persisted in their odd transformation. Vaulnik's army also paused in their onslaught as the flames spired high into the sky. It was clear to him that they were just as afraid of the sight before them as his men.

"What is it?" he questioned Viszerak.

"I am as yet unsure," the great blue dragon told him.

On they watched as the flames began to organize themselves into a face. An evil, vile, twisted face. In a flash Clavorn recognized the image in the conflagration. It was that of Zagnor, just as in his dream. The image continued to grow and change.

Alethea and Maltak turned to face the now complete form of the god of Zezpok. But to his amazement he no longer saw Alethea as Alethea, rather she appeared to be Alhera, just for a moment. He blinked and looked again, but the image was gone, melted into the melee of battle. Yet for that one fleeting second he could have sworn she appeared just as the goddess herself, like in the stained glass

Fires of Life

image he had seen in the broken remains of the temple at Kisensgraw. The two clashed and fought, Zagnor and Maltak with her champion. It was like watching some ancient battle from the legends of old play out before him.

Light fought darkness. Bright light intertwined with smoke, flames, and an eerie darkness that seemed desperate to consume the light. Great magic on both sides mixed and mingled. Occasionally, Clavorn caught sight of Alethea, her sword glowing as Maltak twisted and turned, maneuvering, battling the god of Zezpok. Time seemed to stop as the two fought, and he wondered how a mortal could ever defeat a god, but then she was no mere mortal. She was the Shaddorak.

On and on the odd mix of light, flames, and darkness fought. All the while darkness threatened to consume the light. As Clavorn watched, his heart began to sink, for before his eyes the darkness began to grow, turning all its initial flames into shadows, dark vortexes smelting into one large black cloud sucking in all the light, and flames that Maltak and Alethea appeared to be putting forth. Viszerak moved them back from the growing darkness.

Suddenly, there was a great giant burst of light so bright that it nearly blinded him. Both he and Viszerak had to turn away for a moment. Its radiance engulfed the entire field of battle, welling up into the sky as if to touch the Shardon Lands. When the light dimmed the sky was clear, the smoke gone along with the darkness. The stars and moon shined down on the scene below.

Clavorn looked down where the great battle had just taken place. There was nothing, no sound, no movement, all was silence. The blackened remains of scorched dark earth silently sizzled as his eyes found the only contrasting element in the picture before him, the faint glow of a great green dragon lying, splayed on the ground. It was Maltak. On her back was the lifeless body of Alethea.

Chapter 51

"NOOO!"

Every nerve in his body screamed as he and Viszerak hovered momentarily. A great silence filled the battlefield, neither side moving, neither side seeming to know what to do. Horror, sorrow, and grief filled his heart. For a brief second he starred in complete shock. It was not the outcome he had expected. He wanted her alive. Every fiber of his being said she had to live. He shook himself, not allowing despair to overtake him.

"Come on Viszerak!" he shouted as his senses returned.

Down they flew, fast and furious. Viszerak came to an abrupt stop as he alighted beside Maltak. As they landed, he could see Alethea. Her lifeless body appeared broken and spent. Her beautiful long dark hair splayed out over Maltak's one wing, and the ground beneath them.

The dragon appeared as lifeless as Alethea, except for a faint glow that kept emanating from her scales. He was about to dismount when suddenly Viszerak rose up on his hunches, startling Clavorn out of his grief, and forcing him to grab hold. That was when he saw him, Vaulnik, approaching the spent body of Maltak, his sword raised.

Flames burst forth from Viszerak while Clavorn raised his sword, ready to slay the foe that had wreaked so much pain and suffering on his people, the land, and every living thing. But vengeance was not to be his. For suddenly the earth beneath them began to tremble. Viszerak alighted into the air just as the ground gave away under them, taking the bodies of Maltak and Alethea with it.

Once again horror and shock filled his heart at the loss. However, as they continued to watch from their place in the sky, they could see Vaulnik. Terror gripping his face as he stumbled about struggling to keep his balance while the ground shook beneath his feet. Then, just at that moment, a great burst of light shown forth. Seconds later a great cry was heard from Vaulnik as the earth gave way from under him, and he was swallowed into the abyss of light. Before long more areas of light rose from beneath the earth as great holes opened up, swallowing all the evil vile men and creatures from Vaulnik's army.

When the dust finally settled, and the light was gone, only a few of Vaulnik's men were left standing. They quickly dropped their swords in a gesture of surrender. Clavorn saw Sefforn, and what was left of his men along with the remainder of the Hindolin, begin to approach them. In the distance, he could just make out the Kalmak as they paused on their unicorns while the Ornskyterraks landed nearby. All were silent.

Finally, out of the quiet of the moment, there arose from the center of the huge abyss where, Alethea and Maltak had descended, the sound of a great wind. Louder and louder it roared, echoing off the cavernous walls. Every being paused in their actions as the sound grew. Till at last its source was revealed. All looked on in awe as before them arose the great Mother of All Dragons, Maltak, with Alethea on her back, her hair flowing out behind her while she raised her sword in victory.

Chapter 52

    Clavorn felt himself overcome with elation as he witnessed her rise out of the earth. At that moment the sky became crystal clear as the sun's first rays of light shown down upon the scorched soil of the battlefield. Bodies of dead Zoths lay strewn up on the ground along with those of many a brave soldier and steed. The image brought another wave of emotion from Clavorn, though very different from the first, as he felt for the loss of life before him. Suddenly, the sun caught the blade of her sword and reflected down to the earth below.
    Clavorn watched as her sword began to sparkle and shimmer in the sun's light; its rays refracting off the crystalline formation of the Kriac stone, and fracturing off into all the different colors of light as it directed the sun's light to the earth below. To his amazement the ground where the light hit suddenly began to become green with life. As the sun continued to rise and grow in intensity, so too did the light from her sword. Till it was more than just her sword alight and sparkling with the light of the sun, but her entire body as well. He continued to watch, astounded by what he was witnessing. For before his very eyes it seemed that all the earth was coming alive again.
    Suddenly, Maltak flew down, breathing her Flames of Life upon the land. Wherever they hit the ground flowers sprang up. Dead men rose. Horses, unicorns and other beasts that were once gone to the realm of the gods returned, and all those present rejoiced.
    Yet the bodies of the dead vile dragons known as Zoths still littered the area. Their gray lifeless forms, which were strewn everywhere, contrasted dramatically with the life that was springing up around them. Clavorn could not help but take note of the disparity as he watched the remarkable display before him.
    At that moment both Maltak and Alethea paused in midflight. The light glinting off The Great Dragon's scales, Alethea's dark hair billowing out behind her, as Maltak hovered a second over the field

Fires of Life

of battle. Clavorn observed as Alethea then took out The Stone of Alhera, and lifted it to the Shardon Lands.

Sunlight glinted and sparkled off of it, reflecting the light rays down to the surface of the earth in all their myriad of colors. This time, however, a great and wondrous event happened. One by one, as the rays found their quarry, the dragons, known as Zoths, who had once served Vaulnik, began to come to life. However, as they did their color changed, apparently reflecting their transformation back to their true selves. Now, they were no longer dark, sooty gray beasts but beautiful blue or green creatures whose iridescent scales reflected a rainbow of colors.

Then one by one the dragons rose from the ground, lifting their now fully restored selves off the ground, and into the sky. As Clavorn watched the sky became crowded with the beautiful beasts as dragon joined up with Ornskyterraks in marvelous flight.

Soon the sky was alive with wondrous dragons which flew and dove, breathing the Fires of Life down up the earth. Before long the whole battlefield and the lands beyond were transformed from scorched, lifeless patches of earth, to lush green forests, with rivers and valleys teaming with life as the newly resurrected dragons helped restore the lands that Vaulnik had them destroy.

Chapter 53

A great cheer began to rise up from the earth below as the men, who had once been engaged in battle, now witnessed the dramatic power of the dragons before them. Elation spread everywhere as gradually the realization swept far and wide that the oppressor, Vaulnik, and his evil reign was over.

Viszerak alighted on a patch of earth in the heart of the great congregation of rejoicing men. On a hilltop not far from where he and Viszerak alighted, back away from the crowd, he saw Ferrterrak with the rest of the Hindolin. The great leader nodded his head in acknowledgement and gratitude. Clavorn did the same. Then the Hindolin made off into the woods, he assumed to return to their home in the swamp.

Glancing down about the riotous crowd gathered before him, he noticed the Kalmak and Ornskyterraks were conspicuously missing. Their task completed, he presumed they had returned to the unknown lands they were charged to protect. Then he spied Shalmaray on the ground in front of Viszerak. Her red hair rippling with the gentle breeze as Skytak remained on the edge of the gathering, his noble eagle head proudly arched as he looked on.

"*Well done, Clavorn Remmaik, son of Favorn. Well done. Our world is free. You have the gratitude of the Kalmak should you ever need us again,*" she told him in his head and then she was gone.

Briefly his eyes searched the throng before him, but there was no trace of Shalmaray or Skytak. However, before he had time to consider what had just transpired between him and the leader of Kalmak, his men rushed in about him, quickly filling the space they had made to allow for their landing, cheering and shouting with joy. Clavorn dismounted to the great ovation and merriment.

Sefforn and Melkiar were some of the first to find their way to him. Immediately, the men embraced. Sefforn gave him a big slap on the back in congratulations. No one mentioned the Kalmak leader, and he presumed it was because no one had seen her. A trait he was gradually becoming accustomed to. Even so he searched, and searched the throng of warriors for the real heroin of the moment, but she was nowhere to be seen. His heart sank.

Where is she?

As he lifted his sword in victory, with a smile on his face, his eyes and his heart continued to search the crowd for the one woman who had captured his soul and saved his people, his land, his country, the world. But she was nowhere to be seen.

Then suddenly there was a great gust of wind, and a hush fell over the multitude. Clavorn stood in silence while he watched as the throng of warriors began to part. Another rush of wind from the north blew in. His eyes followed the parting crowd before him. As the last man stepped aside he saw her. She was coming towards him, the wind in her hair, the lioness at her side, the eagle overhead, and the sun glinting off of her armor. In the background The Great Green Dragon, Maltak, could be seen. Her head arched as she proudly surveyed the scene before her. Both Viszerak and Maltak looked on. This was her moment. It was his.

Silence once again filled the battlefield, but this time it was the silence of reverence as Alethea approached. But Clavorn did not notice his men. The only thing that had his attention was her. Her green eyes trained on him as she closed the gap between them.

Suddenly, she was standing right before him, and he could not resist her power any longer. He reached out and took her in his arms, his lips meeting hers, her flesh pressing against his as his passion could no long be contained.

In that moment, a great cheer rose up from the multitude present. However, Clavorn never even heard his men as he held the woman he loved.

Chapter 54

That night great rejoicing was heard across the land as celebration upon celebration took place all across Avivron, and the surrounding kingdoms. Clavorn and Alethea rejoiced together with his men. Much wine flowed and foods of all sorts were everywhere. Dancing and music could be heard all throughout the encampment, as men and women gathered about a great fire in commemoration of their victory. Even the moon and stars seemed to rejoice in their triumph. The dragons, Maltak and Viszerak, watched from a distance, their part in these affairs basically over. Suddenly, from the multitude a great chant started to rise.

"SHALTAK! SHALTAK! SHALTAK!"

Clavorn looked at Alethea. "This is your moment," she told him, "Take it."

"But what about you? If it had not been for you…"

"It was you who led them into battle," she interrupted, gently placing her fingers over his lips to stay his words. "You found the dragon. You gave them hope when they had none. If it had not been for, you there would have been nothing I could have done. For without hope, without your belief, your belief in them, in me, in the dragon, and much more, I would only have had power, but no one to give it life. It is you who have made this all possible. You, Clavorn, Shaltak, Slayer of Dragon Killers, Defender of Maltak, who are their hero, reap the reward they bestow on you." With that said she stepped back as the throng of warriors and peasants melded around him.

His eyes searched for her, but she was gone as the cries of "Shaltak!" filled the air.

A few moments later a sound like thunder could be heard on the wind. Within seconds the ground began to shake at their feet, and the crowd went silent. All turned in the direction of the ominous noise as

Fires of Life

several riders thundered over the hillside above them. The great hush continued as the standard they bore came into view, flickering in the light of the pyre. Soon the riders dropped down to a trot as they neared the scene of their mission, finally coming to a stop in front of Clavorn.

The familiar green standard with the golden dragon on it furled and rippled in the night wind. He noted the golden dragon which should have been one of silver. Silver had always been the color of the dragon which emblazoned the standard of Avivron, but King Sevzozak had changed that. He had changed a great many things. Now the golden dragon rippled in the evening wind.

"Shaltak, Slayer of Dragon Killers, Defender of Maltak and Dragons," the voice of the one holding the standard boomed out, "your presence is requested by King Sevzozak, Ruler of Avivron."

Chapter 55

"Shaltak, Slayer of Dragon Killers, Defender of Maltak and Dragons, your presence is requested by King Sevzozak, Ruler of Avivron," the head of the guard and standard bearer had announced as Clavorn had stood amongst his people to receive their laud. Now, he was being escorted into Escadora by King Sevzozak's high guard. And though their apparent reason for the King's summons was to congratulate him on his victory, he had the distinct impression that there was more to it. In fact, as he rode into Escadora through the dragon gate, Clavorn had the increasing sensation that he was going more as a prisoner than as a hero.

The somberness and soberness of the guards who were with him did nothing but add to his suspicions. He could not help but wonder if Alethea had known this was about to happen. The great dragon gate to the city closed behind them as they passed. The pair of dragon sculptures that formed the gate now faced each other. Their mouths open, breathing fire, their wings upright as they sat, supposedly guarding the city from any malevolent foe that dared to enter, seamed together perfectly as they shut; effectively sealing him in, or so it felt like. Clavorn could only wonder if their power applied to evil from within as well.

The city's inhabitants were out cheering in the streets, torches in their hands, as he and his escort trotted their horses in on the cobble stones. The sound of their horses hooves clicking and clacking off the stone streets could barely be heard above the din of their voices. Their flickering torches gave the city an odd feel as the light reflected and danced off the walls of the surrounding buildings.

Soon the great castle, where his father had severed as First Knight to King Dakconar, came into view. Its tall spires reaching upwards to the sky, their tops adorned much as the little temple in Kisensgraw had been, only much more richly. The fires from the mouths of the dragons, which were mounted on the corners of every roofline on the castle, flickered and fluttered in the evening breeze. Gilded golden

Fires of Life

dragons of various forms, which decorated the imposing building, glinted in the night and felt odd to his eyes

He had not noticed them the night he had ridden in with Melkiar. His cloak had hidden them from his view. Now they appeared as nothing less than the symbol of decadence Sevzozak had become. During his youth they had been gilded in silver or perhaps platinum, for it withstood the weather better and retained their silver nature without tarnish. He did not know which. All he remembered was that they used to be silver; not gold.

The drawbridge lowered at their approach, and they were allowed to enter the castle proper. Soon his somber friends rode up to its entrance where they dismounted. Clavorn did the same. A stable boy came by to take his horse and give him water. The horse snorted at first, but Clavorn gently reassured him that all would be fine, despite the niggling feeling in the pit of his stomach to the contrary.

A brief moment of sorrow pinged at his heart as he missed his trusted equine friend, Hawk. He still had not seen him since he left him on the mountainside. Yet at the same time he was glad that he was not here. If something bad was going to happen to him, he did not want him to wind up in Sevzozak's hands. He gave one last pat to the horse which had brought him to the castle before handing the reins over to the stable boy and joining the waiting guards.

As he entered the castle, flanked by guards, he had the distinct feeling that his hour had come. He would either show the king and his son for the traitors his knew them to be, or be accused of being a traitor himself. Their boots echoed down the corridor that led to the Great Hall. Memories of that night, not so long ago, when he had strode down this very same hall as Mentak, crossed his mind. This would be a very different night than that one.

Once again he noted the huge paintings of long dead ancestors interspersed with tapestries of ancient scenes, legends, or tales. Their eyes seemed to follow him as they marched down the long elaborately decorated hall with its large gold framed mirrors. He could not escape the feeling that even the dragons which adorned those frames were watching, waiting, anticipating whatever outcome would transpire here on this ominous night.

They stopped in front of the golden brass doors that led to the Great Hall. A series of relief sculptures depicting the origins of Avivron, the arrival of her dragons, and other legends embellished their surface. Clavorn's eyes roamed across them, spying all the familiar tales his grandfather used to tell him. An odd sensation crept over him as he stood there in front of those doors behind the high guard with his cloak of green velour trimmed with gold.

The head guard removed his helmet. Its emerald green plumage shuddered in the act. He then took a hold of one of the large dragon knockers and knocked on one of the doors while they paused for admittance. Its great booming sound reverberated throughout the hall and into the chamber before them. The many voices emanating from the Great Hall within suddenly went silent.

"You may enter," the king's voice boomed in reply. Then the doors were opened to reveal the large opulent room filled with nobility from all over Avivron. All of them elaborately attired. Clavorn's eyes immediately took in his surroundings, assessing and processing the situation before him.

"May I present to you, my lord, and your court here present, the Great Shaltak, Slayer of Dragon Killers, Defender of Maltak, and Dragons," the guard announced as they crossed the threshold.

"You may. It has been a long time coming," the king commented as he waved them forward. Clavorn noted that the hall was filled with nobles from every house in the land. They stood silently as he and the guards moved into the room, finally coming to a stop in front of the king himself. Clavorn and the guards all gave the king a ceremonial bow. Then the king dismissed them all, all that is, except Clavorn himself. He now stood alone in front of the men he considered traitors to his people.

Almaik, his son, stood at his father's right side as the king now rose to acknowledge his presence. The great Crown of Ages adorned his head. Its large center ruby glistened in the torch light. The

Fires of Life

diamonds surrounding it only seemed to accent the beauty of the center stone. Gold trim with rubies festooned his rich black garments. A red fur trimmed cloak unfurled out behind him as he stepped forward. The Dragon Heart Stone, or Stone of the Dragon as it was also referred to, hung green and glistening from about his neck.

Legend held that the stone had been given to, Elshardon, the first of King of Avivron, by, Saltak, Avivron's first dragon for his valor and dragon like heart in his defense of life in putting an end to the Tarmian Wars. It was said that the stone carried the power of the dragon and brought great luck and prosperity to the land.

Clavorn noted that it had been recently embellished with a huge golden dragon that now held the original pendant. The Stone of the Dragon was historically held in place by two silver dragons which represented the First Dragons of old. The fact that now they were clutched by the claws of this new golden dragon was disturbing. Sevzozak's black garments only served to accent the stone and its changes. The ruby eyes of this disquieting embellishment stared out at him as he stood alone before the king.

"Well now, it has been a long time in coming, Shaltak, but I must say that you have the gratitude of all of us present when I say, thank you for liberating us." The king gestured widely as he spoke, so as to be all inclusive of those present.

"You are most welcome, my liege," Clavorn began, briefly bowing his head in deference. Then upon lifting his head he continued, "Tell me though, sire, would you have been so grateful of Clavorn Remmaik if he had delivered your kingdom to you thusly?"

King Sevzozak stared at him obviously taken back by his question.

"Why of course? What would possibly make you wonder at the integrity of this court?" he questioned.

Clavorn paused a moment before continuing, "Perhaps, sire, it is because there is one amongst you who I know to be a traitor, a traitor to Clavorn, and by extension to this court, and therefore to Avivron as well."

The king stared at him, but it was obvious to him that Sevzozak was doing his best to maintain his composure.

"Surely this cannot be so, but if you know this to be true, then please do not keep such information from us," Sevzozak told him.

"It is my intention to elucidate on the subject, but first I have a couple of questions for which I need to be certain of the answers, if my liege does not object?"

"Of course, this court has no objections," Sevzozak replied, waving Clavorn on, "please ask them, so that we may all be illuminated."

"Certainly, my lord. The first question should be one of relative ease," he paused a second, and the king nodded for his continuance. "Would you all agree that, Clavorn Remmaik, son of Favorn, was a true and loyal servant to this court?"

As Clavorn glanced about, he could see various nods coming from those in attendance.

"Yes, I believe I speak for this entire court when I say he was certainly a most true and loyal servant of this court," replied the king apparently mystified by Clavorn's question.

"Then would you also say that anyone who then betrayed him to the enemy was then a traitor to this court, and to this country for which he served?"

The king looked at him and for a moment he said nothing.

"Yes," he answered slowly, "Yes, I would have to say so. Unless this person had information that would prove Clavorn Remmaik was such a traitor as to cause this court to think differently."

"But then why not just bring him before the court. There would be no need to betray him or turn him over to the enemy. I mean after all, if he were working for the enemy, handing him over would merely be like giving back a favored pet."

Loud riotous laughs arose from the crowd in attendance at his last statement.

Fires of Life

"Unless, my good Shaltak, our beloved Clavorn wished to take over my crown and rule Avivron himself; without, of course, the aid of our enemy," countered the King.

"True. So, for the sake of argument, you agree that Clavorn Remmaik was, for a time at least, a great hero, a true and loyal servant to this court, and that anyone found guilty of betraying him to the enemy is, by default, an enemy to this court, unless of course he can prove just cause for his actions."

"I do," the king replied clearly still a bit puzzled by his questioning and obviously unnerved.

Clavorn then turned his next question to Almaik.

"So tell me, Almaik, how was it that you came by betraying Clavorn Remmaik, son of Favorn?"

A collective gasp could be heard around the room as Clavorn shot the question at the man who had once been his friend and ally.

"Excuse me?" Almaik asked clearly befuddled, "I don't know what you are speaking of. Clavorn was my friend. Why would I betray him?"

"Why indeed?" Clavorn asked, "Perhaps for power. Perhaps…"

"Perhaps you had better substantiate your claim, Shaltak, before this court takes back the title of Liberator it was about to bestow," the king interrupted.

"Gladly, my liege," Clavorn replied, "The proof I have is that I *am*, Clavorn Remmaik, son of Favorn." A huge gasp could be heard around the room at the sudden revelation of his words. "I was there. I clearly witnessed his handing over of myself to Vaulnik's guards. But then I am not surprised by your astonishment?" he continued turning his attention back to Almaik. "You did not count on my over hearing you and the guards speaking. You thought I was out cold from the drink you gave me."

"What? Wait! I was here the whole time," Almaik protested.

"Surely you jest. Can anyone substantiate your claim?" he pressed. He could sense he had his quarry cornered now. All he had to do was drive it home.

"Hold on," Sevzozak interrupted, "What proof do you have that you are, Clavorn Remmaik, son of Favorn."

"I have his ring and…" Clavorn produced a small knife, "If you will allow me, my liege, I shall shave this beard, and then you will know that I am who I claim to be."

Before the king could object, Clavorn began to shave his beard from his face. There was a series of gasps about the room as his true identity became clear.

"No!" the king's son cried out in utter shock as his feet temporarily gave way under him, and he slumped down into the throne beside his father's.

"Yes, it is I, my old friend," Clavorn asserted, but then as the words left his lips he noticed something about his old friend, something he would normally have missed.

His friend looked up into his eyes with clear astonishment and bewilderment.

"But I was here in the castle. I swear, but…," Almaik replied as his demeanor suddenly changed, and Clavorn could clearly see a deeper realization had crept over his old friend and ally's face, "but you father, you were out…out on business. You hated Clavorn." His attention had now shifted to his father as he continued, "You were jealous of his growing popularity." His eyes narrowed with accusation, "You came back late that day…"

"I don't like your insinuation. Of course I had business. I have a kingdom to run, which you will one day understand…"

"…Oh, I already do understand," Almaik replied as he stood up, "Perhaps all too well." And before anyone could say another word Almaik rushed at his father plunging his dagger straight into his father's chest.

"Ahh!" The king cried out in pain. Then through the pain of his wound he remarked "Oh, I think it is a shame that my weak and insolent son should only now understand."

That was when it became clear to Clavorn what Sevzozak had done as he watched the shock, pain, and sorrow cross his friend's face just before he expired on the floor before him. For while his son had attacked him with his dagger; the king had had the presence of mind to counter with his own, clearly poison tipped blade.

Almaik's body slummed to the floor at his father's feet with the lethal dagger still protruding from the place where his father had stuck him. The king looked down in disgust before he pulled the blade his son had used laboriously from his own chest.

Anger and rage took over Clavorn as he rushed the king, but Sevzozak brandished his sword as the high guards rushed to secure him.

"You think you can rule, you pathetic dragon lover? Ha! Ha! Ha! He was right. It was me. I hated your growing popularity."

He stumbled backward as Clavorn once again tried to approach, but by now Sevzozak's guards were at Clavorn's side preventing him from coming any closer to the king. Blood began to spew out Sevzozak's mouth as he spoke.

"I tortured a Dragon Witch to put a spell on me..." His breathing became more labored, "...so I would look like Almaik."

"No!" Clavorn shouted, "How could you do that to your own son." He could hardly believe the words he was hearing, yet he knew they were the truth. As difficult as they were to accept, he could see that what Sevzozak was saying was what had happened.

"Ha! Ha! Ha!" the king spat, wiping the blood from his face, "And you think yourself worthy to rule? You cannot see...You have no **vision**." The contempt in his voice was unmistakable.

"No. I have no such aspirations," Clavorn told him. But Sevzozak only laughed as blood splattered and sputtered out of his mouth.

"Figures, for a *weak* dragon lover," Sevzozak choked, then turned and looked down disdainfully on the body of his son. "He was weak! Just like my father." he spat again, the contempt clearly audible in his voice.

How the man hated his own father and son. It was clear now to Clavorn that he had been behind the death of King Dakconar, and most likely his father's as well.

"I wanted you to think it was him. I wanted…" the king's voice labored.

"You wanted me to think it was him. You wanted everyone to think it was him, so you could denounce him later. But why? He was your only son and heir."

"A weak heir!" Sevzozak spat as he stumbled to the ground, barely catching himself.

"You had someone else in mind to take your place." Clavorn could see his thoughts in his mind. The Tears of Maltak had opened his eyes, and now he understood the true vile nature of the man they all called king.

"Ha! Good!... Ha! Very good," came a voice from behind the king.

Clavorn lifted his head and looked to the young man who had been standing to the left of the king. He was known as Rendorian, a tall handsome sort with short dark brown hair who clearly enjoyed a certain air about him. Almaik had spoken of him occasionally. According to his friend, his father had taken him in years ago, raised him as a son. Then the thought occurred to him. What if he was his son, illegitimate, yes, but his son none the less? What if the king favored him? Again he could see the truth of his thinking.

"You!" Clavorn accused his eyes narrowing as he stared at Rendorian.

"Yes, very good Clavorn," Rendorian replied silkily, "It was I, and my father who planned to eliminate both you, and that sap of a son of his, Almaik."

Clavorn recognized the silky, slithery way Rendorian spoke, "So it was you who posed as Almaik at Kisensgraw. You had the Dragon Witch place the spell on you, so you could pose as him."

"Very good," Rendorian praised sarcastically, "Yes, I promised troops to that sap of yours Mentak and that other …"

"Melkiar," Clavorn put in, not bothering to point out it was him who was really Mentak.

"Couldn't have Shaltak, oh excuse me, you win. That was not part of our deal."

"Deal?"

"Yes, we had a deal with Vaulnik. Sacrifice you, and a few lowly peasants, let him rule while we keep our crown, and watch over his territory for him. Small price to pay for power, wouldn't you agree?"

Clavorn would not agree. He thought the whole deal disgusting.

"I am curious. How did you plan to deal with Vaulnik, or were you just going to let him rule over you like a puppet master?" Clavorn inquired.

"No. We were never going to be ruled over. When the time was right, I, or my father would have dealt with him and taken all his power," arrogance seeped forth from Rendorian's lips like poison from the sap of a vine. "However, I must thank you, for now…well, we don't have to deal with all that messy nonsense. Now we can just take Vaulnik's place."

"Good, my boy…go…od," the king remarked as blood poured from his mouth.

Then suddenly he could no longer maintain his strength and collapsed fully to the floor, his crown falling to the ground, rolling away from his head as it hit the cold hard marble.

Chapter 56

"I am king now," Rendorian announced, "Thank you so much Clavorn. Once again you have proven useful to this crown and saved it from the messy trouble of having to kill off its predecessors. It seems a shame now to have to arrest you."

"NO!" Clavorn shouted and with one quick motion he arrested the sword from the guard standing nearest him. The other tried to stop him, but Rendorian quickly halted his advance, choosing instead to brandish his own blade.

"I see you will not go down without a fight," Rendorian egged.

"You see correctly. The trick is, are you up for it?" Clavorn challenged.

"A poison tipped sword always evens the odds, my hero," Rendorian told him as he descended the stairs.

The guards fell back, and everyone in the room made way for the dual that was about to ensue.

"Now it is time for you to die," Rendorian remarked evenly.

"We shall see," Clavorn countered, positioning himself for the conflict while Rendorian coolly took his place in the center of the Great Hall.

Seconds later Rendorian attacked and Clavorn countered. The sound of steel meeting steel echoed off the walls of the hall as the two men fought to the death.

Clavorn was keenly aware of Rendorian's blade. He could not afford to let it so much as nick him. As they fought, it soon became clear that the king had spared no expense in training this usurper to the throne.

CLANG!

Their blades locked as Rendorian forced his way into Clavorn's space. Clavorn shoved against Rendorian's sword, but Rendorian threw his weight into their blades.

Fires of Life

"I think you tier, Clavorn. I am fresh, but you are already worn from the battle of the day."

"We shall see," Clavorn told him through his teeth, "Justice has a way of correcting all mistakes."

"The only mistake that shall be corrected here today is the one in which you lived."

Rendorian pushed back against the locked blades and the sword play began again.

CLANG! CLANG!

Steal met steal as on the dual waged around the center of Great Hall. Up the steps, near the bodies of the fallen king and his son did their battle continued. Suddenly, Clavorn stumbled and Rendorian swung up with his sword. It was all Clavorn could do to tuck his body away from the poisonous tip. The action in combination with his loss of balance caused him to nearly fall.

CLANG!

He caught Rendorian's sword. Out of the corner of his eye he saw the broken body of his slain friend. Anger suddenly pulsed through his veins. Visions of his imprisonment, broken bodies of his men on the field of battle, burnt forests, raped women, all the injustices that had been done in the name of power suddenly pulsed through his mind.

"Time for you to die!" Rendorian shouted as he swung with his sword, but Clavorn caught it, and in a series of fast maneuvers arrested the sword from Rendorian, sending it flying across the marble floor. Now he had him at blade point.

"Go ahead," Rendorian jeered, "Kill me."

Clavorn was breathing hard. He could do it. He held his blade at Rendorian's throat. One swift motion was all it would take. But as he looked at Rendorian something stopped him, a feeling that revenge was not worth it. That he was not worth it. Slowly, he began to lower his sword.

"Ha! Arrest him!" Rendorian shouted, but no one moved. "Arrest him!" he shouted again, and again no one moved.

"I see that no one honors your claim," Clavorn told him as he took a step back, "It will be interesting to see if you *can* rule."

"I **will** rule!" he shouted as he pulled a dagger from his side and lunged for Clavorn. But, with one swift instinctual motion, Clavorn caught him with his blade. Surprise and shock graced Rendorian's face as he clutched the lethal blade that had mortally wounded him before he slumped to the floor in defeat, dead by his own doing.

Chapter 57

Silence fell about the room as the broken body of Rendorian lay splayed on the marble floor. Not far from him lay the body of the king and his only legitimate son, Almaik. Clavorn stood tired and speechless. He had always suspected the king of being behind his imprisonment. But to discover that he was solely responsible for his betrayal came as a total shock. What had surprised him even more was the discovery of Rendorian.

Now, as he glanced about the remains, his eyes could not help but fall on the broken body of his friend as he lay slumped in a heap before him. A great sadness crept over him, and he became suddenly a wash with regret; regret for having suspected his friend of such an act, regret that this was how their friendship should end, regret for his passing.

For several minutes it was clear no one knew what to do. Suddenly, The Stone of the Dragon, which lay about the king's neck, began to shine. Soon its radiance became so bright that no one could look upon it without fear of burning their eyes. The light grew, filling the Great Hall with its intensity. Then almost as quickly as it began to glow it stopped. All was as it had been except, when Clavorn looked up, there on the steps before him stood Alethea, her green eyes staring into his.

The guards immediately came up, turning their swords on her.

"NO!" he cried out as he grabbed the arm of the soldier nearest him, "She's the Shaddorak!"

The men immediately froze in their tracks. Silence again reigned as Alethea stood before them arrayed in all her battle regalia. Then she bent down and took The Stone of the Dragon from the chest of the fallen king, but to Clavorn's amazement it was no longer held by the golden dragon. Instead, it was free. Only the silver dragons embraced its excellence as the stone sparkled and glistened in the torchlight. As Alethea lifted the stone, a light shown from within it, but tame by comparison to its brilliance of before.

"It is time for Avivron to choose a new ruler," she announced, "One chosen by her people, then and only then, will I give this back to you. For only a true, just leader, chosen by the people is fit to wear The Stone of the Dragon."

Then in a flash of light and whirl of wind she was gone. All stood in silence and awe at the events of the evening. Moments later a nobleman, claiming to be next in line for the throne, came forward and announced, that until such time as a new ruler was chosen, he would be in charge. Then he ordered that word be sent out to all the land to meet 'here,' in the central city of Avivron, Escadora, in three days' time, so that a new king could be chosen as the Shaddorak had said.

Chapter 58

In three days' time Clavorn returned to Escadora mounted upon his trusted equine friend, Hawk. Hawk had appeared back at camp the night of his return from the castle. Clavorn could not forget his joy at seeing his favorite steed's return. Now, he sat mounted on Hawk as he rode into the capital of Avivron with Melkiar and Sefforn at his side. Kevic, Clovak, Sayavic, and Sorenavik brought up the rear as did Yolondon, Heffron, Thalon, and Falor. None of them were going to miss this day. As soon as they reached the designated area for the announcement they dismounted. A stable boy came quickly and took the reins of his horse, as well as those of Melkiar and Sefforn, while his companions came and took care of the others. He smiled up at Clavorn.

"You're Clavorn right?" he asked shyly.

"Yes, why do you ask?"

"Oh, no reason just...ah wanted to know is all. Ah, I'll take good care of your horse," he said, smiling up at him once more.

It was clear to Clavorn that the boy felt awkward in his presence, "Thank you, and your name is?"

"Tillon, sir," the boy announced proudly, "Tillon, son of Raymorvon."

"Well, Tillon, son of Raymorvon, I am glad Hawk is in such capable hands," Clavorn told him.

"Yes sir, thank you. Oh, and I'll take good care of your friends' horses too."

Clavorn smiled down at the boy, "I'm sure you will," and with that he clasped the boy on the shoulder and proceeded into the gathering crowd with his friends.

It was high noon. A huge throng of people from all throughout Avivron were gathered outside the castle for the choosing of their new ruler. Fendane, the man who had come forward on the night of the king's death, claiming to be the next in line to the throne, soon appeared from one of the balconies above the crowd. He was dressed in his ceremonial garb which denoted his rank and status amongst the nobility. His dark hair rippled in the wind as the sun shined down on the crowd below.

"So how are they planning to let the people choose?" Sefforn asked.

"I have no idea," Clavorn replied.

"My bet is they'll use the time honored tradition of picking from the bloodlines and then letting us vote from there," Melkiar commented with an edge of sarcasm.

"Well, why don't we wait and see," Clavorn suggested as Fendane began to quiet the crowd.

"My friends, we all know why we have been assembled here today," Fendane began, "It is sad but true, our one true king and his only son are dead. Unfortunately, it has fallen to me to confirm the rumors that our once illustrious king did, in fact, betray us."

"There's an odd juxtaposition of ideas, illustrious and traitorous, humm," Melkiar commented in hushed tones to Clavorn.

"I presume, by now, that you have also heard the rumor that, Shaltak, Slayer of Dragon Killers, Defender of Maltak, and Liberator of Avivron, is also none other than, Clavorn Remmaik, son of Favorn Remmaik, First Knight to King Dakconar." Fendane paused.

A voice from the crowd shouted, "Yes!"

"I suppose you are wondering if this rumor is true," Fendane continued.

Clavorn could see from the corner of his eye that many around him were nodding their heads in agreement, others just turned and looked at him. Clavorn kept his eyes trained on Fendane, his expression blank.

"Well, it is true," Fendane went on, "The man who you thought was dead is alive,"

A combination of gasps, cheers, and murmurs rippled through the assembled throng.

"Shaltak and Clavorn are one and the same." Fendane's voice boomed above the crowd. Suddenly, from the back of those gathered, a chant began. Within seconds it had moved forward so that the whole of the assembly had taken it up.

"CLAVORN! CLAVORN! CLAVORN!"

The chant grew louder and louder till it became so loud that Clavorn could hardly hear himself think. It took a bit of time for Fendane to calm the people and quiet them down so that he could continue.

"Now, we have been told by the representative of Alhera herself, the Shaddorak, that it is time for Avivron's people to choose their next king."

A great cheer went up from the crowd. Fendane waited for them to calm down again before he continued.

"So who is your choice?"

This time the chant was so loud that is seemed as if it echoed off the walls of the castle and the surrounding mountains.

"CLAVORN! CLAVORN! CLAVORN!"

"Well, it looks as if you are now our new king," Melkiar told him as he patted him on the back.

"Congratulations!" Sefforn exclaimed with a smile as he clasped his friend in a brotherly embrace, and then raised Clavorn's hand above the crowd. A great cheer went up from the crowd at Sefforn's act.

"I believe you have a new king!" Fendane announced, and with that a huge roar went up as Clavorn was hoisted onto the shoulders of Sorenavik, Sayavic, and Clovak. Thalon and Falor stood by clapping and congratulating as did Yolondon and Heffron. Flowers, hats, and all manner of things were thrown into the air by those gathered as they rejoiced over their new king. Kevic congratulated him as cheers welled up around them.

Suddenly, from high above in the sky there appeared the great shadow of a dragon. Her green scales glistening, reflecting the light of the noontime sun. On her back was a woman, her dark hair flowing out behind her in the wind.

Silence overcame the crowd as she lifted her sword, the light of the sun catching it and reflecting downward, spotlighting Clavorn. Suddenly, his garments changed to fine cloth in shades of green, and upon his head there appeared a silver diadem of hawthorn leaves with a central silver dragon. Its wings open as if in flight, its eyes were of flaming rubies, and clutched in its claws was the famed Stone of the Dragon.

Chapter 59

It was a beautiful night as he stood on his balcony overlooking the Mountains of Kilmeia. The moon was full, and the stars seemed to sparkle and shimmer even more brightly than usual, yet he could not help but wonder where she was. The last time he had seen her was on the day he was declared the new ruler of Avivron. She had appeared with Maltak and adorned him with the Diadem of Alhera. He thought she might appear today; since it was the day of his official coronation, but she had been conspicuously absent save for Maltak and Viszerak, both of whom had been present for the coronation.

Special room had been made for them at the outdoor ceremony. They had stood behind him as Fendane had crowned him King. Ferrterrak, and Shalmaray had been present too as they witnessed his coronation near The Great Dragons. Initially, the Hindolin's appearance had caused a bit of a stir, but once it was made known that he meant them no harm, and was merely there for the day's events, the people calmed down. Skytak had stood to the right of the Great Beasts, his noble eagle head looking down upon the ceremony as he called out when Fendane declared him king.

Later dragons from all over Avivron had given a fine display of dragon aerobatics as part of the celebration. The people had cheered as they watched them fly over Escadora. Flowers of all colors had rained down profusely as part of their event. It was truly a spectacular sight. But her absence was beginning to make him wonder if, since he had achieved what she had wished, he would ever see her again.

Moonlight was glistening off the far distant mountains and the walls of the great castle around him, including the city of Escadora down below. The wind was gentle, the air sweet and fresh. Freedom had finally come for his people and those beyond. The world was safe now. Vaulnik vanquished. Peace flourished across all the lands.

In the wake of that peace he had ordered the destruction of the giant crossbows which had been used in the final battle against Vaulnik. Viszerak had been all too eager to assist him there. He could hardly blame him. The knowledge of the menacing arrows and their poison would die with him when his time came. All of which suited him just fine.

As a gesture of goodwill, he had sent word to all the kingdoms under Vaulnik's rule that he wished to honor their sovereignty, and they had responded in kind. Now, delegations from all over were gathered. Soon someone would come to fetch him for the coronation dinner and celebration. He should be happy, but somehow it all felt a bit incomplete, as if he was missing the better part of himself.

As he stood looking out over the mountains, he found himself thinking back on the day he had met her. Her green eyes staring out at him from beneath the coverings of her face, her white skin and supple body as it contrasted against the dark rocks of the waterfall, the taste of her lips, and the feel of her flesh as it pressed against his.

Oh, where is she?

No other woman would ever fill his mind, his heart the way she did.

Suddenly, there was a great gust of wind. It blew open the balcony doors behind him, causing the window coverings to furl and billow out the opening. The great torches which flanked the entrance to his bed chamber flickered and danced at the pronounced disturbance.

"Why are you not at the celebrations?" he heard a familiar voice say from behind him.

He turned and there she was, standing inside his room, arrayed as he had never seen her before. Dressed in a beautiful white flowing gown that clung about her body, around her waist she wore a wide purple sash with a large sliver dragon on it. The dragon was also holding a green Kriac stone, its wings out stretched, with silver hawthorn leaves as gentle links of a chain which fell gracefully over the sash and around her waist.

Upon her head she wore a simple silver diadem much like his. About her neck was a beautiful silver necklace of hawthorn leaves and green Kriac stones; the largest of which fell as a single tear drop in its center. The verdant color in the stones seemed to reflect the color in her eyes. Her eyes that were so perfectly framed by her beautiful long flowing black hair.

"I don't know. Missing you I suppose," he replied.

He was not sure how he should answer her question, so he chose honesty as he stepped inside the elaborately appointed room.

"Oh?" she replied as she took a step towards him, the wind rippling her gown so as to accent her figure even more. Her green eyes stared into his.

"Yes," he replied taking her in his arms and pulling her close.

As he stared into her deep emerald green eyes, he felt overcome with emotion. Gently, he removed a lock of hair from her face as he softly held it in his other hand and began to kiss her. Clavorn could feel her lips as they melted into his, smell the perfume in her hair. He pulled her closer. Her body melted into his as their passion grew. Her arms gently wrapped around him. Suddenly, he pulled her away.

"I want you to be my wife," he announced his eyes staring deep into hers.

"I want to be your wife..." she replied, but Clavorn could sense there was more to her statement, a 'but' somewhere, an idea he hated.

"...but you can't" he spoke the dreaded words as his arms dropped down letting her fall away from him.

"Please understand I belong to no man. I am the Shaddorak..."

"...part goddess, part woman. I know the stories. I've heard the legends. But surely it is not out of your purview to take a husband." He could not see how the gods could deny her that, could deny them that.

"No, Clavorn. I am for all men and no man. I am the bringer of life to the earth in the name of Alhera," she put a hand gently on his lips to stay his protest, "I can, however, choose a consort, to be my husband by night, and champion by day," she told him her eyes sparkling in the silver moonlight as it shined in through the open balcony doors.

Hope burned in Clavorn's heart as he listened to her words.

"I will gladly be such a man for you," he told her his heart pounding in his chest. Did she not know how much he loved her?

"I know Clavorn, but does not a kingdom need a queen?"

"What greater queen than you? It would be unfair of me to take another, for no other could compare to you. She would suffer every night we were together. I could never allow such a fate for any woman in my kingdom or beyond," he told her, hope slipping away in his mind. Had he traded love, for leadership? Could not a man be good at both?

There was a pause.

"Then you shall be my husband in Shardon and the gods shall marry us, but of the earth I am no man's. Here we are consorts. Lovers till the end of time. Our children shall grace your kingdom and beyond, renewing the world they touch, and they shall bare The Mark of the Dragon, so that all may know that they are ours."

Clavorn had no words to follow hers. He simply took her in his arms and kissed her. Their passion took over the night and they were married in the eyes of the gods, but to the world of men they remained only secret lovers.

No one ever came to call Clavorn to dinner, and he never asked how it was that they had not missed him. He did not care. To him it was just one of those mysteries that only she could explain.

That night, as they lay in bed, Clavorn could not help but stare at her sleeping peacefully next to him. The moonlight played off her ivory skin. Her dark hair glistened like the surface of a deep lake in the night. He thought he could never feel such happiness as he did at that moment. She stirred. He leaned over and kissed her tenderly, then placing his arm about her, he closed his eyes to join her in the realm of dreams.

Outside the moonlight shimmered off the scales of The Great Green Dragon as she flew high above the castle. Suddenly, she let out a thunderous roar across the land, and breathed The Fires of Life into the night, while the world awaited the dawn of a new day.

Glossary

Alhera's Forest - forest not from Shyloran Forest to the east of it

Alhera- goddess of the earth; daughter of Allethor and Thelenor; bringer of life to the earth

Allethor - king of the gods; husband of Thelenor

Altak- Maltak's mate and Father of all dragons the First Dragons; and therefore Father of all Dragons created by Alhera

Battle of Quantaris or The Great Battle- the final battle in The Dragon Wars

Battle of Yonis- a battle fought early on in the Dragon Wars after King Dakconar's death.

Castle Shalhadon- castle in the main city of Shalhadon in the land of Ishalhan

Darzors- assassins in the art of slaying dragons

Death Lake- a lake on their way to Kisensgraw once known as Mirror Lake, now with the shadow of death all around it, its lifeless waters only reflected the dismal depths of waist and sorrow.

Demonrak-demonic dragon created by Zagnor from a lost scale of Altak

Dragon's claw- when referred to as a unit of measure it would be the approximate length of our 1 foot or 12 inches.

Dragonglass- a type of spy glass, said to give the viewer almost as good vision as a dragon.

Dragon's head- as a unit of measure approximately 7 of our feet.

The Dragon's Heart Stone or the Stone of the Dragon - a large flawless blue green Kriac stone said to be the color of Maltak's scales, given to the first King of Avivron, Elshardon, by, Saltak, the first dragon of Avivron for his valor in putting an end to the Tarmian Wars and for exhibiting a dragon like heart in his defense of life during the wars. It has been passed down over the centuries, but is said that only one with a dragon heart can truly be its keeper. Any other was sacrilege and would be cursed by the dragon. The stone was said to carry the power of the dragon and bring great luck and prosperity to the land. If, however, the land fell into a time where the people of Avivron fell out of favor with the dragon, the stone could be taken from them and the land and her people cursed until such time as goodness and justice returned.

Dragon's jaw- as a until of measure much like our dozen on equal to the number of teeth in a single dragon's jaw 34

Dragon's Lair- An area of rough terrain and forest in Avivron where an Ornskyterrak is said to live

Dragon lengths- a unit of measurement equivalent to the length of a dragon from nose to tail or approximately one hundred of our feet

Dragon Seeing- a sort of dejavue or a feeling that one has been in a place or been in a specific situation, or seen something before even though they have not.

The Dragon Wars- the war against Vaulnik, started by the dragons which ended with their virtual extinction.

Effora- Power of the Stones- the unique power held within each stone. In regards to the Kriac Stones it was their power of creation, the power of life.

Escadora - capital of Avivron

Escadora Castle- main castle in Avivron where King Sevzozak dwells

Forest of Calhador- legendary magical forest; said to be as old as time its self

Forest of Herlona- forest on the outskirts of Escadora

Forest of Klestovak- forest just to the north of the Krimian Ridge

Forest of Thestaera- forest near the castle of Vaulnik

Hindolin – smaller cousins of dragons, breath fire, part alligator, part dragon, with a pack mentality a kin to a wolf. They live in bogs and swamps. Are known to eat various creatures that stray too close to their habitat, including creatures as big as horses or humans when fully mature.

Hindora-land to the far west of Avivron where Clavorn had first gone to join the fight during the Dragon Wars-shipping country-rich before the war

Ishalhan – the name of Vaulnik's kingdom before he took over which lies to the south of Avivron

Kalmak- a sect of Dragon Witches tasked with protecting the sacred places of the earth.

Kazengor Castle - Vaulnik's castle in Zvegnog a kingdom once known as Ishalhan

Kisensgraw- ghost town in Avivron cursed by the dragons for mining Kriac Stones.

The Krimian Ridge - a ridge of mountains in Avivron that are in the southern quadrant they sit in front of The Mountains of Shylaharon which lay due south in Ishalhan.

Kriac Stones-clear emerald green to blue green stones, harder than diamonds which fell to earth in a great shower from the sky sent by Allethor, and which the legendary dragon Maltak is said to also have created at one time as a show of gratitude to Thorlon for his bravery and honor. They hold the power of creation and healing.

Maltak- The First Dragon, Mother of the First Dragons, and thereby the Mother of all dragons; created by Alhera

The Mountains of Kilmeia-mountains that sit west of the Escadora in Avivron

Ornskyterrak- a creature with the head of an eagle, the body of a dragon, the forelegs and often coloration of a panther- a protector of ancient woodlands (can be black, or tan like a panther), breathes fire. They are smaller than a dragon and more agile in the air. The falcon of flying beasts. Known to be able to see into men's souls.

Passage of Allethor - a great cleft or mystical passageway which connects the Forest of Calhador with Avivron

Shaladorn Forest- forest of angry trees to the south of Kisensgraw

Salhera-mountain lion friend of Alethea

Salvahook-land to the south of Avivron where the Dragon Wars began

Sespon-Zagnor's name before he was banished from Shardon

Shaddorak- woman who legend holds will be able to wield the power of all the Kriac stones, the dragons and be Alhera's presence on earth

Shalhadon- Capitol of Ishalhan before Vaulnik took over

Shardon- heaven

Shardon Lands-heavens

Shyloran Forest- Ancient Willow Grove – forest in Avivron with stream

Tarmian Wars- One of the first wars of men.

The Mountains Shylaharon are located in Ishalhan in behind the Krimian Ridge.

Thelenor-queen of the gods and Allethor's wife

Thorlon- legendary warrior and hunter

Valhera- equivalent to our angel

Vigoths – gray shadow creatures created by Zagnor and released on earth to destroy all life

Vingali-large shaggy boar like creatures with huge fans

Viszerak- The Last Dragon; The Dragon of the North

Fires of Life

Whimpernickles- short, dwarf like creatures about two dragon claws high with large pointed ears which they use to hear the smallest of sounds, red hair that grows up out their head like a tuft of grass, and intensely deep blue eyes. From their arms grow small sprouts of tree branches and about their legs are patches of bark. They live alone, but desperately enjoy company to the point of often sequestering their guests for an untold amount of time. They are well-meaning creatures who can speak with all the life of the forest which is their charge.

Zagnor- god of the dark world, nearly equivalent to our devil or Satan

Zezpok- the dark world, nearly equivalent to our hell, or underworld

Zoths- evil dragons

ABOUT THE AUTHOR

Maria N. McMillan lives in the Pacific Northwest with her daughter, two horses and assorted feline friends. Influenced by the natural world around her and her interests in history, art, and archeology, she writes her stories to lift us out of our everyday lives and take us to places we have never imagined. Where we can laugh, dream, cry, hope and be inspired to better versions of ourselves. For more about her and her upcoming projects visit her website http://falkhan.wix.com/marianmcmillan

She is also an avid photographer. You can view some of her work at http://falkhan.wix.com/mnmcphoto

FROM THE AUTHOR

"One thing I enjoy about writing is telling stories; stories for all kinds of people, of all ages. I hope you enjoy reading my work as much I have in writing it. See you within the pages, on the other side of imagination."

Made in the USA
Charleston, SC
25 September 2016